YUKON REVENGE

A Novel

Ken Baird

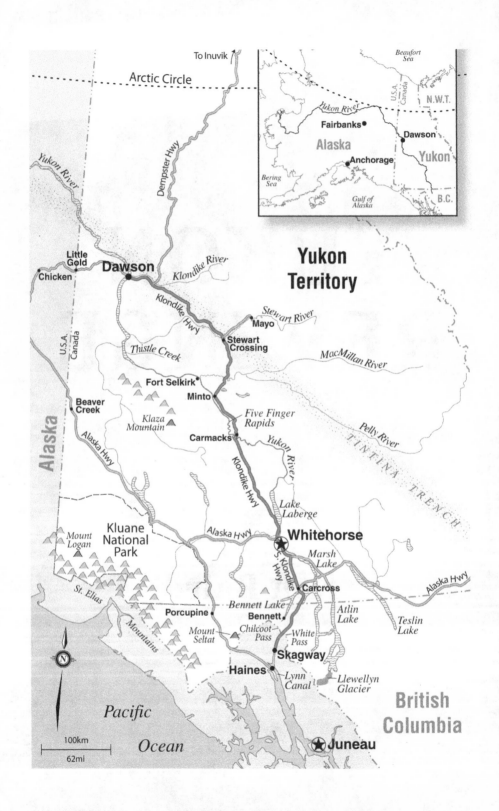

DeHavilland Canada DHC-2

General Characteristics

Crew: one pilot
Length: 30 ft 3 in (9.22 m)
Wingspan: 48 ft 0 in (14.63 m)
Height: 9 ft 0 in (2.74 m)
Wing area: 250 ft² (23.2 m²)
Empty: 3,000 lb (1,360 kg)
Loaded: 5,100 lb (2,310 kg)
Useful load: 2,100 lb (950 kg)
Powerplant: 1 Pratt & Whitney R-985 Wasp Jr. radial engine, 450 hp (335 kW)

Performance

Cruise speed (w/floats): 110 mph (180 km/h)
Range: 455 miles (732 km)
Rate of climb: 1,020 ft/min (5.2 m/s)
Service ceiling: 18,000 ft (5,500 m)

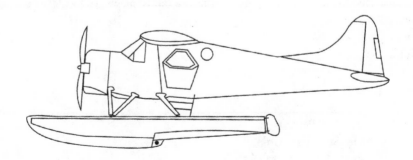

Yukon Revenge
Copyright © 2019 by Ken Baird
All rights reserved

First Edition

ISBN: 978-0-9973175-2-7

Cover Photo by Mark Perry
Cover Design by Streetlight Graphics
Map by Chrismar Mapping Services

*"...it isn't the gold that I'm wanting,
so much as just finding the gold..."*

—Robert William Service

*He is your friend, your partner, your defender, your dog.
You are his life, his love, his leader.
He will be yours, faithful and true, to the last beat of his heart.
You owe it to him to be worthy of such devotion.*

—Unknown

Praise for YUKON AUDIT

*"...a brilliant novel...one of those page turners
that's impossible to put down..."*
- Readers' Favorite

"...a gripping, entertaining ride..."
- Jonathan Harr, NY Times Best Selling Author

"... a super pace and flow..."
- Brian Stewart, Gemini Award Winner

"...a page turning thriller... Fast paced and masterfully written."
- Urban Book Reviews

"A thrill a minute..."
- Book Lovers Book Reviews

"Wow! Wow! Wow!"
- Eyes and Ears Book Blog

To the memory of Erna Monica Baird
1930-2011

ONE YEAR AGO

In desperation the big man in the river grabbed a floating tree and could only watch as his canoe was swept into the rapids.

It bounced off a rock, spun around, rode up a boulder, sailed into the air, and jettisoned the little man at the front. It landed upside down, rolled upright, and stopped momentarily with a ton of water in the hull. Then the current took hold, accelerating it downstream, slamming it into rock after rock, rolling it over and over, purging its precious cargo. Seconds later everything disappeared into a wall of white water: the canoe, the little man, and three styrofoam boxes. Three million dollars was in the Yukon River.

Everything was in the Yukon River.

The tree he was clinging to was thick and heavy, moving slowly and haltingly through the rapids as it toggled from one rock to the next. Its long branches kept it from rotating and he managed to mount and straddle it, raising most of his body out of the frigid water. But time and time again another wave would rise and fall over him, thoroughly soaking him to his skin, inducing a great shudder that rippled down his torso and resonated through his bones. His feet were his greatest concern, he couldn't find a way to keep them out of the water, and they were beginning to feel dead and unattached as a numbing pain crept up his legs. He knew he didn't have long, he could only survive another few minutes before succumbing to the ice cold grip of the river.

He had to get to shore.

Halfway down the rapids, the top of the tree plowed into a narrow gap between two boulders, stopping it dead, hurling him forward into a nest of branches, cutting a deep gash across his brow. With blood in his eyes, he couldn't see what had stopped the tree, but now that it was stationary, the torrential river engulfed him. Flattened to the trunk by tons of water gushing over him, he gasped and thrashed and kicked out at a rock. With a mighty push of his left leg, the tree began to swing to his right in a long slow arc. When it was at right angles to the current, it released from the boulders and began a slow drift sideways, skidding and sliding along a row of rocks toward the right side of the canyon. He turned his head and saw the river bank was not thirty feet behind him, getting closer by the second as the tree tracked across the current. The water between him and the shore was fast and smooth, and though a poor swimmer, he knew this was his one and only chance to survive.

The rocky shore was twenty feet away when he fell more than leapt from the tree, and began windmilling his arms wildly. He realized immediately something was wrong, for as much as he tried to summon his great power, the strength in his body had left him. But though the frigid water might have won his energy, it could never defeat his resolve, and he gasped and thrashed for his life until his hand came down on a rock. He pulled himself forward until he felt another rock, pulled on that one too, then another, and another. When his knees finally scraped bottom, he stumbled to his feet, took a few steps, fell back to his knees, and with the roar of the rapids behind him, crawled onto land.

He would live.

* * *

Ten minutes later the big man had climbed halfway up a rocky bluff and was standing on a narrow ledge. Cold and exhausted, bleeding and shaking, he turned and looked down at the Yukon River. He was at the north end of a pillar of rock about as high and long as a battleship. To his left and right the river rushed past him through two narrow canyons, but in the distance beyond it lay wide and flat and calm. He squinted his eyes against the low sun, and using both hands to shade his face, scanned the sparkling water for any sign of the little man.

What he saw made his blood boil.

A man in a canoe was stopped beside the little man who was in the water. The little man was lying on a white box, clutching it to his chest. The white box he was clinging to was one of the three styrofoam boxes they'd been carrying in their canoe.

Inside the box was a million dollars in cash.

The man in the canoe seemed to be talking to the little man, but then he abruptly paddled away.

Leaving the little man to die.

The big man knew who was in the canoe. It was the pilot who had led them into the rapids. The pilot who would be thinking he had killed them both. But he was wrong about that. Dead wrong. Because only one man would die that day.

The pilot would have to pay for what he did.

But first the big man would make him miserable.

Then he would make him suffer.

Then he would kill him.

ONE

Life is full of mysteries.

Like why would a man with a pickup, a plane, a cabin on the river, and two dogs to keep him company, not be happy?

I was mulling over the possibilities while peering up into a dark deep recess in the car above me.

Another mystery.

It seems there's one in every job, a single nut or bolt that's impossible to access, but has to be removed to change a part.

I wonder why automotive engineers design cars like that. To discourage do-it-yourselfers? To keep car dealers in business? Or is it simply a disdain for mechanics in general?

It was then I caught a whiff of smoke.

Now there was a problem.

In the Yukon we don't have hurricanes, tornadoes, tsunamis, sinkholes, or volcanoes. And on the rare occasion when the houseplants sway a little, well it's hardly what you'd call an earthquake. But when you smell smoke in the air up here, you find out where it's coming from.

Fast.

I left the car on the lift and walked out of my rough timber shop with a wrench in my hand. The wind was out of the south, cool and light and steady. I took a long deep breath. A forest fire in the Yukon is rare in early June, but smoke was on the wind.

Wood smoke.

The dense spruce forest surrounding my shop blocked every view of the horizon, so I headed across the gravel lot to my old Chevy half ton. I dropped the tailgate, got in, and turned the key. The engine started and ran nicely. It had better run nicely, I have the only auto repair business for forty miles and the engine in my truck is my whole advertising campaign.

I dropped the wrench on the seat, wiped my hands on my jeans, lowered the windows, looked in the mirrors, and started counting. One, two, three, four...and didn't get to ten before two Jack Russell terriers came charging out of the woods, leapt into the box, and skidded to a stop at the cab window. I put the transmission in drive, idled out of the lot, and started up the two track lane leading out to the Klondike Highway. A cloud of dust kicked up and followed like it didn't want to be left behind. Branches and bushes scraped the sides of the truck and I made a mental note to do some spring pruning.

Russ and Jack—they're my dogs—were eagerly anticipating some action. They'd each picked a corner of the box and were up on their hind legs with their front paws draped over the sides, craning their necks ahead, filling the big western mirrors with their portraits, surveying the air for anything with a heartbeat.

A minute later we reached the highway. I stopped and waited for the dust to sail past, then got out and looked up and down the empty road. And smelled the air again. The pungent aroma of smoke was even more tangible now, though the sky still clear as a bell.

The source had to be close.

My boys eyed me carefully when I strode out and stopped in the middle of the tarred gravel road. The gold rush city of Dawson is a hundred and eighty miles north of where I was standing—a left turn out of my place—and the city of Whitehorse, the Yukon's capital, a hundred and fifty miles south. That would be a right turn. There are no traffic lights in Dawson but Whitehorse has plenty, probably a dozen by now, and whenever I ever get the urge to see one, it's a two and a half hour drive from my cabin. I generally avoid places with traffic lights, though, so living where I do, near a dot on the map called Minto, in the middle of nowhere as people tell me, well that suits me just fine.

I scanned the horizon in all directions and saw nothing but pale blue sky. Other than the engine idling in my twenty year old pickup, not a rattle or tick in it by the way, there was barely a sound to be heard—a rustle from the trees, the caw of a crow, a chattering squirrel, a whisper of wind.

Just another Monday morning rush hour in Minto.

But with smoke in the air.

Russ and Jack were wary, watching my every move, getting antsy.

"Stay," I commanded, knowing well that neither would even think about jumping out with the motor running, and risk missing a drive down the highway. Unless of course they spotted something with fur and four legs, in which case they'd both be gone in the blink of an eye.

For a good two minutes I stood there in the middle of the Klondike Highway, scanning the sky, sifting the air, waiting and watching. Then I glimpsed a faint plume of smoke rising over the tree line. It was low in the sky to the south. Not far. Probably from the village. I jumped into my truck and spun the tires.

Two minutes later I knew what was burning.

* * *

The hundred or so aboriginal Canadians who live in Minto today are the direct descendants of the people who walked into North America.

More than twelve thousand years ago—eons before today's carnival men began touting LED lights as a panacea to stop our oceans from rising—the world's sea level was hundreds of feet lower than it is today. It was the peak of the last ice age, a time when so much of the earth's water was locked up in glaciers and ice fields that a narrow strip of land lay exposed between Siberia and Alaska. The Bering Land Bridge—a walking path from Asia to North America now submerged under the Bering Sea—lay high and dry above the Pacific Ocean, covered in grass and plants, populated by birds and animals migrating out of Asia. The people of Siberia joined the migration, chased eastward by the glaciers advancing behind them, pursuing and harvesting the birds and animals that sustained their nomadic way of life. But when these nomadic tribes arrived in the Yukon, they could go no farther. All routes south and east into the new continent were blocked by a great wall of ice. It was the northwest extremity of the massive icefield that at the time smothered two thirds of North America, and it was over a mile high in places. For the newcomers there was no going back, no forging ahead, no other choice but to settle where they were.

They were the first Yukoners, the first North Americans, and the new world's First Nations.

Today, on a Monday morning in early June, ten thousand years since the earth's temperature began rising, thousands of years since all but a few of North America's glaciers and icefields had melted away—creating the Great Lakes, forging new rivers, and replenishing the world's oceans to their current level—the First Nation of Minto was still preoccupied with ice. This particular ice would be perfectly smooth and flat, a sheet of it exactly 200 feet long and 85 feet wide, and they intended to keep it that way all winter long.

Construction of the new Minto hockey arena had begun two weeks ago. An acre of land was cleared and a pad for the 300 by 150 foot steel building had been graded. Last week a trench was excavated for the concrete footings. Two days ago three trucks from Whitehorse rolled onto the site and unloaded a couple of tons of reinforcing bar, ten stacks of plywood, a dozen bundles of two by fours, and a whole bunch of pipe to circulate the refrigerant. The stacks of plywood and lumber had been uniformly distributed around the trench, ready to cut into concrete forms. In a couple of weeks the footings would be poured, and the week after that when the pipes had been plumbed over the pad, the rink would be poured.

Everything was coming together, everything was on schedule, everyone was working hard. If the weather cooperated, with a little luck we'd be skating inside a building this fall.

But when I braked hard to turn left off the Klondike Highway, into the village of Minto, my heart sank. The stacks of plywood and lumber surrounding the site were no more. They'd been reduced to soaking wet piles of charred wood.

Someone had set them on fire.

* * *

Other than all the fire hoses strewn all over the place, and all the burnt stacks of lumber and plywood, it might have been a Yukon wedding. There were at least twenty pickups, a bunch of ATV's, a motorcycle, lots of bicycles, a school bus, two front end loaders, a backhoe, a grader, two water trucks, and as always for this kind of occasion, the nicest four by four in town. The flagship of the Minto RCMP detachment—an enormous blue and white SUV, and a Chevy Yukon at that—was parked with its engine idling and every one of its lights blazing, blinking and flashing.

Just about everyone from the village was milling about the site: kids of all ages, adults of all ages, dogs of all ages, and as usual a cluster of dishevelled men congregated for yet another meeting of the minds.

The five men who comprise the Minto Highway Department, with little or nothing to do until it snowed again, were holding another one of their private symposiums. They all wore identical yellow hard hats and fluorescent orange vests, fully unzipped to let their ample bellies protrude, proudly displaying them as if they were prestigious awards. Two of the men were standing together, smoking cigarettes, surveying the damage, pointing at things, doubtless discussing the possibility of spontaneous combustion. Arlo and Andy nodded in unison when they saw me roll in and I reluctantly acknowledged them with a tip of my cap.

There was nowhere to park. I was evidently the last one to arrive at the scene, not unusual for me when it comes to social events. But I wanted to be close to the action because I was having trouble walking today. One of the laces in my boots had gone missing this morning. My dogs had feigned ignorance when I asked them what had happened to it, and in particular, what a well chewed boot was doing on the couch. Until I got a new one, a short piece of rope would have to suffice.

I stopped on the rear bumper of the RCMP vehicle and got out. Russ and Jack jumped to the ground and dashed off to check out their four-legged girlfriends in the village, eager to see who was pregnant and who might still be available for a dog date.

Minto's one and only cop had his back to me and was leaning on a front fender of his big blue jail on wheels. He was talking to a forestry guy coiling a fire hose. The guy coiling the hose didn't seem interested in what he was saying. Constable Daryl Pageau of the Royal Canadian Mounted Police turned his head, looked at my truck, and five strides later was in my face.

"You can't park there, Brody!" he yelled, waving his hands over his head.

I looked up at him like I was trying to read a street sign.

"How come? You leaving?"

Daryl towered over me, casting a great dark shadow and delivering an officially sanctioned cop glare. He brushed off the lapels of his shiny blue coat, put his hands on his hips, puffed out his chest, and splayed out his elbows. The image of a condor came to mind. Daryl is a very big guy. I'm six feet and a hundred and eighty pounds but feel like a school kid next to him. A couple of years ago I watched Daryl break up one of Minto's semi-annual bar fights, separating the combatants and casually tossing them into piles like he was sorting dirty laundry. He has at least ninety pounds and a good five inches on me. Add another three inches for the hat on his head, and one more for the heels on his boat-sized shoes, and you can appreciate why no one messes with Daryl.

Well almost no one. I maintain his big blue truck.

With menace in his voice he said, "As a matter of fact, I *am* leaving. And real soon. Going to the airport to pick up some very important people, not that that's any of your business. But that's not why you've got to move your truck. You can't park less than six meters behind an emergency vehicle when its lights are flashing. Mine are flashing and you're on my bumper. Now park somewhere else!"

"How many feet is six meters?" I asked, stepping around him and walking up to the smoldering pile of two by fours in front of his truck. The boards had been reduced to briquets.

"Twenty," he shouted after me as I stumbled my way along a muddy trench toward a pallet of charred plywood. I stopped in front of it. All the sheets in the soaking wet stack were badly burned and coated in a gooey mixture of wood ash and congealed plywood glue. Every piece was a write-off. Daryl's shoes squeaked like only a cop's shoes squeak when he stopped beside me. We studied the stack of burnt plywood for a while.

"This sure looks like arson, Brody," he managed to utter between breaths.

"Gee, Daryl, do ya' think?"

Still winded, he glared at me and said, "Any idea who might have done this?"

"No. Not a clue. Why would I?"

"Maybe it was one of those scoundrels from that mess you stirred up last summer."

"I stirred up that mess? Don't you think it was a bunch of crooks and cops who stirred up that mess?" I shook my head and said, "No. Those guys from last summer are all dead. Or in jail. This is someone else."

I could feel his eyes on me for a long time before he said, "You seem awful sure about that. But one of those guys didn't go to jail. And maybe he isn't dead."

I glanced up at him to see if he was serious.

"Are you talking about that gorilla, Kay? Come on, Daryl, really? Do you think a man can survive ten minutes in the Yukon

River in June? No chance. The water's too cold. He drowned. He's dead. Just like his boss. You may not have found him yet, but he's dead."

"Staff Sergeant says maybe he's not dead."

"Staff Sergeant Robson? What does he know? I was the one who was there, not him. I watched those guys go into the rapids and spent a long time looking for them after I got through. They both got tossed into the river and were in the water way too long to survive. The only reason I couldn't find their canoe was because it wasn't floating anymore. No way they made it through that middle channel without dunking. That's wild water in the spring and they ended up in it."

I sighed and shook my head again. Daryl shrugged his shoulders. We studied the stack of burnt plywood some more. The man we were talking about was a thug and professional enforcer, who with his boss—a crook named Wei Lee—was chasing me down the Yukon River last June in a canoe. I'd been in another canoe and the two men were planning to kill me. But when we reached a treacherous part of the Yukon River called Five Finger Rapids, an infamous and dangerous white water hazard forty miles upriver, we took different routes into the rapids. I'd been lucky and went down the one and only channel considered navigable by an amateur paddler, and even then had barely made it through safely. But the two men following me had gone through another channel, the one in the center, a maelstrom of roiling water rushing over rocks and boulders, presenting an impossible challenge to navigate in an overloaded canoe. It was beyond me how any canoe wouldn't have flipped over in that white water and tossed its occupants into the frigid river.

"But Brody, you never saw their canoe capsize, and you never saw either man go into the water. And you also never saw their canoe after it went into the rapids. You lost sight of it when those two entered the center channel, that's what you said at the inquest. That's what the Staff Sergeant told me. That's why he thinks that big guy might have survived."

"How, Daryl? How could he have survived? We all entered the rapids at the same time. I would have seen their canoe come out if it had still been floating. But you guys found it submerged to the gunnels miles downstream, close to where you found Lee's body. So isn't it obvious what happened? They went into the rapids, their canoe capsized, they both went hypothermic, they both drowned. End of story. But Robson wants you to believe what? That Kay got tossed into those rapids but somehow survived? That he managed to swim to shore and walked out of the Yukon? Come on, give yourself a shake. Think about it. Just because you never found him doesn't mean he's alive. There's no way he's alive. He drowned or died of hypothermia just like his boss. He's in the river, he's dead as a door nail, and he's stuck under a log somewhere. It's only a matter of time before some kayaker finds his bloated body. You'll see."

Daryl grimaced and rubbed the back of his neck.

"I hope you're right about that, Brody. I really do."

TWO

A heavy gray sky pressed down on the city, weighing on the spirits of Monday morning commuters. So this is Ottawa, thought Sarah Marsalis, sipping rich coffee from a fine china cup, cooling her forehead against the window, watching traffic crawl through a fine Scotch mist.

Her flight out of Washington had been delayed last night and landed late in a thick fog. She'd cleared customs, then taken a taxi into the city—by herself—all the way downtown to the Chateau Laurier, one of Canada's grand old hotels. She'd checked in at midnight, declined a nightcap with her colleagues, and slept poorly in the big soft bed.

With her bearings now she gazed west at the Parliament Buildings—the Peace Tower, the West Block, the Commons, the Senate—then the War Memorial to her left, all standing like great Gothic sculptures, each soaring high and mighty into a somber spring sky. Everything here seemed so neat and clean she mused, so civilized and established, far too peaceful for a major city on a weekday morning.

She wondered why the sidewalks were empty, only cars and buses were out, plying the wet streets with courtesy and care. Why weren't there people on the streets? Had everyone left for some reason? Was today a Canadian holiday? Maybe it was just early.

Or maybe it was the weather. She looked at the clock beside her bed. Seven a.m. She set her cup down on the silver tray. Time to get ready for her meeting. She stepped into the shower and thought about Brody.

Long lost Brody. She wondered how he was. What he was doing. Whether he'd be flying today. Whether she'd ever see him again.

Why she couldn't stop thinking about him.

* * *

The heels of her shoes clicked and clacked on the polished granite floor and echoed through the arches down the long marble hallway. She thought fleetingly about the architects of history who'd walked this same hallowed path—kings and queens, presidents and prime ministers, robber barons and titans of industry. The concept was inspiring and she raised her chin, heading toward the tall brass doors that opened onto Rideau Street, and the three men standing in front of them.

If she was right, and she usually was, they'd been waiting at least ten minutes. They were ten minutes early for everything. She could never understand their compulsion to be early. The rendezvous was scheduled for eight. She glanced at her watch.

Right on time.

The men turned in unison when they heard her footsteps and watched with unabashed fascination as she approached them with long confident strides.

Sarah Marsalis was wearing a black pinstriped suit that clung to her body like paint. At a slender five feet nine inches tall she'd been created for haute couture, and this morning had poured herself into a creation by Dior. It was obscene what it had cost her, but what else was a lonely girl from Washington to do with an income tax refund? There'd been enough left over for the silk blouse, and a two hour styling of her short auburn hair, but the rest of the package couldn't be bought—the flawless complexion, the intelligent brown eyes, and a charisma that could conquer a country.

At that particular moment, though, it was her legs doing the talking, providing pure entertainment for at least two of the men waiting at the doors. The other man, the short fat one with the comb-over in the rumpled gray suit, well legs weren't really his thing. That was a shame, he was her boss.

She slipped her black attaché from one arm to the other and shook hands with F.B.I. Special Agent in Charge, David Owen.

"Nice to see you again, S.A.C.," she said with a beaming smile, emphasizing each letter of his new title. "Congratulations on the promotion."

"Thanks, Sarah. You look great. Been a while, huh? Thanks for coming. We've got another interesting one for you today."

She held her smile and said, "I'm looking forward to hearing all about it, David."

'David'.

Sarah liked just about everything about David Owen. Owen was about forty, a few years older than she was, very handsome, very polite, and a very reasonable guy to work with, even if he *was* FBI. In fact about the only thing she didn't like about David Owen was that he was a happily married man.

Oh well.

She turned to the next man, and with a familiarity that went far deeper than the three years they'd worked together at the US Department of the Treasury, said, "Morning, Stan."

"Morning, Sarah."

Special Agent Stanley Kurtz was her closest colleague, a good guy and attractive in his own right, and the two had a lot in common. He too was a CPA, the same age as Sarah, unattached and available, and as always, dressed to impress. Kurtz was tall, fit and trim with a fully paid gym body she'd seen every inch of during a one-night stand a year and a half ago. It had happened after the Christmas office party and still haunted her to this day. She'd had far too much to drink and made the biggest mistake of her professional life by going to bed with him. It would have been easy to blame the booze, but booze wasn't the problem. She was the problem and she knew it. She'd been steadfast ever since in making sure the episode stayed a 'one and done' deal, but it *had* happened. To have slept with a colleague had been utterly unprofessional and clearly the stupidest thing she'd done in all her ten years working for Uncle Sam. She still regretted their indiscretion, if for no other reason than Stan had become emotionally invested in her, reading far more into their roll in the hay than he should have. She'd lamented his disillusionment ever since.

Guilt. Pain. Drink.

Guilt.

"Cutting things a little close this morning, don't you think, Special Agent?"

It was S.A.C. Harry Polichek speaking now, the little man in the rumpled suit, the little man who happened to be her boss, and of all the people in this world, the one and only person she needed to impress to get ahead.

Polichek raised his wrist to her face and tapped his watch with a finger.

It was one minute before eight.

"Sorry sir. Didn't sleep well."

He gave her a look of admonishment, then looked outside and said, "Jesus, where are they?"

Sarah resisted an urge to roll her eyes. The little twerp drove her crazy. Polichek was the most uptight person she'd ever met. He was constantly agitated and started every second sentence with 'Jesus'. Every mundane challenge had to be treated like a crisis. He fretted incessantly about the time of day. She wondered how someone with his disposition could have possibly managed to rise so high in an organization of cool calm professionals. If ever there was a walking heart attack, he was it. Thankfully he was retiring in a few months. The day couldn't come soon enough as far as she was concerned. Of course a heart attack would work well too.

"There's our ride," said Owen, calmly nodding at a soaking

wet Cadillac Escalade that had just pulled up to the curb. A crisply dressed RCMP Constable jumped out and opened all four doors for the four American dignitaries. He took extra care to make sure the lady was comfortably seated in the seat behind his. Extra good care. Polichek held his watch up for all to see, tapped it with a stubby finger, then marched around the front of the vehicle to the front passenger door, huffing and muttering the whole way. Owen and Kurtz climbed in through the far rear door and sat beside Sarah. The big SUV drove off into the rain.

Right on time.

THREE

There were six of them, all cops, all seated in a spacious room on the fourth floor of a sparkling new building with big green windows.

Introductions had been made and business cards exchanged. The four sleuths from America were waiting to hear how they might help their Canadian counterparts bust some bad guys.

A young woman in uniform who'd been introduced as a Corporal Taylor sat stoically in a chair by the door. The rest of the group were comfortably spaced around an oversize boardroom table. Sarah had chosen a seat with a perfect view of the park across the street. If things got dull she could always look outside at the trees and the grass, watch the squirrels scamper through the rain, and daydream about another place.

Or so she'd thought.

"Corporal, lights and blinds please," said the tall gray haired man in a sharply pressed blue suit to the short young woman in the blue pants with wide yellow stripes. Corporal Taylor got up and turned on a projector, then walked over to the windows with her shiny shoes squeaking and closed the blinds.

The man at the head of the table had introduced himself as Staff Sergeant John Munroe, but he was no rank and file street cop, and certainly nothing like the Staff Sergeant that Sarah had met in the Yukon last year. Munroe was pure detective and the urbane Canadian cop was now poised to brief his American friends on a case he was leading.

Sarah sensed the presence of a man in charge. She guessed Munroe might be in his early fifties, and like most Canadian cops she'd met, clearly took care of himself. Munroe told the group he lived in Vancouver where the case was centered, but that he always enjoyed visiting Ottawa, his hometown and the place where he'd signed on with the RCMP twenty-nine years ago. The room went dark with the flip of a switch. Corporal Taylor returned to her seat. Munroe clicked the remote in his hand.

"The man you're looking at is one Cheng Li," he said. "Mr. Li is forty-two years old, Asian, a naturalized Canadian who lives in Vancouver."

Munroe paused a second so everyone could take a good look at the man portrayed on the wall. It was likely a passport photo, a head and shoulders shot of a very average looking oriental man. He had small dark eyes and the hint of a smirk at one corner of his mouth.

"Cheng Li was born in China, moved to Hong Kong when he was three, then to Canada when he was six. Among other things, he owns a small independent stock brokerage house in Vancouver, though he's rarely seen on the premises. For years Mr. Li has been a real bad apple in the penny stock business, making millions financing and promoting dubious mineral exploration projects on both US and Canadian junior exchanges. His 'pump and dump' boiler room campaigns are legendary and his scams are well known to every exchange commission north and south of the border. Li was once known as the 'tipster' in the local penny stock community and that monicker soon morphed to 'Tippy'. Ask anyone in Vancouver's Chinatown if they know where Tippy Li is, and they'll just smile and nod and walk away. Because even if they happen to know where Tippy Li might be, they know better than to tell you. That's because Tippy—Mr. Cheng Li—is one bad dude. And here's why.

"First, Li is much more than a stock promoter. He is, in fact, the boss of a major crime syndicate, a Hong Kong triad with well established operations in both Hong Kong and Vancouver. We believe he was responsible for the street executions of at least six people in Canada last year. He owns or controls a labyrinth of Vancouver and Hong Kong companies that appear legitimate at first glance—real estate, shipping, waste disposal, restaurants, the list goes on—but every one of those enterprises is little more than a front for one of his criminal rackets: drugs, prostitution, human trafficking, extortion, numbers, money laundering, smuggling, you name it. There are a lot of gangsters in the Vancouver area who'd just as soon kill him as kiss him, depending on whether they made or lost money on one of his recent pump and dumps, or if he happens to be expanding into their turf with one of his rackets. Settling turf disputes for Mr. Li is usually done wild west style and we've recently learned that he's recently become a gun runner too. Which explains why his cavalry of well armed thugs wins most of the gunfights around Vancouver.

"That said, charging and prosecuting Li for any of his criminal enterprises has been next to impossible. He's a challenge to keep tabs on, very hard to track, let alone locate, always moving around town from one residence to the other, or taking off to parts unknown in his private jet. And whenever or wherever he's seen, he's impossible to approach, constantly surrounded by a large entourage of enforcers. He's been as slippery as ice for as long as we've been investigating him, and no agency on either side of the border has ever been able to pin him down for a conviction. That's because he never dirties his hands in his own illegal activities, and maintains an impermeable fortress of slick lawyers and offshore companies to shield his financial affairs from scrutiny. Most significant, though, is that no sane individual will testify against the man. In a word, to put it metaphorically, Li is 'bulletproof'.

"However, we do remain committed to putting Li where he belongs—in jail. If we can put him behind bars for any reasonable amount of time, then a lot of fruit can be shaken from the trees and we can neutralize a whole bunch of other bad people operating in our country. Doing that would break up Li's organization and the organizations of others. It would give us a whole new ball game on the streets of Vancouver. So that's our objective, lady and gentlemen. Put Li away for just about anything we can come up with, even for just a couple of years, and we can score a major victory against organized crime in Canada."

Munroe looked around the table. He had everyone's attention now and waited as they digested the information. Sarah realized she wasn't the only one at the table to have taken a long deep breath. She exchanged glances with Owen and Kurtz, though not Polichek. Polichek was playing with his watch. Everyone turned their gazes back to the man on the wall.

Munroe spoke again. "So how do we get this guy? And how can the US Department of the Treasury and the FBI help the RCMP do that? Well, there's an interesting new scenario that recently presented itself. As I already pointed out, no agency to date has ever been able to build a decent case to prosecute and incarcerate Li. It seems that every time we get close, we always come up short attaining that single critical piece of evidence necessary for a conviction. So we recently decided to revise our strategy and investigate the people Li does business with, to see if his illicit business dealings with other sordid characters might yield enough evidence for an indictable case. And…an opportunity arose last month that just might provide a way to do that, and tilt the playing field in our favor."

Munroe paused to let that sink in. Everyone was quiet, waiting for him to continue. Almost everyone.

"So what's the opportunity?" Polichek blurted out. Sarah caught Owen and Kurtz rolling their eyes. She stifled an urge to do the same.

"Well, S.A.C. Polichek, it appears that Mr. Li has fallen in love."

"Love? So what?" asked Polichek.

Staff Sergeant Daniel Munroe raised a hand and said, "I'll get to that now, S.A.C."

He clicked the remote and a new face appeared on the wall. It was a woman with the same unenthusiastic look as anyone else getting their picture taken for a drivers license. But Sarah knew a beautiful woman when she saw one, and the exotic eyes and full lips belied any notion that this woman wasn't an extraordinary beauty.

"Meet Lynn Chan, President of the Lucky Star Trading Company and owner of Vancouver's newest and most desirable luxury condominium building," said Munroe. "More significant to us, though, Ms. Chan is Mr. Cheng Li's new lover.

"Miss Chan has dual citizenship, Canadian and American, she's highly educated with a law degree from Stanford, speaks Mandarin and Cantonese, as well as English of course. She's obviously Asian, thirty years old, single, and last but not least, rich. Miss Chan made her money the old fashioned way. She inherited it. A man named Wei Lee, her former boss and lover who I'm sure you're all familiar with, left his entire estate to her after drowning last spring."

"Is that the Lee who drowned in the Yukon River last spring?" asked Polichek.

Sarah exhaled with exasperation.

Yes, you moron, it's the same man.

"It is sir, the very same man," replied Munroe. "As I said, Lee bequeathed Chan his entire estate which among other things included her brand new luxury condominium building in Vancouver. She was his executive secretary in Los Angeles at the time of his death, and it came as some surprise to us that he would leave all his assets to his secretary, until we discovered that Lee had no one else in his life—no wife, no kids, no siblings, no relatives—no one. So lucky Miss Chan. She was Lee's sole beneficiary for all that he owned, including two briefcases full of gold that were recently delivered to her by the Yukon Government. Last year those two briefcases were seized as evidence for a murder trial, but that trial never took place after a plea bargain was negotiated. The gold in those briefcases was worth over two million dollars and belonged to a Yukon gold mine, a mine she now owns courtesy of the late

Mr. Lee. So last month Miss Chan got even richer. But none of this information explains why we're so interested in the woman you're looking at."

Munroe paused to sip from his glass of water and clear his throat. "As best as we're able, we're always monitoring Mr. Li's movements around Vancouver, which by the way and for obvious reasons, has now become Chan's new home. A few weeks ago we noticed Li was frequently spending the night at Chan's residence, the penthouse suite in her new building. We can only speculate whether Li is doing business with Chan, but we're almost certain the two are having a romantic relationship. If that's true, then we think their relationship warrants our scrutiny because a hole in Li's armor may have been created. Chan certainly won't have anything close to the security measures that Li employs, and so should the two ever do any kind of deal together, well we think that might be a good opportunity to expose Li's side of the transaction. Of course we know that Miss Chan is no angel, at least not based on the businesses she inherited from Lee, which includes fifty massage parlors in California that she continues to operate, and a Yukon gold mine that was run last year as a money laundering scam. But Chan is young and inexperienced, and therefore a prime candidate for Li to take advantage of in one of his scams.

"And therein is the opportunity. Should Chan ever find she's been burned in one of Li's deals, which is always a likely outcome for any of his partners, we think she'd be more than happy to give him up in exchange for staying out of jail. Remember, just one conviction is all we need to incarcerate Li. Our strategy is certainly speculative, but we think it's a good approach and justifies our time and resources. And your time and resources as well, Mr. Owen, and yours too, Mr. Polichek. Because whatever deal these two scoundrels might cook up together, it would almost certainly involve cross-border financial transactions, and those transactions will be of mutual interest to all agencies concerned. That's why we're seeking your assistance and cooperation on your side of the border, gentlemen. And lady."

Munroe nodded with reverence at Sarah, paused, then said, "Corporal."

The young woman sitting at the door rose to her feet and opened the blinds, then turned on the lights.

Everyone blinked and looked down, waiting for their eyes to adjust to the light. Sarah eventually looked at Kurtz who acknowledged her with a nod, then at Owen who was chewing on a pencil. Owen caught her gaze and nodded too. The wheels were turning inside, thought Sarah, though she had no idea what he might be thinking. Polichek was still squinting at the faint image of the woman on the wall. He reminded Sarah of a college student who'd missed the first three classes of a course and had no idea of what was going on.

After some pause for thought, Owen spoke.

"We're certainly interested, Staff Sergeant. We know Chan and have been trying to keep tabs on her ever since she moved to Vancouver. We know she's running the same prostitution ring in California that was owned by her former boss, so she must still be recruiting girls from some human trafficking source. But what that current source is, we have no idea. And based on her last tax return, we know she's not banking her profits. Where she's hiding those profits, which will all be cash, is also a mystery. She certainly needs to launder it somehow. We know there's been a lot of recent exploration activity around the mine she owns in the Yukon, but she closed the mine last year and it's no longer in production. That's perplexing to us. Her former boss was using the mine to launder *his* cash, so if she's not operating the mine, how's she laundering *her* cash? That's something we need to find out. So your investigation of Li, and any business he might have with Chan, are indeed of mutual interest. You want Li, we want Chan, and you say they're sleeping together. We all need to find out what they're up to. Working with you would make a lot of sense. We're in."

"Thank you, S.A.C. Owen. I'm glad you see it that way. S.A.C. Polichek? Can the RCMP count on the US Treasury to share any relevant financial information on Chan that you might dig up south of the border?"

Polichek looked like a deer in the headlights.

"Relevant financial information? What relevant financial information?"

Sarah put her head in her hands and and rubbed her temples. *Moron!*

She could throttle the idiot. But instead she recovered and composed herself, then said, "Sir, I think what the Staff Sergent is asking is whether we're prepared to commit resources to investigate any suspicious financial transactions conducted by Lynn Chan in the US, and share information on those transactions as they might relate to the RCMP's investigation of Mr. Li's crimes in Canada."

Polichek gave Sarah a blank look, then said, "Right. Of course. We're in too."

Staff Sergent Daniel Munroe seemed very pleased and said, "Good, thank you, S.A.C. Polichek. Gentlemen, your government's contributions to our investigation of Li will be much appreciated. You can count on the same cooperation from the RCMP to share any intelligence relevant to your investigation of Chan south of the border. Tomorrow I'll send each one of you a complete dossier on Mr. Li by secure email. We'll also issue you security clearances for ease of entry into any port in Canada, should your investigations lead you north of the border."

Everyone smiled and stood and there were handshakes all round. There was an uncomfortable pause when everyone realized the meeting had taken only twenty minutes. The American contingent now had time on their hands. Their ride to the airport wasn't scheduled until noon.

What to do?

FOUR

"Staff Sergeant Munroe, our flight to Washington isn't until two," said SAC David Owen. "Is there somewhere we can sit and do a little work?"

"Of course, SAC. This room isn't booked for the rest of the morning, you're welcome to work here. The Wi-Fi is secure and the Corporal will give you the password. Coffee's down the hall. I have to run but Corporal Taylor will remain at your service." Munroe was almost at the door when he stopped and turned. "Mr. Owen, just a thought, but if you'd like I could email you Cheng Li's dossier right now."

"Great idea," answered Owen, "we can go through it while we're waiting."

Sarah moved to another chair with an even better view of the park. Owen and Kurtz decided they needed a break and left together with Munroe for a guided tour to the men's room. The young Corporal followed them out. Polichek had moved to the end of the table and was emptying his briefcase.

Sarah unzipped her attaché and pulled out her tablet. She turned it on and waited as it searched for the network. Corporal Taylor returned to the room and handed her a card with the password. Across the street two birds were taking turns dive bombing a squirrel that was running for its life. Sarah watched them for a while and thought how different her world was from theirs. Or maybe not. She looked at Polichek who was making a racket trying to open his laptop, then back at the birds and the squirrel. No way she was getting up to help him. The Corporal walked to the end of the table and opened it for him. When an icon flashed on the screen of her tablet, Sarah entered the password.

The email from Munroe had come in and she opened it. There were five files attached. She was curious about the third one. It was labeled 'hallwaylc. jpeg'.

'lc'.

Lynn Chan?

She tapped the file with a finger and it opened. 'hallwaylc' was a slide show of black and white photos. She began tapping the arrow on the screen and randomly scanned a few photos. Time and date stamps were imprinted at the bottom of each photo and she realized they were organized in chronological order. The images were soft and grainy and had likely been taken with a motion sensitive surveillance camera, probably a battery powered micro model with a short range transmitter. All the photos were of people in a long wide hallway with a formal entry door at one end. The photos were all slightly off kilter and she guessed the camera had been hastily stuck on a wall by someone in a hurry. Sarah wondered whether the surveillance had been authorized by a court.

Each image she viewed was of such low resolution that none of them would be much use to anyone, unless they knew who they were looking at. What was obvious, though, was the absence of doors along the hallway, as well as the framed art and ornate sconces adorning the walls. She surmised the photos might have been taken on the penthouse floor in Chan's new building. Only one way to find out.

Sarah went back to the beginning of the slide show and began scrolling through them. The first twenty photos were of an Asian woman alone, coming and going from what she assumed was likely a residential suite. She had to believe the woman was Lynn Chan, judging by the fit of her clothes, varying hairstyles, and the most telling clue, a different pair of shoes for every outfit. The next two photos were of the same woman, but this time with a man.

The two were entering the suite. The time stamps were just before midnight. The next two photos were taken eight hours later and showed the same man and woman leaving the suite together. She noted the date stamp was exactly a week ago, on a Monday morning. The images were so grainy it was hard to discern their faces, but their body language and physical proximity implied an intimacy. The couple had to be Chan and Li.

Who else?

The twenty-fifth photo was time stamped 9:02 a.m., on the same day. A man in a suit was leading three workmen wearing white coveralls and painters caps toward the door of Chan's suite. One workman carried a short ladder, another a tool box in each hand, another a large box. The man in the suit carried nothing. The three workmen were of average height and weight, but the fourth man, the empty handed one, looked grossly obese. The next photo, also time stamped 9:02 a.m., showed the obese man working a key in the door while the other men waited behind him.

The next to last photo in the file was time stamped 10:08 a.m., a little over an hour later. The three workmen were leaving the suite, walking toward the camera in single file. They were wearing the same white coveralls and painter caps, and carrying the same equipment and box as when they'd entered the suite. The obese man had his back to the camera and was evidently locking the door.

In the last photo, also stamped 10:08 a.m., the obese man had turned away from the door and was walking toward the camera. Sarah leaned in for a closer look.

And gasped.

FIVE

Problems for me on a Monday morning are never in short supply, and when I left the village, I had twice as many as an hour ago.

One problem was my dogs were AWOL. Apparently they had better things to do than come home with me and had ignored my calls and whistles. Oh well, I've chased a few women myself and could relate. I'd have to make a special trip to retrieve them later, maybe at noon when they were hungry. It's about the only time they come when I call.

A more pressing problem, though, was being at a loss to understand why anyone would sabotage Minto's first new building in over sixty years. Everyone in the village was excited about the new arena. Not only would the Band have an indoor rink for skating and hockey, but also an off-season facility for all kinds of other activities. Like bingo. Now who doesn't want to play bingo in a brand new arena?

I was driving a steady sixty miles an hour with my window down, reveling in the majestic colors of a Yukon spring day—the vibrant greens in the valleys, the mauves and magentas on the mountains, the riots of purple fireweed dancing in the fields. Hawks and ravens soared high in the sky and occasionally a gopher or rabbit would make a mad dash across the road in front of me. The

land was alive again and on any other day the renaissance would
be uplifting.

But I was depressed, preoccupied with who might be so dead
set against a new arena that they'd try to halt its construction. The
arena was never going to be a money maker so it couldn't be a
commercial competitor. And surely it couldn't be someone with an
emotional beef like jealousy or resentment. The Minto Band was
the sole owner of the land and had been for ten thousand years. So
who might begrudge a small community of aboriginal Canadians
for building an ice rink on their own property?

Yet another mystery.

Then I had an occurence.

I get them now and again and knew exactly who to talk to.
Maybe she could tell me if my hunch was worth investigating.
Besides, I was hungry.

* * *

Daryl roared past me with his lights flashing when I slowed
and turned into the Minto Café parking lot. Actually it's not really
a parking lot, more like a wide dirt clearing in front of an old
wood building with a couple of ancient gas pumps standing guard
out front. At the north end of the lot is an eclectic assortment of
junk that no one wants to deal with—numerous wrecked cars and
trucks, a crumpled plane missing its wings and motor, a stripped
bulldozer sitting on logs, and the rusty artifacts of various doomed
mining ventures—all haphazardly scattered along the edge of
a dusty spruce forest. At the south end lies the energy center of
Minto—a solitary diesel pump, a heating oil tank, a cage full of
propane tanks, and a fenced enclosure securing a dozen barrels of
aviation fuel. The barrels are mine.

As for the building itself, well it's hardly what most people
would call a Café, more like a parched and weathered two-story
box preserved in a petrified layer of road dust.

But we call it the Café.

The rough timber building is owned and operated by the Minto

First Nation Band and currently serves as the village's main purveyor of food, fuel and drink. Years ago the second story developed a list and the plumbing in the six rooms upstairs started to break apart. The tilt in the upstair walls has been noticeably increasing over the past couple of years and I say it's only a matter of time before the whole works collapses and falls to the ground. However imminent that possibility might be, it's never concerned the Minto First Nation. A few years ago when repairing the plumbing upstairs became a daily chore, they simply shuttered off the stairs and built some leaky log cabins out back for their infrequent highway guests.

In any other jurisdiction the Café would have long been condemned, but this is Minto, and it's under First Nation management. The Band owns the building and they don't give a damn 'how they do it outside'. So long as the first floor adequately serves its purpose as a restaurant, grocery store and bar, the Café will remain open for business until nature takes it course.

Damn the torpedoes.

I idled into the lot and gave a wide berth to two muddy four-by-four pickups parked in front of the Café's big front windows. Both trucks were a faded yellow with plenty of dents and scrapes, spider cracks in the windshields, and the pedigree of vehicles with a lifetime of off-road use and abuse. The one on the left had three bumper stickers. One said 'The Moral Majority is Neither', another 'Nuke the Whales', another 'If It Doesn't Grow, Ya' Gotta Mine It'. I'd have to agree with two of the three. Each sat low on its axles, overloaded with bulging cloth bags in the back. The bags were bound closed with wire ties and labelled with metal tags. It would be a good guess the bags contained rock samples.

I parked on the south side of the building and walked down a wooden boardwalk protected by a dozen ancient gold dredge buckets. Each cast iron bucket had a new coat of glossy black paint and was overflowing with freshly planted geraniums. At an easy two hundred pounds a piece, they were never going to blow over in the wind, let alone get cherry picked by someone scrounging free flower pots. The Café's gardener would have to be one strong dude to have arranged them so nicely. A battered old tow truck parked beside a light pole told me he was around.

I stopped at the front door and wiped my boots on an old straw mat with a hole in the middle. A faded piece of paper was taped on the door. It was a hand written notice that had been put up last fall. At the top it said 'Mens Baseball', and below that, 'Tonight is cancelled due to Darkness'.

When I walked into the Café, the Chief of the Minto First Nation Band was on the radio. Minnie McCormack, a very large and rotund native woman with thick glasses and a braid of jet black hair running down her back, was sitting at her usual station, a tall swivel stool behind the cash register.

"RCMP Otter, this is Minto Café Radio," she bellowed into a corded mike. She had her eyes locked on two dials mounted on the wall behind her. "Winds ten at one-eighty, pressure thirty point one, you are clear to land, over!"

She slammed the mike down on the VHF radio, spun around, and looked at me.

"Brody!"

I rolled my eyes. Minnie always yells my name when I walk into the Café. When I stopped in front of her, I said, "Minnie, you don't clear a plane to land at an uncontrolled airport, just the wind and air pressure is all you're supposed to tell the pilot, it's up to the pilot if it's clear to land."

"Mister, that airport is on *our* land and I'll damn well tell whoever wants to land at *our* airport if they're clear to land at *our* airport! By the way, Daryl just called in on the radio. Says he's pickin' up a bunch of cops on that plane comin' in, says they're comin' over for coffee, says they want to ask you some questions about the fire, says you're supposed to wait here for them. I think they want to know if you had anything to do with that fire. Did you have anything to do with that fire?"

I studied the two communication radios and a bird's nest of wires on the greasy counter behind her, then said, "No, Minnie, I did not have anything to do with that fire and I don't have a clue who did. But I'd sure like to know."

"Me too. Who would do such a thing? Anyway, Daryl says you're not to leave here until they get here. He says they need to talk to you about something very important. That's what he said, just like that. So if you're eatin', you better eat fast, if you're intendin' to run off like you always do. They'll be here soon. Want the usual, hon?"

"Yeah, Minnie, the usual," I muttered with a sigh.

Damn cops. I hate talking to cops. Especially when they're on one of their fishing expeditions. What could I tell them about who torched all that lumber? I wanted to talk to Minnie about my hunch but there wasn't going to be time. Not with the cops on the way. I had to dine and dash.

Minnie spun around her chair and bellowed through the kitchen window, "Leah! Order up! Breakfast for Brody! Pronto!"

I headed toward my favorite table on the far wall but stopped at the end of the counter to peruse the junk food inventory. No sour cream and onion Pringles. Pringles in Minto are like cops, never around when you need them. I lifted the lid of an old freezer to see what I might cook for dinner.

A shadow fell over the freezer as if cast by a great creature.

"Hey, Brody."

"Hey, Reg," I replied, not looking at the bear of a man who'd approached me with the stealth of a cat.

Minnie's son Reggie, my best friend and the heir apparent to the chiefdom of the Minto Band, stood at my shoulder. He had on the same work boots, blue jeans, black T-shirt, and red and black checked jacket he wears every day. Reg is twenty something, a little shorter than me, but wide and thick and solid, and unbelievably strong. He wears his straight black hair short these days, but when I met him five years ago it hung in a braided rope halfway down his back. One might assume the scars under his eyebrows are from fighting but it's been a long time since anyone picked a fight with Reggie. The scars on his broad brown face are actually self-inflicted from opening beer bottles with his eyes. The twist caps they put on beer bottles these days has thankfully put an end to that pointless bravado.

Most days Reg can be found puttering around the Café, doing whatever his mother tells him to do, but occasionally he'll go out on the highway in his old tow truck to pick up a broken down vehicle. He also gets a fair share of work from me, doing all kinds of odd jobs, and doing them well. He's never disappointed me and always turns up on time. I'm not sure if Reg has ever been outside the territory, he rarely leaves Minto, but no one I know is more competent in the bush and he's the best guide I know. No one goes hunting with Reg and comes back without a so-called 'trophy'.

For a while we stood in silence, staring through an ice fog hovering over a couple of hundred pounds of frozen food.

"Beef's just in. The lake tomorrow?"

"Yeah, Reg, the lake tomorrow. Ten o'clock, okay? Do me a favor and throw a couple of those porterhouse steaks in a bag for me. And a bag of peas."

Reggie reached down and picked up my order with a hand that resembled an industrial tool. He walked away without a word.

I sat down at my favorite table. It's the last one against the wall at the back of the room, separated from the next table by a big wood stove, but still affords a good view of the barren stretch of land across the road, aka the Minto Airport. The Minto Airport really isn't an airport, just a half mile gravel strip that parallels the highway. Its midpoint lies roughly dead center through the Café's big front windows and is marked by a tattered windsock swinging on a rusty steel pole. Seems that with each passing year the pole leans a little farther south. I sat down knowing I'd be able to see the RCMP plane land with plenty of time to eat, and leave before the cops arrived.

Two men were sitting at one of the front windows, mopping up what was left of their breakfasts. I assumed they belonged to the pickups out front. Both men had ballcaps and beards, working man's hands, dirty stiff clothes, and experienced muddy boots.

They'd obviously been in the bush for a while, I could tell because they weren't talking. The only thing on their minds would be a shave, a shower, and the touch of a woman. One of them looked familiar but it took me a while to put a name to his face.

I got up and walked over to their table, taking care not to kick over an orange traffic cone sitting in the middle of the floor. Whenever one of the Café's floorboards pops up, Minnie puts the cone over the board. Eventually Reggie will find time to nail it back in place.

"Mike, long time no see, everything good?"

Mike Giguere was a geologist and a good guy. A number of times in the past five years I'd flown him into some pretty desolate places north of Minto. Mike was tall, lean and sinewy, maybe in his early fifties, though he looked much older with deep creases lining his heavily weathered face, the price paid for a lifetime working in the Yukon bush. He was one of those old school geologists who had chosen to practice his profession outdoors, searching for minerals where they were, not philosophizing about them in an office. I've always liked doing business with Mike, he's always on time and pays me promptly, and never turns up at my plane with more than it can carry.

He looked me up and down and said, "Hey, Brody, how you been? Thought that was you I saw walk in. Glad I ran into you, just the man I need to talk to. This is Dan Sanders from Fairbanks. Dan's working with me on a new exploration project up at Thistle Creek. Dan's a blaster, an explosives expert. We just finished a surface sampling program up and down the creek valley. Hey, pull up a chair and join us."

Thistle Creek. Just the mention of the place made my heart skip a beat. It had been the focal point for all kinds of trouble in the Yukon last year and I had to wonder why Mike was working there. And for whom. The man named Dan Sanders didn't seem like the friendliest guy. He didn't offer his hand or say anything to me, barely managed a nod, just stroked his beard and gazed out the window.

"I got breakfast coming, Mike, just thought I'd say hello. But thanks. Who's your client?"

"Some brand new venture called Thistle Creek Resources. One of those penny exploration companies with a couple of million bucks in the kitty. They optioned the hard rock rights from the owner of a placer mine that was operating there last year. The shares trade under the symbol TCR. Might want to buy some, bought myself a bunch last week at five cents a share and it's doubled already.

"Dan and I are running their exploration program. We're looking for the source of the gold in the creek. We just finished a stripping program along the creek sides, sampled the surface along a one mile strike, and everywhere we looked there's epithermal material with disseminated pyrites and quartz in altered sediments, lots of oxidized breccia and quartz stockwork too. Yesterday we blasted out some samples in an old adit on a hillside. Found a nice smoky quartz vein the old timers were working with visible gold all over the face. Once we figure out the lithology, you never know, maybe we'll be looking at another Carlin deposit. Some grab samples we assayed ran half an ounce of gold per ton. Bit of copper and silver in them too."

I nodded my head like I had a clue what Mike was talking about, but could tell he was excited about his new project.

"Sounds great, Mike."

"I'll say. If we find enough rock with that kind of grade, we could have another open pit mine for the Yukon. Open pit is what the big companies want these days, so it could mean a bunch more mining jobs for the territory. Couple of years ago they found a pretty good-sized deposit about twenty miles south, so chances are there's another one real close. Anyway, we've got a couple of million dollars to spend this summer and can't be wasting our time driving rock samples to Whitehorse. Whenever we have to drive samples south to the assay lab, we lose two days out of our exploration schedule. So I was wondering, would you be interested in doing a couple of trips for us? About a thousand pounds a load?

All you have to do is pick up the samples at Thistle Creek and fly them to Whitehorse. The assay company will take delivery when you land at Schwatka. That's the job."

"I can do it, Mike, but you know flying's not the cheapest way to move rocks. It'll cost you a lot more than driving them out with a truck. I'll need $3,500 a trip."

He nodded and said, "That's kinda' what I figured and your price sounds fair. But time is money and this company, TCR, well they seem to have lots of money and not much time. They're always in a big hurry to get assay results for their press releases. The boss in Vancouver calls me almost every day on the satphone, always wants to know when the next samples will be shipped to Whitehorse. I told him the only way to speed up the process is to fly our samples to town and he gave me the go ahead. Your first load would be Friday. If it's okay with you, I'll fax you the contract when I get to Whitehorse. Got a fax?"

I pointed a thumb over my shoulder. "I don't but the Café does. Ask Minnie for the number when you pay your bill."

"I'll do that," he said. "Here's my card. You got one yet?"

"Nope."

"Some things never change, huh? But I'll need your phone numbers."

"Numbers?"

"Home and away. You must have a cell phone by now."

"As a matter of fact I do have a cell phone, but I don't know the number."

"You don't know your cell phone number?"

"Nope. And if I did, I wouldn't give it out to just anyone. Hardly ever use the damn thing anyway. Minnie knows what it is, ask her. But don't be surprised if I don't answer. And please don't give it to anyone else."

"What if she's tall and gorgeous?"

I laughed and said, "Well, maybe then."

Mike stood and we shook hands.

"Glad I ran into you, Brody."

"Me too, Mike. See you Friday morning at Thistle Creek."

When I turned to go back to my table, I caught a dirty look from Dan Sanders.

SIX

Last June on the Yukon River a man handed me a styrofoam box with four hundred thousand dollars inside. The box was loaded into a canoe I was to paddle alone. Then the man loaded three more styrofoam boxes into another canoe, a canoe he would share with his boss. We all set off on a river trip to Dawson.

They didn't make it.

So what happened to the four hundred thousand dollars in the box in my canoe? Well between you and me, I gambled it away. Every dollar of it.

On lottery tickets.

When the Minto Band finally decided this was the year to build a new ice arena, someone came up with the bright idea to hold a lottery to help with the cost. I've got to admit, I was the someone.

First prize is a new four-by-four pickup truck, a coveted asset for anyone living in the north, even if it's rumored to be a Dodge. So far the tickets have been an easy sell. People around here can't wait for the draw at the Band's annual Canada Day birthday bash, held the first day of July every year, just down the road at Two Spirit Lake.

Close to sixty thousand tickets have been sold so far and I bought and paid for two thirds of them. Unfortunately for me, I can't remember where I put the stubs, and if the stubs don't get put in the drum, well I guess I can't win the truck. Tough luck for me because a lottery is one of those 'no ticky, no laundry' deals, so last week I bought one more ticket at the Café to make sure I have one stub in the drum. You only need one ticket to win anyway, and there will be so many ticket stubs in the drum, no one should notice that a mere forty thousand are missing.

All that matters is that Minnie was pleased as punch when I handed her two cardboard boxes with the four hundred thousand dollars inside. I told her I'd sold the tickets down south and would give her the stubs later. I doubt if she's losing any sleep wondering when and if that will happen. I also doubt if anyone around Minto has a clue that a certain criminal organization from California is missing the same four hundred thousand dollars, rumored to have been in a styrofoam box that happened to go missing on the Yukon River last year. As long I'm right about that, it should suffice that I'm very good at selling lottery tickets but incompetent when it comes to mundane matters like lottery ticket administration.

Everyone in Minto will be sure to believe it.

As of last week the Minto Arena Lottery had raised close to six hundred thousand dollars—almost the total budgeted cost of the new arena—and I couldn't be happier about that achievement. But I did have a growing concern that some nosy bureaucrat, or a certain cop for that matter, might get wind of the number of tickets sold and start wondering how a small Native community in the middle of nowhere could have possibly accomplished such a feat.

Fortunately it's none of their business. The Minto Band is a sovereign nation living on their own land with their own government and their own financial administration. The financial affairs of the Band are off limits to the Canadian authorities and that includes nosy cops. I may happen to know that the six hundred thousand dollars is currently sitting safe and sound in a bank account in Whitehorse, but the cops don't, and they don't have to.

Even so, the specter that they might start prying into the Band's lottery receipts was just another thing on my mind when I walked out of the Café and headed for my pickup.

Cops. Snoopy and suspicious, never around when you need them, always there when you don't. I wonder how you say that in Latin. It would be a good motto to put on the doors of their cruisers.

As soon as I left the parking lot, Daryl appeared in the mirror as a blue speck on the horizon about a mile behind me, probably headed to the Café with the VIP's who'd just landed at the airport. Of course they weren't going to find me there. No way I was going to stick around when all they wanted to do was grill me about things I knew nothing about, like who set those piles of plywood on fire. With better things to do, I was out of there as soon as I saw their fancy plane land. Daryl would know where to find me if his guests really needed to talk.

First things first was the car on my lift.

It needed two new driveshafts and I was now officially behind schedule. The old ones had to be removed, I didn't have a clue how to remove the bolts to get them out, new ones would have to be ordered from Whitehorse, and the job had to be finished today.

Then there was my old float plane. It's a 1952 DeHavilland DHC-2 Beaver, serial number 108, and my pride and joy. Yesterday morning Reggie and I went out to Two Spirit Lake to fill it with gas and prepare it for its sixty-fourth year of flying people and things into the Yukon wilderness. We noticed immediately it had a profound list to its port side, and when I checked the left float, discovered a lot of water inside. That seemed strange as it had been in the lake less than a day. Floats leak, but not that much.

It took us half an hour to pump out the float, then we winched the old plane out of the lake with Reggie's tow truck. We jacked up the left side, and after a long time inspecting every seam on the bottom of the float, saw nothing that might be a leak. We left it on the beach and drove away stymied, planning to return tomorrow with an air compressor. Pressurizing the float with air would quickly reveal a leak in a riveted seam, though the possibility was hard to fathom as both floats had been replaced only three years ago, and they'd never been abused. I should know, no one flies my plane but me.

If all that wasn't enough to deal with, I had another problem, and it was bigger than all the rest. It was the worst kind to have because there's never a satisfactory solution, at least as far as I know. And even if there was a solution, I probably wouldn't have had the courage to implement it. The problem was sitting on the couch in my cabin, devouring everything in my fridge and pantry, watching game shows and soaps all day.

Yes, a house guest, and a woman at that.

Before I braked for the turnoff to my shop, I glanced in the rear view mirror.

A red pickup truck with a white camper was closing fast.

SEVEN

Lynn Chan was livid.

She was standing between two matching Gucci suitcases she'd just lowered to the floor, and with her hands on her hips, was glaring at a gaudy monstrosity hanging over her dining room table. It was supposed to be a fine crystal chandelier but what she was looking at wasn't close to the one she'd ordered.

Not even close.

With a kick of her heel she slammed the door behind her and stomped over to her opulent walnut desk, grabbed the phone from the handset, and plopped her perfect derriere into a plush leather chair. Still seething, she punched a button on the receiver and gazed through a wall of glass at the Pacific Ocean. Tall buildings scattered along the perimeter of West Vancouver partially blocked the view, but from her fourteenth floor penthouse she could make out two container ships anchored on the flat gray waters of English Bay. They were sitting low in the water, exactly where they'd been last week, still waiting their turn to unload more crap for the Canadian economy. One ring, two rings, three rings, then "Good afternoon, Miss Chan."

"Jeremy, get your ass up here right now!"

"Yes, Miss Chan."

Chan slammed the phone down, spun around in her chair, and

glared again at the ball of rubbish hanging from her ceiling. She'd just spent a week in the choking smog of Los Angeles and the whole time there had been looking forward to admiring the crowning touch to her new home in the sky. She'd commissioned an Austrian artisan of world repute to create a masterpiece in lighting, a custom creation in a classic Baroque motif, multiple tiers of polished crystal teardrops dazzling and glittering in a magical trellis surrounding a polished silver candelabra. Her choice had been exemplary, elegance defined, an overt expression of her exquisite taste and uncompromising desire for the best of what life had to offer. A hundred grand worth of uncompromising desire.

Instead, what she was gawking at looked like a haphazard collection of cheap christmas tree ornaments, dangling from something that looked like a wagon wheel. Gaudy and tasteless, it was nothing more than a collection of chintzy bric-a-brac, probably slapped together by an amateur welder in a Bejing backyard.

Her phone rang.

"What!" she screamed into the receiver.

"Baby, you're back!"

"I'm back," growled Chan with a sigh of resignation. She swiveled around in her chair to face the ocean again, then said, "Hello, Tippy."

"You don't sound happy, doll. How was your trip?"

"Fine. Fine. The trip was fine."

"Everything good in L.A? San Fran?"

"Yeah, great, business is booming, better than ever. Everything at the bank went well. Deliver my package?"

"I did, signed, sealed and delivered. All is good, but you're not happy."

She sighed once more and took a moment before saying, "Oh it's nothing, just tired I guess."

"Well this should cheer you up. We've got a press release coming out tomorrow and it's an absolute bombshell. Your phone will be ringing like crazy as soon as it hits the wire. Every broker and promoter in the world will want to talk to you. And by the way, we're going out to dinner tonight to celebrate."

"Tippy, what do you mean *we* have a press release coming out tomorrow morning? I'm the president of Thistle Creek Resources, not you. Don't you think I'm the one who ought to decide when we issue a press release? And what exactly is this news *we* are announcing in this press release?"

"The latest sample assays from Thistle Creek, that's what. And wait 'til you see them, doll, they're off the charts! The stock will soar!"

Lynn Chan took a deep breath and realized her foray into the stewardship of a public company was not something she was enjoying. For one thing, she didn't have the control she assumed went with the job of president, let alone a clue about the mineral exploration business, or how to manage a company whose shares traded on a public stock exchange. But more than that she abhorred the protocol, constantly under the scrutiny of so many watchdog agencies and constituencies to whom she was now accountable: a board of directors, shareholders, auditors, the stock exchange, transfer agents, stock brokers, security regulators, exchange commissions, and oversight committees out the ying-yang. And the lawyers! They were driving her crazy! Every week they would send over yet another stack of documents for her signature, documents that no one cared about, documents no one read, documents she didn't understand, all seemingly created for no other reason than to feed a regulatory bureaucracy with an insatiable appetite for paperwork.

In her heart she knew she'd made a mistake going into business with Tippy, though it had seemed like a good idea at the time. Buying seed stock in Thistle Creek Resources had been a quick and simple way to deal with all the cash sitting in her safety deposit boxes in LA—cash that had just flown away with Tippy on one of his monthly business trips to Hong Kong. In exchange for her cash she'd received ten million of shares in the new company, which were now safely vested with a Cayman bank. So for the time being at least, she was home free from the taxman. That was a relief. And since she was now in charge of Thistle Creek Resources, she wouldn't have to operate that damn Yukon gold mine this summer, a mine that her former boss had been so proud of yet had ultimately been his demise. That too was a big relief because she knew nothing about mining, let alone the Yukon.

The Yukon! Wilderness! Mining! Mud and dirt! Ugh!

So now she could look forward to making some serious money the easy way, selling her shares after Tippy worked his magic. But when his latest scam had run it's course, that would be it for running a public company. Never again. There had to be an easier way to launder money. She wouldn't be Tippy's patsy again.

Even if he knew how to take her breath away.

* * *

Stupid bitch.

She made him nervous with all the whining. As if she could write a press release. As if she knew the business. As if she knew the game.

Tippy Li shook his head, replaced the phone in the armrest, and looked down the gleaming silver wing of his brand new jet. Eight miles below him the Pacific glowed like bronze under the setting sun, flowing like a river under the Dassault Falcon 8X as it sped east toward a dark horizon.

Thirty-six years ago he'd made the very same trip from Hong Kong to Vancouver in an old slow boat. That first journey to the new world had taken eighteen days. Today, at over six hundred miles an hour, he'd do it in ten hours. Soon he'd be home for dinner with the hottest woman he'd dated in years. Hopefully he could cheer her up.

Of course he knew how to do that, provided she didn't insist on ruining the evening complaining about press releases. But a few drinks and a fine meal should take the wind out of her sails, then it would be straight to bed. He'd been gone for a week and knew exactly what she needed. And what she needed he would gladly supply. Until such time she became just another liablilty.

He knew exactly how to deal with that situation too.

EIGHT

I can fix just about anything.

Except a woman.

If I had an inkling how they work, I might have been able to keep one.

Two worn out driveshafts were lying on the bench in front of me. I was rolling and twisting them back and forth, tweaking the constant velocity joints, deciding whether they could be repaired with a kit. I'd removed them as easy as pie after coming up with an ingenious way to remove those inaccessible bolts. Life's no fun unless you know how to get a kick out of yourself, and you couldn't patent the combination of levers and wrenches I'd rigged to get them out.

I was about to reach for the phone on the wall when it started ringing.

At that very same instant, Daryl's big SUV came roaring into my lot, going far too fast, spraying and spitting out gravel, skidding to a stop with the wheels locked. Four doors opened in unison, four doors slammed in unison, the phone was still ringing, and I made an executive decision to ignore the call.

Armed with only a rag in my hand, I walked out to the open bay door and watched four uniforms and a civilian approaching. They were spaced out in a wide line, crunching through the gravel like

Clydesdales, staring me down with their best cop glares, poised for trouble with their arms splayed out, ready to draw firepower if I tried anything funny. When they stopped in a semicircle in front of me, I was hemmed in by a fence of pressed pants and shiny black shoes.

Showdown at the Brody Corral.

"Hey boys, car trouble?" I asked, not looking at any of them, working a line of grease under a fingernail.

Daryl jabbed a finger at my chest and said, "You were supposed to wait for us at the Café, Brody."

"I was?"

"You know you were. You were supposed to…"

Staff Sergeant Alan Robson, a man I'd met before and didn't like, held out a hand and stopped Daryl before he tore a piece out of me. Robson was also an imposing figure, thick and strong, very fit, a little over six feet, maybe two hundred and twenty pounds, with a fresh buzz cut and piercing blue eyes that he used for one of the best cop glares I've ever seen.

"The more things change, the more they stay the same, right Mr. Brody?" When I said nothing, he took a step forward and asked, "Got a minute?"

Ignoring his first question, I replied, "Sure, what can I do for you today, Staff Sergeant?"

"How about we step over to that bench of yours, have a little chat, just you and me."

"Alright," I said, trying my best to appear relaxed as I walked to the bench with Robson breathing down my neck.

When we got there, I turned around and found myself looking directly into his eyes, barely a foot away. He had his face in mine as usual, but as intimidating as that was, I managed to stand my ground. The phone was still ringing.

"You gonna answer that?" he asked with a scowl, jutting his chin at the phone on the wall.

"Nope."

He nodded and rubbed his chin, then said, "Could be important. Whoever it is, isn't giving up."

"If it's important they'll call again," I said.

Robson was apparently one of those people who just had to answer a telephone. It was clearly an irritant to him and he was compelled to put an end to it. He lifted the receiver an inch off its cradle, then dropped it with a clunk. The ringing stopped.

"So, Mr. Brody, any idea about who might have set all those fires at the village this morning?"

"Not a clue. Why would I?"

"Thought it might have something to do with those shenanigans of yours last summer."

"Shenanigans?"

"Yeah, you know, poking your nose into all kinds of things that were none of your business. Like money laundering, and two murders, and then making a so-called emergency landing on the Yukon River, and then that so-called canoe trip to Dawson, and then a drowning, and oh yeah, the biggest little lottery I've ever heard of."

Biggest little lottery. Robson was no dummy.

"A drowning?" I said. "Like just *one* drowning? Don't you mean *two* drownings?"

The big cop cocked his head to one side, gave me a suspicious look, rubbed his chin again, then surveyed the bench.

"Driveshafts," he said.

"That's right. Driveshafts."

Robson nodded again. "Watched my brother change a pair of those a few years back. Hell of a job. Bastards to get out. The rubber boots on the axles get brittle in the cold and they crack and split, then the dirt gets into the bearings and in no time they chew themselves up. Always gotta keep your eye on driveshaft boots in the Yukon."

He nodded some more as if seeking concensus, then looked at the car on the lift and went quiet.

"Sergeant, er, Staff Sergeant, did you come in here to talk about driveshafts? And what do you mean one drowning?"

"Oh, see that fella' over there in civvies?" he asked, pointing outside.

I sighed with impatience. "Yeah, I see him."

"Maybe he can help you with that. That's Staff Sergeant John Munroe from our Vancouver detachment. He leads a special task force that investigates organized crime on the lower mainland. He wants to take a quick look at the Thistle Creek mine and is hitching a ride with us to Dawson this morning. We've got other business up there but Thistle Creek, well it's right on the way to Dawson. Course you know that, don't you Mr. Brody? Anyway, we're always happy to assist our colleagues from Vancouver so naturally we were more than happy to oblige Mr. Munroe's request for a bird's eye view of the mine. As soon as we've taken a quick look-see at the fire scene in the village, we'll be on our way. But seeing as we were in town, I thought if you had a minute to spare, well maybe you wouldn't mind answering a few of the Staff Sergeant's questions. Sure would appreciate it."

"Questions."

"Yeah. Just a few. I told the Staff Sergeant all about you, how you were involved with all the goings-on at the Thistle Creek mine last summer, how you were...shall we say... familiar with the players involved. He said he'd like to ask you a few questions about the people running the mine, if that's okay with you."

I shook my head in disgust. Robson was being condescending and reticent. What was he up to? It was obvious he was working closely with Munroe on something to do with the Thistle Creek mine and was setting me up for a Q and A session with his buddy cop from Vancouver. But what was going on up there now that would be of any interest to the cops? The mine was closed. The 'players' from last year were all out of the picture. Could this have something to do with the exploration program?

"Okay," I said. "I'll talk to him. But not for long. Just a few questions. I'm busy."

Robson gave me a wry grin and started to walk away, then raised a finger in the air, turned and said, "Oh, one more thing, Mr. Brody. I hear you've got a contract to fly rocks out of Thistle Creek. Job starts Friday. Is that right?"

Damn. Minnie and her broadcasting. Mike Giguere asks Minnie for the Café's fax number, Minnie asks why, Mike tells her about our contract, and Minnie tells the cops. The Yukon may be a hundred and eighty six thousand square miles of pristine wilderness but it's also the biggest little town on the planet. Less than an hour ago I make a deal with a geologist in the middle of nowhere to fly rock samples out of an exploration camp—also in the middle of nowhere—and now the RCMP knows all about it. And who else? The FBI? The CIA? Interpol? How ridiculous. I had to remind myself that there's no such thing as a secret in the Yukon. I guess that explains why there's so much lying up here.

After leaning against the bench for five minutes I was gnashing my teeth. The two staff sergeants were taking their time and it was getting on my nerves. They'd moved out to a spot in the middle of the parking lot and had been in a deep and protracted private conversation ever since. For a while I watched them nodding to each other in constant agreement, exchanging top secret information in whispers, occasionally glancing my way to make sure I didn't make a break for it. When I'd finally had enough of doing nothing, I called my favorite parts guy in Whitehorse.

"Yukon Auto Parts, this is Christine, how may I help you?"

"Christine! What's happening?"

"Hey, Brody. We picked some fresh lettuce and tomatoes in our greenhouse this morning and the grocery store just got in a big load of California grapes and peaches. Want some?"

"Sure do. I think I'm getting scurvy up here. Send me lots of everything. And I need a set of driveshafts too."

I gave her the specs for the driveshafts. She said they were in stock and promised to ship them on the noon bus to Dawson. I'd have them by two o'clock, as well as a box of fresh fruit and vegetables.

Christine is not only the best parts 'man' in the Yukon but my main supplier of fresh produce. She and her boyfriend live on a large rural property south of Whitehorse. Christine works in town at an auto parts store and her partner, Bruce, is a stay-at-home Dad, tending to a five year old boy and a burgeoning hydroponic business he runs out of a greenhouse behind their home. The currency of our relationship is barter and I pay my account with everything from salmon and Chinese food, to fly-in fishing trips for Bruce and his buddies.

I hung up the phone just as the two cops were adjourning their top secret summit. Staff Sergeant Munroe was heading my way and I sized him up from fifty feet. He was a little older than Robson but equally well turned out—fit, slim and tall—with a full head of salt and pepper hair that he wore neat and short. He was wearing a pair of dark pressed slacks, a gray collared sweater, and a black leather jacket. His shoes were regulation RCMP, very black, very shiny, and of course, very big. When he stopped in front of me the first thing I noticed were his steel gray eyes. They exuded a certain intelligence I'd never seen before in a cop. He held out a large hand and smiled. I didn't return his smile but reluctantly shook hands with him. It didn't seem to bother him that his right hand might have gotten a little greasy from the mutual courtesy because he slid the same hand inside his jacket and pulled out the biggest cell phone I've ever seen. Or maybe it was one of those tablet gizmos. Whatever it was, he placed it on the bench between us.

"Mr. Brody, my name is Munroe, Staff Sergeant John Munroe. I appreciate your time. Just a few questions, shouldn't take long. I can see you're busy."

He glanced around the shop—at the car on the lift, the tools on the floor, the driveshafts on the bench.

"Busy enough," I said. "What are your questions?"

Munroe tapped his high tech gizmo. An image appeared on the screen. He slid the device toward me.

"Do you recognize this man?" he asked.

Show and tell, here we go. A 'few questions' and a whole bunch of photos for your viewing pleasure. I'd been through this kind of exercise before, last spring in Dawson at an interview with half a dozen cops in a windowless room. It had been a veritable dog and pony show and I'd talked far more than I should have while analyzing a steady stream of photographs being shoved under my nose. The ploy is to keep you distracted with something to look at while they pepper you with way more than just a 'few questions'. The distraction of the photos takes your eyes off theirs, a mollifying tactic to put you at ease and get you yacking. Loose lips sink ships and I'd talked way too much for my own good in that interview. Live and learn, I would not be fooled again.

I took a quick look at the image on the screen, didn't have a clue who I was looking at, and said, "No".

"Take your time. Are you sure?"

"I did take my time and I am sure," I said, folding my arms and turning away from the bench to study a broom hanging on the far wall.

Munroe folded his arms too, turned and leaned against the bench, and joined me in a thorough appraisal of the same broom. After a pregnant pause he said, "You know, if I was to show that very same photo to someone in Vancouver's Chinatown, they'd give me the very same answer as you just did. But I think you're being honest when you say you don't know the man because anyone in Chinatown would be shaking like a leaf right now."

"Really."

"Really. How about you take another look at that face, then I'll tell you who he is."

Munroe didn't move. I shrugged my shoulders, decided it wouldn't hurt to humor Staff Sergeant Munroe, and turned around for another look at the photo on his tablet. The man on the screen was Asian, probably Chinese, and his image was likely lifted from a passport or driver's license. After a long second look, I was even more certain I'd never seen him before. All I knew was that this stranger was in his early forties and seemed to be sneering at the camera. Closer inspection revealed a profoundly disagreeable

countenance, probably the result of a strange pucker at one corner
of his mouth.

"Okay," I said. "I looked again and definitely don't know him.
Who is he?"

"His name is Cheng Li, better known as Tippy Li. He's the
dragon head of a Hong Kong triad that's recently made big inroads
into Vancouver's criminal underworld. Anything illegal, Mr. Li
can smuggle into the country and supply to you. Guns, drugs,
undocumented people, rhino horns, ivory, you name it, he'll move
it across the border and deliver it to your door. And he's obviously
very good at it because we haven't been able to catch him yet. He
also has a penchant for killing his competitors."

"Dragon head? Triad?"

"The leader, the boss. And a triad is a Chinese criminal
organization, usually based out of Hong Kong."

"Oh. Well I repair cars in Minto. Why show me his picture?"

Munroe smiled. "Maybe you'll understand after I show you the
next one." He turned and tapped the screen. Another face appeared.
"How about this woman? Recognize her?"

Munroe let me study the photo while he resumed his analysis of
the broom on the wall. For an instant the face on the screen seemed
familiar, then my impression waned. The woman on the screen was
also Asian, also Chinese, about thirty, definitely attractive, even if
the government photo didn't do her justice. I shook my head.

"Nope."

"Take your time, Mr. Brody. You've seen her in person, right
here in the Yukon."

I gave Munroe a puzzled look and stared once more at the
woman's face. Munroe then tapped the screen and another photo
appeared. This one was grainy and poor quality, a black and white
shot of a woman taken from behind as she walked down a hallway.
Her physical attributes were obvious: great legs, great figure, tightly
clad in a hip-hugging outfit, definitely an expensive package that
would be of interest to any well-heeled bidder. All the same, and

as red-blooded as I might be, I had no recollection of ever having met her.

"Are both pictures of the same woman?" I asked Munroe.

"They are."

"Well I've never seen her before."

He nodded and replied, "I think you have. Want a hint?"

"Sure."

"The coroner's inquest into the death of Wei Lee last year in Whitehorse. You testified at that inquest. She was there."

"That's right," I said, almost pleased with myself. "She was sitting in the gallery while I was on the stand. Who is she?"

"Her name's Chan. Lynn Chan. She *was* Wei Lee's executive secretary until he died, then she inherited all his assets, including the Thistle Creek mine."

There were those words again. *Thistle Creek.*

"That's nice but so what? What do these people, Chan and...?"

"Li."

"Right, Chan and Li. What do they have to do with me?"

The tall cop took a deep breath and studied my face for a while, then said, "Mr. Brody, whether you realize it or not, you have a very serious problem presented by these two individuals. But lucky for you, so do we. I'm hoping we can work together to solve our mutual problem."

"*Our* mutual problem? What mutual problem? What problem do I have with these two? And what's yours?"

"Let's deal with yours first, shall we?" Munroe straightened himself up and gave me an 'I'm in charge here' look. "The week after Lee's death last year, Miss Chan took possession and control of his massage parlor business in Southern California. And without skipping a beat, it's been business as usual ever since. She's running the same sleazy business as he was, including the sexual exploitation of young undocumented women. So all you really have to know about Lynn Chan is that she's just as much a criminal as her former boss was, and a criminal who just happens to have recently gone into business with another criminal named Tippy Li. Chan and Li are now partners in that mine I'm about to visit."

"You mean they own the Thistle Creek mine together?"

"Something like that."

Something like that.

For a moment I pondered that information and the possible ramifications. I couldn't come up with any.

"Okay. So what?" I asked. "How is that a problem for me? I don't know either of one of these people and couldn't care less who owns the mine. I was hired by the geologist running the show. I'm just supposed to fly rocks out of there."

"Right," he said.

"Well, that's the way I see it."

"May I speak frankly, Mr. Brody?"

"Sure."

"Where's the missing styrofoam box?"

"The missing styrofoam box?"

Munroe scratched the back of his head, then with the same hand pulled down the corners of his mouth.

"Okay," he said. "Maybe this will help you recall what happened to the missing box. Ever meet a man named Jack Kolinsky?"

"Yeah, he's a fisherman, lives in Haines."

"Used to live in Haines."

"Where's he live now?"

"He doesn't live anywhere now. He's dead."

"Dead?"

"Dead. The Coast Guard recovered his body three days ago. It was floating in the ocean about a mile from his boat. Coroner says the cause of death was drowning. But Kolinsky had a head wound and a fractured skull. Alaska State Police are treating the case as a suspicious death. But unless they can find some evidence to support foul play, it will have to be ruled an accident. You know, man on a boat hits his head, man gets knocked out, man falls in the water, man drowns. Been known to happen I guess. But given that the very same thing happened to another fisherman in Haines two years ago, maybe Kolinsky's death wasn't an accident, maybe it was just meant to look like an accident. Know what I mean?"

I didn't answer Munroe's redundant question and shifted my eyes to the driveshafts on the bench. Who would want Jack Kolinsky dead? The last time I saw Jack, a thug named Tommy Kay was roughing him up. But it couldn't have been Kay who killed him because Kay drowned last spring in the Yukon River. So who killed Jack Kolinsky?

Munroe dropped his cop stare and tapped his tablet again. Another face appeared on the screen.

"Know this man?"

NINE

Answer the damn phone!

With the punch of a button, Special Agent Sarah Marsalis of the US Department of the Treasury terminated her third call to the Yukon in the past hour, blew the air out of her lungs, and threw her headset on the desk.

He was in his shop! She knew it! He'd picked up and hung up on the second call, a dead giveaway. And the first and third calls—at least twenty rings each—he'd simply ignored. What on earth is wrong with the man? It wasn't a case that he was avoiding her, he had no idea who was calling. She'd been in his shop last year and had seen his one and only phone. It was thirty years old and didn't have call display. Or messaging.

Who doesn't have a phone with call display? Who doesn't have messaging? And for that matter, who doesn't answer their damn phone? She folded her arms, slumped back in her chair, and gazed out at the bumper-to-bumper traffic inching toward the Potomac.

"Bastard," she muttered. "No wonder you're single."

"Sarah? Everything okay? I'm going downstairs. Want anything?"

Special Agent Stanley Kurtz was standing behind her with an arm over the partition that separated their desks. She wondered why all men couldn't be nice guys like Stan, and then why she never seemed to have any interest in them. What was it about the self-centered ones that she found so attractive, and in particular, one incredibly ornery Yukon bush pilot? What was it about him that had gotten so deep under her skin it just wouldn't go away?

"Sarah? Earth to Sarah?"

Without turning around she replied, "Nothing Stan, thanks."

"Don't forget our meeting at four."

"Can't wait," she said with a glare out the window.

* * *

"Jesus, he's alive?"

"Appears to be, sir," replied Kurtz. "The RCMP and FBI are proceeding on that basis and we've issued a BOLO nationwide and in Canada."

Special Agent in Charge Harry Polichek carefully set the mugshot down on the table, as if being careful not to upset the man in the photo. The man was Asian and his name was Tommy Kay. His head was the size of a basketball and he had no visible neck. His shoulders were immense, running straight out from his ears and sloping beyond the edges of the picture. He had a wide smooth face with a small mouth and flat nose but his most striking feature were his eyes. They were dead and vacant, barely visible under drooping eyelids, fixated on the camera with a reptilian stare.

"Is he as dangerous as he looks?" asked Polichek.

Sarah couldn't help herself and said, "Only if he gets close to you, sir. He doesn't carry weapons."

Polichek nodded with a vacuous glaze in his eyes, then looked up and said, "Well, he can't have any bearing on our work, right? We work for the Treasury Department, we're after money launderers and con artists, not thugs like him. Jesus he looks mean."

Polichek leaned forward and studied the mugshot some more. The three agents were seated around a small round table in a glass wall office in the center of a vast floor of agents and analysts. Sarah hated visiting Polichek's office. It was like being on display in a terrarium as a steady flow of office traffic constantly circled about them, with every passerby compelled to steal at least one peak at the creatures inside. The least Polichek could do was close the blinds during a meeting but she knew he craved the attention, especially having the whole floor know he arrived early for work, every single day.

Polichek lifted his eyes from the photo, held up his watch, and said, "Okay, ten minutes before S.A.C. Owen calls. Where are we at? Agent Marsalis?"

Where are we at?

Sarah cringed. She detested the butchered grammar of modern office vernacular.

She pulled a pad of paper from her attaché and scanned her notes.

"Okay, sir, this is 'where we are at'. First, Thistle Creek Resources. Thistle Creek is a public company listed on the TSX Venture Exchange. Its shares trade under the symbol TCR. The Venture Exchange is a Canadian stock exchange for micro-cap companies—new companies with little or no income that are barely past the incubator stage. These juniors have nothing of real value when they're initially listed for trading other than a little money in the bank and 'the next great thing', perhaps a patent or a revolutionary drug, or an internet idea, or some oil and gas rights, or in the case of TCR, a gold prospect. They're incredibly high risk investments and with few exceptions are doomed for failure. One in a thousand might ever amount to anything, but that's the carrot for speculative investors—the specter of a possible moonshot return on a penny stock. Dreams do come true of course but the odds for these companies are worse than Vegas. The only people who consistently make money on penny stocks are the insiders, the pump and dump hucksters who get cheap seed stock and peddle it to the public with hype and dubious promotions.

"Okay, so now the Thistle Creek property. It's comprised of more than two hundred claims, both surface and hardrock, and is located approximately eighty miles south of Dawson. That's in the Yukon, sir, you were there last year. You'll recall a surface gold mine was being operated on the Thistle Creek property by the infamous Mr. Lee, but as we suspected, the mine wasn't making money. Lee was only running it as a scam to launder his income from his California brothels. When Lee died last June, he left the mine and all the claims, and all his other assets as well, to his secretary, Lynn Chan.

"Okay, so as soon as Chan took possession of the mine she promptly closed it, laid off the workers, and disposed of all the dirt moving equipment. However she did leave the camp intact, which includes two personnel trailers, a kitchen trailer, and a maintenance building. So fast forward to this spring because this is where things get interesting.

"In early April, Chan sold all her Thistle Creek mining claims to TCR. According to documents filed with the exchange, Chan received one million shares of TCR for her claims. Then a month later, in May, she paid cash for another nine million shares of TCR at five cents a share—that's four hundred and fifty thousand dollars, sir, which increased her holdings to ten million shares. A week after that, at the company's first shareholder meeting, she voted those shares to appoint herself president of TCR and replace the board with the company's lawyers. But then, ten days later, she filed another document with the exchange declaring that she'd sold all her shares—all ten million of them—to a private investor for exactly what she paid for them. Now why would she do that?

"So after all those transactions, if nothing else, we know the official story. Thistle Creek Resources, aka TCR, has approximately thirty million shares issued and outstanding, two million dollars in the bank, Chan is the president, and she reportedly owns a grand total of zero shares.

"And I say that's hard to fathom. Any president of a start-up is an ambitious and optimistic entrepreneur. He or she will want to own at least thirty percent of a new company, not zero. I say Chan and Li are in bed together in more ways than one, and that includes being up to no good when it comes to revealing how many shares of TCR they actually own. Which of course is mandatory under exchange regulations. So several things bear investigation.

"First, we know Chan is likely romantically involved with this man Tippy Li, a notorious Vancouver stock promoter. We also know Chan has no experience running a public company. So let's assume Li is helping her run TCR, 'holding her hand' so to speak, sir. The questions are, how is he helping her and why? I'm sure our Canadian friends at the RCMP are dying to know the answers as much as we are.

"For example, where did Chan get the four hundred and fifty thousand dollars to buy her TCR stock? Did it come from her California massage parlors? And if so, does that mean she's now using Thistle Creek Resources stock to launder the cash she earns from her prostitution business? We know she's not running a gold mine anymore, so she must be doing something to hide her illicit income. And why would she buy nine million shares of stock in a company she's in charge of, only to sell them a week later at the same price she paid for them? The answer to that last question may answer all the rest.

"So, that's 'where we are at' sir. Now we get to work. I spoke with S.A.C. Owen at the FBI this morning and he agrees it's time to start pounding the pavement and following the money. He recommended we start with a trip to Vancouver."

Polichek pursed his lips and said, "Agent Kurtz?"

"Sir, I agree we have to go to Vancouver to find out what Li and Chan are up to. But before we do that, we need to take a look at Chan's bank accounts in California. We'll need warrants and I can prepare them this evening. We'll also need to ask the RCMP to get the necessary Canadian warrants so we can look at TCR's and Chan's bank accounts in Vancouver. So first things first, sir. First we get the necessary warrants on our side of the border to look at Chan's bank accounts in LA and San Fran, *then* we go to Vancouver. The horse before the cart, sir."

Sarah was floored by what Stan had just said. Not that any of it didn't make perfect sense, but the the way he presented it was an affront. Of course they had to get warrants stateside. That was a given. But did he have to spell it out for Polichek like she didn't know what she was doing? Was Stan trying to convey that she was being impulsive or negligent, or that she wasn't competent? She could barely contain her fury with him. He was showing her up! It was the only explanation.

Polichek was about to retire and would have a big influence on the selection of his replacement. Sarah always believed she had a shot at the job, and naturally Stan would have the same aspiration. Clearly they were both qualified, both had the experience and credentials, both were front runners for the job. But had it come down to this? Making a fool of her in front of the boss to advance his cause? Politicking and undermining her efforts after all the years they'd worked together? She couldn't believe it!

But then she thought, *No problem, Stan, if you want to play it that way.*

She glared at Kurtz who wouldn't meet her eyes, then addressed Polichek.

"S.A.C. Polichek, sir, we don't have time for 'horses and carts'. Not if we're going to bust Chan for money laundering. S.A.C. Owen told me this morning he's already liaised with the RCMP and they'll get the necessary bank warrants for Canada. He also told me the FBI got the warrants for California last week and have already executed a bank search for Chan. It was he who suggested we all meet in Vancouver next week. So we're good to go for the trip to Canada, sir, *right now*. If Stan would like to join us, I'll include him when I make the arrangements. With your say-so, sir."

Kurtz ignored the sarcasm. He was studying a framed picture of Polichek's wife and kids. It was sitting on a credenza next to a bowling trophy. Polichek studied Sarah with a blank look, opened and closed his mouth, clearly at a loss for something to say. The instant he opened his mouth again, the phone at the center of the table rang. With overt relief, Polichek punched a button.

A bored voice on the speaker said, "Call from the FBI, sir, an S.A.C. Owen on line one."

"Polichek."

"Good afternoon, S.A.C. Polichek. How are you?"

"Fine, fine. Right on time, Mr. Owen. I'm sitting here with Special Agents Kurtz and Marsalis. We've been discussing the Chan case. I understand you've already been discussing strategy with Special Agent Marsalis, in a phone call you made *to her* this morning."

"Hardly what I'd call strategy, Agent Polichek. These are early days and we only discussed the elementary stuff. In fact it was you I called, very early this morning in fact, to confirm this telephone meeting. But you weren't in yet, sir, so I took the liberty of asking for Agent Marsalis. She happened to be available and I advised her when you might expect this call. I gather she gave you the message. We also spoke about something else. I assume you've seen the photo I sent you. But the real reason I'm calling now, Special Agent in Charge, sir, is to inform you all that we just received a very enlightening piece of information."

"And what's that?"

"Last week our people in LA observed Miss Chan making a personal visit to her bank out there. Evidently she emptied out three of her safety deposit boxes. We immediately procured the bank's surveillance tapes of her visit, under authority of a warrant, of course. I'll email the video to you as soon as it's been sharpened by our techs. After you review the video I think you'll agree there's no need for any of us to travel to California now. Vancouver is where we need to be."

Sarah was exalted. Owen had delivered a concise but firm message with slick jabs like 'elementary stuff', 'you weren't in yet', and 'Vancouver is where we need to be'. There was nothing to rebuke, nothing to discuss. Stan had to be humiliated and Polichek utterly disarmed.

"When do we see this video?" replied Polichek with overt irritation in his voice.

"Hopefully by the end of the day, sir. Call me anytime with

your questions. And let me know your plans as soon as you can. I'm leaving for Vancouver tonight. Hope to see you all there soon."

* * *

"Don't talk to me, Stan! Not now!"

Sarah was on the warpath. She was headed to her office but all she wanted to do was get the hell out of the building. Stan could barely keep up.

"That didn't come out right, Sarah, it's not what you think."

"Bullshit!", she barked. "And I said don't talk to me!"

She stomped into her office, stuffed a stack of papers into her attaché, and slung her coat over an arm. When she whirled around to leave, Stan was standing in front of her, blocking her egress, searching for something to say. She stepped into his face and glared. He knew that glare, knew he was wasting his time, and retreated to his office. She stomped off, still in a snit, though smiling inside.

Thank you, David Owen.

At the elevator she stood with half a dozen people for what seemed like forever, watching floor numbers illuminate and go out at a turtle's pace—on-off, on-off—*come on!*

Exasperated and out of patience, she decided walking would be faster and was well on her way to the stairway when an impulse seized her. She backtracked to her office, threw her things on a chair, and looked at the phone on the desk.

One more try.

TEN

I hate surprises.

I'd just opened the door and had a foot inside my twenty year old truck when the phone in the shop started ringing. It was the third call today. Some kind of record.

I looked at the big bay door of my shop, wide open and fifty feet away, then down at my boot with the missing lace, then at an old watch hanging on the gear shift. It was one o'clock and Jack and Russ would be hungry. I decided that whoever was calling would call back—if it was important. Besides, I really didn't feel like talking to anyone because I had a brand new problem.

I made off for the village.

Five minutes earlier Staff Sergeant John Munroe had left my shop after showing me three photos of a man he thought I might know. I did.

After studying the grainy images on his tablet, I confirmed his assumption. The pictures were of a man named Tommy Kay, a man I thought was dead. But Munroe convinced me Kay was in fact alive and well. He hadn't drowned in the Yukon River. He'd somehow managed to escape certain death, left the Yukon undetected, made it all the way down to Vancouver, then unbenownst to him, had his picture taken three times in Lynn Chan's building last week. Naturally I was shocked. How Kay could have survived that frigid water was beyond me, but as implausible as it was, I took Munroe at his word.

Kay's current whereabouts were anyone's guess, including that of the RCMP who were looking for him in Canada, and the FBI who were searching stateside. The cops wanted him for at least two murders in the Yukon last year, and at least one more this year given the suspicious death of Jack Kolinsky in Haines. Hopefully they would arrest him soon. About the only thing I could feel good about after Munroe left my shop was not having yielded any information about 'the missing styrofoam box'—a box that no longer existed.

So was I concerned that Kay was alive?

You bet I was. For all kinds of reasons, none the least of which was my very survival. Kay was a professional enforcer and a killer for hire. As Munroe explained, when an organized crime boss is killed on the watch of someone paid to protect him, that someone has a score to settle. Same if you stole from him. I was with Lee last year when he dropped three million dollars into the Yukon River and subsequently drowned, and even though I didn't steal his money, or kill him for that matter, Kay wouldn't see it that way.

Kay had a score to settle with me.

So that was my brand new problem. And a big one it was.

* * *

At two o'clock I returned to my shop after meeting the bus on the highway. I walked inside with my two dogs, two driveshafts, two burgers to go, and one large box of fruit and vegetables. The plan was for a quick stop to make sure the new driveshafts were the correct ones, feed my dogs, then drive down to my cabin on the river to feed the woman on the couch.

Russ and Jack were on my heels when I reached up for a bag of dog food high on a shelf. The shelf is six feet off the floor. My boys are only a foot at the shoulders but can jump straight up and grab things off a five foot shelf. That's five times their height at the shoulders. I've watched them jump for twenty minutes trying to get at their food on that six foot shelf, over and over and over, until they're exhausted. No wonder they eat three times the calories per pound as I do and stay skinny as ropes. I poured equal amounts of food into the two bowls at my feet and it was gone before the bag was stowed.

A crack and a snap from the woods made me jump. Bear? Tommy Kay? I whirled around and looked outside.

"Hi, Brody!"

Surprise!

A mop of long blond hair was swinging like a pendulum as she approached me with her head down, struggling to close the fly on her jeans. Once she was buttoned up, she raised her head and greeted me with a wide smile and mischievous blue eyes.

I waited for the adrenalin to subside, then said, "Damn, Amy. You scared the crap out of me. What were you doing in the woods?"

"Bathroom. Yours is locked."

"It's not locked, just tricky to open."

"Oh."

We stared at each other blankly.

What?

Amy's last name is Vanderbilt, I think that's what she told me, which is all I really know about her, other than she's twenty-six years old, wears a lot of makeup, grew up in Alabama, says she's a dancer, was heading to Dawson to look for work, and just broke off with her boyfriend because he didn't understand her.

Whatever.

I met Amy last year in an oceanside restaurant in Haines, an Alaska fishing town on the Pacific, a hundred miles south of Minto. I was waiting there for someone and Amy was my server. She poured me three cups of coffee, never stopped smiling, and asked me a lot about my plane that was tied to the dock out front. Other than leaving her a healthy tip, that was the sum total of our 'relationship' until she walked into my shop three days ago and threw her arms around me like we were long lost friends.

So how did she find me? Easy. The letters on the tail of my

plane. It didn't take her long to find out where it was registered, and once she got to Whitehorse and found the right bar, someone told her where I lived.

I made two mistakes when she turned up unannounced. The first was to offer the poor soul a place to unroll her sleeping bag and stay warm for a cold night coming, the second was to feed her. What do they say about feeding strays?

Actually, truth be told, I did make one more mistake. After a fine meal prepared by yours truly, and finishing what was left of a bottle of lousy wine, I didn't protest as much as I should have. My bad, my fault, and the next thing I knew there was a tiger in my bed. I'll fix the leg we broke after she leaves, but in the meantime the concrete block I shoved under the corner seems to be holding up.

"Hungry?" I asked.

A rhetorical question if ever there was. In three days Amy had eaten everything in my cabin that you didn't have to cook including every piece of bread, every cracker, all the peanut butter, all the honey and jam, all the fruit, all the cheese, and six tubes of Pringles. If I was cynical I'd guess the boyfriend dumped her because he couldn't afford to feed her.

"Starving," she answered.

Go figure.

We ate our burgers standing at the bench, drank water from the sink, devoured a bunch of grapes, then I said, "Okay, Amy, I've got work to do. See you down at the cabin around seven."

She seemed hesitant and said, "Brody?"

"Yes?"

"Can I talk to you about…something?"

"Amy, I have a job to finish here, can it wait?"

"It won't take long, I promise."

"Okay, go ahead."

"Well, you've been really great and everything, and I had a lot of fun hanging out here with you, I mean that, I really do, it's just that…"

"What?"

"Well, this isn't working for me."

"What is 'this'?"

"This. You know. Us. Look, I'm sorry, it's not you, it's me, but I'm just not feeling it, you know? I don't want to hurt you but I can't stay here. I need to move on. I just can't do…*this*…anymore. Please don't try to stop me, Brody, I've made up my mind. I'm leaving tomorrow."

Leaving? Halleluja! How can I help?

"Are you sure?"

"I'm sure."

With that she kissed me on the cheek, then with great ceremony turned and raised her chin, ran her hands through her hair, and with long deliberate strides proceeded to make the grandest of exits through the big bay door. My dogs and I followed her outside and stopped to witness the rest of the melodrama, a performance for the ages, at least around these parts. She knew I was watching but didn't look back, her mind was made up and there was no stopping her now. With a nonchalant wave of the hand she proudly pressed on, disappearing behind the trees, heading down the trail to the river.

'Fare thee well, my love'.

On a sunny afternoon in the middle of the Yukon, all I could think of were red velvet curtains closing on a packed house rising to its feet.

Bravo!

Enjoy your stay on earth, Amy, but please don't miss your return flight to Neptune.

When she was out of sight, Russ and Jack looked up at me with curiosity.

"Don't worry about it," I muttered.

ELEVEN

At four o'clock in the afternoon the little Honda in my shop had two new driveshafts, clean engine oil, and all four wheels on the ground.

Almost ready.

Almost.

After checking everything under the hood, I backed it out into the lot and headed for the highway. I test drive every car I work on and if they don't run like they should, diagnose the problem and tell the owner what's needed. Most appreciate the advice though never the estimate for a surprise repair. But there's never any point in driving a car that's not right. One bad part quickly leads to another and keeping a car in good condition is the cheapest way to run them. That, and it's a lot nicer driving experience when everything is functioning as it should.

Out on the highway I accelerated to seventy miles an hour and the fourteen year old car ran as smooth as silk. The owner would be pleased. You could hardly hang on to the steering wheel when she'd brought it in. With time to kill before I cooked 'the last supper', and nothing to do that couldn't wait, I decided to deliver the little car to its owner.

Not a soul was around when I walked into the Café but there

were two fresh pots of coffee on the burner. I went behind the counter and helped myself.

Someone said, "You're not supposed to be back here, Brody."

"And you are," I replied. "Where is everyone? Your car's ready. It's out front."

"Really? Is it fixed now?"

"Sure is. Runs like a top."

"What's a top?"

"Never mind, you'll love it."

"Will it go to Whitehorse without all that shaking?"

"A million times."

Leah McCormack jumped a foot off the ground and pumped a fist in the air.

"Yes!" she exclaimed.

"Glad you're happy, Leah. Can someone watch the place while you drive me back?"

"In twenty minutes. Charlie and Lisa come in at five, that's when I'm off. Can you wait?"

"I guess I'll have to," I said, looking at the clock on the wall while making my way back to the customer side of the counter, selecting a stool that wasn't too sticky. I poured enough sugar into my coffee to make it sweet as candy, then gave it a good stir and took a big gulp. Perfect. Love sweet coffee.

Leah leaned her elbows on the counter opposite me and clasped her hands together. She was Minnie's daughter alright with raven black hair cut short and straight, and though no classic beauty, had a twinkle in her eyes and an effervescent spirit that was irresistible to a slew of suitors. Like most young aboriginal women, her skin was fine and soft, and at eighteen she was bulging in all the right places. It was hard to believe she was the same person as the shy little girl I'd met when I arrived in Minto five years ago. Now she was a woman staring life in the face.

Leah was one of the more worldly kids in the village, one of the few I knew who read books, and she'd spent the last four winters in Whitehorse going to high school. Over that period she had traveled to all kinds of places on class trips including Vancouver several times. She loved Vancouver and with high school now behind her, was headed there in the fall to attend nursing college. I knew she'd do well, she was independent and ambitious, enjoyed the structure of school—and big city life too—and would probably never live in Minto again. Good for her.

"Brody?"

"What?"

"How much is the bill going to be?"

"It isn't *going to be* anything, Leah. It *is* four hundred dollars and that's a hell of deal, young lady."

"A hundred dollars a week, okay?"

"Yeah, fine. Maybe you can make the first installment by giving my plane a good spring cleaning. What do you say?"

"No thanks. I hate cleaning your plane. It rocks in the water and I'm always afraid I'll fall in."

"It's sitting in three feet of water, Leah. You fall in, you get wet, you stand up, you walk out. Big deal. You could clean it tomorrow night. Reggie and I will have it serviced by then."

She rocked her head back and forth to convey her noncommitment, then went quiet for a moment, thinking about something else.

"Brody?"

"What?"

"Can I ask you something?"

"As long as it's not about sex or women."

She gave me a look of disgust and said, "It's not about sex or women."

"Okay, ask away."

She took her time with a scan of her surroundings, making sure no one else was around.

"Okay," she said.

"Okay, what?"

"Okay," she repeated, then after a deep breath, "How do you know when you're in love?"

"Oh, that's easy."

"It is?"

"As pie."

"Well, how do you know?"

"Leah, I can't just give out that information. It's...it's like the secret to life. Do you know how long it took me to discover that? Sorry, too valuable. Ask your mother. Maybe she'll tell you."

"Come on, Brody, tell me. Please?"

"Clean my plane?"

She heaved a sigh and said, "Alright!"

"Promise?"

"I promise."

I took another gulp of coffee, savored its sweetness, looked into her big bright eyes, and laughed.

"Brody!"

"You ache," I said.

* * *

A little after five o'clock Leah brought her car to a stop in front of my shop. She was thrilled how well it ran. I got out and walked around to the driver's side, and looked down at her with my hands on the roof.

"Don't forget to clean my plane."

"I won't."

"Remember what I told you about how to stay alive when you're driving a car?"

She huffed. "Yes, I remember. Concentrate."

"Concentrate what?"

"Concentrate all the time."

"Right. Drive carefully, Leah."

"I will. Thanks for fixing my car."

"You're welcome."

I patted the roof and she drove off, then I walked to the back of the shop to get my steaks and peas. I'd left them in an old fridge that was just slightly newer than the washer and dryer sitting beside it. The fridge had been in exactly the same spot for forty years, still working as well as the day it was plugged in.

'Don't make 'em like they used to' is an adage that's never rung truer when you're talking appliances these days. For one thing, the old ones weren't stuffed with all that electronic gadgetry that beeps and blinks and reminds you to brush your teeth before going to bed. As soon as that crap quits—and it's always the first thing that does—that gorgeous stainless steel fridge you bought five years ago isn't worth repairing.

Progress.

I surveyed the mess on the floor and the bench, and figured the easiest way to deal with it was to close the doors. Russ and Jack didn't appear when I drove the half mile down to the foot of the trail. That was unusual. Even though they spend most of their time in the woods they always emerge when they hear my truck rumble by. I assumed they must have treed a pretty good-sized critter and weren't going to leave it alone for a while.

I opened the door of my truck and placed a foot on the familiar dirt that was home, my sanctuary and sanity, a place where everything wrong, everywhere else, simply doesn't matter. I grabbed the steaks and peas and walked twenty feet through a copse of tangled poplars to the edge of the Yukon River.

The ice had broken up only a week ago and the swollen spring river was gorging itself on the high water mark, tugging and grabbing at its muddy banks, liberating everything it could, carrying off its plunder for the fifteen hundred mile journey north and west through the Yukon and Alaska, all the way to the Bering Sea. The powerful river was at least a thousand feet wide where I stood, flowing five miles an hour, hissing and gurgling and bubbling as it rushed past my feet. The sounds were hypnotic and I thought this spot could use some seating, perhaps a few thick logs neatly cut across, stood up on end, strategically placed around a ring of rocks. With the majestic mountains and scenery all around me, it was the perfect place for some fire gazing and a cookout this fall. Yet another summer project to put on my 'to do' list.

Halfway up the rocky path leading to my cabin I stopped where I always stop, whether out of ceremonial habit or some other innate compulsion—never been sure—and took another look at the muddy brown river below me, flowing thick and heavy as soup, saturated with thousands of tons of silt and sand and flotsam. It would be like that for a few more weeks then the spring melt would ebb and nature's yearly cleansing of the river valley would wane. By summer's solstice the water would be crystal clear again and I could spend my evenings sipping beer on the deck, gazing at an emerald green ribbon running into the sun.

I stood perfectly still for a moment, enjoying the tepid breeze, admiring the deep green forests and snow glazed mountains, savoring the cleanest air in the world, letting the ubiquitous scent of spruce linger in my sinuses. The sun was high and white and would barely touch the horizon for another two months. I turned to face it and let its radiation pierce my clothes and warm my bones. It was spring again in the Yukon. The doom and gloom of another long and cold dark winter was over.

About time.

I climbed the last five feet of elevation on the eight wood stairs that rose to the deck of my cabin.

"Amy! Steak for dinner!"

I held up the bag for her to see but the supine lump on the deck didn't move. Amy was wearing sunglasses and she had her face tilted toward the sun, lying on her back with a pillow under her head. Her body was covered to the neck with her sleeping bag and her shock of thick blond hair was spread out like a fan on the bleached wood planks. She was catching some rays, tanning her face, enjoying the warmth of the sun, evidently fast asleep after a long hard day of watching TV and eating too much.

I decided to leave her alone. There was no point in waking her up, I didn't need any company and besides, dinner wouldn't be ready for at least an hour. I sure wasn't hungry and assumed she wouldn't be either, not yet anyway, we'd just had lunch. First things first, it was time to clean up. I entered my one bedroom, one bath cabin through the screened porch door which had been left ajar to sway in the breeze. I was about to say something clever about leaving doors open in mosquito country, then thought the better of it.

Let sleeping dogs lie.

A suitcase might have exploded in the bedroom for all the mess in there, and I had to tiptoe over and around all kinds of female paraphernalia to access my walk-in closet for a change of clothes and towel. The tiny bathroom had been annexed in similar fashion with every surface occupied by enough lotions, potions and creams to pave a highway.

'*I'm leaving tomorrow*'.

Ten minutes later I'd showered and shaved, had two pots of water heating on the stove, and two seasoned steaks lay on the counter ready for heat. I wheeled my little gas grill out to the deck, fired it up, then returned to the fridge for a well-deserved beer. There were two in there this morning, now there were none. I was officially upset and went outside.

"Amy," I said, standing over her, casting a long shadow across her face, no longer concerned about her beauty sleep. "I'm going up to the shop to get some beer. Can you watch the pots on the stove?"

She didn't stir.

"Hey, hear me? Can you watch the stove?"

No response. I leaned over and gave her a poke.

"Come on, wakey, wakey, say something."

Still no response. I crouched down, put a hand on her shoulder and gave it a gentle shake.

"Amy!"

Something was wrong. She wasn't responding. Then I noticed her open mouth and the pallor of her skin. I lifted her sunglasses and looked in her eyes. I'd seen eyes like that before.

Amy Vanderbilt was dead.

TWELVE

"What color was her hair?"

"Her hair?"

"Yes, her hair. What color was it?"

"I don't know, like blonde."

"Blonde?"

"Yeah, blonde."

"Short or long?"

"Long."

"How old was she?"

"How old?"

"How old was she!"

"I don't know. What's with the questions? Job's done."

"Pull over."

"What for?"

"I said pull over."

Seven miles north of Minto on the Klondike Highway, a red pickup truck with a white camper and Alaska plates slowed and turned into an empty gravel lot bordered with log curbs. The sign at the entrance said it was a campground but there wasn't much there except two picnic tables, two garbage cans, and two outdoor toilets set well back in the trees. Between the toilets a narrow dirt lane disappeared into a dark spruce forest. The truck rolled up to a log curb and stopped, facing the trees. The two men in the truck were Asian. The driver was small and wiry, the passenger big and grotesquely muscular.

"Last chance, how old was she?" asked the big man.

"I don't know. Hey, what do you mean last chance? I did my job. The woman is taken care of. Doesn't matter how old she was."

The big man reached over and grabbed the driver's ear, then gave it a twist. The driver howled in pain and tried to break the vice-like grip by pressing his thumb on a nerve under the big man's wrist. No reaction. The wrist was like an iron bar.

"I asked you how old she was."

The big man twisted harder. The driver screamed louder.

"I rip it off if you if you don't tell me how old she was."

"Twenty!"

"Twenty?"

The big man let go of the driver's ear and looked around. They were alone. He looked at the outdoor toilets, a his and a hers, two tiny wood buildings barely visible in the shadow of the forest, spaced wide apart, on opposite sides of the single track lane.

Perfect.

The driver was still bellowing with his hand on his ear.

"You son of a bitch! Why'd you do that? You almost ripped it off! I'm gonna lose it! You goddamn son of a bitch! Damn you!"

In a rage of pain the driver plunged his hand inside his jacket and found the grip of his gun. But too slow. Much too slow. A fist smashed into the side of his head like it had been shot from a cannon. A flash of light exploded in his brain. It was the last light he would ever see.

The big man took a pair of gloves off the dash, put them on, then pried the gun from the smaller man's hand. He studied it and smelled the barrel. It had just been fired. He ejected the magazine. Three rounds missing.

Three.

He shook his head. The big man had never liked guns. They made things too easy for cops and prosecutors. Besides, who needs a gun? What's easier than killing someone with your bare hands? And a woman?

Child's play.

There was no traffic on the highway and that was good. After driving the truck fifty feet down the lane, he stopped and carried the driver into the ladies toilet. He broke his neck, lifted the toilet seat, and shoved him head first through the hole. The big man leaned back when he let go of the driver's feet and there was a splash when he landed in whatever was at the bottom. There was another splash when he dropped the gun in after him. The big man bent over and looked down the hole. It was so dark down there you could barely make out the shape of a person—even if you were inclined to look. And the smell was horrible. It would be some time before any self-respecting woman would use that toilet.

The big man lowered the seat, closed the door, got back in the truck, and continued down the dirt lane toward Two Spirit Lake.

* * *

Lynn Chan didn't thank the neatly dressed waiter when he slid the chair under her posterior and took his sweet time to make sure she was comfortably seated. She sensed his lascivious inspection of her thighs as her short leather skirt flexed and stretched and rode up her legs. The lurid image should be thanks enough. She placed her silver sequined purse to her left, her phone to her right, then admired how nicely they bracketed the white table setting in front of her. She watched between two silver candles as Tippy Li sat down across from her.

"You look great, doll, I missed you," said Tippy, smiling and smoothing his tie, reaching for his napkin.

Lynn admired his fine dark suit and the crisp collar on his sparkling white shirt.

"Nice to see you too, Tippy."

But cool and formal. And no smile. Not tonight.

Lynn Chan was definitely not happy. Precisely why, she wasn't so sure. She hadn't been sleeping well, that never helps. Then there was that damn chandelier, that was infuriating. And the police, they'd dropped by the office twice last week when she was in California, looking for Tommy Kay. Police were never a good thing.

But then, staring at the man across the table, she realized what was making her unhappy. It was him. There were simply too many things about Tippy Li that bothered her. For one, she didn't like being called 'Doll' and 'Baby'. Those might be monikers of affection to him, but as far as she was concerned they were anachronistic and condescending. She would have to let him know. And soon. Then there was his arrogance, the way he man-handled TCR business without ever consulting her. Admittedly Tippy knew what he was doing when it came to promoting the company's shares and clearly she didn't. But so what? The exploration of Thistle Creek was being conducted by a company of which she was president. She intended to start reminding him of that little detail as many times as necessary, until such time he understood who was in charge. From now on he wasn't going to do anything for TCR without her say-so. She was the boss, not him, it was her neck on the line, not his. She resolved then and there that he'd better get used to doing things her way, or not at all.

A service trolley draped in white linen rolled up to their table.

"On the house, Mr. Li," said the maitre d' with a self-deprecating smile, raising a chilled bottle of Dom Perignon from a bucket of ice, proudly holding it up in a white towel like a newborn.

'On the house'.

As if, thought Lynn.

Tippy and his ego and his power plays. He knew she didn't like champagne. It made her burp and gave her headaches. Now or never. She smiled at the starched man with the bottle in his hand and said, "I'm sorry sir, but I prefer wine, a good beaujolais if you have one."

"Of course, madam," the maitre d' said while looking at Li with trepidation.

Li managed a wan smile but Lynn could tell he was offended. Never mind, this was just the opening salvo, there'd be more.

"Beaujolais it is, doll."

Li snapped his fingers and the cart rolled away.

Lynn's phone buzzed. She looked at the display. The call was from the Yukon. She stood up. Li didn't. He just leaned back, folded his arms, and glared at her.

"Excuse me, Tippy, but I *must* take this call. I'll have the filet, rare."

She left him sitting by himself with a glass of water. He was clearly unhappy about it but she didn't care. She left the dining room to the inquisitive stares of a large table of graying gentlemen and their heavily pearled wives.

* * *

The lobby was as dark and intimate as the dining room but Lynn couldn't help notice three very large Asian men standing in the shadows. They were young and strong, alert and intimidating, finely dressed in made-to-measure suits that accentuated their bulk.

Tippy's army.

He'd have another man stationed in the kitchen, another in the alley, another out front, and another sitting somewhere in the dining room. Lynn raised her phone to her ear.

"Yes?"

"Hello, Miss Chan."

"Tommy?" she whispered. "Is that you? Where are you?"

"The Yukon."

"The Yukon? What are you doing in the Yukon? You should be out of the country by now."

"I had to go to Dawson, Miss Chan. And Haines. And now I must speak with Mr. Li. One of his men had an accident. Do you have his phone number?"

"One of Mr. Li's men had an accident? What kind of an accident?"

"You know, an accident. Mr. Li will know which man. I will explain it to him."

Lynn could barely breathe.

"What happened?"

"He was supposed to take care of the pilot's girlfriend, but he got the wrong woman. Stupid. So he had an accident."

Lynn started shaking and prayed no one noticed, including Tippy's men who were fixated on her. She sat down in a red velour chair to compose herself, turned her head, and lowered her voice even more.

"Why do you do these things, Tommy?"

"For Mr. Lee, Miss Chan."

"Tommy, listen to me. Mr. Lee is dead. He's gone. The pilot and his girlfriend don't matter anymore. You have to drop this vendetta thing. Please stop it right now. Mr. Li will be very upset when he finds out what happened to his man. I will try to help you with that but the police know you are alive and they are looking for you. They came to the office last week asking questions. They will not give up. I told you, Tommy, you must leave Canada right away. I cannot help you if you don't leave. I will keep paying you, but you do not work for me anymore. Don't you understand? I'm very sorry. Now please, call me when you have left Canada and tell me where I can send you money."

"One more job, Miss Chan. One more job. Then I will leave. Then I will call you."

Lynn's hands were shaking so badly she could barely stow her phone in her purse. She couldn't believe Tommy would dare kill one of Tippy's men. It was a death sentence for him. And maybe for her too. After a few deep breaths, she got up and walked over to one of Tippy's gorillas.

"Tell your boss his date just left."

THIRTEEN

Death is always a shock, always a surprise, never expected.

Amy Vanderbilt's body lay on the deck behind me covered in a sleeping bag. With my hands clasped over my head, I stared across the river, seeing nothing, hearing nothing, overcome with disbelief. What the hell had just happened here?

One minute the girl was alive and well in my shop, the next thing she's dead on my deck. Three hours ago she was a vivacious young woman in the prime of life, now she was no more for this earth. Why? What had suddenly ended her life? A bee sting? Food poisoning? Diabetic shock? An embolism or aneurysm? Had she fallen and hit her head? What?

And what difference would it make?

Death is absolute. Death is the end. For Amy there was no going back, no second chance, no remedy. My disbelief and wanting for answers were self-centered and irrelevant. It was her life that was over, not mine.

Amy's had ended on a glorious spring day in the Yukon and nothing could ever change that. Thousands of miles away safe and secure lives were about to be rocked, dreams shattered, hearts broken. Parents would be devastated, siblings and friends stunned, and all that any of them could do was grieve her loss, console one another, honor her memory, and wonder why. Eventually they'd pick up the pieces, go back to their routines, and press on without her. Life would go on—it had to—it always has and always will, though for many it would never be the same.

Perhaps down the road someone would explain to me what happened to Amy Vanderbilt. In the meantime, the bad news had to be reported to the authorities.

With no phone or communications at my cabin, I stumbled in a daze down the path to my truck and drove up to the shop. There was no one else to call but Daryl. His phone rang five times before a recording said press one for an emergency, or two to leave a message.

I pressed one and got the 911 operator in Whitehorse.

"Yukon 911, what is the nature of your emergency?"

"The nature is there's a dead woman at my cabin in Minto. My name is Brody."

"Is she breathing?"

"Not since she died."

I hung up.

'*Is she breathing?*'

The phone rang again. I let it ring for a while. The cops were calling back to confirm she wasn't breathing. If they could be assured of that, they could finish their pizza before coming out. I picked up.

"What?"

"Brody?"

"Just a minute, I'll see if he's here."

Yet another surprise and yet another cop. But this one wasn't the genius from 911. How many cops had I talked to today? There should be a law, a daily limit. Maybe there is. Something to look into.

I laid the phone down on the bench and walked outside, thinking about whether I wanted to talk to this one. After a lap around the lot, something compelled me to return to the phone.

"I'll have to call you back, Sarah."

* * *

An hour later there was a crowd of cops on my deck. The more the merrier for a death investigation.

Daryl was on the highway when he heard the news about a dead woman at my cabin. He'd been ordered to pick up Staff Sergeant Robson at the Minto airport before coming over. Robson had been airborne, returning to Whitehorse from Dawson, when he got the news and decided it was an opportune time to drop by for another visit. Daryl, Robson, and Staff Sergeant Munroe arrived in two vehicles. When their doors finally stopped slamming, three other men joined a solemn procession of cops climbing the stairs to my cabin. Two of the men were the uniforms who'd accompanied Robson this morning on his sightseeing trip to Minto. The other man, like Munroe, was dressed in civvies. I'd seen him before.

He was the coroner from Whitehorse. Robson introduced him as a Dr. Reid. He gave me a cursory nod but didn't seem interested in social formalities. Reid was thin, a professional looking man in his forties, bespectacled with readers perched low on his nose, and he carried a well-travelled leather bag. The last time I saw him he'd been wearing a suit in a court room. Today he was wearing blue jeans, a shirt, a windbreaker, and looked like he could use some sleep.

"Some room, gentlemen, please," Reid said with overt irritation, circling then kneeling beside Amy Vanderbilt, and opening his bag. He drew back the sleeping bag and revealed her face. Her lips were drawn into a grotesque smile and I turned away in horror. Everyone moved back a few feet.

"Gentlemen please, a little respect for the deceased. Staff Sergeant!"

All eyes but mine were fixated on the scene, waiting for a view of the body, but Robson got the message and issued an order.

"Everyone, down to the vehicles, now!" he barked, stabbing a finger in the air.

Of course that included me and I was more than happy to join the two uniforms and Daryl in a hasty exit from the deck. Munroe and Robson were allowed to stay because they were Staff Sergeants.

"Who is she?" asked Daryl, watching my third failed attempt to skip a stone on the river.

"A friend."

"A girlfriend?"

"No. Just a friend."

"From where?"

"Haines."

"Was she staying with you?"

"Yeah."

"For how long?"

"Couple of days."

"What happened to her?"

"Daryl, I don't have a clue what happened to her. I found her like that when I got home. That's all I'm going to say about it."

"This doesn't look good for you, Brody."

"Why do you say that?"

Daryl shrugged and I threw another stone. It made a splash and sunk.

"How did the coroner get here so fast?" I asked.

"He was in Dawson."

"What was he doing up there?"

"There was a murder."

"Another murder?"

"Yup."

"When?"

"Saturday, and that's all I'm going to say about it."

I nodded and looked out at the river. Daryl picked up a stone and threw a six skipper.

* * *

Ten minutes later Robson and I were standing alone on the deck. He'd beckoned for me after the two uniforms had zipped up a body bag and carried Amy's body down to Daryl's big SUV. Daryl drove off with the coroner.

"It just follows you around, doesn't it Mr. Brody?"

Robson was in my face again and really had his cop glare going.

"What just follows me around?"

Robson shifted his eyes to my cabin and walked over to the kitchen window. He cupped his hands around his face and pressed his nose against the glass.

"Mind if we take a look inside?"

"Inside?"

"Yeah, inside. Outside too. All around."

"Why?"

"Okay, Mr. Brody. Two choices. One, you say 'yes' and we look around your place while you stand out here taking in the scenery. Or two, you say 'no' and I cuff you, get a warrant, and we look around your place while you sit in the cruiser. Now what's it going to be?"

"Cuff me? Can you do that? I didn't do anything."

"Maybe you didn't, maybe you did. That woman we just took away? She was murdered."

"Murdered?"

"Someone broke her neck."

* * *

I was lying in the narrow bed in the apartment above my shop, staring up at the rafters, contemplating the day that was, wondering about a whole bunch of things, including where my dogs might be. Like their master, they avoid cops whenever possible and generally disappear when big men in big cars with blue lights come knockin'. But notwithstanding our common prejudice, their empty stomachs should have brought them home by now. They hadn't come when I whistled and I had to wonder if they were okay.

Two hours ago Daryl and his buddies had wrapped enough yellow tape around my cabin to line a parade route. A team of forensic experts had arrived from Whitehorse to analyze the hell out of everything. Staff Sergeant Robson told me I could use my cabin again tomorrow, provided he hadn't arrested me first. He told me to stay in the shop until he 'dropped by' in the morning, that I was not to leave Minto until then, and under no circumstance was I to leave the Yukon without his permission. No chance of wanting to do that in June, so no big deal.

I thought about what Daryl had said about a murder in Dawson. Murder is a rare occurrence in the Yukon and it was a fair assumption it was connected to the murder of Amy Vanderbilt. But with no idea who the other victim might be, there was no sense in analyzing it.

I thought about Amy some more and wondered why anyone would kill her. It was a short leap to surmise Tommy Kay might be in the area and might have murdered my innocent house guest to make me miserable. But then I wondered if that was his style. Surely he could impart more misery simply by snapping my fingers and breaking my legs. But who else? Who else would sabotage the new arena by burning all that wood? The more I tried to come up with another name, the more I came up with Kay.

My stomach was growling because I'd missed dinner. Hopefully the cops didn't seize those nicely seasoned steaks for evidence. I imagined one sizzling on a plate with three fried eggs and a pile of toast for breakfast. Robson said he'd put them in the fridge and he had damn well better have turned off the stove or he'd be sifting for murder clues in the charred remains of my cabin.

Sarah Marsalis would have to wait for her call back. It was ten o'clock when the cops finally let me go and she lived three time zones east. Maybe tomorrow I'd call her. Maybe. Any fleeting desire to see or talk to her again rode on an ebb and flow tide. There was so much to say yet nothing to say. Our whirlwind romance in the Yukon last summer led us to a white beach in Mexico last December, but after six days under a hot sun, everything fell apart. We flew home on separate flights and hadn't spoken since. Whatever we had was gone.

I think.

So why would she call today? What did she want? To reach out?

To make amends? A daunting concept to say the least. The woman had got me into more trouble last summer than any man deserved.

I like my life because it's simple—at least I try to keep it that way—and it certainly was when I woke up this morning. Now, just sixteen hours later, it was complicated. I closed my eyes and hoped tomorrow would be a better day. Hopefully the cops would be gone, my dogs would come home, Tommy Kay would be arrested, and I could fly my plane again.

That would make for a great day, even if a woman named Sarah Marsalis wasn't going to be part of it. Can't have it all I guess, though I fell asleep wondering why that still bothered me.

FOURTEEN

When I parked in front of my plane at Two Spirit Lake, I knew the left float didn't have a leak. I knew because the left and right windshields were smashed. Whoever was responsible had to be the same saboteur who pumped water into the float.

"Looks like they used a hammer."

"Be my guess, Reg."

"Someone's got it in for you."

"Yup."

"Wonder why."

"Don't know."

We walked back and forth under the nose for a while, appraising the damage. The two acrylic windshields were pockmarked with dozens of round dimples. Someone must have spent a fair amount of time swinging a ball peen hammer. A mosaic of spider cracks radiated from every point of impact all the way out to the frame, and everything in between was an opaque, cloudy haze. Flying was out of the question. You can't fly a bush plane if you can't see where you're going. At least not very well.

I was furious and depressed at the same time. This was exhausting. A fire, a murder, and now my pride and joy had been vandalized. When would it stop? I knew whoever the culprit might be was unlikely a local. No one around Minto would do such a thing. An aircraft on floats or skis is a sacred beast in the north, even for a town served by a highway. Pilots have been extolled in the Yukon for almost a century, ever since the first deliveries of mail and medicine were dropped from open cockpit airplanes onto the streets of Dawson. Whether transporting people, food, or supplies, or making an emergency medevac to save a life, an aircraft in frontier country has always been an ethereal connection to the outside world and a revered asset for any community.

So there was little doubt in my mind that an outsider was responsible and I had a pretty good idea who it was.

For what seemed a long time I stood with my hands on my hips, staring across the dark water of Two Spirit Lake, absorbing the beauty and serenity of the mountains in the distance, trying to calm myself down.

Reggie broke my reverie by saying, "Won't get fixed just standing there, Brody."

"I know, Reg. I need to go back to the shop to make some calls. Can you do the checks?"

"The checks?"

"I won't be long. We'll put it in the water when I get back."

"Easier to fix on the beach."

"Not going to fix it on the beach. I haven't got time to wait for windshields. I'll fly it to Whitehorse now. Get it fixed there."

"How can you fly it like that?"

"You'll see."

"You better tell Daryl what happened."

"You tell him. After I take off."

Reggie gave me a resigned look, then shrugged his shoulders and shook his head. Without another word I walked over to my pickup and before I'd even opened the door, resolved to find whoever was out to get me—and stop them with whatever it took.

* * *

Minnie McCormack had an intense look with her chin propped on a hand, sorting through a stack of mail. She hadn't acknowledged me when I walked in the front door and didn't look up when I sat down at the counter in front of her. Unusual. The place was empty.

Without lifting her eyes she said, "You know, Brody, five years ago when you came up to work for old man MacPherson, to work in his shop and fly his plane, everyone here was happy. And after he died and you bought his business, we were even happier to have you and his plane stay in the community. We trusted and liked you, that's why my father gave you the lease on that land you live on. But after what happened around here last summer, and now with a fire in the village, and a murdered girl at your cabin, well maybe it turns out we made a mistake, maybe we should have found out more about you first, done some digging about who you really are."

She looked up with a challenge in her eyes.

"Minnie, I told you, I did not start any fires in the village and I certainly did not kill that poor girl. And I sure as hell can't be blamed for anything done last year by a bunch of strangers who were up to no good. That's not fair."

She shoved her mail aside, nodded, stared out through the big front windows, but said nothing.

"Hey," I said, "Who told you about the girl at my cabin?"

"You mean the *murdered* girl at your cabin? That big cop from Whitehorse with all the stripes, that's who told me. He came in here for breakfast with Daryl a couple of hours ago and started asking me a bunch of questions about those fires at the arena, then about some murdered girl at your cabin. Of course I couldn't very well tell him anything about a murdered girl at your cabin, now could I? It was news to me, I'd never laid eyes on her or knew anything about her so I told him she must be just another one of those women you like to hide at your cabin."

I rubbed my forehead and rolled my eyes.

"Minnie, I don't hide women at my cabin."

"Oh, is that so? And by the way, that big boss cop that came came in here lookin' for you? He said you were supposed to wait for him at your shop this morning but said you weren't there. Seemed pretty mad about it and asked me where you were."

"What did you tell him?"

"I said I didn't know where you were. Oh, and he also asked me if I knew where you were two days ago. He asked me if you'd gone to Dawson."

"Dawson?"

"Yes, Dawson. Did you go to Dawson?"

It dawned on me why he would ask her that. The murder in Dawson was two days ago. Was I a suspect for that one too?

"No, Minnie, I did not go to Dawson. Haven't been there this year. I've been here all week working in my shop."

"So you say."

"Well it's the truth."

She studied me for a moment then said, "Look, I'm busy Brody, what brought you in?"

"Well, while we're on the subject of things like fire, I had a thought yesterday and wanted to ask you about that church that burned down here years ago."

Minnie's eyes closed to slits and she leaned forward.

"That was sixty-five years ago and we don't talk about that around here. Why do you want to know about the church?"

"Because all that's left of it are the footings and they're about to disappear under a layer of concrete when they pour the pad for the new ice rink. So I was thinking, maybe whoever owned the church... well maybe they're not too happy about it. I mean, maybe they think the new arena is being built on their land or something. Maybe someone from the church started those fires to send a message."

Minnie responded with a growl. "First of all, that church was built on our land and it's never been anyone's land but ours. Two, those people are long gone and so is their damn church. And three, they're not coming back to build another one, not ever, so end of story. Now I told you, we don't talk about churches around here and you can forget about your dumb theory."

"How come you don't want to talk about it?"

"We just don't, okay? That was then, this is now, leave it be."

"Leave what be?"

"Brody, enough with the questions about the church! Now, why did you come in?"

I sighed and asked, "You got a fax for me?"

She reached under the counter and slapped it down on the counter. It was three dog-eared pages and had obviously been passed around. Who knew how many people had read it?

"What else?" asked Minnie.

"What, what else?"

"Brody, if you're going flying you need something to eat. And Reggie will be wanting his lunch."

* * *

We were sitting on the tailgate of my truck, eating our sandwiches, swatting mosquitoes, gazing at the lake and the sky, watching trains of northbound geese honking over our heads.

Then we got to work on my DeHavilland Beaver.

With a battery powered saw I cut a rectangular hole in the damaged left windshield, placed a small piece of plexiglass over the hole, and taped it in place. For the next ten minutes Reggie was cutting and handing me piece after piece of duct tape while I stood on the float ladders, applying the tape like bandages. When the roll of tape finally ran out, both windshields were completely covered save for a ten by twenty inch patch of clear plastic. Hopefully everything would hold together for my trip south to Whitehorse, a two hour flight that would have to be navigated through a letter slot view of the world.

Once done admiring our patchwork, Reggie and I installed a freshly charged battery and filled the engine reservoir with six gallons of new fifty-weight oil. We pumped a barrel of aviation gas into the rear and middle tanks, and after hand turning the prop through a few revolutions to make sure the engine hadn't seized over the winter, we attached a gin pole to Reggie's tow truck and skidded my old silver plane into the lake. It looked strangely ominous with its windshields plastered with black tape, but after seven months sitting high and dry on the beach, it was inspiring to see it floating again, back in the water where it belonged. After tying it to the dock I began the procedure to start the engine, the very same procedure used to start it for over sixty years.

The DHC-2 is not a 'turn-the-key' kind of machine. Bolted to the fuselage a few feet in front of me was a 640 pound, air cooled, supercharged behemoth—a 'radial' engine—so-called 'radial' because its cylinders are arranged in a circle around a short crankshaft at the center. Designed in the 1920's, commercial production of Pratt and Whitney's Wasp Jr. engine began in 1930 with the last of almost forty thousand built in 1953. The Wasp Jr. has a remarkably different design and technology than the fuel injected, computer controlled, in-line engines of today, but this particular antique engine still powers planes all over the world. And for good reason. It's compact, powerful, simple to maintain, and rock solid reliable.

With my door open and Reggie on the dock below me, I turned on the master switch, worked the wobble pump lever until the fuel pressure was four pounds, reached down to the floor and pumped the primer to spray fuel into the cylinders, turned on the master switch, pushed the mixture lever ahead to full rich and the prop lever to fine pitch, rocked the throttle lever back and forth, lifted the starter toggle, and watched the propellor turn. After counting two revolutions, I turned on the magnetos.

After a couple of more pumps of the primer, and working the throttle lever some more, and after a few big pops and puffs of thick black smoke, the old radial came to life. Nine cylinders displacing 985 cubic inches were now producing power with nine enormous pistons firing in the circular sequence of 1-3-5-7-9-2-4-6-8—five power strokes in the first revolution, four in the next—around and around, over and over.

Thump-thump, thump-thump.

You've got to hear one to believe it.

The Wasp Jr. radial engine is a marvel of engineering and metallurgy, a complex assembly of finely machined and polished components, working in perfect choreography, compressing air and fuel, igniting and burning it, belching out hot gases with a loping, thumping rumble that sounds like nothing else. A DHC-2 Beaver in flight can be heard from miles away and the signature sound of its throaty exhaust is as intrinsic to the north as the cry of a loon, or the howl of a wolf, and arguably, just as forlorn.

Now for the waiting. It would be ten minutes before the six gallons of engine oil warmed to a temperature of a hundred and forty degrees. Ten minutes before the big engine was ready for flight.

I got out and followed Reggie back to the beach so we could hear each other talk.

"Thanks for your help, Reg. Mark yourself down for four hours, okay?"

"Okay."

"Oh, and when you get back to the Café, could you file a flight notice for me? Minto to Whitehorse direct. ETA about four, okay?"

"Okay."

"And tell Leah not to come out tonight. I'll overnight in Whitehorse. She can clean my plane tomorrow. Okay?"

"Okay."

"And hey, my dogs? Haven't seen them since yesterday. Could you find and feed them?"

"Okay."

'Okay' was all I ever needed from Reggie. When Reggie said 'Okay', you had his word. And his word was as good as gold.

"You can go now if you want, think I'm all set. Thanks again."

He was quiet for a moment, studying the old plane, then said, "I'll wait. Watch you take off."

I went over to my pickup to get my backpack. On the way back I had the feeling I'd forgotten something. It came to me as I stepped on the dock.

I turned around and said, "Say, Reg, can I ask you something?"

"What?"

"You know where the new arena is being built?"

"Yeah."

"Well, I was just talking to your Mom. There used to be a church in the village way back when, but then it burned down. The new arena is being built exactly where it stood. I asked her about that, whether she thought someone from the church might be against building something else on the very same spot, whether they might be upset about it, you know, like maybe upset enough to try to stop anything else from being built there. She didn't think so. What do you think?"

"We don't talk about the church, Brody."

"We don't have to talk about the church, Reg. Just wondering if you think it might have something to do with the fires yesterday."

"No."

"No?"

"No."

"Sure?"

"Sure."

Reggie had a thousand yard stare going and I figured he wasn't prepared to say another word on the subject. More perplexed than ever, I left him standing on the beach and walked out to my plane, wondering why no one wanted to talk about a church that had burned down so long ago. I untied a couple of ropes and was about to push off when Reggie grabbed the wing strut.

"Ask Mrs. Deerchild about the church," he said. "She lives in Whitehorse. Now go."

"Who's Mrs. Deerchild?" I asked, climbing into the cockpit.

"Go, Brody. Safe flight."

He put a hand on the wing strut, walked my plane down the dock, and pushed it out into the lake.

FIFTEEN

There's nothing like sex to relieve tension.

But whoever said it first must have meant good sex because the tension was still there, hanging between them like a rancid carcass.

An hour ago Tippy Li had swallowed his pride and summoned his chauffeur to drive him to her building. He'd used his key card to let himself in, stripped and slipped into her enormous bed, ravenous for a carnal feast.

What he got was crackers and cheese.

He gave her butt a shove and she collapsed in a heap on the satin sheets. He fell to her side, rolled onto his back, gazed up at the ceiling, and waited to catch his breath. She lay beside him with her back to him, her head buried under a pillow, already tightly wrapped up in a sheet with her arms clutched across her breasts. He could see she was barely breathing—no surprise there—she'd barely moved or made a sound through the whole ordeal.

Frigid bitch.

But the message had been loud and clear. Last week she'd been a tiger, tonight a bag of potatoes. No matter. No woman was worth analyzing when they behaved like this. There were others who would gladly take her place.

So why worry?

But he did.

Tippy Li needed Lynn Chan. He needed her because she was the president of Thistle Creek Resources and had a critical role to perform tomorrow. The stock promotion was about to start and there was big money at stake.

The press release would go out at noon and his friends in Hong Kong were ready. As soon as the news hit the street, they'd start buying and selling huge volumes of TCR stock, trading its shares amongst themselves through a complex network of offshore accounts, utilizing convoluted transactions that the authorities could never unravel. Each trade would be a tick higher than the one before, ratcheting the share price up a penny at a time, drawing in the suckers. Buying begets buying and when the suckers joined the frenzy, the number of shares changing hands would soar into the millions. Lynn Chan had better be prepared for a busy day.

As soon as the press release hit their screens, every penny stock broker on the continent would be calling the office, if for no other reason than they could then say to their clients, "Hey! Just got off the phone with the president of Thistle Creek Resources. Have you seen their latest press release? The assays are fantastic! You gotta own this stock!"

And all Lynn Chan had to do was tell them what they wanted to hear. Just give them the hype, short and sweet, the standard ten second blurb, and regurgitate it over and over, all day long. "Everyone at Thistle Creek Resources is ecstatic about these results, we start drilling in two weeks, this could be big! Sorry, have to let you go, we're swamped with calls, email us if you'd like a property visit."

'A property visit'. Brokers loved property visits. Sell enough TCR to your clients and you've earned yourself an all expense paid trip to the property, or at least a trip to a city near the property. Tippy knew most brokers couldn't care less about visiting an exploration property, especially one in the middle of nowhere like in the Yukon, just to look at a bunch of rocks and dirt of which they knew nothing about. But they sure liked an excuse to get out of the office, out of town, away from the boss, and away from the wife.

Head off to another place for a few days of partying and blowing off steam. Get drunk, get laid, and get away with it. Tippy knew nothing sold stock like a bunch of booze, hookers and brokers in a hotel miles from home. He had never disappointed anyone who had signed up for that perk and could expect the usual crowd of hucksters and hustlers.

But invitations had to be made.

"Baby?"

Silence, then, "My name's not 'Baby'"

Tippy turned his head and looked at her.

"Okay, Lynn?"

"What?"

"Is something wrong?"

"No."

"Sure?"

"I'm sure."

"Then look at me."

"No."

He sighed and decided to deal with the pressing issue.

"Lynn. Tomorrow our first big press release goes out at noon. The world will want to talk to you. You must be at your phone all afternoon. Count on a lot of calls. In the morning we'll go over what to tell anyone and everyone who calls. Have your assistant... what's his name...?"

"Jeremy."

"Yes, Jeremy. Tell Jeremy he'll be spending his day reading emails. He'll be making a list."

Another long silence.

"What kind of a list?"

"We're throwing a party."

* * *

When the wheels of the big jet touched down at Vancouver

International Airport, Sarah was still pondering why she was there, and why she was traveling alone.

After she got home last night, Polichek had called. That was a first, and so was his issuing last minute marching orders over the phone, dispatching her on some 'urgent mission to Canada' that he didn't have time to discuss. He told her she'd be briefed when she got there. He said he wouldn't be joining her because he was needed somewhere else. She assumed that meant one of his bowling tournaments, though any excuse was fine with her, the man was exhausting. But then Polichek told her Stan wasn't going either.

That was a surprise. Stan was her partner and he loved field trips to the west coast. In fact Stan had always welcomed any change of scenery, let alone any opportunity to distance himself from Polichek, if only for a few days. So even if things between her and Stan were currently cool, it seemed odd he would voluntarily forego a chance to go with her. Perhaps he'd been dispatched on another mission. But what and where? There was no way of knowing without calling him and she wasn't going to do that. So there she was in Vancouver, on her own for some 'urgent mission', whatever that might be.

She had packed in a hurry and left her Georgetown condo in the darkness before dawn, caught a six-thirty flight to LA, then boarded another flight to Vancouver. Twelve hours later it was barely midafternoon on the west coast of Canada, and all she wanted to do was check into her hotel and get some sleep.

. She wove her way through several long lines of disheveled travelers waiting to clear customs, and took a place in a short one that processed V.I.P.'s and airline crews. On the other side of a glass partition stood S.A.C. David Owen. He was waiting for her according to plan, leaning against a wall with his hands in his pockets, wearing a dark blue suit with the jacket unbuttoned, as usual looking relaxed, refreshed and composed.

She felt anything but.

"How was your flight?" he asked as they made room for an oncoming family with five kids and two luggage carts piled high with bulging luggage.

"Long and dull, David. They're all the same."

"Even the ones in a DeHavilland Beaver?"

"What?"

Sarah blushed after catching his mischievous grin. Owen was more than familiar with that particular aircraft, and a certain Yukon pilot.

The two agents had met in the Yukon last summer while working the same case. Sarah needed to do some aerial reconnaisance and had hired a bush pilot who flew a plane called a Beaver. Owen had subsequently hired the same pilot and plane for another job, but by then Sarah had become romantically involved with the pilot. That indiscretion became a poorly guarded secret amongst her peers, and had created quite the controversy. She had barely managed to avoid a suspension and reprimand, and only because the case had ended abruptly. Evidently, though, Owen just found the whole episode amusing.

He would, of course. David Owen was an entirely natural person with no airs about him, invariably at ease with the world, slow to judge others, and nothing ever seemed to bother him—except the transgressions of the criminals he was pursuing. Maybe that's why she liked him so much.

"Here we are," he said, picking up her bag and pointing at an RCMP cruiser at the curb.

Sarah did a double take. The driver had a long bushy beard and a turban on his head, but when he got out of the car to open the trunk, she clearly recognized the uniform. The dark skinned man was an RCMP officer.

No problem with his color, but a turban and beard? Really?

When the constable got behind the wheel, Owen reached for her door and whispered in her ear, "Wait 'til you see the cab drivers here, they wear Mountie hats."

She smiled and they headed off for the city, stopping at countless intersections, crossing bridges, winding through neighborhoods of grand old homes, eventually joining heavy traffic on a wide boulevard. Her impression was the place could use a freeway.

The car was quiet until she said, "So, David, why am I here?"

SIXTEEN

Reggie McCormack must have been wondering what I was doing.

Four times he watched me apply full power and start a takeoff run, get the floats up on step, accelerate to fifty miles an hour, then cut the throttle back before the plane took off, slow back to a crawl, work the ailerons, flaps and rudders, and turn around to do it all over again.

What I was doing was making sure my plane would fly. Someone had just attempted to sabotage it, and in spite of our best efforts to check everything that could be checked, I wanted to make sure we hadn't missed something.

Because I hate surprises.

There are old pilots—and bold pilots—but no old, bold pilots. Which was why I was second guessing my windshield repair job. The plexiglass patch should have been placed lower. All I could see was a rectangular swath of sky unless I tortured my thighs and raised my butt off the seat. The cockpit had an eerie hue and the unusual ambience reminded me of learning to fly with instruments. The instructor would tape a sheet of paper on the windshield in front of me, and there would be no choice but to fly with the indicators and instruments on the console. Flying blind, as it were.

Hated those lessons. Hate flying blind.

But I was determined to go to Whitehorse, even with the view ahead severely compromised. With two last glances at the lake on either side of me, and after poking my head out the open cockpit door for one final look ahead, I pointed the nose into a west wind, latched the door shut, tightened my seat belt, adjusted my head phones, checked the gauges and settings one last time—rudders up, prop pitch fine, mixture full rich, flaps and trim at takeoff position—then held the yoke back and shoved the throttle lever ahead.

With a great roar from its 450 horsepower engine, my trusty old DeHavilland Beaver rose up on the water and accelerated down the lake like it was running from the law. At sixty miles an hour I gave the wheel a little turn to lift a float off the water, then pulled back on the yoke and took off.

The feeling never gets old.

It's an exhilarating experience to leave the earth in an airplane under your control, to climb an invisible highway of air into the sky, to head for the heavens and watch your world transform from trees and rocks and water into landscapes and mountains and lakes. I can only imagine the euphoria of the man who made the first flight in a heavier-than-air machine, even if it was only a hundred and twenty feet and lasted just twelve seconds.

But what two brothers from Ohio—two bicycle mechanics with nothing more than high school educations—managed to accomplish on a gray and windy day in December of 1903, was nothing short of extraordinary.

They'd flown an airplane.

It was something that had never been done before and the remarkable thing about their achievement was how they managed to do it.

The miracle of flight was borne out of vision, tenacity, and pure unadulterated genius. With a table top wind tunnel they built in their shop, the two men spent years studying the behavior of air flowing over numerous model wings, searching for the secret to aerodynamic lift. They knew it was theirs to discover, for years they'd watched birds soaring effortlessly on the wind without flapping their wings. So how did the birds do it? What was their secret? It all boiled down to the contour of their wings. The brothers' discovery of how to shape an airfoil, and their successful test of a motorized aircraft on a desolate beach in South Carolina, would forever change the world. Every time I take off, I have to tip my hat to the Wright brothers.

With the push of a pedal and a nudge of the wheel, I veered toward the dock. Reggie was a couple of hundred feet below me when I flew over him under full power and acknowledged his wave with a rock of the wings. A few minutes later I was over my cabin on the river, admiring its metal roof flickering in the sun, three thousand feet below me.

From my lofty perch high in the sky I peered through the slot in the windshield. The weather ahead was changing. Seventy miles south, precisely where I was headed, a thin ribbon of nimbostratus clouds were building on the horizon. The low line of dark clouds stretched across the sky and marked the leading edge of a front, probably a low pressure system laden with moisture, moving in from the Pacific, climbing over the coastal mountains and rolling into the Yukon.

It would be a rainy day in Whitehorse.

* * *

Near the north end of Lake LaBerge, I slipped under a canopy of gray wet clouds that instantly drenched my plane. For the previous hour I'd been dodging showers, flying lower and lower under a steadily descending ceiling, trying to keep the ground in sight through a maize of swirling mists, eventually deciding to abandon the straight and narrow path to town and follow the Yukon River the rest of the way in. If worst came to worst, and the clouds ultimately descended all the way down to the water—a full-fledged fog by anyone's definition—at least I could land before running into something.

For twenty minutes I flew straight south down the big lake,

barely a hundred feet off the water, through a mist the color of lead, in a drizzle that wouldn't quit. Thirty-five miles later the banks of Lake LaBerge converged and funneled into the Yukon River, and there I began the final fifteen mile leg to Whitehorse in rapidly deteriorating conditions.

The next five miles went agonizingly slowly as I made turn after turn to keep the winding river below me, eventually catching a murky view of some old buildings scattered along the right bank. The buildings marked the north end of the city. I knew where I was and needed to keep things that way. With ten miles to go I checked the compass and GPS to confirm my location, then called Air Traffic Control in Whitehorse and told them who I was, where I was, and what I wanted to do.

And kept going.

ATC approved a straight in approach for landing on Schwatka Lake, the local float plane aerodrome located on a flooded section of the Yukon River, immediately above the Whitehorse power dam. The guy in the tower reported local conditions—as if I didn't know—light rain, no wind, patches of fog, poor visibility, and 'no conflicting traffic'. Which was a subtle way of saying I was the only idiot out flying around in a thick fog with a hundred foot ceiling. But there was no turning back, the weather was the same every which way, and I needed to land.

No big deal, I thought. It was only five minutes to the safety of the lake and all I had to do was navigate the final twists and turns of the river with a little piece of plastic for a windshield, keep the plane level in a pea soup fog, stay away from the mountains looming on the left, clear a power line that crosses the river, and avoid running into the dam.

"Piece of cake," I muttered to myself with a clenched jaw, turning on the carb heat, the nav and landing lights, the console lights, then adding power and pulling the yoke back to gain a little altitude. For the immediate challenge ahead I needed to be at least a hundred and fifty feet over the river.

Even if I couldn't see where I was going, it was not an option.

As expected, and not a minute later, three big orange balls hanging from the power line flashed under the floats, barely fifty feet below me. One hurdle down, one more to go.

The power dam and its ancillary power lines and towers were now less than two miles south. I needed a plan to clear them. The highest tower was at least a hundred feet above my current altitude, the visibility wasn't getting any better, the ceiling had all but collapsed into a cloud, and more and more I found myself using the plane's instruments and GPS to maintain my bearings. Looking down through the cabin door window, I noted the river was still coming and going from sight on a sporadic basis, but the clusters of mist were getting taller and wider, thicker and more frequent.

I glimpsed a long line of haloed headlights crawling over a low vehicle bridge, but as quickly as they had appeared, they dissolved into a milky white soup. But spotting the bridge had been a good thing. It confirmed my location. Now for my plan.

With a mile to go I pumped the flaps down to fifteen degrees, shoved the throttle ahead, pulled the yoke back, climbed three hundred feet, leveled off, pointed the nose a few degrees east of south, reduced my airspeed to eighty miles per hour, used the artificial horizon to keep the wings level, made a quick calculation, and watched the clock on the GPS. I flew entirely blind for the next twenty seconds, then pulled back the throttle, pumped the flaps down a few more degrees, and let the plane sink.

Somewhere in the last half minute the Whitehorse power dam and an assortment of towers and power lines should have passed under the belly.

Should have.

I was now on final approach, descending four hundred feet a minute, waiting to break out of the clouds, hoping I hadn't messed up.

Really hoping.

Seconds later Schwatka Lake rose up out of nowhere, looking like a dull sheet of pewter, flat as a table top, mottled with rain, not a hundred feet below me. I watched through the cabin door window

as my trusty old plane sank to the water until the floats touched
down, slicing the surface into two glorious wide fans of hissing
white spray. I pulled back the throttle, let the floats settle down,
lowered the rudders, and looked at the clock on the GPS. It was a
few minutes before four o'clock in the afternoon. Right on time.

Mission accomplished.

Piece of cake.

I pushed a button on the wheel and said, "Whitehorse Tower,
Papa Papa Alpha Golf, on the water."

"Copy that, Alpha Golf. How's the visibility out there?"

"What visibilty?"

"Roger that, Alpha Golf, welcome to Whitehorse."

I let go of the wheel and wiped the sweat off my hands.

* * *

A wise old pilot once told me, "Get the weather or it'll get you."

I couldn't shake the feeling that I'd just tempted fate and gotten
away with something. Too many things could have gone wrong.
While I might have congratulated myself for a perfect performance
in horrible conditions—conditions that have spelled the final flight
for many a pilot—all I could muster was an overwhelming sense
of guilt. Taking off from Minto without a weather report had been
utterly stupid, but flying into a line of ominous dark clouds was
unforgiveable. And without a windshield to boot. A drink might
alleviate some of my anxiety but what I really needed was to vow
never again to test the limits of my abilities. I would rack up my
poor judgement to experience, file the last hour of my life in that
nebulous place—the razor thin zone between really good and really
lucky—and move on.

The flight trajectory over the dam had taken me well down the
lake and it would be all of twenty minutes to taxi back to the docks.
I opened both cockpit doors to see where I was going. The rain had
morphed into a weightless drizzle, the air was mild, and without
a breath of wind, the water lay as flat and smooth as a pool of oil.
Tufts of white cotton mist hovered around me like frozen ghosts,

restricting the line of sight to barely fifty feet. I turned right to find the shoreline. It would be my guide. Out of nowhere a pair of shiny black ducks appeared in front of the prop. They were heading the same direction, paddling as fast as they could, weaving back and forth, frequently glancing back to see if I was gaining on them. When a gravel bank emerged out of the haze, they stopped and turned to face me. I turned right again and watched them watching me, bobbing up and down on my wake as I idled past them. One of them returned my farewell salute with a haughty glare and a few quacks.

Probably the male.

A soaking wet forest cloaked in a cotton candy fog skirted the shoreline and would lead me to the dock. I was taking my time, puttering slowly northward, taking great care not to run into anything. It would be a long slow taxi in, but there was plenty to think about as I wobbled in and out of the contours of the lake's edge, still with the cockpit door open, keeping my eyes peeled on the trees off the end of the wing.

A growing sense of unease had been festering inside me and I knew why: too many questions without any answers. Like who killed Amy Vanderbilt? Was it Tommy Kay? Had he actually survived and come back to the Yukon? Or had it been someone else? And if so, who? And regardless of who, why? And why at my cabin? Then there were the cops. What were they up to? Did they really consider me a suspect for a murder? Were they waiting to arrest me? Did I need a lawyer? And then, of course, there were my dogs. Where were they, what were they doing, and were they okay? Had Reggie found them?

There were other questions too, but the backburner kind, the kind a man sorts out when he has the time, like when he's fishing, or gazing at a sunset, or grilling steaks, or chopping firewood. Questions like how come I had time in Minto to call the boys at the hangar in Whitehorse to come out and replace my windshields, but not an extra two minutes to call the weather office? And why hadn't I called Sarah Marsalis back?

Maybe tonight.

Maybe.

At least one question was about to be answered. Would the guys with my new windshields be waiting to greet me? It would be no surprise if they didn't turn up, who could expect anyone to go flying in weather like this?

But surprise, surprise, when I turned off the engine and glided up to the dock, there they were. Two tall skinny guys in blue coveralls, standing with their hands in their pockets, tool boxes at their feet, and two new windshields beside them.

In front of a crowd of people I didn't know.

SEVENTEEN

"Treasury will not promote you, Sarah."

The words seemed insignificant and irrelevant and she deflected them like a snippet of conversation overheard from another table.

'Will not promote you'.

Two hours ago Sarah Marsalis had checked in at the Westin and begged off a happy hour drink with David Owen. She was still stumped why she'd been dispatched to Vancouver, but that could wait until dinner. She was exhausted and needed a nap and went up to her fifth floor room to do just that. But after a moment of daydreaming at all the joggers out in force, she decided sleep could wait. Exercise was what she needed.

An hour and a half later she had showered and changed clothes, and though her six mile run around the Stanley Park Seawall had hardly been an inspired effort, she felt rejuvenated and refreshed.

"Sarah?"

"Hmm...?"

Her eyes had a watery glaze as they wandered around the dining room, then outside at the panoramic view of Coal Harbour and the dark blue mountains to the north.

"Look, you've had a long day, we can talk about this in the morning," said Owen, savoring the last piece of his poached salmon before leaning back and inspecting the glass of wine in his hand. He watched her drain a whole glass of water.

"No, David, we'll do this now," she said, dabbing her mouth with a napkin. "You say Treasury will not promote me. How on earth would you know that? And you still haven't told me why I'm here."

"Officially?"

"Officially, unofficially, what's the difference? Talk to me!"

Sarah had a fierce look going and Owen was wary.

"Right," he said. "Let's do this somewhere else."

* * *

They were shown to a corner table in a long and spacious room surrounded by tall windows that provided an expansive view of the cityscape to the east, and the seascape to the west. The motif was ultra-modern—everything chrome, black or silver—the carpet, the fixtures, the tables, the pictures, every piece of fabric and trim. Sarah and David blended in perfectly, two chic and affluent professionals dressed for success, she in black slacks and a white blouse with shiny black pumps, he in a dark suit and white shirt with shiny black Oxfords. They were alone save for an amorous couple huddled together in a booth near the bar. Closer scrutiny revealed a silver-haired businessman with busy hands in constant motion, sliding them all over a young Asian woman who giggled a lot and might have been twenty. Sarah watched them for a moment. He couldn't wait get into her pants and she couldn't wait to get into his wallet. The escort business was alive and well in Vancouver.

The bartender took their order, a virgin caesar for Sarah, a ruby red port for David.

"Nice bar," said Sarah.

"Quiet," said David.

They waited in silence. A few uncomfortable minutes later their drinks were placed on the onyx table in front of them. The two cops raised their glasses, sipped, and set them down.

Sarah wasn't going to say anything until David did, the place had been his idea, the ball was in his court. She would wait him out and was content to stare at her impotent drink. With no idea of what he was about to say, she would have preferred a vodka tonic, a double given the circumstance, and then maybe another, and perhaps one more for the road. Which was always the problem. She simply couldn't have just one drink. It was why she hadn't had one since the last day of last year, five months and five days ago. The day that damn Yukon pilot had just picked up and left her alone in a tiki hut on a beach in Mexico.

She had never blamed him, though, she would have done the same.

On Christmas day they had met as planned, at the airport in Phoenix, and flown to Acapulco. There they hired a taxi to drive them two hours up the coast to a tiny seaside village. The place had little to offer, not even a modern hotel, just a few palm frond huts on the ocean, a restaurant that closed at seven, a cantina that boasted authentic margaritas, and a brilliant white beach with nary a tourist around. It had all seemed so perfect to her. She hadn't picked the place to meet people or play tennis.

For two days they ate shrimp and salsa, drank sweet drinks, held hands in faded hammocks, took long walks through the surf, and exhausted themselves with world class sex. On the third day the pilot decided he needed something to do and took up surf fishing under the tutelage of a local kid who didn't speak a word of English. Sunburned and with no interest in joining them, Sarah found shade and solace in the cantina across the road, which just happened to have the best daiquiris in Mexico. And that marked the end of the honeymoon. For the next four days she got stoned drunk every afternoon. And every day, just before five o'clock, he'd walk into the cantina to retrieve her. Pluck her out of her chair, throw her over his shoulder, carry her back to their hut. When she woke up parched and hung over in the early evening of the last day of the year, he was gone. The note on her suitcase was short and sweet.

'Sorry, Sarah, doesn't work for me. Happy New Year.'

* * *

"So I talked to your boss a couple of days ago."

Sarah jumped at the sound of his voice.

"Polichek?"

"Yes."

"And?"

"Well, I called him because I wanted permission...to talk to you about something. I was impressed with the job you did in the Yukon last summer, and with what's going on with Li and Chan and that ruse they're working at Thistle Creek, well I thought we really ought to have a presence up there, to keep an eye on things."

"A presence."

Owen clasped his hands together and leaned forward with his elbows on his knees.

"Look, Sarah, we need someone to fill a critical role in the Yukon this summer. I thought you'd be the perfect candidate for a UC role up there. You've been up there before, you seem to like it, and you know your way around the place. I was hoping you'd be interested."

"Me? Undercover? Ha! Come on, David, I'm a CPA. I crunch numbers and do financial forensics, not that FBI cloak and dagger stuff. Which cost my brother his life, by the way."

"I know, and I'm truly sorry about that. There's not a day I don't think about him. But this is a much safer gig. Altogether different."

"David, no UC job is safe. Anyway, what exactly did SAC Polichek say when you asked permission to talk to me? Don't tell me he sent me all the way out to Vancouver just so you could pitch me on some undercover job. And what's this about me not getting promoted? What did he tell you?" She leaned forward and said, "Come on, spit it out. What's going on here?"

He stared at her for a minute, then said, "I shouldn't tell you any of this but the impression I got was that neither you or Stan are in line for his job, at least not so long as you're both working in the same department. There's no such thing as a secret, only things people haven't found out yet. Apparently you and Stan had a roll in the hay a few years back, and Polichek, well...he knows. He said he won't stand to have either one of you supervising the other, given that mutual history. And..."

"And what?"

Owen leaned back and looked at the ceiling as though searching for something.

"He also told me that if push came to shove, he was leaning toward Stan because..."

"Because what?"

"An issue."

"An issue? What issue?"

Owen took a deep breath and said, "He said it had to do with your drinking."

"My drinking! What drinking? Do you see me drinking? In all my years at Treasury I've never had a single drink on the job. Not one. What drinking is he talking about?"

He held up his hands in defence. "Hey, it's just what he said. Don't shoot the messenger. But sometimes perception is reality."

She took a deep breath and watched the silver-haired gentleman and his 'date' get up to leave. Silver hair had a hand firmly planted on the young lady's behind. Wouldn't want to let it get cold.

"Perception, huh? And what does a UC job in the Yukon have to do with this perception?"

"Nothing as far I'm concerned. I want you to come work for me."

"For the FBI?"

"Yes."

"No, David. I don't think so."

"Look, here's why you should at least consider it. Donna... my wife...Donna and I are both from the northwest. We've always missed it. Our son was born out here. We've been planning to go back for a long time, get out of the heat and humidity and gridlock in DC. Last year I put in for a transfer. We'll be moving to Seattle in September. The office there is expanding and we'll be hiring a lot of new agents over the next few years. There'll be plenty of opportunities for you to move up the ranks out there. I'll make sure you get a raise. You could take the job in the Yukon for the summer, then come work for me in Seattle. You'll have way more fun in the FBI than Treasury. It would be a fresh start and definitely a great move for you."

"I don't know, it would be such a huge change."

"It would. But what's the alternative? Stay in DC? It doesn't look like you're going anywhere there. And if Polichek decides to promote Stan, then you're certain to be transferred. And who knows where? Some cold windy hick town in the Midwest? Come on, Sarah, think about it. You're done in DC. Seattle is a great place to live and work. You'll love it out here."

She sat back and gazed out a window. A float plane was landing. It looked exactly like the one she'd flown in last summer. Maybe it *was* time for a change. There was nothing holding her down in Washington, other than her daughter, a freshman at Virginia State. There'd be long plane trips on the holidays but she could deal with that.

"So what's this job in the Yukon?"

EIGHTEEN

"Mr. Brody! Mr. Brody! Did you kill Amy Vanderbilt?"

"What? No!"

The instant I stepped on the dock, there were half a dozen cell phones in my face and I was besieged by a gaggle of young women in raincoats and rubber boots. They were excited and aggressive, like a gang of trick-or-treaters on uppers.

"Mr. Brody, what was Amy Vanderbilt doing at your home?"

"Eating. Now if you'll excuse me ladies, I need to tie up my plane."

I tiptoed past them along the edge of the dock and crouched to tie a rope to the front float. There were so many cell phones floating around my head, I could barely see what I was doing.

Another voice: "Are you here to turn yourself in, Mr. Brody?"

"What?"

"The police are here. Are you here to turn yourself in?"

"No."

Another voice, "Why are they here?"

"How should I know? Maybe crowd control."

I stood and looked toward the rear of the plane, waved a hand above the cell phones, and pointed at the rear float. The two guys in coveralls had me covered and were already securing it.

Another voice: "What happened to your plane, Mr. Brody?"

"No comment."

"Why won't you comment?"

"That would be a comment."

The shortest of them stepped under my chin, shoved her phone in my face, and asked, "Mr. Brody, how well did you know Amy Vanderbilt?"

"That would also be a comment. Now all of you, go away."

When none of them moved, I yelled, "Hey, everyone here wearing a life jacket?"

"What for?" from the back.

"Because in one second I start tossing people into the lake."

That worked better than expected. They shuffled off en masse, a clump of soaking wet raincoats with rubber boots squeaking and creaking, heads down, tapping their phones with their thumbs. I watched them walk up the jetty and gather at the top, then turn to take pictures of the mad pilot from Minto in front of his strange looking plane with the black tape plastered all over the windshields. Beyond them in the parking lot was my favorite cop leaning on his blue batmobile with his arms crossed, watching and waiting. Parked right behind his cruiser was a green pickup truck with 'Thurson Ames Assayers' painted on the door. Mike Giguere. My ride to town.

"Hey guys," I said to the two young men in coveralls. "Can't believe you turned up in this weather."

"And miss that?" said one of them.

Tim and Jim Crothers are identical twins and I can't tell them apart. No one can. The two aircraft mechanics have the same lanky builds and brush cuts, work for the same company, and wear the same company issued coveralls. The only way I can establish who's who is by reading the names on their lapels, but even that's no sure thing, they think it's funny to occasionally switch uniforms.

"Say boys, how do you suppose those reporters knew I was coming to town?" I asked.

They both shrugged. Tim or Jim said, "Beats me, someone must have an inside source with the cops."

"Yeah, or maybe someone was monitoring flight plans," said the other one.

And I said, "Yeah, or maybe someone up at the hangar told them I was coming and when I was expected."

They both shrugged again and gave me a 'Who me?' look.

"What the hell happened?" Tim or Jim asked, gawking up at the windshields.

"Birdstrike," I said.

They nodded in unison and the one on the left said, "Must have been a pair of Kamikaze geese. Big ones."

The one on the right said, "For sure." Then he looked at me and asked, "How could you see where you were going through that little piece of plastic?"

"In this weather? What difference would it make? Couldn't see a damn thing anyway"

"Right," said the one on the left.

"Gotcha," said the one on the right.

I grabbed my backpack and handed one of them the cockpit key.

"Lock it when you're done, boys. Leave the key with the bill. I'll drop by the hangar tomorrow to pay it—Tim."

'Tim' didn't blink. Guess they hadn't switched coveralls today.

* * *

Staff Sergeant Robson had his cop glare at the redline when I approached him. He was still leaning on the door of his cruiser with his arms folded and a mean unwavering glare.

"You like to live dangerously, Mr. Brody," he growled.

"Yeah, bit of a surprise out there today with the fog. But I wouldn't call flying in this stuff dangerous, I'd say it's downright insanity. Never seen it this bad in Whitehorse."

"Neither have I," he said. "But flying in the fog isn't what I'm talking about."

"Oh?"

"You weren't at your shop this morning. I told you to stay put until I came by. *That's* living dangerously."

"Oh, sorry about that. I was pretty hungry. Missed dinner last night and went to the Café for breakfast. Thought you might look for me there but I guess you didn't have time. I know you're a busy man."

Robson straightened up, put his hands on his hips, and moved into my face.

"Damn right I'm a busy man! I've got two murders in a week and no one to arrest. I'd drag you in for questioning right now if half the cars in this city hadn't run into each other today. Now here's your last chance to stay out of jail. Be at my office tomorrow morning at eight. No excuses, eight o'clock sharp. If you don't show up, I'll impound your plane, hunt you down, and throw you in jail. And you'll stay in jail until we find out who killed two people in the Yukon this week. Is that clear?"

After a hard dry swallow, I managed to get out, "Yeah, sure."

"Good. Now, what brings you to Whitehorse, Mr. Brody?"

"Shoelaces."

"Shoelaces."

"Yeah, shoelaces. Need new ones. Boot laces, actually. The leather kind. My dogs chewed mine up. See?"

I pointed at my boots but Robson wasn't interested.

He studied my face for a while.

"What time do you see me tomorrow?"

"Eight."

He nodded once, then squinted through the haze at the dock. Tim and Jim were removing the pilot side windshield.

"What happened to your plane?"

"Birds," I muttered.

He looked me up and down, and growled again.

"Birds, huh? Know what, Mr. Brody? If you don't want to get thrown in jail tomorrow, you'll have to do better than that. I'll ask you again in the morning."

And with that he got in his cruiser, slammed the door, and drove off. I watched him disappear into the fog to the sounds of doors closing and engines starting. The trick-or-treaters were leaving too.

The engine in the little pickup truck started and I walked around to the passenger side. I opened the door and blurted out, "Man, that guy needs a beer more than I do. How are you doing, Mike?"

When I sat down and reached for my seat belt, a woman laughed and said, "I'm Jennifer. Mike sent me. There's beer at the house."

NINETEEN

Jennifer was the picture of health.

She had a wide round face with plump pink cheeks and I stifled an urge to squeeze one. They were the perfect compliment to her pale blue eyes and light brown hair drawn back in a pony tail. She wore a John Deere ball cap, a hooded rain coat, a red flannel shirt, blue jeans and black rubber boots. I guessed she might be thirty, but with that baby face she probably got carded everytime she walked in a bar. Seemed like a happy young woman.

"So yeah," she said, "Mike is working on some press release or something and asked me to pick you up. Where to, or do you just want to go to the staff house?"

"What staff house is that?"

"Oh, you're staying at the Thurson staff house tonight. Mike had some surprise house guests turn up this afternoon. He said he was sorry for the inconvenience but will meet you for breakfast tomorrow. He said he'll call you tonight. We have to talk anyway."

"Oh yeah? What do *we* have to talk about?"

"Rocks," she said, glancing at me with an infectious smile. "Let me explain."

She put the truck in drive and hit the gas with confidence.

"Okay," I said. "Explain away. I'm Brody, by the way."

"You better be," she said with a laugh. "Jennifer Kovalchuk, president of Thurson Ames Assayers."

"President, huh?"

"Damn right."

Without taking her eyes off the road, she held out a large hand and mine was tingling when I let it go. Jennifer was one strong woman.

The fog over the road was as thick as over the lake and the visibility no better. But Jennifer was competent, driving not too fast, not too slow, getting us safely down the narrow gravel road that led out to the highway. We turned right and headed for town at less than half the legal speed limit with the wipers sweeping off a layer of drizzle every five seconds. I could barely see the Yukon River to our right so turned the other way and studied her for a while. She was quiet, concentrating on what she was doing.

"So we need to talk about rocks, huh?"

She smiled and replied, "We do. We have to go over the protocol for shipping exploration samples. Thurson Ames is doing all the assays this summer for Mike's project on Thistle Creek, and every sample we receive from him must have a documented chain of custody. Whenever rock gets passed from one person to the next on its way to our lab, like those samples you're picking up on Friday, two parties have to sign off at the transfer point. I'll show you the forms at the house. Easy stuff but it has to be done."

"How come?"

"Stock exchange rules. Ask Mike to explain but sample control is a big deal these days. Basically it's to prevent, or at least discourage, people from tampering with samples."

I nodded and said, "Like discouraging people from adding gold to rocks before the rocks get tested for gold."

"Exactly. That's called salting and it's fraud. Stock exchanges hate fraud." She smiled and looked at me. "Gee, Brody, you're not just a pretty face."

I shook my head, smiled, looked away, and thought about someone else.

"Hey, Jennifer?"

"What?"

"Did you hear that a young woman was murdered in Minto yesterday?"

"Of course, who hasn't? It's in all the papers and on the radio. A man was murdered in Dawson, too."

"Well, did you know the woman was found at my place?"

"Sure, at least that's what the paper said. You're the talk of the town, by the way. Or didn't you know? Kind of explains that welcoming committee you had back there."

"Well, aren't you the least bit concerned that I might be responsible for...?"

"Oh, please, give me a break. Like the cops go all the way up to Minto to investigate that poor girl's murder, then come back here without you? Leave you there with your plane to fly away somewhere? I don't think so."

"Glad you see it that way."

"How else? It's obvious you didn't kill her. Why would you call the cops if you did? Why not just dump her in the river and let her float away? Or take off in that plane of yours? Anyway, Mike says there's no way you did it and that's good enough for me."

"You're a trusting soul, Jennifer."

"Tell me about it," she said, rolling her eyes.

"Well, for the record, Mike is right. I didn't kill her."

"Look, I know you didn't. Now let's not talk about it, okay? Gives me the creeps."

We drove through a traffic circle and past the SS Klondike, a grand old paddle wheeler that last plied the Yukon River in 1955, then turned left on Fourth Avenue and joined rush hour traffic, or at least a long line of cars inching through the fog.

"What's with this weather?" she complained. "Never seen anything like it up here, least not in the afternoon."

"Definitely a freak event," I replied, reflecting on my harrowing flight from Minto. "So where's this staff house?"

"North end of town. Not far from Mike's place. Do you want to eat before you start drinking?"

I looked at her.

"Actually, all I had in mind is one beer. So yeah, I can eat first. Is there a restaurant near the staff house?"

"Hey, know what? I could eat too. What do you say we go somewhere for a burger, then to the house for your beer."

"Sounds like a plan."

Twenty minutes later we were standing shoulder to shoulder at the counter in my favorite burger joint. Jennifer had left her raincoat in the car and was an impressive sight on her feet. She was tall, only an inch shorter than me, but what really gave her a presence was her broad shoulders and narrow waist, not to mention some very long legs and a very, very nice front garden. Not that any of that mattered to me, as of yesterday I was sworn off women.

"Two cheeseburgers, large fry, large root beer," I said to the kid behind the cash register.

"Same for me, please," said Jennifer, thrusting a fifty into his face.

"Whoa, allow me, for the airport limo. And that beer you're going to buy me."

Too slow. The kid grabbed her fifty before it took out his eye.

No point arguing when everyone's smiling.

"Thanks," I said.

"Thank Thurson Ames."

When she'd finished inhaling her meal, I caught her looking at my fries.

"Help yourself," I said, sliding them toward her.

"Better not," she said, slumping back in her chair, patting her belly. "Watching my weight these days."

Really?

I wondered if she had an inny or an outy.

*   *   *

The Thurson Ames staff house sat at the foot of the cliffs at the west end of Cook Street. It was vintage forties, probably built during the Second World War, a time when the best you could hope for was to get what you needed. The tiny blue and white gingerbread sat close to the street on a deep lot, bordered by a decrepit wood fence that had long lost its battle with nature. Its parched gray pickets and posts were warped and split, with tall grass and wildflowers flourishing between them, and ran all the way around the property. A dirt driveway led back to a new steel building that occupied most of the backyard.

Jennifer Kovalchuk parked on the narrow street in front of the little house, leaving room for traffic by dropping two wheels into a shallow ditch.

"You travel light," she said while opening her door, pointing at my backpack.

"Got everything I need," I said while opening mine.

"The world by the tail?"

"Sometimes."

We smiled through the truck at each other. I followed her through a gap in the fence where a gate once swung, then up a cracked concrete walk to the front door. She opened it and I followed her in, and was greeted by a big wood stove standing guard front and center, and the smell of fresh paint.

The whole interior had just been renovated. I stopped on the entry mat and looked down at a gleaming hardwood floor, then up at a lofted ceiling, then to my right at a modern U-shaped kitchen, then to my left at two leather couches with a whole bunch of pillows, and a TV on the wall. A tall plant stood in a corner by a long front window. All the plaster was new, the window sills, the baseboards, even the light switches. Were everything not crammed into such a tiny space, it might have been a sales model in the 'burbs'.

"Nice," I said.

"Thanks. The contractor just left. He started the job last fall and told me it would take six weeks. So do the math. The project was a six month nightmare of delays and excuses. I could write a book. But he did do a good job."

"He did."

"This fall I'll tackle the outside. A new fence, maybe a few trees, paint the trim. Definitely going to use a different contractor, though. You coming in?"

I looked down at my boots, took them off, followed her into the kitchen, and pulled out a heavy wood chair from a stout round table.

She opened a shiny new fridge and yelped, "Bastard! Damn you Tony!"

She slammed the door.

Whumph!

"Who's Tony?"

She hesitated before saying, "Oh, never mind, one of my techs. Son of a bitch took my beer. You'd think he'd know by now that paybacks are hell with me."

She stomped down the hall toward the back of the house and I heard a screen door open and slam shut. Curiosity overcame me and I followed her, stopping at the door just in time to watch her put a key in the door of a travel trailer. She disappeared inside and emerged a moment later with two cokes and an almost empty bottle of a dark drink. I held the door open and she blew past me, muttering, "Hope he doesn't think this makes us even."

I left that one alone. A few minutes later we were back in the kitchen, sipping Jack and Coke. I was seated and she was standing beside me with a hand on the back of my chair. She had just pulled out a stack of fill-in-the-blanks forms from a large envelope.

"Okay. So this is a sample control log form," she said, palming one with a wide hand and sliding it under my nose. "You need to complete one of these for every load of samples you transport. Press hard, you're making three copies. Never mind this column," she said, pointing a long finger at a list of printed numbers. "These are Thurson's internal control numbers. But this column on the right is where Mike will enter all the tag numbers he's using for a particular shipment. Thurson supplies the tags and we've already given him all he'll need for the summer. With me?"

"Yup."

"Good. Now, for every bag or box or container of samples being shipped, it must have a tag attached. Mike will take one of our pre-numbered tags, thread a steel wire through it, then loop the wire through the sample bag or container. Then he'll crimp the wire with a tool. The wire is now a closed loop with a tag on it, and the sample container is officially sealed. If you see any container with a wire that's cut, or has more than one crimp, or is missing a tag, or in any way looks tampered with, don't load it 'cuz we won't process it. Got it?"

"Got it."

"Good. So all that's required of you is to read the tag number on a bag or container, find the same number that Mike entered on the control log, and initial in the space beside it. Now you can load it. Again, don't load any container unless it's properly sealed with a crimped wire and tag, and the tag number has been recorded and initialed in the log. Last, once you've matched all the container tags to all the numbers entered in the log, and have initialed each one, sign here at the bottom. Get Mike to sign here, then separate the pages. You take the top two copies, Mike gets the other two. Now you're good to go. And please, do not forget your copies when you take off. We need at least one to take delivery. Got all that?"

"Piece of cake."

"You're sure."

"I'm sure."

"Great. Give this envelope to Mike when you see him in the morning," she said, stuffing the the forms back inside and licking the envelope with a delicious red tongue. "Another drink?"

"No. I mean yes. Yes, I'll give the envelope to Mike. No to the drink. I'm good."

"Come on, there's barely enough for one more. Let's finish the bottle."

I opened my mouth to say something but she had already turned her back. I watched her set our glasses on the counter and pour out the last of the Jack Daniels. More in mine than hers.

"So, Jennifer. If we drink these, will you be even with Tony?"
"Not even close," she growled.

* * *

The big man put on the boots and walked around the room. They felt dry and stiff, like the rest of the used clothes he'd bought at the Mission of God.

He'd paid eight dollars for a checked shirt with a frayed collar, a canvas coat with a stain on the front, a hunter's cap with tattered ear flaps, and a pair of blue jeans two sizes too big. He put on a pair of scratched eyeglasses and looked at himself in the mirror. Not bad. He should blend in nicely with the city's vagrants, like those drunks hanging around the liquor store, or the beggars in front of the post office.

The casualties of colliding cultures are as intrinsic to Whitehorse as any other city. For the next hour he would be one of society's discards—the downtrodden, the disenfranchised, the invisible.

He walked out the back door of the geologist's house and scooped up a handful of dirt. After working it between his hands, he wiped some on his face. He pulled out a small bottle of cheap whisky, filled his mouth with a slug, gargled for a few seconds, and spat it out on the lawn.

He was ready.

He walked out of the yard and into the mist, heading for the house where the geologist said he could find the pilot.

Tommy Kay shoved a hand in his pocket and felt for the knife.

* * *

Jennifer had gone for a shower and had left me alone in front of her television. Some news show was on and two politicians were accusing each other of lying. I turned it off and dug inside my pack for my pay-as-you-go flip phone. I gave it a wipe and turned it on. While it was searching for things, I went over to the front window and looked outside. The drizzle had stopped but the fog was still thick. I could barely make out Jennifer's truck and a large man walking down the other side of the street.

A maritime fog is a bizarre and rare meteorological event for Whitehorse, but it was only a matter of time before the wind picked up and blew it away. Soon the midnight sun would break out and light up the city with its mystical light.

I sat down again, found the fax from Mike, flipped to the last page for his number, and opened my phone. The screen said '10 missed calls'. I hadn't used the phone for a month and scanned the numbers, recognizing just one. Someone at the Café had called me a few hours ago. It was now after nine and the restaurant would be closed. The bar would be open but they rarely answered. I decided to call back in the morning. The rest of the numbers were foreign to me and I deleted the whole lot. Nothing like a fresh start for the summer.

I called Mike and he didn't pick up so left a message to call me back. Jennifer walked in wearing a thick white robe with a white towel on her head. She had fluffy white slippers on her feet.

I looked her up and down and said, "You sell ice cream, too?"

Jack Daniels can make you stupid in a hurry.

"Very funny," she said. "Bathroom's all yours."

I felt sheepish when I left the room.

Idiot. Shut up with the corny jokes. You hardly know her.

Blame the Jack.

The house was chilly and all I wanted was a hot shower and a warm bed. It had been a long day, a dangerous one too, and in spite of two stiff drinks my anxieties still lingered like skunk. Where were my dogs, what did Robson want, who had called from the Café, who had smashed my windshields, and where was Tommy Kay? And then there was Amy. Poor, poor Amy. Damn whoever had killed her. What a senseless crime. She didn't deserve to die. Deep inside an incipient sense of guilt was beginning to knaw. I wanted to disappear from myself, hide from life, sink into the void of sleep, fast forward to the other side of night, see what a new day would bring. Tomorrow had to be better.

Had to be.

I ran the shower as hot as I could stand, shampooed and shaved, then leaned against the wall and bowed my head under the spray, letting its heat flow into my body, watching soapy water circle the drain.

The door opened.

"Yes?"

"Towel!"

"Thank you!"

The door closed.

Then the curtain moved. Two hands slid around my waist and stopped on my belly. She pressed her breasts into my back, nibbled on my ear, ran her chin up my shoulder, and nestled one of those big soft cheeks into the nape of my neck.

"Jennifer?"

"Yes?"

"What are you doing?"

"Getting even with Tony."

TWENTY

It took Jennifer about half an hour to get even with Tony, and I was more than happy to oblige. Then she let me sleep for a solid seven hours. The clock beside her bed said six-thirty when I opened my eyes to the clatter of breakfast and the smell of bacon. When in Rome. It was time to get up.

I snuck a quick shower, then rummaged through my backpack for the greatest luxury in travel—clean underwear—in this case, boxers and a T-shirt.

What bliss.

Jennifer's ex-fiancé had to be some kind of an idiot. When I sat down at the kitchen table, she was shovelling mounds of bacon and scrambled eggs onto two big plates. A stack of waffles sat on the table. A percolator was bubbling away on the counter. All she had on was a big grin, those silly white slippers, scanty panties, and an oversized T-shirt with Mickey Mouse on the front. It all worked for me, especially when she bent over to open the oven.

Eat your heart out, Tony, whoever you are.

She set a plate down in front of me, planted her face on mine, and kissed me until my lips were numb.

"Good morning," she said, patting me on the cheek.

"Goo mornung," I replied with a drool, gingerly putting a hand to my face to check if all my teeth were still there, hoping there was no permanent damage to my jaw.

She went to get her plate and sat down across from me.

"In case you're wondering about all this," she said, gesturing at the feast in front of us, "Mike just texted and said he can't meet you for breakfast. He said to meet him at Trans-Pacific at nine-thirty."

"Where's that?"

"Front and Main, second floor, northside."

"Never heard of them but I know where that is."

"I think they're stock brokers."

"Oh."

We dug in and ate everything she'd made. If Jennifer was watching her weight, I wouldn't want to carry her groceries if she went off her diet. We studied each other with quiet contentment while sipping the last of her superb coffee. I thought about how much we'd eaten in the last twelve hours, then admired her broad shoulders and long arms. Last night I'd conducted a thorough topographical survey of the rest of the terrain, and other than the obvious places, found nothing but solid muscle, save for those chubby cheeks of hers.

"Know what?" I said, wiping my rubbery lips with a paper towel.

"What?"

"This is one hell of a staff house you're running here."

"We at Thurson Ames *aim* to please," she said, beaming about our little secret.

"Well keep on aiming. Breakfast was outstanding, by the way. Thank you very much."

"You're very welcome."

"Say Jennifer, can I ask you a question?"

"What?"

"Who's Tony?"

She put her coffee down, leaned back, laced her hands over that nice belly of hers—she had an inny by the way—and looked around at everything but me.

"Well, I guess I owe you this much. He *was* my fiancé."

"Oh. And when was 'was'?"

She looked at the clock on the wall and said, "Officially? About eight hours ago."

"What?"

She laughed but then went serious. I waited her out.

"Alright. Here's the Reader's Digest version. My parents were the fourth generation to farm a square mile of lousy soil in northern Manitoba. My two older brothers and I hated farming, and my folks knew a hard life on a Manitoba prairie wasn't in their children's future. So when I left the farm for Regina to study chemistry, they sold the farm and moved to town. Then for some strange reason, my Dad goes out and buys this little assay company called Thurson Ames. We had no idea why he did it, he didn't know anything about geology, let alone assaying, but the business was on the verge of bankruptcy and he only paid a song for it anyway. So after he bought Thurson, he kept one member of the staff around to run things, a young tech named, you guessed it, Tony. My first summer off from college, my Dad convinced me to come home and work in his new business, and that's where and when I met the guy. When Tony wasn't seducing me in the lunch room, he taught me how to assay. It was quite the internship.

"Anyway, then I get this scholarship to Stanford and off I go to California. I stayed there until I got my engineering degree in materials science. Took me all of another four years."

"So *you're* not just a pretty face."

"Actually," she said, acknowledging my barb with a smile, "swimming was what got me the scholarship."

"Oh."

Swimming. That explained a lot of things. Like the shoulders.

"Okay, so there I am in San Jose, all finished school with a P.Eng. and I need to make a decision. Either go to work for some big international company, or try to make something of my Dad's business. There was no future for it in Manitoba, mineral exploration was in the doldrums there, but things were booming in the Yukon. So three years ago I decided to load up all of Thurson's equipment and ship it up here. I set up shop in that new building out back and was open for business. I had so much work from the get go that I called Tony to give me a hand. He came up a month later and next thing I know we'd picked up exactly where we'd left off seven years earlier.

"Then last month, he asks me to marry him. We had everything but the date picked out when I caught him last week, how should I put it, grazing in the wrong pasture. Turns out he's hardly marriage material. Seems he prefers sleeping with women he doesn't know very well. And I've since found out there have been plenty of them. So I tossed him out. His new home is that old trailer out back, if he ever he comes back to town."

"You let him stay in your back yard? He cheated on you."

"Damn right he cheated on me. Hurt me and embarassed me in front of my parents, and my clients, too. My Dad can't believe I still employ him, but he is a good tech."

"You still employ him?"

"Yes, but in Dawson, not here. He'll be working up there for the summer, then I'll review his extremely bleak future with Thurson Ames. But right now I need him. We're opening a second lab up there because of all the new exploration south of town. Our new Dawson branch will put us a couple of hundred miles closer to the action, which is a big deal for a lot of the smaller companies. It's a short season, they have small budgets, and want their assays fast. It's why Mike pledged all his business to us for his Thistle Creek project. So yesterday I sent Tony and two other techs packing off to Dawson in two trucks hauling trailers full of equipment. We're setting up our new lab out near the airport. As soon as I find someone to run the office, we're open for business. Hopefully by the end of next week."

"And where will you spend the summer?"

"Mostly here, miles from what's his jerk. I like life in Whitehorse and there's still plenty to do here. But I'll go up to Dawson now and then, if and when I'm needed. Play it by ear, I guess. Why do you want to know that?"

I shrugged my shoulders and said, "Just being nosy."

She nodded and gave me a mischievous smile.

* * *

At exactly seven-thirty we dried the last of the dishes and Jennifer left the kitchen. The RCMP building was a fifteen minute walk and I had a few minutes to kill. I took out my phone and turned it on. This time while it was searching for things, I went over to the kitchen window for a look outside. To the west a thin layer of haze was hovering halfway up the cliffs, but the streets were now clear. Soon the sun would break through. I went to the table and checked my phone. Three more missed calls. One from the Café, two from some other number I didn't recognize. Still no call from Mike. I called him again and he didn't answer so left another message to confirm our rendezvous at Trans-Pacific. I called the Café.

"Brody? That you? Are you in Whitehorse? Did you talk to Leah? How's Jack?"

A shiver went down my spine.

"Minnie, what do you mean 'how's Jack'? Did something happen to him?"

"Oh, Brody, you don't know."

"Know what? What happened?"

I could hear heavy breathing. It's a rare occasion when Minnie is at a loss for words.

"Minnie! What happened to Jack!"

She sighed.

"Someone shot him."

"Shot him? What do you mean someone shot him? Who shot him? Is he alright?"

"All I know is he got shot."

"But is he alright?"

More heavy breathing.

"Minnie! Is Jack alright?"

"It doesn't look good, Brody. Leah drove him to town last night. You better call your vet. That's where she took him. Talk to your vet."

I slapped the phone shut, whirled around, and ran down the hall. The bathroom was empty. I pounded on the bedroom door.

"Hang on!"

The five second wait was excruciating. The door opened.

"Jennifer, someone shot my dog, I need a ride to the vet."

"Someone shot your dog? Why? Is he okay?"

"Never mind that, can you drive me or not?"

"Take my truck. Keys are on the wall in the kitchen."

"What if you need it?"

"I'm not going anywhere this morning, just go."

I ran back to the kitchen, grabbed the keys and my pack, and made a mad dash out the front door. I jumped in her truck, started it up, and hit the gas.

Something didn't feel right. It barely made it out of the ditch.

Flat tire?

I got out and looked.

It didn't have a flat tire. It had four flat tires.

They'd been slashed.

TWENTY ONE

I had to call the vet.

And Leah to see if she could drive me there. And Robson to tell him I'd be late for his meeting. And the cops to report the slashed tires. And a tire shop to replace the slashed tires. And Mike to let him know I'd be late.

I left the truck parked askew on the street and ran back into the house. It was empty. Jennifer was in the building out back, sitting on a stool at a bench, peering under the hood of some fancy instrument, rotating knobs with both hands. She had on a white coat and safety glasses, and without taking her eyes off her work, murmured, "That was fast."

"Jennifer, someone slashed your tires last night. Do you have a phone book handy?"

She whipped around and said, "Say what? Did you just say someone slashed my tires?"

"Yes. They're ruined."

"Ruined? Holy shit. Who would do such a thing?"

"I can only guess. But don't worry, I'll pay for whatever it costs to replace them."

"Why should you pay?"

"Because it probably has something to do with me. I should have known."

"Known what?"

"Look, never mind that, I'll tell you later. Right now I have to make a bunch of calls and I need a phone book. You can call the cops about your tires, but wait 'til I'm gone, okay? And don't tell them I was here last night."

"How come?"

"Jennifer, please, trust me. You don't want to know. Just don't tell the cops I was here last night, okay? Now do you have a phone book or not?"

She gave me a fierce look, then slid off the stool, stomped to the end of the bench, and pulled out a drawer. The phone book may have been thin but it stung like hell when she slapped it against my chest. Her big blue eyes were blazing behind her safety glasses.

"Brody, I'm hardly in the mood to trust any man these days, so God help you if you're messing with my life. Now give me my keys."

She made a hasty exit and I watched through a window as she stomped down the driveway to the street.

I called Minnie again to get Leah's number. It was one of the numbers on this morning's missed call list. Might have guessed. Her phone rang six times before she picked up.

"Hmm..."

"Leah, it's Brody."

A long silence before, "Time is it?"

"Almost eight. I know it's early but can you drive me to the vet?"

"What for?"

"What for? What do you mean what for? To see Jack."

"Not until noon."

"No, Leah, now. I want to see him now."

"You can't. The vet said don't come before noon. That's when he'll know."

"Know what?"

"If he can save his leg."

* * *

The RCMP took up half a page in the phone book. They had so many departments and phone numbers I couldn't figure out which one to call. So I didn't call any of them. The Staff Sergeant would have to wait and wonder if I was going to turn up.

But I did call a tire shop. That was easy because they only had one number. I asked the guy who answered to come get Jennifer's truck and install the best tires he had. And to give it a wash and a vacuum, too. He said he'd do everything—the tow, the tires, and his 'super-duper' clean and wax—all for the low, low price of eight hundred dollars. Plus tax, of course. He told me that was a really good deal. I told him it would be an even better deal if he threw in a couple of Tire King ball hats. Done, he said. Pick it up at noon.

Jennifer was happy to hear her truck would be fixed so fast. So happy, in fact, she agreed to wait until I was gone before calling the cops. Hopefully she could figure out which number to call.

Just before eight I set off into the crisp morning air and fifteen minutes later was standing in front of the RCMP building. It was a drab three story box, battleship gray with dark windows, adorned with all kinds of towers, antennas and satellite dishes. I climbed a short set of concrete stairs, walked past a few marble plaques, then entered through a double set of glass doors.

A sleepy woman made me sign a register, then pointed at an X-ray hoop at the end of the counter. She put me through the whole airport drill, made me take off my hat, jacket, belt and boots, and took her time analyzing the contents of my backpack. She kept my Swiss army knife and told me not to forget it when I left. I asked her how come I couldn't keep my knife if everyone else at the meeting was allowed to have a gun.

She gave me a deadpan stare and the silent treatment.

I knew where to go, it was my second visit to see Robson in a year, and headed for the elevator at the back of the building. The woman who confiscated my knife had called ahead to announce my arrival. When the elevator doors opened on the third floor, I was standing face to face with Robson's executive assistant, a short barrel bodied woman in her fifties. I'd met her last year. She was wearing the same polka dot dress and the very same scowl.

"You're late, Mr. Brody."

"Sorry."

"Don't tell me you're sorry. Tell the Staff Sergeant. He's very angry with you."

"He's always very angry with me."

She dropped her hands from where there once were hips, turned, and dug in for launch.

"Follow me," she commanded with the wave of a hand.

I did, though at a safe distance, staying well back of her wildly swinging arms as she set a blazing pace down a long hallway. She turned right at the end, then made a quick left into a conference room. I followed her in.

Three cops with serious cop glares were waiting for me. They were seated on either side of a long boardroom table. The one with the most stripes sat alone. They reminded me of rugby players— big, strong and healthy—with flat bellies and bulging arms. All had brush cuts and fresh shaves, all wore blue ties and pressed beige shirts adorned with badges and stripes, and name tags pinned high and right on their chests. As to be expected, they were loaded for bear, packing big guns in big brown holsters on big brown belts. None of them offered a word.

The chairs at either end of the table were empty. An open door at one end of the room provided a perfect view of Staff Sergeant Robson in an adjoining office. He was sitting behind a large dark desk, talking on the phone. He either he didn't see me come in, or chose not to acknowledge my arrival. The three cops remained stoic and silent. I gave them a nod but not one reciprocated.

The strong but silent type. Or maybe just shy.

"Morning, guys. Sorry I'm late. An issue with my dog. Hey, been watching the finals? Can you believe they're still playing hockey in June?"

No response. Zombies. It then occurred to me that the silent treatment was a tactic, a ploy to break me down with passive-aggressive behavior, drive me crazy with cold stares and deaf ears, turn me into a raving ranting maniac who would confess to anything. But if that was their plan, they were wasting their time.

I love quiet.

Robson's right hand woman pointed to the chair at my end of the table.

"Please be seated, Mr. Brody. And please remove your hat," she added on her way out the door.

The three cops had already removed theirs and had arranged them in a neat circle at the center of the table.

When in Rome.

I took mine off and took a moment to admire it. It was my downtown hat these days. It had two palm trees embroidered on the bill, with *Acapulco* scrolled across the front in big red letters. It was very classy, at least as ball caps go. Cost me twenty bucks at the airport in Mexico. I straightened the bill, brushed it off, then leaned over and placed it dead center in the middle of theirs. The three cops stiffened and glared daggers at me, struggling to stay silent. It was obvious why they were upset. My palm trees were much nicer than the chintzy gold leaves on theirs. But if my hat wasn't welcome at their hat party, so be it, no big deal to me. I picked it up and stuffed it in my pack.

Cops. Zero sense of humor.

I walked over to the window and gazed out at the streets and buildings of Whitehorse, then at the Yukon River flowing past the foot of the city, then beyond at Gray Mountain rising into a vacant silver sky. The air was clear, the fog was gone, the sun was out. I folded my arms and thought about Jack. Couldn't wait to see him.

There was a resounding thump and I spun around to see Staff Sergeant Robson had entered the room. He'd just dropped a thick stack of files on the table in front of him and was stabbing a finger at me.

"You! You're late! Now sit down!"

I did. He didn't. He just stood behind his chair glaring at me.

Then he leaned forward and laid his hands on the table. Everyone was frozen in their chairs, fixated on him. He was taking his time, milking the tension for all it was worth.

"Mr. Brody, I made it clear to you yesterday that our meeting was set for eight o'clock sharp. And I told you the consequences you'd face if you were late. So what do you do? You turn up late. You waste another half hour of my time, as well as that of my colleagues. So before I do what I have to do, do you have anything to say for yourself?"

"Nothing."

"Nothing?"

"Nope. Not if you're going to put me in jail for being late for a meeting."

"Alright, if that's the way you want it."

"Hey, if I'm going to jail, why should I say anything? Except that I didn't murder anyone and you don't have a shred of evidence that I did. You're just another bully with a gun, Robson, all dressed up with nowhere to go. So screw you."

I looked out the window again, stunned by my own audacity, incredulous that I was about to be put behind bars for turning up late for his meeting. I thought about Jack, what he was going through, that he might lose a leg today, maybe even his life, and that some irritable cop was going to prevent me from being with him. I was furious.

The three cops were on full alert, waiting for the word, poised to jump from their chairs and shackle the prisoner, haul him off and toss him in the dungeon.

But Robson didn't give the word.

Instead he sighed and said, "Alright, Mr. Brody, I'm going to pretend I didn't hear what you just said. Let's say we start over. Wipe the slate clean. Make a fresh start. What do say we try this again this afternoon? Right here at three o'clock. How about it? That suit your busy schedule?"

I leaned forward and said, "So you're not going to put me in jail? I can leave?"

"If we have a deal."

"Okay, we have a deal. Can I go now?"

"You can go now. But be back here at three o'clock. That's three o'clock *sharp*."

I looked at the other three cops. Same stares, same poker faces. I got up, grabbed my pack, and hustled toward the door.

"Oh, Mr. Brody?"

I stopped and turned around.

"What?"

He reached in his pocket, pulled something out, and held it up high.

"Know what this is?"

I did.

It was the key to my plane.

TWENTY TWO

Staff Sergeant Alan Robson was quiet, staring out the open door, tapping his fingers on the table. The three cops remained seated, silent, waiting.

He sat down.

"Think he'll come back?" asked Sergeant Arcand.

"Oh, he'll come back," replied Robson, rubbing his face with both hands.

"How do you know?"

"Because I have the key to his plane."

"Maybe he has a spare."

"Probably does. But he got the message. He may be a smart ass but he's also smart. He needs to make a living. He has a contract to fly rocks out of Thistle Creek starting Friday and I can't see him jeopardizing that. He may know we've got nothing on him but he also knows that if he doesn't turn up this afternoon, I might just go down to Schwatka Lake and shoot so many holes in that damn plane of his, it'll never fly again. So he'll be back."

"You don't think he's good for the girl?"

"No. Just got off the phone with the coroner. She was killed between four and five in the afternoon. The pilot is golden. He was drinking coffee in a restaurant up on the highway. Has a witness, a young woman named Leah McCormack who served him. So the dead girl at his cabin has got to be connected with the two murders last week, and the two last fall at Thistle Creek. We know Tommy Kay was good for the ones at Thistle Creek, so he's probably good for all of them. Kay was probably tidying up loose ends when he killed that gold trader in Dawson on Saturday, and the fisherman last week in Haines. The man in Dawson and the fisherman were our key witnesses for the Thistle Creek murders, and with them out of the picture, our case just got real weak. But why Kay would kill a woman the pilot barely knew, now that I'm not sure about."

"Maybe some kind of message."

"Be my guess. But the message would have been a lot stronger if the victim was someone the pilot cared about. So here's what I'm thinking. Minto's too small a place for Kay to visit in the middle of the day. He'd risk being spotted and he's impossible to forget. If you've ever seen the guy, you'd know what I mean. The man is a physical freak, reminds me of the Incredible Hulk. In a little place like Minto, he'd stick out like a turd in the front hall. So I say he sent someone else to do his dirty work. Probably a hired gun. And whoever that was killed the wrong girl."

"So who was the right girl?"

"A woman named Sarah Marsalis. A real looker, a US Treasury agent working out of D.C. She was up here last summer working on a money laundering case and that's when she met the pilot. Their eyes met and the proverbial sparks flew. Kay met them both in Dawson last summer and he knows they were love birds. Last fall, when the coroner declared Kay missing and presumed dead, we suspended the investigation of the Thistle Creek murders. As soon as Marsalis heard that, she jumped on a plane and flew all the way up here, just to see her Yukon boyfriend. Craziest thing. Those two are a mismatch if I've ever seen one. When I drove her up to his place in Minto last fall, she was more excited than a kid at Christmas. Anyway, my guess is if Kay wanted to send a message to the pilot, he'd kill Marsalis, not some waitress from Haines passing through town."

"This Marsalis woman, she still with the pilot? Sounds serious."

"Serious? Ridiculous is more like it. You see the guy? He's a bum. You should see her, she looks like a movie star. Anyway, I'm not sure if they're still an item, but Kay wouldn't know or care about that. He had no use for either one of them."

"So where do we go from here?" asked Arcand.

"We focus on what we know. We know Kay is back with the living, we know he's back in the Yukon, and we know he's definitely our guy for at least four murders. We want him for killing two scumbags at Thistle Creek last summer, and we want him for those two in Dawson and Haines last week. Pinning any one of them on him is all we need to put him away. But we need evidence, gentlemen, so keep digging."

Robson leaned forward, looked around the table, and stared each cop in the eyes. Orders sent and received.

"Good. Now I have a question for you, Sergeant."

"Sir?"

"Where the hell is Kay?"

"We're looking hard, sir."

"Well look harder. He's on the run. I want him locked up in the basement, not wandering around the territory like a loose cannon."

"Yes, sir."

Robson looked back at the other two cops. Corporal Harris and Constable Monahan were his top grunts.

"Corporal Harris, did the pilot say why he was late?"

"Yes, sir."

"Well, what did he say?"

"He said he had an issue with his dog, sir."

"An issue with his dog? What was the issue?"

"Didn't say, sir."

"You didn't ask?"

"No, sir."

Robson shook his head and sighed, then folded his arms and leaned back in his chair. It creaked as he made himself comfortable. The room was quiet again. Robson studied the ceiling, thinking.

Last fall when he drove the girlfriend up to Minto, he'd met the pilot's dogs. He remembered them all too well, two snarly little things that buzzed around his legs like bees. He remembered suppressing an urge to kick them.

Yesterday the pilot didn't have any dogs with him. So he must have left them at home. But if one of the pilot's dogs had 'an issue'—like being sick or injured—then someone in Minto would have been sure to call the pilot. The pilot would have asked that the dog be taken to a vet. The closest vet was in Whitehorse. So one of the dogs might be in town.

'Keep digging'.

"Constable Monahan."

"Sir."

"Call every vet in Whitehorse. Ask them if they've got a small dog that just came in from Minto. Belongs to a guy named Brody. Find out what's wrong with it."

"Yes, sir."

* * *

Main Street was just waking up but the stores and banks wouldn't open for another half hour. I had twenty minutes to kill before my meeting with Mike. Time enough to get my mail.

I crossed the street to the post office.

No one ever sends me money. As far as I'm concerned, mail is just a bundle of bad news to be dealt with twice a month. On a good day there are a lot of bills and a lot of junk. On a bad day there will also be a letter from some government agency, threatening me with fines, terminations, suspensions, penalties or imprisonment if I don't fill out a form and send them money. I say any letter from the government is a poorly veiled guise for a shakedown. It's always 'money for nothin' and never 'chicks for free'. I wondered if it was going to be a good mail day, or a bad mail day.

I climbed two stairs and was walking across a pebbled concrete terrace when an aboriginal man intercepted me. He was one of the usual crew stationed out in front of the post office, a certified member of the city's homeless citizenry, a man with little more to do than watch people all day, talk to his friends, beg a little money, kill a little time, find a bottle, get drunk, and live to do it all over again tomorrow.

This particular fellow was solidly built but more scruffy and disheveled than most. He reminded me of a burly troll. He could have been thirty, he could have been forty, there's no way of telling when it comes to street people. His mismatched clothes were as good as rags and the ball cap perched backwards on his straggly black hair was filthy and frayed. I was five feet away when he jumped into my path, planted his feet in a pugilistic stance, and raised his fists to my face.

"You owe me a buck!" he yelled.

I stopped in front of him. He had a freshly split lip, a few missing teeth, and the typical red raw complexion of a street alcoholic.

"I do?"

"Yes!"

"This buck I owe you, does that include interest?"

He dropped his hands to his hips and looked around. He was thinking, assessing the possibilities. Then he looked at me through his sunken red eyes and said, "No."

"No? Well, how much is the interest?"

He put a leathery hand to his unshaven chin and took some time before saying, "Two bucks."

"So I owe you three bucks?"

"Yeah, three bucks."

"Okay, three bucks. My name's Brody, by the way. What's yours?"

"Ray."

"Okay, Ray, here's the thing. The smallest I've got is a five. Could you wait here while I go inside and get my mail? Then we'll go to the coffee shop. We can get change there. Okay?"

Ray looked around, unsure of himself. I waited while the wheels turned.

Finally he said, "Okay."

I entered the building and went over to a wall of shiny post

office boxes. A minute later I was standing at a counter with three
stacks of sorted mail in front of me. The biggest stack was junk and
I slid it along the counter until it fell off the end into a recycling
box. The next stack was bills and a bank statement. I put those
in my pack. The last stack wasn't actually a stack, just a single
envelope from the Yukon Water Board. I held the envelope up to
the light. No check inside.

Go figure.

I didn't have a clue what the Water Board would want with me
but stuck it in my pack anyway. It was now officially a bad mail
day.

When I went outside, Ray was sitting on the edge of a concrete
flower tub full of freshly planted pansies. He was staring at the
ground with his elbows propped on his knees, holding his face in
his hands. He seemed dejected. The morning breeze had grown
into a blustery cold wind and I zipped my jacket up to the collar.

"Come on, Ray, let's go."

The trip to the coffee shop was slow going. I only had half a
lace in one of my boots and both of Ray's yawned at the toes each
time he lifted a foot. The soles had separated from the uppers and
the tape he'd wrapped around them had worn away. They flapped
with every step.

"You ought to glue those before they come off, " I said, pointing
at his feet.

"You got glue?" he asked.

"No."

"Neither do I."

Two blocks east we stopped for a light at the hub of the Yukon
financial district, the corner of Second and Main, where three
different banks occupy three of the four corners. A block south of
the light we walked into a coffee shop. Two men and a woman in
business attire were seated at a window table, appraising us intently
as we approached the counter. We were greeted by a friendly
teenager standing behind a feast of bagels and donuts in a long
glass case. High on the wall behind her, backlit screens displayed

fancy sandwiches and soups in glorious colors. The aroma of freshly brewed coffee dominated the air.

"Say, Ray, how about a coffee?"

He shrugged.

"Hey, know what? I could eat something, too," I lied. "How about you? You hungry?"

He shrugged again. I caught the threesome at the window still staring. Not at Ray, at me.

"Come on, how about a soup and sandwich? What do you say?" I asked him.

He shrugged again.

I ordered, paid, and carried a full tray over to a table that Ray had picked out. It was in the far corner, a poor target for prying eyes. I offloaded what I ordered—the same for both of us—a bowl of chicken soup, a tuna sandwich, a small double-double coffee. Ray gave me a suspicious look when I sat down.

"Man's got to eat, Ray. You buy next time, okay?"

He nodded without a word and dug in.

* * *

Across the street a red pickup truck with a white camper and Alaska plates was parked with the engine running. Sitting behind the wheel was Dan Sanders, waiting for instructions. He was alone in the cab, but not alone.

In the camper behind him sat Tommy Kay who was peering out a curtained window. Kay and Sanders had been following the pilot since he left the police building. They had watched him go in and out of the post office, talk to some Indian outside, then a few minutes later walk into a coffee shop with the same Indian. Kay wondered what the pilot was doing hanging out with the drunken Indian he'd punched in the face last night. The Indian had threatened Kay with his fists, said he owed him money. Kay had knocked him out with a love tap. No one threatened Tommy Kay and got away with it. The Indian was lucky to be alive.

Kay waited and watched. Ten minutes later the pilot walked out of the coffee shop. He was alone and in a hurry, heading toward Main Street.

Now where was he going?

Kay tapped the cab window.

Sanders put the truck in gear.

TWENTY THREE

I left Ray in the coffee shop with the three dollars I owed him and my soup and sandwich untouched. Dollars to donuts he would eat them. Which was the plan. Alcoholics have only one priority when it comes to financial choices, and booze always trumps nourishment when money is a constraint. Whatever might befall Ray today, at least he'd start it on a full belly.

One of the oldest structures in Whitehorse sits at the foot of Main Street. Built just after the railway came to town in 1905, the ground floor of the funky two story wood building hosts a variety of local eateries, art and souvenir shops, with a slew of small offices upstairs. I surveyed a directory at the foot of a staircase to make sure I was in the right place. After climbing a long flight of creaky stairs, and walking down several long hallways that bounced hollow under my feet, I eventually found Trans-Pacific's office at the north end.

The reception area was the size of a broom closet. The door barely cleared a chair inside and I almost tripped over the legs of the old-timer sitting in it. A small table smothered in magazines separated him from another old-timer in another chair. They both lowered their morning papers and looked up to assess the visitor. I had to turn sideways to clear their feet and avoid brushing the TV on the wall to get to the office at the back.

A good looking young man sprung from a chair behind a cluttered desk. He was slim, clean shaven, with a perfectly cut shock of thick black hair, and was dressed to impress in a white shirt with a striped tie. His black frame glasses completed the image of a young professional on the move.

Clark Kent, incarnate.

He beckoned me in with a wave and professional smile, then extended his hand between two large computer screens.

"Good morning, sir. Dave Sorenson, Trans-Pacific Securities. What can I do for you, Mr...?"

"Brody. Sorry to interrupt you, Dave, but I was told to meet someone here at nine-thirty. His name is Giguere. Know him?"

We shook hands over his desk and he gestured for me to sit in a chrome chair wedged in the corner.

"Mike Giguere? Sure do," he said, falling back in his chair and glancing at one of his screens.

I ignored his offer to sit. Dave stuck a well chewed pencil in his mouth, tapped something on his keyboard, took the pencil from his mouth, scribbled a few things on a printed form, and skewered it on a desk spike. He looked at the other screen, tapped his keyboard again, picked up another form, filled that one in too, and skewered it over the same spike.

He looked back at me and said, "Sorry about that. Yeah, Mike. Spent a few months in the bush working for him up in Old Crow. That was a few years ago when I was studying geology, a summer field job when I was in university. Mike's a great guy. He was just in here, you missed him by five minutes. Said to tell you he was real sorry but he had to run, said he had to go back to Thistle Creek. But he did leave an envelope for you. Hang on, got it here somewhere."

While Dave was ransacking his desk for Mike's envelope, I stepped over to the only window and gazed down at a short gravel alley. It was uncharacteristic of Mike to miss an appointment and lately it had been impossible to get hold of him. Why? I checked my phone to see if he'd called. He hadn't. I wondered what to do with the envelope that Jennifer asked me to give him. The phone on Dave's desk rang and he picked it up.

At that very instant, Mike appeared below me. He had just exited the building from a door below me and was heading out the alley. He wore a ball cap and had a coffee in his hand, but that was it—no backpack, no briefcase, nothing. I tried to open the window but it wouldn't budge. I looked back at Dave. He waved a hand in the air and mouthed, "doesn't work". There was no way I could catch Mike on foot, there simply wasn't enough time to get down the hall and descend the stairs before he got to the street, even if I ran. I had a brainwave and called him with my phone.

It rang four or five times while I watched him. He didn't break stride, never reached for a pocket, just kept walking. I checked the number I'd dialed. Definitely Mike's. The call switched over to his voicemail. I listened to his greeting but didn't leave a message. Maybe there was something wrong with his phone. Maybe he hadn't paid his bill and his account was suspended, or maybe he didn't have his phone with him. But none of that made sense. Mike was always connected. Whatever you used—a cell phone, a VHF radio, a satellite phone—one way or the other, you could always get in touch with him.

Something didn't seem right.

Then a red truck with a white camper rolled up on the sidewalk at the entrance to the alley, sealing it off from the street. The driver was alone. He got out and walked around the hood to the passenger side, stopped and leaned against the passenger door, and waited. It was Dan Sanders.

When Mike got to the truck, Sanders seemed to have a lot to say. Mike kept shrugging his shoulders as if to convey something wasn't his fault.

The first surprise came when Mike turned sideways to get in

the truck. It was his face. Even from two hundred feet away I could clearly see white tape plastered over a metal splint on his nose.

The second surprise came when Mike put his hand on the passenger door handle. Sanders stopped him and pointed to the rear. The two men walked to the back of the camper. Sanders opened the rear door and Mike climbed into the camper. Sanders got in the cab and drove away.

Now I was sure something wasn't right.

* * *

"Found it, knew it was here somewhere," said Dave Sorenson with a grin.

Still perplexed about Mike's appearance, I turned toward the voice. Dave was leaning over his desk with an outstretched arm. I took a plain white envelope from him.

"Thanks," I mumbled. I sat down in the chair in the corner to think. It was so low that the view out the window was nothing but blue sky. I held the envelope up to the light and saw the shadow of a small piece of cardboard inside. The only thing written on the outside was my name. I decided not to open it in front of Dave and slipped it in my pack with the rest of my mail.

I thought about Jack and couldn't wait to see him. The clock on the wall said ten o'clock. Two hours.

"Say, Dave?"

Dave was tapping keys again, concentrating on his screens.

"Yes, sir?"

"You said Mike was just here."

"He was."

"Did he say what happened to his face?"

"Yeah, he said he broke his nose. He said he was unloading his pickup on some wet grass yesterday and his feet slipped out from under him. Says when he fell he caught his nose on the tailgate. Looks like he smashed it up pretty good. Said he spent half the night in hospital."

I looked at the sky for a while, doubting if that was the truth. Did Mike have something to hide? Why was he avoiding me?

"So Mr. Brody, own any TCR?"

"TCR? What's that?"

"Thistle Creek Resources, Mike's project."

"Right. He told me about it on Monday."

"What did he say?"

"Nothing that I understood. Seemed pretty pumped about it, though. Told me to buy some."

"Did you?"

"No."

"How come?"

"Wouldn't know how. Never owned a stock in my life."

"Really?"

"Really."

"Buying stock is pretty simple."

"Oh, yeah?"

Dave studied me for a moment, then asked, "What do you know about the stock market, Mr. Brody?"

"Nothing, why?"

"Well, if you wanted to buy your first stock today, TCR would be a good choice."

"And why's that?"

"Well, for one thing, the guy running the project personally recommended it to you. Two, it has an excellent promoter. And three..."

He hesitated and smiled.

"What?"

"It has news coming out today and the market's going to like it."

"How do you know that?"

He smiled again and said, "Let's go with the first two reasons and buy you some TCR before it takes off."

* * *

Dave Sorenson was a hell of a salesman.

I'd walked into his office to meet up with someone and half an hour later he'd sold me a penny stock.

Before I'd even left his office, he'd done some tapping on his keyboard and bought me 40,000 thousand shares of Thistle Creek Resources at thirteen cents a share. He told me that was a great price, as if I would know. I wrote him a check for a little more than five thousand dollars and wondered if I needed my head read. Every spring there were a ton of expenses to cover before the money started coming in, and I was already worried about my bank account. Five grand to buy stock wasn't in the budget, and neither were two new windshields, four new tires, and what would be a significant vet bill. There are days in life when you just have to grit your teeth and press on.

I was reaching for the door knob, about to leave Trans-Pacific's office, when a voice croaked behind me.

"Say, Mister?"

I turned and looked down at the old fellow sitting next to the door. He was well into his eighties but his bright eyes exuded an aura of health. He seemed unsure of himself, looking back and forth from the newspaper in his hands to me.

"Is this you?" he asked with a raspy voice, tapping a knarled knuckle on the front page.

With shaky hands he held out the paper and I took it from him. It was me alright, dead center in a large black and white photo plastered across the top half of the morning paper. I was standing on the dock at Schwatka Lake, talking to Tim and Jim in front of my plane. One of the trick-or-treaters from yesterday must have taken the shot from the top of the dock. The mist lent an eerie hue to the scene, but no doubt it was me in front of my plane. You could even make out the letters on the tail.

Great.

The headline over the story was in big bold letters, four words, and had probably sold a lot of papers.

MURDER SUSPECT THREATENS REPORTERS

Special to the Yukon Times
By Ellen Burke

Yesterday in Whitehorse, a prime suspect for the murder of a woman in Minto threatened to throw reporters into the icy cold waters of Schwatka Lake.

The bizarre incident occurred just after C.E. Brody of Minto had landed his float plane at the Whitehorse Water Aerodrome. He was tying up his plane to the public dock when several reporters asked him if he had killed the woman found dead at his home on Monday. Brody offered only a curt response, replying "No." When asked for more information, Brody quickly became agitated and threatened to start throwing reporters into the lake.

"I was terrified," said one of the press corps on the dock at the time, speaking on condition that her name not be used for her own safety. "He (Brody) looked crazed and we all ran off before he could carry out his threat. Thank God the police were there, who knows what he might have done? I'm just relieved to have escaped a very dangerous situation."

The dead woman found Monday evening at Brody's home in Minto has been identified as twenty-six year old Amy Vanderbilt of Haines, Alaska. According to an RCMP spokeswoman, Vanderbilt was an overnight guest in Brody's home for the two days preceding her death. Police say her neck had been broken and have ruled her death a homicide.

It remains unclear if Vanderbilt's

murder is connected to the murder of
Ralph Braun, a sixty-six year old man
found strangled in his Dawson home last
Saturday.

The RCMP are continuing their
investigations into both murders. No
charges have been laid for either crime.

An RCMP officer was seen questioning Mr.
Brody as reporters prepared to leave the
scene yesterday. It remains unclear if he
will be charged for uttering a threat.

TWENTY FOUR

The first thing I did on my way to the bank was stop in front of a store window.

The image in the glass was a familiar man: six feet, a hundred and eighty pounds, ball cap, aviator sunglasses, windbreaker, blue jeans, boots, backpack. The question was, how familiar would he be to others? Who else might recognize the man in the window as the man on the front page?

Probably plenty. If some old geezer could identify me from a picture in the morning paper then so could anyone else. Everyone in town would now be on the lookout for the crazed murderer from Minto. The Yukon has its fair share of people who can't mind their own business and I thought of the threesome in the coffee shop who had given me the dirty eye. Maybe I ought to lose the ball cap, get an overdue haircut, change sunglasses, change my jacket, change my footwear…but then I thought, no. Deception was the wrong tactic. I hadn't hurt anyone and decided to tough things out with my head held high.

The notoriety shouldn't last long anyway. The press has the attention span of a pre-schooler and by tomorrow they'd have manufactured another sensational story, featuring a brand new pariah for their readers to loathe. Besides, soon the police would arrest Amy's true murderer and I'd be exonerated.

So I hoped.

My phone rang and I dug it out of my pack.

"Hello."

"Hi!" said a friendly and familiar voice.

I almost responded with 'Hi hon', but checked myself. We weren't quite there yet.

"Hello there, Jennifer."

"Hey, guess what?"

"What?"

"The guy at the garage just called and said my truck will be ready at eleven thirty."

"Great. I'll pick it up for you. "

"Where are you?"

"Downtown."

"I have a better idea," she said. "How about I pick it up and meet you downtown for lunch? I'm closer to the garage than you are."

Lunch? She wants to eat again?

"Sorry, can't do lunch, Jennifer. Got to go to the vet."

"Oh, Brody, I'm so sorry. I didn't ask about your dog. How his he?"

"Not good. I'll know better when I see him."

"Do you need a ride?"

What I needed was to borrow a vehicle.

"Actually, if I could borrow your truck and drive there myself, that would be great, Jennifer. How about I pick up your truck for you? The walk to the garage is no big deal."

"Okay, let's do this. You pick up my truck, then you come get me, then you drop me off at the pool, then you go to the vet, *then* we'll go for lunch."

"Sounds like a plan."

Lunch.

I needed some cash.

* * *

The bank was empty but I had to weave back and forth through one of those ubiquitous cattle runs of chrome posts and velvet ropes to reach the counter. Two tellers were on duty, poised for paper work at opposite ends of the counter. I stopped and waited for a cue. The teller closest to me was a fixture at the branch, a friendly old gal who was undoubtedly someone's grandmother and had always served me well. But when I looked at her today, there was no smile for the customer. Instead she was delivering a scathing look of disapproval, and with no greeting forthcoming, I assumed she'd seen the morning paper.

The alternative to dealing with Grandma was to take my business to the pretty young lady marooned twenty feet away. She looked like a kid at a lemonade stand who couldn't wait for her first customer. I decided to deal with her.

Grandma's eyes tracked me like surveillance cameras when I walked past her admonishing glare. She didn't respond when I tipped my cap. But the pretty young woman seemed pleased to have a customer. She welcomed me with a broad smile and held it until I handed her my withdrawal slip. Then her face went slack and her eyes grew big as dinner plates She fixated on the slip like it was a holdup note. In a flash Grandma was all over the crisis and grabbed the slip from her catatonic protegé.

After a careful and judicial appraisal, she said, "Mr. Brody, in future the bank would appreciate advance notice when you wish to make such a large withdrawal."

"How come?"

"Because it takes time to count that much cash."

"That's weird. It didn't take you long to count it when I deposited it last fall."

The two women left with the slip and disappeared down a hall. Probably off to call the cops. The murderer from Minto was planning a getaway and had to be stopped.

But eventually the two returned with Grandma battleaxe in the lead. The young woman was all smiles again and ten minutes later there was ten grand sitting at the bottom of my backpack.

The money was this year's spring budget, though a fair chunk of it would be gone by the end of the day. I hoped what was left over would get me through the next three weeks. It better.

I was well ahead of schedule and had only one more thing to do before starting my hike to the tire shop. I found a chair near the front door, pulled out Mike's letter, and looked it over. The envelope had Trans-Pacific's return address at the top left corner. 'Brody' was scrawled in pencil on the front. I wondered again why Mike hadn't answered my call in the alley, let alone any of the others I'd made in the last twelve hours. Why write a letter when all he had to do was call me? I opened the envelope. Inside was a small piece of piece of cardboard. It had been torn off a cereal box. There was colorful factory printing on one side, handwriting on the other. The note was in pencil.

> Brody, there's a big Chinese guy out looking for you. Danger, stay clear! See you Fri am at Thistle. Don't walk up to camp, lots of bears, wait at the dock. Mike   p.s. no police, will explain

'No police'?

Why would I call the police? Mike was scared of something.

Or someone.

I was too.

Of course I knew perfectly well who Mike was describing when he referred to 'a big Chinese guy'. It had to be Tommy Kay who was in fact a Korean-American. But what mattered was the message. Kay was definitely in the Yukon and officially on the prowl for me.

Then I wondered how Mike would know that. Had Kay tracked him down for information on my whereabouts? Had he broken Mike's nose to get answers? Did this have something to do with Thistle Creek? I considered the last possibility, that it might have something to do with Mike's exploration project, then thought it unlikely. This was personal, it was about money, it was about that box full of cash Kay gave me on the Yukon River last year. Kay wanted his four hundred grand back, plain and simple. The threat had escalated and I was more nervous than ever. And afraid. Afraid that Kay might be waiting to ambush me at Thistle Creek on Friday. Mostly though, I was afraid for anyone who knew me. Mike had already paid a heavy price for my acquaintance and Amy had lost her life for it. Poor Amy, she'd done nothing more than cross paths with the wrong guy at the wrong time. I thought about Jennifer. And Jack. And Leah. And everyone else I knew in Minto. The situation was intolerable. Kay had to be caught and locked up. The sooner the better.

Sorry, Mike, the cops have to know about this.

* * *

Tippy Li was sitting on one of the long leather couches in Lynn Chan's living room. In his hands he held the final version of today's press release. He'd just pulled it from the printer. The paper felt warm in his hands. Ironic in this digital day and age, he thought.

'Hot off the press'.

He scanned the list of assays and intervals. They were twice what they were yesterday, a big improvement over the first version. He had to hand it to Tommy, the geologist had done what he'd been told. It had taken some persuasion, but in the end he'd done what was best for Thistle Creek shareholders. Now the assays weren't just great, they were downright fantastic.

Tippy smiled. What the punters wanted, the punters would have. He knew the penny stock market was nothing more than a casino, that buying shares in an exploration company was nothing more than a bet on exploration results.

Tippy didn't know a damn thing about gold mining and only slightly more about exploration. In fact about all he knew was that assays were a test of what was inside a rock, what minerals it contained, and how much of them there were. Assays provided an indicator of what the rock might be worth. The more minerals inside a rock, the higher the value of the rock, the higher the value of the property. What more did anyone have to know about the business? It was so simple.

High grade gold assays meant a high grade share price.

And who didn't want that? So what if the assays were a little optimistic? Who cared? Give investors what they want. Fans of Tippy's promotions weren't in for the long haul. Everyone knew it took years and years and billions of dollars to develop a mine, and none of his followers were interested in that. All they wanted was a bet on finding one.

Gold exploration was about dreams, about drilling for treasure, and maybe even finding one. It was about making a fast buck. Tippy's business model was simple: host the game, set the table, drill lots of holes, broadcast great results, pull in the suckers, and take bigger and bigger bets on the next press release. When the share price got high enough, and the market was in a frenzy, he'd sell his shares and move on to the next one.

He looked at the Tag Heuer on his wrist. Ten o'clock in the morning in Vancouver, one o'clock in the afternoon in Toronto. The markets would close in another three hours. In twenty minutes he'd pull the trigger and the press release in his hands would circle the world at the speed of light. The latest Thistle Creek gold assays could be read on every broker's screen from Johannesburg to Sidney, from London to New York, from Vancouver to Toronto. Then the calls would start. Lynn's phone would light up like a Christmas tree.

She had better be ready. It was party time.

He gazed across the expanse of thick white carpet to the end of the room. Fifty feet away Lynn Chan was sitting at her desk in front of a wall of glass. In front of her she had a fancy desk phone, two bottles of water, a pad of paper, a pen, and on her right—in case she forgot her lines—the card with her ten second spiel. She looked ready, even with a major league pout going. If nothing else, she was good at that, thought Tippy.

He studied her for a while. She'd been doing an excellent job of ignoring him. When she wasn't inspecting her nails, she was daydreaming at the ships in the harbor. Whenever she swiveled her chair from one side to the other, Tippy would admire the exquisite profile of her ass. Every time she moved, it flexed like soft putty. A week ago it had been his to fondle on a whim, as easy as sampling a melon in a grocery store. But not anymore.

Something had changed and he doubted he'd have the pleasure again. Overnight she had turned to ice, now barely speaking a word to him.

Why? What had happened? What had he done? Was there another man? Surely she knew that would be a fatal mistake. For both of them.

He laid his head back, spread his arms across the back of the soft Italian couch, contemplated the ceiling for a while, and pondered the mysterious behavior of women. Then his eyes drifted to the chandelier in the dining room.

He had to agree with Lynn, the damn thing *was* ugly. Whoever bought it had absolutely no taste. But Tippy knew why it was there. And why the chandelier she'd ordered was not.

The switch had been made as a matter of necessity, a requirement for function over form, to serve a special purpose. Somewhere in all that brass and bronze junk was a video camera and Tippy could now monitor Lynn from anywhere in the world. He wasn't sure where Sanders had placed the charges but was assured there was enough C-4 in the thing to blast a hole through the roof. Sanders had demonstrated how with the press of a button on his phone, Tippy could blow Lynn and her desk out those tall windows to the street below. Pity anyone else in the place, including boyfriends.

There'd be nothing left of them.

His phone vibrated. He looked at the screen and recognized the number. The call was from one of several burner phones purchased in Alaska last week. He got up and walked down the hall, went into a bathroom, closed the door, and raised the phone to his ear.

"Yes?"

"Hello, Mr. Li"

"Hello, Tommy."

TWENTY FIVE

It was a two mile walk to the tire shop and I wasn't going to do it with a piece of rope for a boot lace.

A hundred feet from the bank, on the same side of the street, I entered a sporting goods store that sold everything you'd need to climb Everest. On a wall at the back was a display with every kind of hiking boot imaginable. There must have been fifty of them, all lefts, each one sitting on its own little shelf, brightly lit under an array of spotlights on the ceiling, enticing customers to touch and squeeze and make judicious appraisals. I was scanning a rack of laces when a skinny kid emerged from a back room. He looked at my boots and asked if he could help me pick out a new pair. I told him mine were fine and asked where they kept their leather boot laces. He said they didn't sell leather boot laces. I left the store shaking my head, crossed the street, and went into the drugstore. They didn't sell boots but had leather boot laces.

Go figure.

I dodged through slow moving traffic and jaywalked across to the sunny side of the street, found a bench, and in no time was admiring two newly relaced boots. I was good to go but wondered how to get to the north end of town, without being spotted by Kay. If he was cruising the streets, I'd be well advised to stay off the sidewalks. Taxis and buses are scarce around Whitehorse, so I considered the alternatives. Some tourists walked by behind me, chattering away in German, heading east toward the river, and it gave me an idea.

I followed them down to the White Pass train station, crossed the old narrow gauge tracks, and stepped onto an all purpose walking, jogging, bicycle path that follows the river's west bank.

The Whitehorse Waterfront Path is the paved section of a series of interconnected trails that runs through the city and along the Yukon River. Wide and smooth, it was virtually empty on a weekday morning. If Kay happened to be on the hunt for me there, I'd see him a mile away. He was so muscle bound he could barely walk, so even if he pursued me, he could never catch me running scared. All of a sudden I felt a lot more relaxed. I headed north with my brand new laces in my comfy old boots.

The path wandered back and forth along the river's edge in long gentle bends, past buildings and docks, through playgrounds and parks, between stands of trees with shiny new leaves. Whenever it took me close to the river, I could hear the dark cold water burbling and gurgling as it rushed northward. I stopped under a tall steel tower and looked up at the three power lines traversing the river, and the three orange balls suspended from their midpoints. They were high over my head, maybe a hundred feet up, and I thought about how close they'd passed under the floats yesterday. Maybe next time I'd fly under them. I paused to consider that scenario, then reminded myself there wasn't going to be a next time.

With barely a whisper a pair of kayakers whizzed by on my right, loaded with gear for a wilderness adventure, paddling over a black sheet of water flowing six miles an hour. I couldn't have kept up with them in a sprint.

I carried on and saw almost no one in the next twenty minutes, at least no one to fear. Two boys on mountain bikes passed me early on, going the same direction as me. Minutes later a smiling woman with a stroller and a dog passed me going the other way, and soon after that a man jogging, and then another woman jogging, also going the other way. Just everyday people out for some fresh air on a sunny spring day. So far so good I thought, though I intended to remain vigilant and aware of my surroundings.

Almost there.

With a thousand feet to go before it ended at a hotel parking lot, the path narrowed into a heavily treed corridor. Were someone to be lurking in the woods in ambush, my only other option was to leave the path, venture into the open, cross a wide gravel lot, then a major intersection, and walk a block down a busy street. I weighed the risks. Fifty-fifty, six of one, pick your poison.

I stayed on the path.

The ground shook. A shrill horn pierced the quiet morning air. Fifty feet ahead of me a set of rails crossed the path and a hundred feet to my right a funky old trolley car was approaching. A young woman was standing on a platform at the front, controlling its speed with a lever in one hand and blowing the horn with the other. A bright headlamp below her blazed the way ahead. The ornately painted white and gold car had a curved tin roof and was adorned with colorful curlicues draping from the eaves. It looked as cute as a Christmas toy and was brimming with sightseers, with as many standing as seated. The trolley rumbled toward me, heavy and slow, clicking and clacking over the rails, sending shudders through the ground as it got closer. It was only going ten miles an hour but I decided to wait and let it pass.

The man who'd passed me jogging the other way stopped at my side. I hadn't heard him for the trolley and was mildly startled, though a glance told me he wasn't a threat. He was young and tall, slim and lean, soaked with sweat, breathing heavily, running on the spot to stay warm, ready for takeoff at the first opportunity. He was wearing a black toque, sunglasses, a long sleeved turtleneck, and skin tight leggings. Obviously he was on the return leg of his run. He ignored me and I ignored him. The trolley crossed the path a few feet in front of us with lots of happy kids and adults leaning out the windows, smiling and waving at us.

Oh what fun it is.

I waved back and started walking again. But the jogger didn't resume his run. Instead he simply began walking beside me, stride for stride, making me feel damn uncomfortable.

Then he wagged a finger at me and said, "Do I know you?"

"I don't think so," I said, not looking at him.

"Yeah, I think I do. I think I know exactly who you are."

"No, you don't."

"Yeah, I do. You're the guy in the newspaper this morning, the one who killed that woman in Minto. Your name's Brody, right?"

I stopped and looked at him and said, "Hey, I didn't kill anyone, okay? The paper has it wrong. Now leave me alone."

He stopped too and replied, "I don't want to leave you alone."

"I don't care what you want. Now leave me alone and go."

He didn't. I started walking again. So did he, matching me step for step, now smiling at me. I looked straight ahead and tried to ignore him, which wasn't easy as he had moved closer, now almost touching my shoulder. The path was veering left through the trees and the noise from the trolley was gone. The river was close to our right and I could hear it again. We walked past a short path that led to a bench on the bank. A man was sitting on it.

As soon as we were past the bench the jogger grabbed my right arm and twisted it behind my back. He was strong, much stronger than I might have guessed. And fast. I should have never taken my eyes off him. He shoved me off the path and wrapped his left arm around my neck. He seemed to know what he was doing and put a leg between mine, then hooked a foot around an ankle. He clamped his arm harder around my neck and pulled my head back, then twisted my right arm even higher, so much higher I thought it might pop out of its socket. He had me in a choke hold and I could barely breathe, managing only to eke out a grunt.

"How's it feel?" he whispered in my ear.

"What do you want?" I gasped.

Tears welled up in my eyes from a seering pain in my shoulder. My vision at the periphery was funnelling down. Stars and mirrors were dancing at the end of a long dark tunnel. I struggled to break his grip but it was no use, he knew what he was doing. I was fading fast.

"What I want to do is break your neck," he hissed in my ear. "I'm going to kill you right here, right now, with my bare hands. Just like you did to Amy."

Amy?

"I didn't kill..." were the last words I got out.

"Yes, you did," he whispered in my ear.

I was about to lose consciousness.

So this is how it would end. Yesterday I'd tempted fate on my own terms, and were it not for a fair amount of luck, my demise would have been assured and entirely my own fault. Now, a day later, my life was once again at the brink but for no good reason. The only thing on my mind when my legs gave way was the irony.

But my luck hadn't quite run out.

Behind me I heard a swish of air and a heavy thud, as though someone had dropped a book on a desk. The arm around my neck and the hand on my wrist relaxed, then they were gone. I heard a gasp, a thump, and a long deep sigh. I fell to my knees, gasping for air, supporting myself on my one good arm on the cold hard ground. My right shoulder was on fire, hanging at my side, useless. I turned my head and looked behind me. The jogger was flat on his back with his upper body lying out on the path. He was dead still.

Maybe because he *was* dead. A small pool of blood was forming under his head. His arms were spread out with his face to the sky. I waited a moment for my vision to clear, then with great effort rose to my feet, took two unsteady steps, and looked down at my attacker. With a finger I slid his sunglasses down his face. His eyes were open, unfocussed, staring up at nothing. There was a clatter to my left. A thick tree branch was rolling down the path, twenty feet away.

I glimpsed a man with long black hair running into the woods.

"You owe me a buck!" he yelled.

* * *

"Ray? Ray!"

I waited.

Virtual silence, save for the breeze in the trees and a hiss from the river.

He was gone. Either he hadn't heard me or wouldn't respond. Whatever the case, it was no surprise he had run away, and I couldn't blame him. Why stick around? For what? He'd just clobbered a stranger over the head with a branch as big as a baseball bat, and maybe killed him at that. It wouldn't matter to Ray that he did what he did to save my life, or that his heroics were justified. He was hardly the kind of guy who wanted anyone's attention, especially that of the police.

The police. Robson. Damn.

Clearly I owed Ray a lot more than a buck. I'd start with the obvious and resolved there and then to protect him from the fallout.

Our little secret, Ray.

I checked the path both ways. No one else was around, just me and my attacker lying at my feet. I kneeled down for a closer look. He wasn't moving and didn't seem to be breathing. I certainly wasn't going to help him, he was no friend of mine, and it was kind of late to let bygones be bygones. The pool of blood under his head was growing larger. What to do?

I certainly didn't need another crisis with the cops. What I needed to do was pick up a truck, pick up Jennifer, and go see Jack. If the man was dead, why do anything?

But better make sure he was.

I stood up and stepped away from him, extended a leg out, and gave him a nudge in the ribs with the toe of my boot. And nearly jumped out of my skin when he moaned and fluttered his eyelids.

Which is exactly when I saw the other jogger. She was young and chubby, breathing hard, standing fifty feet away in the middle of the path, holding out a phone that was pointed at me.

Not again with the pictures.

I walked around the man at my feet and took a few steps toward her.

"Hey, how about using that thing to call 911?"

"Not another step or I'll scream!" she yelled.

"Scream away, no one will hear you," I yelled back, though stopped as ordered. Then, "Hey, come on, quit taking pictures and call 911."

"What happened to him?"

"I don't know but he needs help. Now make the call."

"Why don't you make the call?"

"Hey, you're the one with the phone in your hand."

"You're lying!"

"Lying? About what?"

"You killed him!"

"No I didn't, he's breathing. Now do whatever you want. I'm out of here."

With that I turned, gave her a wave with my good arm, and walked away.

TWENTY SIX

No one attacked me on the rest of the way to the tire shop and there was no sign of Tommy Kay.

But I wasn't feeling great. A little dizzy, a little weak, a little depressed too, but mostly overwhelmed with a throbbing pain in my right shoulder. If I tried to raise my right arm, halfway up a stab of pain stopped me dead. Not good. I wondered if I could fly. Maybe, maybe not.

I also wondered about the woman on the path.

Who stops fifty feet from an injured person on a public path and starts taking pictures? Don't you just run up to see if you can help? What was with that attitude? Maybe she'd been afraid of me, thought I posed some kind of threat to her, that I was somehow responsible for the man's state and was about to attack her too. But if that was the case, why didn't she run away? And calling me a liar? Lying about what? And arguing about who should call 911? Now what was that about? It all seemed very strange.

* * *

The Tire King is run by a couple of slobs named Rick and Ron Granger, the third generation of slobs to own the business. I don't think the office floor has ever been swept or the customer counter cleaned. It always perplexes me how some people can function in filth and chaos. The way Rick and Ron deal with overflowing garbage in the trash cans around their property is to let it fall out and blow away. If they didn't have such a great location, and the best prices in the Yukon, I wouldn't bother with them.

The main building is a piecemeal assembly of concrete block additions that long ago absorbed a two bay garage built back in the sixties. A couple of years ago Rick and Ron got a great deal down south on one of those spinning brush car washes that no one wants to own anymore. They shipped it up to Whitehorse and installed it in a new concrete block building out back. Today the Tire King is your one stop shop for gas, tires, and a drive-thru car wash that'll rip the mirrors off your car in the blink of an eye.

The overhead doors in the main building were wide open and I walked past a faded sign that said 'Employees Only', then into a six bay work shop where I was greeted by a cacophony of screaming air guns, hissing compressors, and tools clunking on concrete. The place looked like a bomb went off with wheel weights and wheel covers and wheel nuts everywhere. Men in coveralls and welder's caps were dragging tangled hoses behind them, shouting at each other. A cloud of dust hung like a London fog and coated everything in a thick layer, including the virtually opaque windows. There were tires all over the place, old and new, stacked in piles, sitting on racks, lying on benches and tables, leaning against vehicles and walls. At the entrance to one bay door, a lone tire lay abandoned like a baby on a doorstep.

Utter chaos.

Rick Granger had a clipboard in his hand and was yelling at some kid with an air gun. The kid had his mouth open and seemed totally confused. When Rick spotted me, he pointed at the office and I followed him in. Rick is a big guy with a fully paid beer belly and an unkempt beard, and as usual was gasping for air like he'd just run a marathon. He wore a dirty blue shirt with his name stitched on the lapel, and greasy eyeglasses perched off kilter on his crooked nose. He was about my age.

"How 'ya doing Brody?" he asked with his chest heaving, closing the door behind us, tossing his clipboard on the counter and pulling out a pack of cigarettes from his shirt pocket.

"Not bad, Rick. That Thurson truck ready?"

"Sure is. It's out back," he said, lighting up. "The boys are just polishing 'er up. Looks great. I'm a little disappointed to see you here, though. Was hoping that tall hot blonde who owns it would come get it, not your sorry ass face."

He hauled on his cigarette, exhaled a cloud of blue smoke, and coughed.

"Life's full of disappointments, Rick. Let's go see what you did."

"How about we settle up first? Then you'll be good to go."

"Hey, Rick. Do I look like I just fell off a tomato truck? Last time I was in here you guys installed directional tires backwards."

"You're a fussy bastard, know that?" He shook his head and said, "Alright, follow me."

He didn't seem pleased about making the hundred foot walk out to the back of the building. But at the Tire King you always make sure you get what you bargained for, *before* paying your bill. We walked through the shop, navigating an obstacle course of junk and old tires. Why move something out of the way when you can just step over it?

The 'boys' who were supposed to be 'polishing' Jennifer's truck had their butts glued to the fenders, gawking at their cell phones. Behind them the car wash was screaming like a jet. They jumped when they saw Rick, whipped out their rags, and started wiping like their lives depended on it.

Or at least their summer jobs.

I walked around Jennifer's truck and did a careful inspection of her new tires.

"Hey, Rick?" I shouted over the racket.

"What?"

"These kids know how to check tire pressures?"

"Course."

"Good, have one of them check the pressure in these ones."

"Already done. The installer does that."

"That's why I want them checked. By hand. And with a decent gauge. Thirty six pounds all round, okay? Last time I got new tires here the pressures were all over the place. And tell them to check the spare tire too."

"Damn, Brody, you're in some kind of mood today."

"You got that right. Now check them."

Rick jutted his chin at one of the kids and we returned through the noise and dust to the office. Rick used a forearm to clear a space on the counter, then placed Jennifer's invoice in front of me. He tapped the grand total printed in the lower right hand corner.

"Eight hundred as quoted," he said, "plus forty for the tax makes it eight forty total. Hell of a deal, I gotta say."

"How about my hats?"

"Hats? What hats?"

"Come on, Rick. Two Tire King hats. It was part of the deal."

"You're one tough son of a bitch to deal with, know that?"

He smiled with yellow teeth and disappeared in a closet behind him.

Just getting started, Rick.

My right arm was useless. I fought off a stab of pain and managed to slide my pack off my shoulder and lower it to the floor, then picked it up with my left hand and put it on the counter. I grabbed my right wrist with with my left hand and rested it on top of the pack, unzipped the big compartment with my left hand, reached in, and pulled out five bills from the stack of hundreds at the bottom. I placed them in a fan on top of the invoice. Rick came out with my hats, one beige, one blue. Home and away. Nice. I shoved them in the pack and zipped it up.

"Thanks," I said.

He nodded, saw the cash on the invoice, and counted it twice.

"Put the rest on a credit card?" he asked.

"There is no *rest*, Rick. That's plenty."

"Now just a minute there, big guy. The deal was for eight hundred. I can't do five hundred, no way. We had a deal."

"We had a deal, alright. Eight hundred for the best you have. But you didn't install your best. You installed those."

I pointed at a big colorful placard leaning against the wall. It advertised a four tire special for some Korean tire. Then I pointed at a line on his invoice which said Michelins. Rick tried to appear shocked.

"You sure about that?" he said.

"Go check for yourself, if you want. I'll wait here."

He didn't move. No surprise.

Busted.

"Well damn, Brody, I'm real sorry about that. I'll have to tune up the installer for that bonehead mistake."

"You do that. Now tell one of those kids out back to bring the truck around."

He picked up his phone while tapping the keys on a filthy keyboard. A printer spit out a new invoice. Five hundred total. He marked it paid. I stuffed it in my shirt pocket and turned toward the door, then had a thought.

"Hey, Rick?"

"What now?"

"You get any other calls today for slashed tires?"

"Nope. Just this one. Which is kind of strange when you think about it. Most times there's a slashing around here, there's a whole a bunch of them. Up and down and both sides of a street. Kids out on a spree, ya' know? That cop that came in here this morning asked me the same question. Why?"

"No reason," I said.

* * *

Bait and switch.

Nice try, Rick.

As soon as he knew Jennifer's tires had been slashed, Rick smelled an insurance claim. He knew most people carry vandalism insurance and could sell her whatever he wanted, at any price, because her insurance company would foot the bill. But Rick went a step farther. He short changed her on the goods. He installed cheap tires and charged her for good ones. She'd never know and neither would the insurance company. Which is why Rick had called Jennifer to come get her truck, a half hour earlier than promised to me. He wanted her to pick up the truck, not me. She would have missed the con. And Rick would have made a tidy profit on the rip-off.

Scumbag.

Jennifer's shiny truck rolled up in front of the office and the kid driving it jumped out and started wiping the mirror, like he couldn't stop working on it. Then he held the door open for me. I threw my pack inside and got in.

The kid resumed his furious wiping, then stopped and looked at me like he deserved a tip. I looked at him like he didn't.

I headed for Jennifer's house and thought about why her truck had been the only vehicle in town to have its tires slashed last night. I didn't like the answer. I remembered the man on the street last night. Could that have been Kay?

I called Leah.

After five rings, "Mmm..."

"Leah?"

"Mmm..."

It was a quarter to noon and she was still sleeping. Teenagers.

"Leah, it's Brody."

"Time is it?"

"Noon."

A long pause, a loud yawn, then, "Need a ride now?"

"No thanks."

"Good."

"You getting up today?"

"Yup."

"Hey Leah, tell me what happened to Jack."

"Wait."

I did. For three minutes. Three minutes of dead air while I assumed she was off to the bathroom. Time enough for me to drive down Fourth, turn right on Cook, and pull into Jennifer's driveway.

"Still there?"

"Still here," I said, turning off the engine with my left hand.

"Okay, so yesterday afternoon Reggie and Buck walked all around the village looking for Jack and Russ, then they took Buck's dogs and went down to your place. They looked around your shop, then walked down to your cabin and looked up and down the river, then Buck's dogs found them in the woods behind your cabin. Jack was lying under a tree and Russ was sitting beside him. They were both in pretty bad shape. Their noses and eyes were all swelled up because they were out all night. Reggie says the mosquitoes really chewed them up. So then Reggie took them up to the Café and told me to drive Jack to town 'cuz of his leg. So I did. He took Russ back to his place. How is Jack?"

I cringed at the thought of Jack and Russ spending a night in a cloud of mosquitoes.

"Won't know until I see him. Going to the vet now."

"Call me when you find out," she said.

"I will. When are you going back to Minto?"

"Later. Have to do some shopping for Mom and visit Mrs. Deerchild."

Mrs. Deerchild.

"Where does she live?"

"In town."

"Is that where you're staying?"

"No, I'm at a friend's place."

"Which friend is that?"

"None ya'."

Oh-kay.

I looked up to see Jennifer bouncing down the driveway with a big grin and a gym bag slung over her shoulder. She was wearing a pair of those skin tight leggings—jet black—with white sneakers and a tight white T-shirt under an unzipped windbreaker. Worked for me. She walked a wide circle around her truck, made big eyes at me, then the grin blossomed into a big smile. I managed a small one when she opened the passenger door.

I looked away and murmured into the phone, "Hey Leah?"

"What?"

"I owe you. Thanks."

TWENTY SEVEN

"Wow, looks like new!"

Jennifer Kovalchuk was beaming, surveying the freshly vacuumed carpets and clean interior of her truck. She scooted across the bench and kissed me on the cheek. I plucked the receipt from my shirt pocket and handed it to her. She gave it a quick read.

"Hey, did you pay for this?" she asked.

"I said I would."

"Well that's weird."

"What's weird?"

"Well first of all, the guy at the tire shop said the bill would be eight hundred and forty, not five hundred. And second, he had me sign some form and said the insurance company would pay him directly, so I wouldn't have to pay anything when I picked up my truck."

"When did you sign these forms?"

"This morning, just after I talked to you. A cop came by and wanted to see the tires that got slashed, so he drove me over to the tire shop. We went in and I showed him my truck and he looked at the tires, then the manager had me sign some form."

Rick, you double dipping scumbag.

Rick was planning to collect another eight hundred and forty dollars from Jennifer's insurance company, after taking my five hundred. I'd have to drop by later and have a little chat with him.

But what bothered me more was why the cop would want to see Jennifer's slashed tires. Cops don't have time to make a federal case out of an isolated case of vandalism. They might not even come out to your house, and if they do, will do little more than take down your name and vehicle info, write up a short report, give you a copy, and tell you to call your insurance company. 'Sorry, nothing we can do, we'll keep an eye out, have a nice day'.

Which is why I wondered if the cop really just wanted another visit with a tall gorgeous blonde. I felt a tinge of jealousy.

Was she under my skin already?

Damn woman.

"Brody?"

"What?"

"Are we going? It's almost noon."

"Right."

I leaned over and turned the key with my left hand, then moved the selector to reverse, also with my left hand.

"What's wrong?"

"Nothing."

"Yes there is. You used your left hand to start the truck."

"Oh, my shoulder, it's a little sore today."

"How come?"

"It's nothing. It'll be fine."

I backed out onto the street and we were on our way.

"Well I know all about sore shoulders. I can take a look at it later if you want. If you're still here, that is. Think you'll stay another night?"

"Do you want me to stay another night?"

She looked down, hesitated, and smiled before saying, "I guess."

I stopped for a red light and looked at her. She had a pretty good blush going in those big plump cheeks.

"I might just take you up on that, Jennifer, thanks. It all depends on how my dog is doing, we'll see."

She smiled at me and said, "Well, I hope you do," and looked away.

We left the downtown area by climbing the 'Two Mile Hill'—which really isn't—crossed the Alaska Highway, then continued uphill on a four lane road toward the Canada Games Center, one of the great multi-purpose sports complexes north of the sixtieth parallel. The place is huge and modern, always busy, housing all kinds of facilities like swimming pools, lap pools, hockey rinks, curling rinks, running tracks, gyms—the list goes on.

Who says the government wastes all your money?

I pulled into the parking lot and stopped at the pool entrance. Jennifer got out and stood facing me with a hand on top of the door, but didn't close it. She was studying me. I studied her back. Not a bad way to kill time—if you have it.

She seemed in no hurry to close the door, scrutinizing me with an inquisitive stare. I was happy to wait her out and stare back. The wind was blowing wisps of her fine blond hair across her face and her sky blue eyes were hypnotic. Rick hadn't lied about one thing, Jennifer was indeed one 'tall hot blonde'.

"Pick me up at one-thirty?" she asked, grabbing her gym bag and slinging it over a shoulder.

"One-thirty sounds perfect," I said.

"Brody?"

"What?"

"What's your last name?"

"Huh?"

"Your last name, what is it?"

"Brody."

"Oh. Well then what's your first name?"

Oh, oh.

"Jennifer, just call me Brody, okay?"

She gave me a long suspicious look, then, "Know something?"

"What?"

"I think you're a man with a lot of secrets."

There was a jolt of pain when I shrugged my shoulders. Maybe I deserved it.

She closed the door. A little harder than necessary.

* * *

I turned right out of the Canada Games Center and continued climbing the four lane boulevard that would eventually take me up to one of the city's new housing developments. Whitehorse has plenty of them. The city is enjoying a steady pace of growth, expanding in all directions, well on its way to becoming another ubiquitous urban sprawl of middle class neighborhoods.

Amazing how time changes a place. A hundred and twenty years ago there was little reason to stop and overnight in Whitehorse, a muddy flat on the Yukon River with a scattering of log buildings and a lot of mosquitoes. Back then everyone on the river was headed to Dawson, another four hundred and fifty river miles north. They were chasing a dream in the greatest gold rush in history, poling and sailing rafts, hoping to make it all the way to the Klondike gold fields. Having just gone through the Whitehorse Rapids—a harrowing and dangerous undertaking—most would have landed at the first available spot downstream on what is now the city's south side, to dry their clothes, check their cargo, and perhaps help bury a stranger who'd just drowned attempting the same feat.

Today a typical visitor to Whitehorse arrives on a jet, grabs a cab, and is chauffered to a hotel with cablevision, internet, and for a few bucks more, an en suite hot tub. If life is about weaving memories, I'll take the 98er's any day.

The road flattened out on a short plateau and a small shopping center appeared on the left. The flat roofed building had five units. The unit at the far end was occupied by my favorite Yukon vet. Two years ago Dr. John Dorval had moved his practice to town after being forced to relocate from his country homestead ten miles north on the Alaska Highway. Apparently his homestead didn't have the right permits and a bunch of neighbors who didn't like his howling sled dogs ganged up on him and put the city on his case. Zoning is zoning and he and his musher wife had to take their hobby out of the city, another ten miles north. Now John has a twenty mile commute to tend to his clients' cats and dogs.

I was slowing in the turn lane with my signal on, waiting for oncoming traffic to clear, about to enter the parking lot, when I saw the cop. He was parked at the far end of the building, close to the road, facing John Dorval's animal clinic. He had the driver's window down with his elbow sticking out, fixated on the front door. He wasn't eating. Any cop in a parking lot who isn't eating is definitely up to something.

But what?

If he was waiting for me, I wasn't going to walk into his arms. I cancelled the signal and drove another five hundred feet up the road, then turned left into a gas station and convenience store. I went around the pumps and parked on the far side of the store, out of his line of sight. I got out and walked to the rear of the building to assess the terrain.

The City of Whitehorse is carved out of a spruce forest and the gas station and shopping center were backed up against a sea of trees. I sidestepped and skidded down a shallow gravel bank, dusted off my hands and blue jeans, and started walking along the edge of the forest, heading back toward the shopping center.

The trees were widely spaced apart and the forest floor was a dry carpet of spruce needles and cones. I could have been anywhere in the Yukon wilderness, save for the empty bottles, drink cans, and paper wrappers that had blown down from the parking lot. The walking was easy and in a few minutes the roof line of the shopping center was visible above me. I climbed up the bank, brushed myself off again, and stood in the middle of a fire lane running down the back of the building.

A small concrete pad enclosed with a wire fence extended out from behind John Dorval's animal clinic. A couple of medium-sized mutts were inside the enclosure, lying on their sides, soaking in the sun, observing me with apathetic eyes. But as soon as I put my hand on the gate, they jumped to their feet and wagged their tales.

"Sorry boys," I said, "someone else will have to walk you."

Walk.

Shouldn't have said it.

I squeezed through the gate to keep my new buddies from escaping, and closed it behind me. Now they were up on their hind legs, pawing my belly, begging for freedom with big eyes and whimpers. All they wanted to do was run off into the forest behind me.

So near, yet so far.

The fire door on the back of the clinic was for egress only. It was flat, smooth and featureless, save for a pull handle. Beside it was a keypad mounted on the wall. But without the code there was no getting in, not unless I was prepared to wait for someone to come out. Just then a woman walked around the corner with a couple of dogs straining at their leashes. She opened the gate and followed them into the enclosure. My new buddies got up on their hind legs and put their paws on her, pleading their case for early release. She struggled to unleash the two dogs she'd been walking. I helped her untangle two leashes and sixteen legs.

"Thank you," she said in a sing-song voice.

"You're welcome," I said. "Could you open this door for me please?"

"Oh, no. You can only go in that door if you know the secret code."

It was then I realized she had Down's. She might have been twenty, was a little overweight, and bundled up in a winter coat and hat on a mild spring day. She had that sweet and innocent disposition typical of people with Down's.

"What's your name?" I asked.

"Henrika."

"Henrika. That's a very nice name. I'm Brody, by the way. Say, Henrika, would you tell me the secret code so I can open the door and go inside to see my dog?"

"Oh no, Brody," she said in a very serious tone. "I told you, the code is a secret."

"But I need to see my dog. He's inside."

"No, no, no, the code is a secret," she said again, wagging a finger at me.

"I see. Well let's do this, Henrika. How about I turn around and you push the buttons when I'm not looking, then I won't know the secret code."

"Okay," she said.

The door clicked and I grabbed the handle.

"Thanks, Henrika."

"You're welcome, Brody."

The meek shall inherit the earth.

If only it were true.

At the very instant I opened the door, John Dorval was crossing the hallway twenty feet in front of me. He stopped to see who was coming in.

"John?"

"Is that Brody?" he asked, squinting through the daylight pouring in behind me.

"Yeah. Hi. Here to see Jack."

He waited for me to walk up to him.

"Henrika let you in?"

"Yeah, but she didn't give up the secret code."

He gave me the hint of a smile. John Dorval was a thin man with a slight build and was a good three inches shorter than me. He always had a sad look, as though the weight of the world was on his shoulders. Maybe it was, he had to put down people's best friends.

"I saw the paper this morning and I'm guessing you saw the cop out front. He's been waiting for you."

"Figured that. It's why I came in the back door. What's he want?"

"No idea. He phoned here about ten this morning. Wanted to know if we had one of your dogs. Then he came in about half an hour ago asking all kinds of questions about why your dog was here. When I told him your dog had been shot, he insisted I give him the bullet we extracted. He asked if we were expecting you to come in. I told him either you or the young lady who brought him in was expected at noon. Sorry, had to tell him."

"No problem, John. How's Jack?"

John Dorval raised his chin, took a deep breath, and looked me in the eyes. He'd had this conversation a million times before.

"Not good. He's alive but in critical condition, which is another way of saying he's just hanging on. He was shot in his left rear leg just above the knee. The bullet shattered his femur. For as much time as it took to get him here, it's a miracle he didn't bleed to death. We operated immediately and removed the bullet—looked like a twenty-two to me—and used a lot of screws and rods to put the bone back together. Not sure how much damage there is to his knee but that can wait. The crisis now is the infection in his leg and whether it spreads or not. It was over twenty-four hours before he had any medication so the infection had a big head start, and unfortunately antibacterials don't work like they used to. He had a fever over a hundred and three when we operated on him last night and it hasn't gone down.

"If we remove his leg now, we'll get most of the infection and he'll probably recover. But if you want to save his leg, and decide to wait and see...well... then there's a good chance you'll lose him. It's a fifty-fifty call, the toughest one there is, and yours alone to make."

The room began to spin and my legs felt like rubber. I had to remember to breathe. I leaned back against the wall and fought an urge to sink to the floor. What had seemed like a surreal scenario an hour ago was now stark reality.

Decision time.

'the toughest one there is...'

"What would you do, John?" I heard myself ask.

"I'd put his life before his leg."

My chin fell to my chest. He was right and I knew it.

"Can I see him?"

John jutted a thumb over his shoulder.

"He's in there. I'll get the paper work."

TWENTY EIGHT

One of nature's great ironies, and mysteries, is that an animal—not a human—is the greatest friend you'll ever have.

From the day you take one home, a dog is committed to you for life. No matter what you do, where you go, how you treat him—he'll never complain, never leave you, never sue you, never divorce you. So why do people do harm to such noble creatures?

After signing a form I didn't read, and handing John Dorval a tidy stack of cash, I left the clinic the same way I got there, with a short, peaceful walk through the woods. All the while I was thinking about Jack, hoping he would forgive me for the decision I'd just made, and hoping everyone would understand when I killed the bastard who shot him.

When I joined a steady stream of city-bound traffic and drove past the shopping center, the cop was still parked in front of the clinic, still behind the wheel, still staring at the front door. I had to shake my head. No wonder they couldn't catch Kay.

Cops.

With half an hour to kill before picking up Jennifer, I decided to make a run to the airport.

* * *

No one was in the trailer that serves as the office for Wesley Aviation Services so I crossed the road and walked into their hangar. It was cavernous inside with an expansive concrete floor that ran out to an enormous overhead door virtually as wide as the building. The door was open to the ceiling and revealed a panoramic view of the airport's taxiways and runways, and in the distance, a ragged silhouette of dark mountains spanning a pale blue horizon. It was as chilly inside as out. A twin turboprop on wheels was parked at the center. The cowling on one engine had been removed and a tangle of disconnected pipes and wires was hanging down underneath, reminding me of a clump of Christmas lights. I hoped whoever was working on the thing knew how to put it all back together.

Tim and Jim were eating lunch at a picnic table in the corner. As usual they were wearing identical coveralls, sitting beside each other, attacking meatball subs with greasy hands. Opposite them sat a young woman poking at a salad. She had on very tight jeans—and in spite of the cold air—a very tight T-shirt. With the predictable physiological result, Tim and Jim were gawking at her breasts. She had to be enjoying the attention or surely would have been wearing something a lot warmer, and a whole lot more modest.

Amanda Wesley was slim and attractive with sharp blue eyes, and according to her father, well on her way to getting a commercial pilot's license. Her grandfather was a pilot, her father was a pilot, and now Amanda was on a mission to perpetuate the family legacy. When she wasn't flying, she managed the office for her father. Tim and Jim were still mentally undressing her when I stopped at the end of the table.

Amanda greeted me with a smile.

"Hey, Brody," she said.

"Hey, Amanda," I said.

Tim and Jim could barely pry their eyes from her bosom when they heard my voice.

"Hey Brody, see our picture in the paper this morning?" asked Tim, or Jim.

"Sure did. Great picture of you guys."

"Thanks. We got a bunch of copies," said Jim, or Tim. "Want one?"

"No thanks. How'd the windshield job go?"

"Perfect. New ones fit like a...uh...perfect," one of them said.

"Great. Where are the old ones?"

"Cops took 'em," the other one said.

"The cops took them?"

Amanda interjected with, "Yeah. Some big cop named Robertson—I think that's what he said—came in real early this morning and wanted to see them. I have his card. Then he took them away. I watched him put them in the trunk of his car, then he left. And he made me give him your keys, too. Sorry Brody, he said you have to go see him if you want them back."

I nodded and sighed.

Robson.

"Sure his name wasn't Robson?"

Amanda clicked her fingers and said, "That's it. Robson."

Twenty minutes later my backpack was lighter another twelve hundred dollars.

* * *

Jennifer jumped into her truck and made herself comfortable with a couple of good bounces on the seat. Her cheeks were flushed and she was as clean as her truck. Her soaking wet hair was tied back in a pony tail and the smell of shampoo filled the cab.

"Whew! I could eat a horse between two mattresses!" she exclaimed with an ear to ear smile.

In spite of everything on my mind, I had to smile too.

"Good swim?"

"The usual, an hour."

"How many lengths?"

"A hundred and twenty."

"A hundred and twenty? Really? How far is that?"

"A little over three kilometers."

"That's like, two miles."

"Sounds right."

"You swam two miles in one hour?"

"Yup."

"That's amazing."

"Well, I have been swimming my whole life."

"Yeah, but it's still amazing."

I looked at her with admiration. The woman was a stud.

"Ah, Brody?"

"What?"

"Can we go? I am really hungry."

"Oh, sure. Where to?"

Once again I had to use my left hand to put the truck in gear.

"Somewhere downtown," she said. "I have to be at the RCMP at three."

"You do? How come?"

"I don't know. The cop that came by the house this morning, he just called. Said he had more questions for me."

I'll bet he does...

"What's this cop's name, Jennifer?"

"Monahan, I think. He gave me his card. Why do you want to know his name?"

I shrugged my shoulders and winced at another stab of pain.

She put her hand on my right shoulder, gave it a gentle rub, and left it there.

"Still hurt?"

"Yeah."

"Poor baby. I can fix it you know. Tonight if you want. Are you staying tonight?"

It was the second time in two hours she'd asked me the same question. I hesitated but knew the answer.

"Well, maybe one more night. My dog, he's..."

"Oh, your dog. How is he?"

"Not good."

"What happened to him? You said he got shot."

"He has an infection."

"Will he be okay?"

"Hope so."

* * *

A block from the RCMP building we sat down in a Chinese restaurant with an all-you-can-eat lunch buffet. I wasn't in the mood for eating but ordered a plate anyway. With Jennifer in the place, it was only fair to the owners.

I joined the line at the food trough by stepping in front of an aggressive beefcake who was lead glutton in a group of six large men. Clearly none of them were with Weight Watchers. They were breathing like buffaloes with their jackets unbuttoned, adjusting their belts for the challenge ahead. With the swagger of out-of-town big shots, I pegged them as government stuffed shirts with great job security and benefits. I put my hand on Jennifers waist and guided her into line ahead of me, which stopped the stampede in its tracks. Jennifer was fast, loading up her plate in a minute, while I on the other hand, took my time preparing a modest assortment of beautifully arranged samples. The more beefcake snorted over my shoulder, the slower I moved.

"Is that all you're having?" Jennifer asked.

"No, I'm also having a glass of water and two pain pills, and maybe a fortune cookie after."

"Not much of a lunch."

"I didn't just swim two miles."

After she returned from the buffet with another heaping plate, she asked, "See Mike this morning?"

"As a matter of fact, no. He'd come and gone before I got to Trans-Pacific. And I was there on time."

Jennifer gave her fork a rest and said, "That's strange, he sounded like he really wanted to talk to you about something. Guess he didn't get my envelope."

"Sorry."

"No big deal, give it to him on Friday. He should have enough forms for the first load anyway. And speaking of samples, what time do I meet you at the lake on Friday?"

"It's a three hour flight from Thistle Creek to here so I'm guessing about three. That work for you?"

"Fine. Hey guess what?"

I learned in public school to never 'guess what', but sometimes I forget.

"What?" I said.

"I think I found someone to manage the office in Dawson. Which means starting next week you can fly Mike's samples up there."

I said nothing.

She studied me for a moment and said, "I hope you come back to Whitehorse soon. It would be nice to see you again."

The slightest blush colored her cheeks and she looked away.

"I'll be back," I said, then after an awkward pause, "Hey, almost forgot, I have something for you."

She perked up at that, like women usually do.

"What?"

I reached down to my feet and opened my pack.

"Pick a color."

* * *

On the Klondike Highway, two hundred and twenty miles north of Whitehorse, Dan Sanders slowed his red pickup with the white camper and Alaska plates, and drove over the Stewart Crossing bridge. On the other side he turned right and drove half a mile up a long hill, then pulled over to the shoulder and turned off the motor. He got out and stretched, and walked to the edge of the road. He looked up and down the Stewart River but saw and heard nothing. He found a good-sized rock to sit down on and lit a cigarette. He was twenty minutes early for the rendezvous and was content to gaze out at the vast country before him. There wasn't a car or truck or boat in sight—or the plane he was expecting.

He waited, watched, and listened.

TWENTY NINE

Jennifer was pleased with her new Tire King ball cap. It had a tire with a crown on top. Now who came up with that idea? She had chosen the beige one and it looked great on her head of damp hair.

I offered her the keys to her truck but she said she wanted to walk and told me it was mine until dinner.

"When's dinner?" I asked.

"When you bring it home."

"What and when?"

"Pizza and a salad would be good. Any time after seven."

"What kind of pizza?"

"Doesn't matter, as long as it's an extra large."

Go figure.

She smiled and I watched her walk away, which was time well spent. I could watch her leaving all day in those skin tight leggings. She was headed to the very same building where I needed to be in fifteen minutes. But she didn't have to know that. I figured the less she knew about my life, the safer she'd be.

With no time to spare I drove a little too fast in the opposite direction, down Main Street toward the industrial part of town. Five minutes later I rumbled through an open gate into a fenced gravel lot full of fuel tanks and fuel trucks. I parked in front of an industrial trailer, went inside, scheduled a couple of fill-ups for my plane, and minutes later was back on the road, heading to my three o'clock appointment, another thousand dollars lighter.

I parked Jennifer's truck where she wouldn't spot it, and at exactly one minute to three, walked through the front door of the RCMP building.

Right on time.

* * *

"Don't forget your knife this time," quipped the bored woman at reception as she waved me through the X-ray hoop. I kept my eyes on her hands when she inspected my pack. There was still enough cash in there for a really fun day of shopping.

I took the elevator up to the third floor and was once again greeted by Robson's fierce assistant. She led me down the hall to the same conference room with the same three cops with the same three hats sitting on the table.

"Hey boys, do they ever let you out for fresh air?" I asked.

Same stares, same silent treatment. The door to Robson's office was closed.

"Sit down, Mr. Brody," said polka dot dress.

"Sitting's unhealthy. I'll stand, but thanks."

She left with a glare that could burn a hole through a brick. I walked over to the window and already had an itch to leave. A minute later, Robson's door opened.

Everyone turned. The man who emerged wasn't Robson. It was Staff Sergeant John Munroe. The cop from Vancouver. He walked down the long table and stopped in front of me.

"Thanks for coming in," he said.

"Sure."

"Mind if I give you a piece of advice?"

"What?"

"Take your hat off and sit down."

I did, in my usual place, in the chair at the end of the table. Munroe sat down too, at the other end, in a chair next to where I assumed Robson would sit.

We waited.

* * *

A few minutes after three o'clock in the afternoon, Dan Sanders heard the distant drone of a small plane. He stood and stepped on his cigarette, put his hands in his pockets, squinted at the western sky, and tried to locate the tiny speck that should soon manifest into the little float plane he was expecting. It should be a Piper Super Cub, flying in from Alaska, a favor from a friend. A five thousand dollar favor. No flight plan, no customs, no record. In and out of Canada in a couple of hours. A special pickup for a special passenger.

Sanders hadn't been precisely sure what he'd signed up for when he took this job, other than the money was too good to be true. At three times what the army had been paying him as an EOD—an Explosive Ordnance Disposal Specialist—maybe it was. But what had seemed like a great opportunity to try something new, well now it didn't seem so great.

They'd found him in a bar in Fairbanks, near the Fort Wainwright base, his home for three years before calling it quits. At first he thought they were with one of those military contractors, offering big bucks to anyone willing to go back to the same killing fields to do the same killing all over again. But after eight years in the mid-east, including three tours in Afghanistan, Sanders was done with that life. He was fed up waging war for something that couldn't be won, and all the close calls and carnage had taken their toll on him. So a chance to work for a mineral exploration company, well now that had been the type of change he'd been looking for. Blowing up rocks in the Yukon—not people in countries ending with '*stan*'— seemed a far more civilized way to make a living.

And for a while it had been until he realized that's not all his new employer wanted him to do. Rigging a bomb in a chandelier was hardly what he'd bargained for when he signed on with Thistle Creek Resources. But he hadn't been given much choice. Some asshole named Adrian had stuck a gun in his face—do it or die—

and he'd done what he'd been told. Now there was another asshole in his face, some muscle bound monster named Kay who was constantly pushing him around. Now he wanted out of this job too.

But first he had to lose Kay. That would be a challenge.

Sanders watched the little float plane taxi into shore. The pilot turned off the motor, got out on the float, gave him a wave, and secured the plane to the trees. Sanders held a finger up to the pilot, walked to the rear of his truck, looked up and down the empty road, dropped the ladder, and thumped his hand twice on the camper door. It opened.

Tommy Kay stuck his head out and looked around, then squeezed through the door and stepped to the ground. He looked like a hunter dressed in a black and red checked jacket, a billed cap with ear flaps, blue jeans and old leather boots. He carried a small bag in his hand. He stood in front of Sanders and got his attention with a few sharp jabs in the chest. Kay's finger felt like a jack hammer.

"Don't let that geologist out of your sight, got that? You call me if he runs."

Sanders tried to appear calm and said, "Got it."

Kay moved his face in closer and said, "And the pilot from Minto. Make sure nothing happens to him. He's mine. I'll be back for him."

Sanders swallowed and said, "Okay."

For a moment Kay glared at Sanders, then turned toward the river. Sanders watched the huge man descend the bank, weaving back and forth through stunted trees and bushes, struggling to maintain his balance on the soft shifting sand. Sanders wondered if such a large man could fit into such a small plane.

He hoped so.

He rubbed his chest and breathed again.

THIRTY

Staff Sergeant Robson walked into the room with the weight of the world on his shoulders.

He tossed a file on the table, leaned over to Munroe, and whispered something in his ear. Munroe grimaced. Robson sat down and placed his hands on the file, then took some time to contemplate his fingernails, as if admiring a fresh manicure.

Five of us—me, the three uniformed cops, and Munroe—waited. I wondered why Constable Monahan was in the room if he had a three o'clock with Jennifer.

Robson finally raised his eyes and said, "You know, Mr. Brody, in twenty years with the RCMP, I have never met anyone in as much shit as you are right now—who wasn't behind bars."

I had no idea what to say so kept my mouth shut.

He went on, "Let's start with some easy questions, shall we? Maybe if we get the truth for those we can try some tougher ones after. And maybe, just maybe, you can stay out of jail."

"Jail? Do I need a lawyer?"

"Don't know. Did you break any laws?"

"No."

"So why a lawyer?"

"Because you guys haven't made an arrest for Amy Vanderbilt's murder. And because you probably think I killed her like everyone else in this town."

"If we thought you killed her, why would we let you walk out of here this morning?"

I shrugged. A jab of pain shot through my shoulder. Would I ever learn?

"How should I know?" I replied, trying not to wince.

Robson turned to Munroe. They were speaking 'cop' with their eyes. He turned back to me and said, "Mr. Brody, let's just say that as of right now, you're not at the top of our list for the murder of Amy Vanderbilt. How's that?"

"Very reassuring," I said. "Ask your questions."

I crossed my arms. That hurt too. I slumped back in my chair and laid them on the armrests. Better.

"What happened to the windshields in your plane?" he asked.

"Don't know."

"What do you *think* happened to your windshields?"

"I *think* someone took a hammer to them."

"And why would someone do that?"

"Because they didn't want me to fly my plane?"

"Any idea of who this someone might be?"

"Tommy Kay comes to mind, but like I said, I don't know."

"Tommy Kay, huh? So now you think he's alive?"

"You do."

Robson nodded.

"When did you discover your windshields had been smashed?"

"Yesterday."

"When yesterday?"

"About ten o'clock in the morning."

He scribbled something in his file and said, "See how easy this is? I ask a question and you answer with the truth. Now let's move on to something else. What happened to your dog?"

"You know damn well what happened to my dog."

"I do?"

"Yes." I jutted my chin at Monahan. "Your man here visited my vet this morning and was told what happened to my dog. He was shot in the leg and you've got the bullet. Now quit with the games, I don't like being set up."

Robson's eyes hardened. "Okay, so you know we tracked down your dog and found out what happened to him. When did you find out he'd been shot?"

"Last night."

"Who told you he'd been shot?"

"The person who drove him to town."

"And that person was...?"

"Leah McCormack."

Robson looked at Munroe again, then back at me.

"This Leah McCormack, is she the young lady who works at that gas stop in Minto?"

"That's right."

"Any idea who shot your dog?"

"Tommy Kay?"

Robson nodded with a wry grin and said, "Have you seen your dog since he was shot?"

"Yes."

"When?"

"Today at noon."

"Today at noon."

"That's what I said."

Constable Monahan turned to Robson. Some subliminal communication was going on. Monahan was shaking his head.

"Noon, you say. You sure about that?"

"Absolutely."

Robson took a long deep breath and exhaled.

"You see, Mr. Brody, this is just another example of what it's like dealing with you. One never knows if you're telling the truth."

"Or what the truth is," I said. "You think because you had your man here stationed out front of my vet's clinic that I couldn't possibly have been there at noon. But I entered through the back door, not the front. And I did see my dog. Feel free to confirm that with Dr. Dorval."

Monahan stiffened and glared at me.

"Check it out," Robson barked at him.

The constable grabbed his hat and bolted to the door.

Robson drubbed his fingers on the table until he was gone, then said, "Alright, let's move on to a more important subject."

"More important than my dog?"

"As far as I'm concerned," he said. "What did you do this morning after you left here?"

"After I left here? Well, let's see. I went to the post office, then to the coffee shop, then to my stock broker, then to the Tire King."

"You have a stock broker?"

"Doesn't everyone?"

He ignored my retort and asked, "Did you buy new laces for your boots?"

I snapped my fingers and pointed a finger at him. "As a matter of fact, I did buy new laces. Thanks for jogging my memory."

"Where did you get them?"

"At the drug store on Main."

"At the drug store on Main." He paused, then said, "See what I mean? Every time you answer a question, you leave something out."

"Sorry, I'll try not to let it happen again."

"Make sure it doesn't. Now where were you this morning at approximately eleven a.m.?"

Damn.

"On the Waterfront Path."

"Doing what?"

"Walking."

Robson leaned forward and said, "You know, we can try this later if you want. In a little room in the basement, just down the hall from your jail cell."

Jail. Can't go to jail.

"Hey, I answered the question. I was walking."

He sighed again with exasperation.

"Where were you walking *to*?"

"*To* the Tire King."

"And?"

"And what?"

Robson opened the file in front of him and flipped through a few pages. He stopped to read one. The three other cops were fixated on me. Monahan re-entered the room and stopped behind my chair. Robson gazed over my head, read Monahan's face, and his eyes went hard. He shook his head, blew the air from his lungs, and pointed at the door. Monahan stomped out.

Banished.

The big cop crossed his bulging arms and rocked back in his chair, then said, "Let me help you recall some more details about this little walk of yours this morning. Right now there's a man in Whitehorse General with a serious head injury. He was jogging on the Waterfront Path when he was assaulted at approximately the same time you were out on your nature stroll. Evidently his assailant clobbered him in the back of the head—we think with a tree branch found close by—about the size of a Louisville Slugger. The man's skull was fractured and he's been unconscious ever since EMS loaded him onto a gurney and took him away. The doctors don't know if he'll make it. Now what I want from you, Mr. Brody, is everything you know about this serious assault. And I mean everything. And be very careful what you say because we have a witness who has identified you as his assailant."

The chubby jogger.

"Me? His assailant? I wasn't anyone's assailant. Your witness is full of shit. Fact is, I was the one who was assaulted, by that jogger you're feeling sorry for. He grabbed me and twisted my arm and shoved me off the path and put me in a choke hold. If someone hadn't come by and bonked him on the head, I think he might have killed me."

Robson and Munroe both leaned forward, apparently interested in my version of events.

"You're saying this gravely injured man who was jogging on the Waterfront Path assaulted you? Is that your story?"

"Damn right it is. He attacked me. The world was going dark and I was fading fast when somebody hit him over the head and saved my ass."

Robson and Munroe looked at each other.

"And who was this person who saved your ass?" asked Robson.

"Don't know."

"You don't know."

"Nope. He ran away."

"Was his name Ray?"

Ray.

"Ray? Who's Ray?"

"Mr. Brody, now is not the time to play games. This is a serious crime we're dealing with here. A man is fighting for his life. A witness says she heard you yell 'Ray'. Now did you yell that name?"

"Why would I yell anybody's name? I never even saw the guy. He'd already run off when I got back on my feet. Maybe I yelled 'Hey', maybe that's what she heard. Yeah, 'Hey'. So who was this jogger anyway?"

"I'll ask the questions, Mr. Brody. Now this man, this jogger you say assaulted you, did you know him? Ever seen him before?"

"No. He was a complete stranger."

"Do you know why he grabbed and choked you?"

"No."

"He never asked you for money or your wallet, or tried to take that backpack of yours?"

"No."

"Did he say anything at all to you?"

"Well, now that you mention it, I vaguely remember him saying something when he was in the process of strangling me. Something about Amy...Amy Vanderbilt would be my guess. Maybe he thought I killed her. Maybe he knew her. Maybe he was out for revenge."

The big cop leaned back in his chair and nodded at Munroe as though he'd just solved the crime of the century. Munroe nodded back, apparently also satisfied.

"Why didn't you report this attack to the police?" asked Robson with an intense look.

"I did. Or at least I told your so-called witness to call 911. She had a phone in her hand."

"But you didn't stick around."

"Why would I? It was over and done with. The guy was down and out, I couldn't help him and had things to do."

"You weren't hurt?"

I thought about my shoulder but said, "No."

"Sure about that?"

"Well I'm sitting right in front of you. Do I look hurt?"

Robson shook his head in frustration, clenched his teeth, then rolled his chair back and got to his feet.

"Staff Sergeant Munroe has some questions for you," he growled. "I'll be back."

The room went quiet as Robson stomped into his office and slammed the door behind him. Munroe sifted through the file on the table and removed a sheaf of papers. He shuffled them into some order and neatened them up, then slid them to his left. Sergeant Arcand relayed them to me. They were black and white photographs.

"Let's start from the top, Mr. Brody. Tell me if you recognize any of these individuals."

The first photo was a head and shoulders shot, likely lifted from a government document. The man in the photo was in his sixties. He had a shock of white hair and a bushy white beard. I knew who he was. The second photo I'd seen before. It was of the same man. It had been shown to me last year in the RCMP building in Dawson. The man was carrying a briefcase and was bent over under the weight of a large backpack. He was walking down a Dawson boardwalk.

"Yeah," I said, "I know who this is. His name is Ralph Braun. He's a gold buyer in Dawson."

"Was a goldbuyer."

"Was?"

"He's dead. He was found murdered in his home in Dawson on the weekend. Someone strangled him. So I have to ask you, sir, have you been to Dawson in the last seven days?"

"Haven't been to Dawson this year."

"Sure about that?"

"Of course I'm sure about that. Haven't been north of Minto since I got back two weeks ago."

"Alright. How about the next two photos. Recognize the person in those?"

'*Please*'.

Munroe must be the good cop.

I looked at the two photographs. Same deal. The first was a head and shoulders government photo, the second a grainy shot of a man standing on a dock in front of a commercial fishing boat. The mountains in the background could only be in Haines, one of my favorite places in Alaska. The man in both photos was Jack Kolinsky. I used to pick up fish from Jack and fly them to Whitehorse.

"I know this guy too," I said. "Jack Kolinsky. You told me on Monday he's dead."

"He is dead. And we're almost certain now he was murdered. Have you been to Haines recently, Mr. Brody?"

"No. Two weeks ago I travelled on an Alaska State Ferry from Bellingham, Washington to Skagway, Alaska, but we sailed right past Haines and didn't stop."

"Who is we?"

"Me and my dogs."

Munroe nodded with a patronizing smile.

"Have you seen Mr. Kolinsky anytime this year, or talked to him at all?"

"No."

I was perplexed why Munroe was interested to know if I'd been anywhere near Braun or Kolinsky recently. Did he really think I might have murdered them? How far-fetched was that? I barely knew either man. What would be my motive?

"Am I a suspect for their murders?"

"Just routine questions, Mr. Brody. Now, if you'd take a look at the last three photos. And please take your time."

'*Please*' again.

Definitely the good cop.

I fanned them out on the table and recognized all three people in the head and shoulders shots.

I leaned forward and once again found myself staring at Lynn Chan, exotic and beautiful, sexy and sultry, with a look of boredom that no amount of money could cure. Then at Tippy Li with his distinctive sneer—a peculiar feature no one would forget—his dark vacuous eyes belying nothing of the man inside. Then there was Tommy Kay with his enormous head, no neck, and reptilian eyes cowled under drooping eyelids, glaring at the camera with a menace that would scatter a crowd.

I slumped back in my chair and clasped my hands over my belly.

"I know who they are," I said. "Chan, Li, and Kay."

"Remember those faces, Mr. Brody. They belong to extremely dangerous people. I expect you to advise us immediately if you see any one of them in your travels."

"Right," I said.

Munroe was still laying on an intimidating cop glare when the door behind him opened. The black cloud that was Staff Sergeant Robson walked back into the room. He sat down and got right to the point.

"Your lucky day, Mr. Brody. Looks like you're temporarily off the hook. The victim of this morning's assault on the Waterfront Path was just induced into a coma and our witness can't be reached. So we're going to have to release you. But I remind you again, you are not to leave the territory without my say-so."

"Terrific," I said, grabbing my pack and standing up.

"Sit down," he barked. "I'm not finished."

I did, laying my pack on the table in front of me, poised and ready to bolt as soon as he gave the word.

"Now what?" I asked.

"Couple of things. First, on your way out, stop and see Mrs. Hodges at reception. You're to give her a full statement of your version of events on the river this morning. Don't leave anything out, and make sure you return here tomorrow to sign your statement, *before* you leave town."

I sighed and shook my head in frustration, then said, "What's the other thing?"

Robson cocked his head to one side.

"Where's Tommy Kay?"

"How the hell would I know where he is? You're the cops."

For a good ten seconds Staff Sergeant Alan Robson gave me another one of his glares, then nodded and said the magic words.

"You may go."

I stood and held out my hand and said, "I'll have the key to my plane."

Robson grinned and said, "No you won't. You're not flying anywhere until you sign your statement tomorrow. You can have your key then."

I was furious and headed to the door, then had an idea. Robson wanted Kay and I was worried about Mike Giguere. I turned around.

"Fine. And I won't tell you where to look for Kay. Have a good one."

"Mr. Brody!"

"What?"

"Where is he?"

"I told you, I don't know. Only where I'd look."

"And where's that?"

"Do I get my key?"

Robson was hesitant. He had to save face in front of his charges and Munroe. I was prepared to help him do that. My priority was to make sure Mike was okay.

"Maybe, if it's good information."

"Maybe, huh?" I took my time before saying, "Alright, there's this guy named Dan Sanders, he works for a geologist named Mike Giguere. Giguere is running the exploration project on Thistle Creek. Sanders is from Fairbanks and is apparently an explosives expert. He drives a red truck, it's a Ford I think. It has a white camper and Alaska plates. I saw him driving it around town today. I saw Sanders pick up Giguere this morning but he wouldn't let Giguere get into the cab, he made him get in the camper. And I noticed Giguere had a broken nose, too. It all seemed a little strange to me, you know, like the hired help makes the boss with a broken nose get in the back? So if I was you, I'd track down that truck and give it a sniff. You never know, maybe Kay is in the back playing cards with Giguere."

"You call that a lead?"

"Better than anything you've got or you wouldn't be sitting here talking to me."

Robson gave me a stern look and said, "Where's this truck now?"

"Not sure, but I think they were about to leave town when I saw them. They probably went north to Thistle Creek. If you hustle, maybe you can intercept them before they turn off on the Bonanza Creek Road."

"What time did you see Giguere get into Sanders' truck?"

"About ten this morning."

Robson was thinking. It was almost four o'clock in the afternoon. It would take all of six hours for a slow moving camper to reach the Bonanza Creek turn off. It would be cutting things close.

He reached in his pocket and held out my key in his left hand, high in the air, well over my head. I had to reach up with my left hand to take it from him.

"Something wrong with your right arm, Mr. Brody?"

Staff Sergeant Robson was no dummy.

THIRTY ONE

The press release had worked its magic.

Thistle Creek Resources closed up eleven cents on big volume and was the star of the exchange—the highest percentage gainer for the day—and the number of brokers calling for a trip to the property had been overwhelming.

Tippy was exultant. The instant the market closed he'd left Lynn's penthouse for his favorite bar on Howe Street, eager to buy as many celebratory rounds as the brokers could handle. And maybe raise some money too.

Shame that Lynn couldn't join him. She may have been exhausted but her job on the phone wasn't quite done yet. The brokers who'd been too busy to call during trading hours would be calling now. She'd be fielding their calls the rest of the afternoon.

Too bad.

* * *

Lynn clicked off yet another call and wondered how much longer before the last of the brokers left their desks for the day. No matter, it was four o'clock and she'd been at this for hours. Enough was enough, she was out of gas.

Screw you Tippy. I'm done.

With that she yanked off her headset and tossed it on the desk, then stood and stretched her arms over her head. The piece of paper with Tippy's spiel lay beside her phone. She'd recited the damn thing so many times it was hardwired into her subconscience. She'd probably be mumbling it in her sleep tonight. She picked up the paper and crumpled it into a ball, then tossed it at the couch. It landed on the very spot where Tippy had been sitting earlier. He'd been on the phone all morning as well, but not with brokers. He'd been doing his own business, probably selling ivory or fentanyl or guns, or whatever else the jerk did for a living.

Lynn decided there and then that working a call center for Tippy was not going to happen again. Lying to stock brokers was not her idea of a good time. She had better things to do. Another light flickered on her phone but she ignored it. For all she cared they could leave a message or call back tomorrow. Then she had an idea.

For a moment she found herself gazing out the tall windows at the ships in the harbor, weighing the consequences of what she had in mind. After summoning up her courage, she leaned over her desk, dialed Thistle Creek's phone number, and logged into the company's messaging menu. She selected the call forwarding option and entered Tippy's cell phone number. There. Now he could field some calls.

She hung up, pressed the speaker button, then the intercom button for the office downstairs.

"Good afternoon. Thank you for calling Lucky Star Properties. This is Jeremy. How may I help you?"

"Jeremy, I need you up here right now. Bring me something to eat. And I want the list of brokers who emailed us for a property visit."

"Yes, Miss Chan."

Lynn turned and leaned against the edge of her desk. She folded her arms, surveyed her palatial surroundings, then the ceiling over her dining room table.

"Oh, and Jeremy."

"Yes, Miss Chan?"

"Bring the paper work for my chandelier."

"Yes, Miss Chan."

* * *

Tippy had just turned off his phone in frustration and returned it to the breast pocket of his suit. He'd had four calls from brokers in the past five minutes. How the hell had they got his number? He could only guess.

He was sitting in a semicircular booth in a dark corner of a quiet bar, flanked on either side by two of the city's finer rent-a-dates. Neither woman was dressed for modesty. Their slick shiny dresses were short and tight, barely making the turn around their buttocks, stretched to the limit across their bosoms, holding back a bounty of flesh threatening to burst the dam. The two young ladies were sipping Neopolitans and giggling a lot, but knew better than to speak. They weren't there to make conversation.

Tippy knew that a man with fine clothes and a perfect haircut could only garner so much attention and respect. But the same man sitting beside two hot women twenty years his junior, well now that gave him a real presence.

The kind that attracted brokers like flies to shit.

Gerry Feldman was a short fat bald man with a flamboyant personality and a perpetual smile. A legendary Howe Street financier of junior exploration companies, he was just the man Tippy wanted to see. Feldman strolled past the wary eyes of one of Tippy's henchmen, slid into the booth, and cozied up hip to hip with one of the rent-a-trophies. He laid a hand high on her bare thigh, gave it a pat, and with the other reached across and shook Tippy's hand. Before their hands uncoupled, a glass of Teachers Scotch was placed in front of him. Tippy knew Gerry appreciated the good stuff, private stock, at least twenty-five years old, always a double, always neat. Gerry downed the glass in one slug and exhaled with a hoarse gasp. The women giggled. Gerry broke out his perma-smile again.

"What do ya' got for me today, Tippy?"

"Can't you read, Gerry?"

"Is it as good as it sounds?"

"Snooze you'll lose."

Gerry laughed.

"How much you need?"

"Two and a half million, ten million shares at twenty-five cents a share."

"Expensive," said Gerry.

"It'll be a lot more expensive next week," said Tippy.

"Still expensive."

"I was thinking of maybe adding a warrant, say at thirty-five cents," said Tippy.

Gerry held up his glass in the direction of the bar. Someone snapped their fingers. Another was on its way.

"Make the warrant thirty cents," said Gerry. "A year to exercise."

"Six months," said Tippy.

Gerry rubbed his chin.

"Throw in one of your girls?"

"I'll throw them both in."

Gerry howled with laughter. So did the women.

"You got yourself a deal there, Tippy. You can have the money next week, net of our usual ten percent, of course. Papers will be ready in the morning. Who's the president for this one?"

"Lynn Chan."

"A woman? She as good looking as these two?"

"Better," said Tippy.

"Throw her in too?"

"Private property, Gerry."

Gerry didn't laugh.

* * *

Lynn was slumped in one of the tall chairs at her dining room table, staring up at the ugliest chandelier she'd ever laid eyes on. The keylock at the front door clicked.

She didn't move when Jeremy Revere—'Ruh-veer' as he would

have you pronounce it—came prancing in on his toes, flapping his hands and arms, talking up a storm as usual.

"My God, isn't that just the most ghastly thing you've ever seen, Miss Chan?"

"Categorically butt-ugly, Jeremy. And it's out of here."

Jeremy dropped an envelope and a brown paper bag in front of Lynn, then pulled out the chair across from her and made himself at home. He was rake thin, about thirty, with a brush cut of tinted pink hair and a large diamond stud in his left ear. Today he was wearing tight white pants and a blue silk blouse, topped off with his signature paisley kerchief tied loosely around his neck.

To describe Jeremy as a flamboyant gay man would be to state the obvious, and totally irrelevant as well, because of who he was and what he was worth to Lynn. He'd come highly recommended and she now coveted him as an indispensible personal attaché. He was reliable, of course, bright and responsible too, but he also happened to be one of the city's most sought after decorators. Lynn could add a hundred thousand dollar profit to the sale of every unit in the building once Jeremy had sunk his cash seeking talons into the lady of the house. Lately, though, what Lynn considered to be his most appealing quality was that Tippy couldn't stand him. She thoroughly enjoyed watching Tippy squirm whenever Jeremy was around, especially in the company of his macho bodyguards.

Lynn reached in the bag and unwrapped a sandwich, took a bite, and daydreamed while she chewed.

After a sip of water she lost interest in eating and said, "So Jeremy, tell me again. Exactly what happened to the chandelier I ordered from Austria, and how the hell did this hideous aberration end up over my dining room table?"

"It's a total mystery to me, Miss Chan." Jeremy reached over and grabbed the envelope, pulled out the papers inside, and picked one out. He pointed at something and said, "Look. Here's the customs form and there's my signature for the box sent from Austria. I picked it up myself at the airport, paid the import fees, loaded it into the van, such an adorable young man helped me load it, the box was so heavy, he was so polite..."

"Jeremy, please try to stay on track."

"Yes, Miss Chan. Sorry. So then I drove back here and parked the van underground in its usual spot and told that boor who works in the basement to install the chandelier. And that was it."

"The boor in the basement you're referring to, you mean Earl, our building maintenance man."

"Is that what he is? My God, he's just the rudest man, Miss Chan, he doesn't seem to do very much and the things he says to me."

Lynn sighed.

"Never mind that, Jeremy. Now exactly when did Earl install this piece of crap on my ceiling?"

"The very next day, after I picked it up, the day before you came back from LA. Mr. Tommy and Earl and two other men came into my office downstairs and..."

"Wait, Jeremy. Mr. Tommy came here?"

"Yes, and two other men too."

"Who were the other two men?"

"I don't know. I'd never seen them before. They were wearing coveralls, white ones like Earl wears, and they had toolboxes too, but I don't know who they were."

Lynn tossed her sandwich on the table and folded her arms. She wondered why Tommy had come to the building. He was supposed to be out of town hiding somewhere. And why had it taken three men to install her chandelier?

"Alright, go on," she said.

"Okay, so then Mr. Tommy asked me for the key to your suite. Naturally I wouldn't give it to him, you told me never to let anyone in your suite unless I was there to personally open the door and watch them do whatever they were doing. But Mr. Tommy squeezed my shoulder and said to give him the key and for me to stay in my office. He was hurting me, Miss Chan, so I did what he said. I'm sorry I never mentioned that before, but Mr. Tommy said not to tell you anything or he'd come back and hurt me. And I believed him."

He looked down in shame. Lynn thought he might cry.

"That's alright, Jeremy. Then what happened?"

"I don't know what happened. I never saw any of them again. And Mr. Tommy never came back with the key for your suite."

"Is that so?" Lynn took a moment to scan her spacious surroundings, admiring the opulence, deep in thought. "Alright, Jeremy. Thank you for telling me all that. Better late than never. So is that it?"

Jeremy stood and put a finger to his chin.

"Well, there was one other thing that seemed rather odd to me."

"And that was?"

"Well, when those two men were waiting for Mr. Tommy to get the key from me, I noticed a big white box lying on the floor between them. It was made out of this cheap shiny cardboard. But the box I picked up at the airport was made out of wood, absolutely gorgeous by the way, for a box I mean, very nicely made, definitely a hardwood, perhaps a maple or maybe an ash..."

"Jeremy."

"Sorry. Well so I wondered why anyone would pack a hundred thousand dollar chandelier into a cheap cardboard box, then put the cheap cardboard box into such a beautful wood box. Doesn't that seem like a weird thing to do? It seemed so...incongruous."

Lynn nodded.

Incongruous indeed..

She looked up at the ceiling again.

"Jeremy, first thing in the morning, I want you to do four things for me."

"Yes, Miss Chan."

"Write them down, I don't want anything forgotten."

Jeremy huffed and cocked his head to one side.

"I don't need to write them down, Miss Chan."

"Alright, for your sake I hope you don't. The first thing you do is get a locksmith up here asap to rekey my front door. Then call the people in Austria who made my chandelier. Ask them if they packed it in a white cardboard box. Then I want you to call one of those high tech security firms. I want to see one of their experts here in my suite, sometime tomorrow afternoon. Last, call Earl. Tell him I want to see you both in the office downstairs, tomorrow morning at ten o'clock sharp. Tell Earl if he's late, he's fired."

Jeremy was smiling ear to ear.

"Yes, Miss Chan."

THIRTY TWO

Dr. John Dorval had left for the day so I spoke with his right hand woman.

She too was a vet and told me Jack's 'surgery' had gone well. I guess vets are mentored in how to describe such procedures, not once did she use the word 'amputation'. But it was what it was, now over and done with, and whatever you called it, difficult to accept.

Jack had lost a leg.

She went on to say my little pal was resting comfortably, that they'd removed most of the infection, and his chances for a long healthy life were as good as ever. He'd be kept under heavy sedation for the night and I could see him in the morning. She said he could go home Saturday.

With blurry eyes I closed my phone and took a deep breath.

Life just sucks sometimes.

* * *

Saturday was three nights away and the prospect of spending them at the Thurson Ames staff house gave me pause for thought.

Jennifer was young and strong, and with my shoulder the way it was, well...another roll in the hay could be painful. Then there was the eating. Recently I noticed my belly was beginning to transform from a six pack to a one pack. Getting fat has never been an option with me and any more time spent at a table with Jennifer would mandate a gym membership. Of course a gift of gratitude would be in order, a token of my appreciation for three days of free room and board, and it would have to be a generous one, commensurate with the big breakfasts, the use of a vehicle, and gratuitous sex all included in the package. I also knew that once the gift giving starts, it never ends, and before you know it you've entered that black hole known as a relationship.

Of course my prime concern was for Jennifer's safety. Tommy Kay was a murderer and out on a mission to settle a score. I didn't think he was the kind of man who took prisoners—and with no idea of where he was, what he was planning, and when he might turn up—hanging around with Jennifer was out of the question. Given all that, and after last night's tire slashing, the choices were simple.

Fly home tonight, or find a hotel room.

I was walking down Fourth Avenue having just left the RCMP building, and raised my arms in front of me as though driving a car. My right shoulder protested with a tinge of pain but it was bearable. I made a steering motion. Not too bad. Buoyed with hope I moved my right arm out to the right and simulated a stretch for the control levers in my plane. A sharp stab of pain stopped me dead in my tracks and I let out a yelp and grabbed my shoulder. A woman coming the other way gave me a bewildered look and a wide birth as she walked around me on the grass.

The crazy man on the sidewalk wasn't flying anywhere tonight.

A hotel room it was.

At the corner of Fourth and Main I walked into the lobby of a big hotel and found myself immersed in a crowd of raucous boys bouncing off the walls. A man at the reception desk was filling out forms in front of a clerk. Now and again he'd turn around and yell at them to settle down, then attempt a head count. There were plenty to count and evidently he was responsible for all of them. The clerk attending to him didn't notice me, she was understandably consumed with a ton of paper work. Just when I was about to try somewhere else, an office door opened and another woman emerged. She waved me over to the end of the counter. The tag on her lapel said, 'Dora'.

Dora was my age, very attractive, and clearly in charge.

"May I help you, sir?" she asked with a professional smile.

"Yes, please. I need a room for tonight and tomorrow."

"Do you have a reservation?"

"I don't."

"I'm very sorry, sir, we're booked solid through the weekend. Four hundred Boy Scouts are in town for a jamboree."

"Don't Boy Scouts sleep in tents?"

She laughed and said, "Not these ones. Half their cell phones don't work up here and they're totally bummed about it."

I shook my head and said, "How things have changed. Guess I'll try somewhere else. Thanks anyway."

"Sir?"

"Yes?"

"I think you'll find every hotel in town is booked solid. But you might try one of the bed and breakfasts. I could call around to see if there's something available."

"That would be much appreciated, thank you."

Dora disappeared into her office and emerged not a minute later. She said a room was available at Maggie's B&B. They'd hold it for an hour.

I looked at the ring on her finger.

"Dora?"

"Yes?"

"Tell your husband he's a lucky guy."

She grinned at me like a Cheshire Cat.

* * *

The sky was a glorious bright blue and the sun was doing its best to kiss and make up for yesterday's gloom. With nothing to do that I wanted to do, and over an hour to kill before dinner, there was plenty of time to walk the five blocks to my B&B. Maybe some fresh air and sunshine would cheer me up.

It hadn't been a great day—not with a tire slashing, a bullshit newspaper article, an assault, two hours with the cops, my dog losing his leg, and now with my shoulder on fire. With or without a change of clothes, a shave and shower might improve my mood.

Unhappy hour was in full swing when I walked past a narrow alley that separates two of the city's more popular watering holes. As usual at this time of day, the alley was crowded with smokers and tokers taking a break from their daily catharsis being served up inside. I glanced furtively at the disheveled congregation, everyone does, but recognized no one. A whiff of marijuana tickled my nose when I heard my name called.

"Mr. Brody!"

It came out like 'Mishta Brogee'.

I stopped on the sidewalk in front of a large window, leaned back, and hooked a heel on the low sill. I was content to wait where I was, soak in some rays, watch traffic drift by, and see if whoever had called my name really wanted to talk to me. If they did, they could come out to the street. The way my day had gone so far I wasn't walking down any alleys.

Dave Sorenson came around the corner of the building with a sloppy grin and glazed red eyes from drink and smoke. The cigarette in his hand and a five o'clock shadow diminished any previous resemblance to Clark Kent.

"Mr. Brody," he repeated, this time pronouncing my name slowly and with painstaking elocution.

Clearly Dave was sloshed, well on his way to a comatose night and a major league hangover.

"Hey, Dave. What's up?"

"TCR, that's... what's...up. Closed at twenty cents. Just talked to the president." He hiccuped, then got out the burp he'd been working on and said, "Drilling starts next week. Course I knew that," he said with pride, stifling another hiccup and tracking a pretty teenage girl walking by.

"Twenty cents? Really? I paid thirteen, right?"

Dave took his time, searched the sky for the answer, then said, "Sounds right."

The math was easy. Forty thousand shares times twenty cents is eight thousand dollars. I was up almost three grand since ten o'clock this morning—for doing absolutely nothing. It was more than what I'd spent all day. Unbelievable.

"Should I sell?" I asked.

"Sell? Hell, no, don't sell. Buy more. It's just getting going. Drilling starts next week. Call me in the morning. Buy more."

Dave was inspecting his feet and swaying. He looked ready to fall over.

"Okay, Dave, I'll call you in the morning."

When you're sober.

He turned to leave. Over his shoulder I glimpsed three scruffy men emerge from the alley. They looked at Dave and he waved at them. One of them returned a weak wave, then all three shuffled back to where they'd come from.

"Drillers," said Dave, studying his feet again. "Just arrived from Arizona. Been on the road for a week. Stopped in town to get drunk. Hauling the biggest drill rigs I've ever seen. They're headed for Thistle Creek. Be there tomorrow night."

"Thistle Creek, huh? I gotta go, Dave."

* * *

Maggie's B&B was an enormous two story house reminiscent of something a banker might own during the Klondike Gold Rush. Though it may have been in the wrong city—Dawson was home to the gold rush and it was more than three hundred miles north of Whitehorse—the building was impressive in its own right.

It was tall and statuesque, clad in vertical wood siding, painted light gray with white curlicues and trim around the windows and gables. A wide porch with swinging benches wrapped the building on three sides and was bordered by low railings and tall pillars that supported a steep metal roof. Flowers and colorful plants were everywhere. An imposing oak door with an ornate glass inlay greeted me at the top of the stairs. A sign hanging beside the door said, 'No Vacancy'.

The place was equally impressive inside with varnished oak floors and intricate wainscoting, textured wallpaper, fine furniture, lace curtains, crystal sconces and stained glass lamps. It had the ambience of a Victorian doll house, not a Yukon B&B.

I shook my head. All I needed was a bed and a bathroom.

A thin woman wearing an apron and kerchief on her head whisked by with a stack of plates in her arms.

"Right with you sir," she chirped.

She disappeared down a hall but as promised, returned in ten seconds. She swept her hair behind her ears and managed a perfunctory smile, then squeezed into an alcove under the staircase and opened a leather bound guest register on a captain's desk. She had the haggard look of someone whose job is never done and I could almost hear her inner voice screaming for a day off.

"You must be Mr. Brody," she said when her finger found my name.

"That's me. Are you Maggie?"

"I am."

The room in the banker's mansion didn't come cheap. The price for a night was as much as a decent hotel, and without a television in the room. Maybe that's why there wasn't a Boy Scout or hockey fan in sight. No wonder Dora had found the place. Breakfast was served from six to eight.

I went upstairs and threw my pack on a frilly bed with enough pillows to stuff a moose. After doing a laundry in the bathroom sink using a whole bottle of complimentary lavender shampoo, I hung up my spare boxers and T-shirt on a couple of hangars, and hooked them over a curtain rod. I wondered if drying underwear in an open window was against house rules.

Sue me.

After a shower and shave, I was good to go.

* * *

The pizza was huge and heavy, and with only one decent arm, impossible for me to handle. I asked the cashier for help to carry out my order. The guy gave me a look, then called over a young woman whom he loaded up like a forklift. She followed me out to Jennifer's truck. The salads and breadsticks were in bags and those went on the passenger seat. I told her to load the pizza in the box behind the cab. I dropped the tailgate and she slid it in like a patio stone. I dug into a jean pocket, pulled out a fistful of coins, and poured them into her hands. She left happy.

"Always return a borrowed vehicle with a full tank of gas," my grandfather used to preach, so that's what I would do. Just before Jennifer's street, I pulled into a gas station. The sign on the pump said 'No Cell Phone Usage When Pumping Fuel' which reminded me I had to make a call. It was one I'd been putting off, but one that had to be made. Soon enough, everyone would know anyway.

"Hello?"

"Leah, Brody here."

"I know."

"How do you know?"

"Call display. How's Jack?"

I was fixated on the pump display, watching the numbers spin, wondering when they'd stop, wondering what to say.

"Brody? You there?"

"He lost the leg, Leah."

"Oh, no. That's terrible."

"It is terrible."

"Will he be okay?"

"The vet says so."

"Where is he now?"

"The vet's."

"When can he go home?"

"Saturday. Where are you now?"

"Walmart."

"When are you going home?"

"Tonight. I have to work in the morning."

"Oh."

"Why do you want to know?"

"No reason."

In fact there was. I couldn't take Jack home in my plane because it's simply too loud, and besides, if the air was bumpy the ride would be too rough for him. I'd have to drive down from Minto Saturday morning and take him back myself.

No big deal.

When I turned onto Cook Street, two yellow pickups were parked in front of Jennifer's house.

THIRTY THREE

They were the same two trucks I saw at the Café on Monday, but without any rocks in the back.

I assumed both vehicles belonged to Mike Giguere, or whoever owned the Thistle Creek project. My first question was, why hadn't Mike driven one of them back to Thistle Creek? Why ride north with Dan Sanders in that red truck with the white camper and leave behind a truck he could use up there? Maybe because Mike wasn't given the option. Maybe because Tommy Kay was calling the shots. The more I thought about it, the more I knew the red truck was the key. Hopefully the RCMP had tracked it down, pulled it over, found out what was going on, maybe even found Tommy Kay inside.

My next question was, who was at the kitchen table with Jennifer? From the street I could see she had a guest. Surely it wasn't Mike, though I really couldn't tell if she was talking to a man or a woman. Perhaps it was long lost Tony, back in town, begging for another chance. I'd find out soon enough. I was expected for dinner after all and there was plenty of pizza to feed another mouth, even with Jennifer at the table.

With nowhere to park out front I rolled down the driveway to the backyard, and backed the truck up to the doorsteps like I was delivering a new appliance.

There was no need to knock on the door, Jennifer was already standing on the little deck when I dropped the tailgate. She was wearing those goofy white fluffy slippers.

"Hi," she said with a big smile. "This a two man job?"

She was laughing as I slid the pizza toward her and she picked it up with ease.

"My arm," I said with enough self-pity to win an Oscar, slamming the tailgate shut with my left hand.

"Oh, your arm. We'll fix that later."

I opened my mouth to say something, but didn't. Telling her my plans for the night could wait.

"Hey, guess what?" she said.

I stepped up to the deck to face her. She looked great, healthy and happy as usual.

"What?"

"I just hired an office manager for our new branch in Dawson."

"That's great, Jennifer. Congratulations."

"Ah...Brody?"

"What?"

"She's inside. Do you mind if she joins us for dinner?"

"Of course not. No problem."

"Good. Um..."

"Um, what?"

"Well, she's not your everyday kind of...woman. She's...a little... different."

"That's okay, everyone's a little different."

Jennifer smiled and swung the pizza out to her side, leaned in and planted a kiss on my cheek.

"I'll put this in the oven. We can eat in five."

"Hang on," I said.

I loaded the salads and breadsticks on top of the pizza, then opened the door for her.

"Heavy," she said. "By the way, her name is Rita."

* * *

Rita was indeed a *little* different—no doubt about that.

She was either a flaming lesbian, or president of the Lisbeth Salander fan club, or both. Not sure if she had a dragon tattoo on her back but I wasn't going to ask.

Her thick hair was dyed jet black, cut army short on the sides, longer on top, standing straight up in spikes like a stiff brush. It reminded me of an attachment for my Shop Vac. She had the raccoon look going with lots of black makeup plastered over, under and around her dark eyes, and then there was the ink. A tattoo of some medieval monster covered one side of her neck with another running down her left forearm and over the back of her hand. For all the piercings and metal stuck in her face, she might have just fallen into a tackle box. Silver studs ran up and down the edges of her ears, with little crosses and daggers and who knows what else dangling from her earlobes. If you still didn't get the message, a ring was stuck through the side of her nose. A chain necklace hung down the front of her T-shirt, with you guessed it, a double-edged razor blade attached. As pendants go it looked damn dangerous to me. Her jean jacket was black, as were her Metallica T-shirt and jeans, and pointy leather boots replete with buckles and spurs.

Spurs?

One thing was for sure, no man in his right mind, including anyone working in the Dawson branch of Thurson Ames, was going to hit on Rita. That would include Tony of course and I had to wonder if Jennifer's choice of new office manager had more to do with payback than merit.

I was standing at the kitchen table with a hand on the back of a chair, looking down at Rita, who was looking around at everything but me. Jennifer walked over and laid a possessive hand on my bad shoulder. Made me feel ten years old.

"Brody, this is Rita Sorano. Rita is our new office manager in Dawson. Rita, meet Brody. Brody's a pilot with his own plane. He'll be flying the Thistle Creek samples up to Dawson. You two will be seeing a lot of each other this summer."

Jennifer was beaming.

Rita wasn't. She gave me a fierce glare, folded her arms, and looked away.

What? No handshake?

"Nice to meet you too, Rita," I said, sitting down with a smile and making myself comfortable. "Look forward to working with you."

"Likewise," she growled through clenched teeth.

Definitely a man hater.

"Pizza will be ready in five minutes," said Jennifer. "What do you guys want to drink? Beer, water, soda?"

"Water for me," I said.

"Ginger ale, if you have it," said Rita.

Jennifer was still beaming. She was on top of the world, entertaining two very important business associates in her cozy little home. I was happy for her. What a lovely young woman she was.

"I think there's ginger ale in the shop," said Jennifer. "Be right back."

She bounced down the hall and the screen door closed with a screech and a clack.

You couldn't cut it with a knife. Maybe a chainsaw, but not a knife.

Rita leaned forward with fire in her eyes.

"What the hell are you doing here?" she hissed.

I leaned back, smiled, and gazed into those big brown eyes.

"I was about to ask you the same question, *Sarah.*"

THIRTY FOUR

Hell hath no fury.

I'd seen that glare before, more than I care to admit, but it was the price you paid to love her. In spite of the makeup, she still had the most beautiful eyes I've ever seen. And if that wasn't enough, there was the flawless complexion and a smile that took my breath away. But beyond those was her charisma, a certain magical presence that filled a room, some inscrutable vibe that stole the show. Don't ask me how it worked but it made my skin tingle.

"You ornery son of a bitch! I asked you first. What the hell are you doing here? A girl is dead because of you. Now leave this one alone and get out of here."

Son of a bitch?

Back to reality. 'Rita' was hissing like a cat.

"Hey," I said. "Leave my mother out of this. And that girl is dead because of Tommy Kay, not me. So do your job. If you cops would get off your fat asses and out of your offices and cars, maybe you could find that monster and put him where he belongs—in jail."

"Is that how you see this?"

"Damn right it's how I see it. Ask a dog catcher. Your quarry's roaming the streets, not hiding under a boardroom table. You guys need to get out and pound the pavement."

She folded her arms, furious, her eyes burning like hot coals.

"Are you sleeping with her?"

"What?"

"You heard me."

"My God, Rita. I am absolutely shocked you would ask such a thing. At a dinner party no less."

"Oh, please."

She rolled her eyes and slumped back in her chair, now pouting and silent. Time to change the subject.

"So, *Sarah*, when did you come out?"

She lurched forward and slapped both hands on the table.

"Idiot! Don't call me Sarah. Can you not put two and two together and see what's going on here?"

"Idiot? Two and two? Oh, I get it. You're not gay, this is just one of your special agent cop disguises. Tommy Kay likes lesbians and you're the bait."

There was a jab of pain in my shin where she kicked it with one of those pointy boots with the buckles and spurs. I counted to three before I had to wince.

"You fuh..."

"Everything okay here? What's wrong, Brody?"

Jennifer was back with an armful of soda.

"Shoulder," I gasped, resisting an urge to rub my shin.

"Poor baby," she said.

'Rita' rolled her eyes.

* * *

Dinner was quiet.

Go figure.

I was in pain, Sarah was fuming, and Jennifer didn't have time for chitchat, engrossed in devouring three times what I ate. Sarah had only one slice and didn't eat the crust. What a waste, it's the best part, especially with jam.

I watched Jennifer use two fingers to carefully pick up the last crumb off her plate, delicately place it on her tongue, and wash it down with the last of her beer. Then she leaned back, groaned, grinned at me, and put her hands on her belly. It was a cue for some conversation.

"So Jennifer, those two trucks out front, they belong to Mike?"

"Yup. Rita and I picked them up this afternoon at his place. We're driving them up to Dawson on Saturday."

"Saturday, huh?"

"Yes, Saturday. Why?"

I thought about Jack. Maybe Jennifer could pick him up and drop him off on her way to Dawson. It would save me a half day of driving. Something to think about it, but then again, maybe not the greatest idea.

"Nothing," I said. "Forget it."

With a quizzical look she said, "So Rita starts her new job on Monday and I thought we'd go up a day early, get her settled in, show her around town. I need to hang out there for a week anyway, make sure everything is running smoothly."

I envisioned Sarah and Jennifer walking side by side down a Dawson boardwalk. It would be quite the sight.

"How are you getting back?" I asked for no particular reason. "Tony giving you a ride?"

I grinned and she laughed.

"Right, like that'll ever happen. Actually, I wanted to talk to you about that."

"Oh yeah?"

"Yeah. Mike says he'll have another load of samples ready to go a week Friday. You'll fly those to Dawson, so I was thinking maybe I could hitch a ride back in that plane of yours. Never been in a float plane. We can talk about it later."

She winked at me.

I could feel the seering heat from Sarah's glare and my cheeks were starting to burn, but no way I was going to look at her.

None of your business.

"So when were you talking to Mike, Jennifer?"

"He texted me at noon."

"Ah."

One of these days I'll have to get someone to explain texting to me. Must be something like email.

Jennifer got up and started gathering plates. Sarah asked if she wanted help but Jennifer said no. I watched her moving around her little kitchen, back and forth, quick and efficient, a blur of long legs and arms, reaching and stretching and stowing. She had on the same skin tight leggings as this afternoon and I sat back to take in the show. The best part was whenever she bent over to put something in the dishwasher. No way I was talking to 'Rita', not then anyway, not with all the jiggling at the kitchen sink.

"Enjoying yourself?" she hissed.

She kicked me again.

The other shin this time.

* * *

Sarah and I were seated on opposing couches in the living room. I felt a lot safer with a coffee table between us. Jennifer had just chased us out of the kitchen and was making herbal tea. I declined a cup of the foul tasting stuff, it's just soapy water to me. Sarah was seething in silence, staring out the window at the quiet street with a leg stretched out and an arm draped over the back of the couch. I kept an eye on her while plotting my escape.

I needed to talk to Jennifer alone, explain why I wasn't going to stay the night. It might be an emotional issue for her and might take some time. But the privacy required would be impossible if Sarah was staying the night. Time to get the lay of the land.

I cleared my throat and said, "So, *Rita*. Been in town long?"

"What's it to you?" she growled.

"Wondering if you had a place to stay or are you just passing through?"

"Don't worry about it."

"You staying here tonight"?

"Are you?"

Okay, Rita, you raging bitch on wheels....

I got up and walked out to the kitchen. Jennifer was bent over a cup on the counter, pouring hot water through a strainer.

"Jennifer?"

"Mmm...?"

"Dinner was great. Thank you."

"Thank you. You bought and brought."

She glanced up and smiled. I smiled back.

"Hey, got a minute?" I asked.

She moved the strainer to the next cup.

"I know. Your shoulder. I'll get to it as soon as Rita leaves."

"She's leaving?"

"After we have our tea. She's staying at the coolest place you've ever seen. It's a bed and breakfast in the north part of town, looks just like an old Klondike mansion."

No.

THIRTY FIVE

A thousand miles south, the Dassault Falcon 8X broke out of a low layer of wet gray clouds and touched down at Sea-Tac International Airport. The gleaming new jet slowed and raised its flaps, then turned off the end of the runway, heading away from the main terminal. Half a mile later it turned again into a large fenced compound and rolled up to the wide open door of a private hangar. Inside the hangar sat a shiny black Mercedes facing the plane. Two large men in suits and ties with sunglasses stood beside its rear doors, hands behind their backs, waiting. The plane stopped in front of the hangar and the pilots went through their shut down procedures, then turned off the engines.

Inside the sleek little jet, Tommy Kay peered out at the rain soaked tarmac and a thick stand of evergreens surrounding the property. They were much taller than the ones in Fairbanks where only two and a half hours ago he'd boarded Mr. Li's plane. Tommy thought Mr. Li's plane was very nice. It was spacious and comfortable, though he was far too big and wide to use the forward bathroom. A young attendant in a short blue skirt had shown him to the master bathroom at the rear where she had also shown him a nice wide bed. She had then catered to his every need, without a word said.

Tommy liked that quality in a woman.

After he showered she'd helped him into a new Armani suit—custom tailored, dark with pale pinstripes, a little tight around the biceps—but that was fine, it was all part and parcel of the image. The Brooks Brothers shirt fit well, as did the Berluti shoes, and he liked the Versace tie too.

From his seat he watched the attendant slip on a pair of white gloves, throw a lever on the cabin door, and give it a practiced bump with her hip. The cabin was instantly filled with a silvery hue and the fresh scent of Pacific air. She stepped out into a light drizzle and opened an umbrella. Tommy stood and dropped a couple of crisp hundreds on his seat, turned sideways, shuffled his way forward, and squeezed out the door after her. At the bottom of the stairs the attendant held out his bag with a smile. He took it from her, ignored her offer of the umbrella, put his hand on her butt, and gave it a friendly squeeze.

"See you soon," he said.

Tommy walked toward the car with his massive arms and legs swinging in great wide arcs, his grotesque bulk oscillating from side to side in a neanderthal gait. He stopped in front of the man on the driver's side. The two men locked eyes and reciprocated the mutual disdain professional enforcers hold for each other. The man on the other side of the car walked around the back, stopped behind his partner, and slid a hand inside his jacket. Tommy knew why.

"No weapons in the car," the man in Tommy's face said in a matter of fact tone. "Hands up, gotta frisk ya'."

"I have no weapon," said Tommy.

"Gotta frisk you anyway," the man said.

Tommy glared at him, then lowered his bag to the concrete and raised his hands over his head. When the man reached out to pat him down, Tommy's right arm came down in a flash, delivering a vicious karate chop that crushed the man's shoulder and snapped his collar bone. The man howled and his knees buckled, but before he fell, Tommy grabbed him by the neck and held him up like a shield. The gunman fired once, twice, then realizing he was shooting his partner in the back, froze in disbelief. Tommy tossed his mortally wounded partner at him. Both men went down in a heap. Tommy stepped on the gunman's hand.

"Let go."

He did. Tommy stomped a heel on his face, then on his chest a few times. The man yelped, curled into a ball, and whimpered and groaned. Nothing like broken ribs and a fractured jaw to take the fight out of a man, thought Tommy. He picked up the gun—a revolver—calmly looked it over, and slipped it into his pocket.

"Get up," he said.

In agony the gunman struggled to his feet. Tommy grabbed his throat and pinned him up against the car.

"Can you drive?"

The gunman tried to nod. Tommy punched him in the ribs, twice, very hard, the second one a well placed shot to the liver. The man buckled over with his face contorted in pain. His jaw was askew and he was making strange gurgling noises.

"Did you hear me? Can you drive?"

"*Yesh*," the man hissed through broken teeth, his face almost purple with his eyes darting about, searching the floor for his partner. "*Ish he dead?*"

Tommy looked down at the unconscious man and kicked him in the head.

"He is now. Put him in the trunk and drive."

Tommy let go of the gunman's throat, picked up his bag, stepped over the dead man, opened the rear door, and got in.

"Hello, Tommy."

"Hello, Mr. Li."

"Nice flight?"

"Very nice flight."

* * *

The tires under the big Mercedes hissed on the soaking wet highway as it rolled north on I-5, heading north toward Bellingham and Vancouver.

Most days the trip to Canada from Seattle took two and a half hours but today Tippy thought the car was traveling slower than usual. He peered over the seat at the speedometer—sixty miles an hour—then at his driver who had a pained expression. He was hunched forward with his arms around the steering wheel, breathing in stuttered gasps, bleeding from his nose. Hardly the image required for a smooth passage through Canadian customs. Tippy pulled out his phone, touched an icon on the screen, murmured a few words, and returned it to his suit pocket.

"First Disposal, Andy."

The driver managed a nod.

A change of cars was in order. Andy needed medical attention but more important, the man in the trunk had to disappear. A new car and driver would be waiting at Tippy's newest enterprise, sixty miles north.

The facility occupied four square miles of a former apple orchard just south of the Canadian border. Tippy knew he'd paid too much for his latest acquisition but the garbage industry was booming, and it was a business he had to be in. Vancouver and its surrounding burroughs were undergoing an explosion in population growth, and with no way to handle the surge in garbage, well that's where America came in, importing tons of the stuff from its neighbor to the north. Tippy smiled to himself. The good old USA, he thought. God, guns, gluttons and glory—and now he could add garbage to the list.

Tippy's new company might break even this year, or so he hoped, and might even make money some day. But that's not why he'd bought First Disposal. It was the hundred and twenty garbage trucks making two cross-border trips a day.

Each one entered the U.S. hauling twenty tons of the foulest cargo imaginable—bags and bags of disposable diapers, rancid food, discarded clothes, broken furniture, and a mish mash of packaging, plastics and chemicals. What better way to move contraband from one country to the next? Even when returning empty to Canada, what customs inspector wanted to poke around a garbage truck?

At the center of the property lay the heart of the operation, a gargantuan incinerator fueled by a steady stream of trucks, dumping a load every six minutes, twenty-four hours a day, seven days a week. Each load was conveyed into a roaring inferno of flame and hot gases, lifting the microscopic elements of yesterday's refuse up a three hundred foot chimney, expelling it high into the sky to become one with the wind. On occasion, fuel for the fire would include the body of some hapless deviant who had dared cross Tippy. He often mused that the process really wasn't actually garbage 'disposal'—*dispersion* was the better word.

Tippy looked at the enormous man on his left. He was quiet and alert, ever the perfect bodyguard, currently fixated on the driver, ensuring he was doing his job.

Tippy had met Kay a month ago.

One night over dinner in Vancouver, Lynn mentioned she had a personnel problem. She needed to hide someone—an employee the police were looking for—a man whose services were no longer required. Of course Tippy was more than happy to help, at the time he'd have done anything for the pleasure of her body, and so had gladly volunteered his services. After a heart to heart with Kay, arrangements were made and he was whisked off to one of Tippy's drug distribution houses in Bellingham. Tippy could keep an eye on him there while deciding his fate.

Tippy had asked his best lieutenant, a hit man named Adrian, to keep an eye on the new houseguest. A week later Adrian reported back. He said Kay was like no other enforcer he'd ever met. For one thing, he didn't carry a gun. He also didn't gamble, womanize, drink, smoke, use drugs, and he never went out at night. He was up early every day and ate the same breakfast—six hard boiled eggs, no juice, no coffee—then spent the morning pumping iron in the garage. At noon he'd walk down to a neighborhood steakhouse where he ate only from the salad bar. Same thing at dinner. Unless spoken to he never uttered a word, and he never ever used his phone. If he wasn't in his bedroom he was in the living room watching TV, usually the Military Channel. When Tippy asked how Kay got along with other men in the house, Adrian said fine, though there had been an 'incident'.

One of Tippy's street dealers, a neighborhood thug named Ringo, had come over to the house to pick up his weekly inventory. Ringo was an oversized and obnoxious street bully known to pick fights. He had turned up early for his appointment and was told to watch TV while his package was being prepared. Apparently Ringo had walked into the living room, and when he saw Kay, told him he was sitting in his chair. When Kay ignored him, Ringo produced a pistol and waved it in his face. Kay took the gun from Ringo, broke his wrist and a few fingers in the process, then picked him up by the neck and crotch, and tossed him down the basement stairs. Ringo stopped screaming when his head hit the concrete floor. Tragically, the hard landing killed him. Adrian said Ringo's body was immediately taken to First Disposal for cremation. Another man was hired to take his place.

Tippy's initial reaction was one of relief. For weeks there'd been a rumor on the streets that Ringo was stepping on house product to support his own habit. Users in the area knew Tippy's drugs were the best in town and he would never compromise that reputation. But with one problem solved another was created. Ringo had some very nasty friends and Tippy knew that paybacks could get ugly, often leading to turf wars. Kay had to be moved, and fast. The best way to facilitate that was to give him a job, ideally an out-of-town assignment.

The next day Tippy dispatched Adrian and Kay to Vancouver for a handy man project, then it was north to the Yukon to meet a geologist. Kay said he had unfinished business up there anyway and was glad for the chance to return. Tippy didn't need to know anything about Kay's unfinished business, so long as he left the lower mainland and ended up far from Ringo's buddies. Of course Tippy never told Lynn he'd hired Kay, or where he'd sent him. No point in having her worry her pretty little head about the travails of a former employee. Besides, before he ever made any hiring a permanent arrangement, Tippy always wanted to know more about a new recruit. Could he handle a field assignment? Was he responsible and dedicated? Tippy had been looking forward to another report from Adrian but it was Kay who had called him from the Yukon. As Kay put it, there had been 'a tragic accident'. Adrian was dead.

For Kay to kill one of Tippy's top lieutenants was outrageous, that he would call in to report it was over the top. Clearly the man had no fear. But there was something about Kay that Tippy liked, some innate and authentic quality he could sense, a notion that he could be trusted. Perhaps Kay had good reason to kill Tippy's most valued henchman, though there was no point in asking him about it. Dead is dead. You moved on.

Instinct had taken Tippy from the back alleys of Vancouver to the top of its skyscrapers, from an old slow boat to a private jet, from a kid stealing fruit to an untouchable underworld kingpin.

Now that instinct told him he'd found a star.

"Tommy."

"Yes, Mr. Li."

"I want you to take charge of my Yukon operations. Can you do that?"

"Yes, Mr. Li."

"Good. There is no need to tell Miss Chan about this. Understood?"

"Yes, Mr. Li."

"Good. Do not speak to her again. Tomorrow you will return to Fairbanks on my plane. You will be picked up by the man who flew you there. He will take you to his home and you will stay there until I call with instructions."

"Yes, Mr. Li."

"And Tommy."

"Yes, Mr. Li."

"If you want a future in my organization, please stop killing my men."

Tommy sighed and looked out his window.

THIRTY SIX

I woke up in Jennifer's bed.

Good idea or not, staying with Jennifer at the Thurson Ames staff house had been a no-brainer. With no other hotel rooms in the city, I'd been down to two choices—either have breakfast with someone who was being nice to me, or with someone who wasn't. Dinner with Sarah had been an ordeal, and with two ripe bruises on my shins, sleeping at the B&B would have been dangerous.

As soon as Sarah had left, Jennifer tended to my shoulder. She directed me to the couch and had me lie on my left side, stood over me with a foot firmly planted in my armpit, and gripped my right forearm with both hands. She then proceeded to pull and push and twist while I whimpered and whined and yelped. She said the objective was to break something up. Whether she accomplished that or not, I'm not sure, but it was ten minutes of hell.

Once done with the physical torture she dropped a bag of ice on my shoulder and told me to lie still while she watched television. I lay in agony for another twenty minutes, trying to take my mind off the pain by staring at her breasts. It helped quite a bit.

The rest of the session went a lot better. Jennifer led me into the bathroom where we had a long hot shower and she massaged the feeling back into my shoulder. Then she took me to bed and got even with Tony some more. She was very gentle this time, much appreciated given my suffering. I'd never had any kind of physio before, and after weighing all the pros and cons, went to sleep thinking I could go for another treatment.

With another big breakfast in my belly, I walked out her front door with the keys to Mike's truck in hand. Jennifer had once again offered me the use of hers but I insisted on taking Mike's. For one thing, I wouldn't have to join her for lunch. For another, my sense of independence had been waning. While it had only been a couple of days since I'd left Minto, it was beginning to feel like a couple of months. Jennifer had been absolutely wonderful but I was now under her thumb and didn't like the feeling. Using Mike's truck meant I wouldn't have to check in at noon.

That, and my day was pretty full anyway. It's always seemed to me that living in a city is nothing more than a lot of running around, doing a bunch of things that have to be done today, creating a whole bunch more things that have to be done tomorrow. I couldn't wait to get out of Whitehorse. Pick up my dog and go home.

But first I had a bunch of things to do.

Go figure.

I headed for the RCMP building thinking about my other pair of boxers. I wondered if they were dry yet. I also wondered if they were still hanging in the window or if they'd been seized and sealed as evidence for a court case.

Mike's truck ran like a piece of crap. It pulled to the left when you drove it straight, to the right when you braked, and rattled like a box of empty beer cans when you stopped at a light. Mike must be one of those people who thought his vehicle was in good condition if it started. I could spend a week on it.

When the elevator doors on the third floor of the RCMP building opened, I poked my head out and looked left and right for the one person I didn't want see. He was nowhere in sight and I tiptoed up to the counter. My second least favorite person in the building was standing there to greet me. Today polka dot dress was wearing a lime green pant suit.

Ninja secretary.

"Mr. Brody, please be seated. I'll get your statement."

She waddled off and disappeared into an office. I sat down in a chrome chair and stared up at a large framed photograph of the Queen. She had a crown and a lot of jewels and was staring down at me. I suddenly felt guilty, though about what I wasn't sure. A minute later Ninja secretary came out of the office and beckoned me back to the counter. I got up and went over. She pushed some paperwork at me.

"This is your statement, Mr. Brody. Please read it carefully. Ring the bell when you're done. You must sign it in front of me."

"I'll sign it now, I'm sure it's fine."

"I must advise you, sir, that's not a good idea. You ought to read it first. There's always the possibility of an error. This is a legal document and your signature will attest to its accuracy."

"Doesn't matter, I didn't do anything wrong."

I looked up at the Queen and winked at her.

"Your funeral," said Ninja secretary. "Sign here."

I did and pushed off the counter for a hasty exit.

"Mr. Brody."

"Yes?"

"The Staff Sergeant will see you now."

Damn.

* * *

"So did you get him?"

Staff Sergeant Alan Robson cracked a wan smile that creased his clean shaven cheeks. We were sitting in his office.

"No, but we did stop that red truck you told us about. Pulled it over late yesterday afternoon a few miles south of the Dempster Highway. Actually had a pretty good excuse to make the stop, it had expired plates. The driver was...let's see..." Robson peered down at his notes. "One Daniel M. Sanders of Fairbanks, Alaska. He's the registered owner of the vehicle, a red 2007 Ford F250. Your friend with the broken nose was sitting beside him, a Michael G. Giguere of Whitehorse, Yukon. But there was no one else in the cab and no one in the camper, just the two aforementioned individuals. So no Tommy Kay and so much for your hunch, Mr. Brody. Now, if you've got a minute, I have a few more questions."

"More questions? I told you everything yesterday. It's all in the statement I signed."

Robson nodded and said, "Won't take long. It's about that truck we stopped yesterday. Ever seen it before?"

"Well yeah, I told you already, yesterday morning."

"I mean before yesterday morning."

I thought for a moment and said, "As a matter of fact, maybe I did. In Minto, three days ago, on Monday morning. A red truck with a white camper was coming up behind me when I was turning into my place. Could have been the same truck I saw yesterday but I can't be sure. Campers on the Klondike Highway all look the same, right?"

"What time of day was this?"

"Midmorning. I'd just left the Café."

"Where you'd just eaten breakfast."

"That's right."

"After skipping out on our appointment."

"Hey, I told you I was..."

Robson waved a hand at me and asked, "Who was driving this red truck coming up behind you?"

"Didn't see."

"But it wasn't Sanders."

"I said I didn't see. Why?"

"Because we'd like to know, that's why. We know Sanders wasn't the driver because he was driving one of Giguere's trucks on Monday. He was drinking coffee with Giguere at the Café when you hightailed it out of there trying to avoid us. The two men were there when we walked in, and they were still there when we walked out. So were Giguere's two trucks. So Giguere wasn't driving that red truck and neither was Sanders. Someone else had to be driving it."

"If it was his truck I saw."

"We think it was."

"How's that?"

"Because when Sanders was pulled over yesterday, he told the constable he'd driven it to Whitehorse on Monday."

"So? Maybe he got his days mixed up. Maybe he drove it down the day before, or maybe the day after."

Robson gave me a look and said, "We're not mistaken. He's lying. For one thing, Sanders' credit card was used to fill up his truck twice on Monday. It was filled up early Monday morning in Stewart Crossing—that's two hundred miles north of Whitehorse— and again in Whitehorse, at six-thirty in the evening. That's when it arrived in town, Monday evening. And Sanders wasn't driving it."

"How do you know?"

"Because according to your girlfriend, at six-thirty Monday evening Giguere and Sanders were drinking beer in her backyard."

"Excuse me, did you say girlfriend?"

"Sorry, Miss Kovalchuk, that young woman you've been staying with, you know—sleeping in her house, eating breakfast in her kitchen, driving her vehicle, and well, if it looks like a duck..."

He gave me a satisfied grin.

Asshole.

"Why were you talking to her?"

"Well for one thing, she called us. Her tires were slashed while you were asleep in her house. Two nights ago, remember? Anyway, we had her come in yesterday afternoon for a little chat. She told us Giguere and Sanders were at her place on Monday evening at exactly the same time that Sanders' credit card was being used to buy gas not a mile away."

I wasn't sure where Robson was going with this but I was losing patience. I stood up and said, "Look, Staff Sergeant, if that's all..."

"Sit down, Mr. Brody! I'll tell you when we're finished here."

I did, reluctantly, wondering why he was telling me about Sanders' truck. As if I knew anything about the guy. Or cared. Robson gave me a cop glare for a moment, then said, "Where was I?"

"You were talking about Sanders' credit card."

"Right. According to Miss Kovalchuk, Sanders and Giguere drove Giguere's trucks into her driveway at one o'clock on Monday afternoon. She said she made them lunch, then watched them unload rocks and carry them into her shop, then they talked some business, then she went back to work in her shop while they opened a case of beer. She said they sat in her backyard drinking all afternoon until they ran out of beer at about seven o'clock. She said she then drove them over to Giguere's house. And..."

"And?"

"She said Sanders' truck was parked in Giguere's driveway."

I shook my head.

"Okay, Robson,...uh, Staff Sergeant...sir. That's some great detective work. But what does any of this have to do with me?"

Robson got up and walked over to the window, put his hands in his pockets, and said, "That's where things get a little complicated. We'll finish this later."

"Later? Look, Staff Sergeant, I have a lot of things to do today, and tomorrow too. If you have more questions, ask them now."

"No. Right now I'm done asking you questions. But there are some out-of-towners coming in here this afternoon who would appreciate a few minutes of your time. How about we meet back here for coffee at..." Robson looked at his watch. "Let's say three o'clock."

Out-of-towners?

THIRTY SEVEN

Lynn Chan was out of patience.

She'd just jumped out of her chair to confront her least favorite employee. He was leaning against the wall next to the door. There was a reason she was wearing five inch heels this morning and this was it. She stepped into the man's face, planted her hands on her hips, and glared at him.

"I've had it with your bullshit, Earl! Last chance. Where's the damn box?"

For the umpteenth time in the last five minutes, all Earl Frye could do was shrug his shoulders, mumble something unintelligible, and try not to let her see him sweat. This was a bad dream. He was in a royal jam and knew it. He had two big secrets and coughing up either one could cost him his life.

The first secret was he knew where the box was, the second secret was he had a key to Chan's suite. The big Chinese guy had given it to him when they'd left, said he might need it later to get into Chan's suite, to change the battery in the phone inside the chandelier they'd installed. Earl had never heard of a phone in a chandelier but that didn't matter, his shoulder was still sore where the big man had poked it. The look in the guy's eyes told Earl he was not a man to be crossed. So what to do?

"He knows Miss Chan. He's afraid of Mr. Tommy, that's all. That's why he won't tell you."

"Shut up, Jeremy," said Lynn, not taking her eyes from Earl's.

Jeremy crossed his arms, pouted, and spun around his chair to face the wall. The three of them were in the sales office of Chan's building, just down the hall from the luxurious street level lobby. They'd closed the door twenty minutes ago and Lynn had been instantly overwhelmed by Earl's BO. The smell was probably in her clothes by now and she couldn't wait to shower. But first she was going to break this excuse for a man.

Earl was fifty but looked a lot older with a soft fat belly and the cherry red nose of a heavy drinker. He belonged in the basement with its bare concrete and pipes, not up here with the tropical plants and thick carpets. Lynn decided it was time to end the standoff.

"Let me guess, Earl. You and Tommy Kay and who knows who else installed that piece of crap over my dining room table and then stole the one I ordered. Now you're afraid to tell me where it is because you think Tommy Kay will hurt you if I find out. Am I right?"

Earl was gulping like a fish. "Look, Miss Chan..."

"No, *you* look, Earl. I paid a hundred thousand dollars for that goddamn chandelier and I want it back. Now either I call Mr. Kay and ask him where you put it, or *you* tell me where you put it. What's it gonna be?"

Earl groaned and looked at his feet.

"Come on, spit it out. I know it was in the van in the basement. You're the only one who had the keys since Jeremy brought it here from the airport. Now where is it?"

Another groan. Earl looked at the floor some more, then murmured, "Out at the airport."

"Out at the airport?"

"I knew it, Miss Chan, I just knew it. He took it!" exclaimed Jeremy.

"Jeremy, please...would you just...shut...up!"

Jeremy spun his chair around for another view of the wall, this time stifling a smile.

"Why take it back there?" she asked.

Earl resembled a cornered coyote with his eyes darting about, swaying from one foot to the other. He swallowed and cleared his throat, then said, "I don't know. That big guy, Tommy Kay, he made me drive him and this other guy, think his name was Adrian, and another other guy too, his name was Dan, out to the airport. We all went in the van and took the box with your chandelier."

"Were these the guys that installed that ugly thing over my dining room table?"

"Yes."

"Okay, then what did you do?"

Earl took a deep breath and said, "Well, then we drove through this gate and over to a place with a bunch of them corporate jets, then we drove around the back of this hangar and took the box out of the van and carried it inside, and left it beside the back door. Some guy working in the office, looked like a pilot to me, he gave us a blanket to put over it. And that's it. We left."

"Left for where?"

"Don't know about those other guys, they got in a car and took off. But I came back here."

"Was there a plane in this hangar?"

"No."

"What did this hangar look like?"

"I don't know, just a hangar."

"Just a hangar, huh? Was there a sign on this hangar?"

Earl's breathing was shallow. He was terrified.

"Look, Miss Chan. I got a wife and kids..."

"And a job too. And if you want to keep it, I suggest you answer my question. Was there a sign on this hangar?"

He took a deep breath and murmured, "New Horizons."

The answer almost floored her.

"Did you say New Horizons?"

He nodded.

Tippy.

Lynn had been to the New Horizons hangar several times, the last time when she and Tippy had flown to the Caymans for a little banking last month. So what was he up to? Why would he steal her chandelier?

"Earl, go home. Take the rest of the day off. Think about whether you want to keep working for me. If you do, from now you shower and shave before you set foot in my building. Every time. Is that clear?"

"Yeah, sure, Miss Chan."

He was reaching for the door when a knock came from the other side. He opened it. FedEx. Earl squeezed past the guy and left in a hurry.

"Package for a Lynn Chan?"

Lynn signed for the thick envelope and opened it. It was from the lawyers. More Thistle Creek crap. The document was half an inch thick with with little yellow tags sticking out everywhere.

'Sign Here'.

She read the cover letter.

A financing? What financing?

She snatched her phone off the desk and turned for the door.

"Jeremy."

"Yes, Miss Chan."

"Leave this door open for a while. It stinks in here."

* * *

I walked into John Dorval's animal clinic with a dry mouth, weak legs, and my heart in my throat.

At the end of a row of chairs sat an old woman with an old dog at her feet. They both looked sad. John's wife was behind the counter at a computer. She looked up and recognized me.

"Well, hello there, Brody," she said with a broad smile, standing to greet me.

"Hey, Evelyn."

We shook hands over the counter.

Evelyn Dorval was a stout strong woman with long gray hair braided in a thick pony tail. She was wearing the only outfit I've ever seen her in—boots, blue jeans, and an unbuttoned and untucked red flannel shirt worn over a white turtle neck. I doubt if she owns a tube of lipstick, but hey, why would the best dog musher in the Yukon need lipstick? Evelyn walked out from behind the counter, put a hand on my shoulder, and guided me over to a chair in the corner.

We sat down, and with her hand still on my shoulder, she said, "He's going to be fine Brody, just fine. Animals are amazing. They adapt to changes like this in no time. The only one we have to worry about is you."

Changes like this.

"I don't know Evelyn. Losing a leg is a big deal."

"More to you than him. Something I learned a long time ago."

"Oh, yeah?"

"Absolutely. When I was a little girl, my parents gave me and my sister a puppy for Christmas. It was a retriever-collie mutt they'd rescued from the shelter and we named it Mandy. She grew up with us. We lived out in the country, deep in the woods, at the end of this long dirt lane that lead out to the highway. Every morning Mandy would walk us down the lane to wait for the school bus, and no matter how dark and cold it was, every afternoon she was there waiting for us when we returned. One summer day we were running through the woods and Mandy stepped on a branch. It flipped up into her face like she'd stepped on a rake. The branch hit her square in the eye, just a freak accident, you know? Anyway, a week later they had to remove the eye. My sister and I were devastated. We thought she'd never be the same. But know what? Nothing changed. She was always the same dog, always at our sides, always waiting for us at the end of the lane when we got off the bus after school. She lived to be seventeen and was happy every day she spent with us."

"Damn, Evelyn, you've got a movie there."

She patted my thigh and stood up.

"Come on. Let's go see Jack."

* * *

Jack was in a cubicle with a wire mesh door in a room by himself. He was lying on his side with a clear plastic cone attached to his collar. It reminded me of a lampshade. A thick bandage was wrapped around his rump with his remaining rear leg protruding. Evelyn opened the wire mesh door and he didn't move. I crouched and put my hand on his shoulder. He opened his eyes but seemed pretty stoned. He acknowledged me with a flop of his tail.

Evelyn said, "He's heavily medicated and we'll keep him calm for the rest of the day. Some good news, his fever was way down this morning. Looks like we have the infection under control. We'll get him eating solid food tonight and keep him for a couple of days. He can go home Saturday."

"When can he get up and walk around?"

"We'll have him walking tomorrow."

I put my hand under his jaw and rubbed his throat. He thumped his tail on the bed again and looked up at me with adulation. He was surely wondering what was going on with his eyes searching mine for the answer, then he gazed down with a sigh.

"I'll give you a minute, Brody. But that's all. He needs to rest."

Evelyn left and I dropped to my knees to massage his ears.

After what felt like a long time holding his head in my hands, I said, "Jack, buddy? Everything's gonna be alright. I'll pick up a couple of steaks tomorrow and it'll be all you can eat for a week. And I promise you this. I'm going to kill whoever did this and feed him to you one piece at a time, until there's nothing left of him."

Jack licked his nose, fell over on his side, and sunk into a deep sleep.

* * *

I had a million things to do and didn't feel like doing any of them. But daydreaming in Mike's truck wasn't going to mitigate my depression. There's no point in feeling sorry for yourself when there's no one around to watch.

It took a few tries to start Mike's truck and when I rolled out to the road, my phone rang. I dragged my pack over to my lap and rummaged through its contents while waiting for a break in traffic. As I closed my hand on the phone, the ringing stopped. It was a toss up whether to ignore the damn thing and be on my way—precisely to where I wasn't sure—or stop and see who had called. Curiosity got the better of me and I threw the truck in park and opened the phone. The screen showed a missed call from the one and only number I know by heart. The Café.

There was also a warning. Big letters were flashing. 'Low battery'.

Damn.

The charger was in my plane.

I thought, what a great excuse to pay it a visit. Check out my new windshields, see if it had been fueled, get it ready for tomorrow, and maybe just do some good old man and machine bonding. Maybe that would cheer me up.

So that's where I headed.

THIRTY EIGHT

A cold north wind was there to greet me, sending sheets of ripples scurrying down the lake, cowing rafts of ducks against the shoreline. When I got out of Mike's warm truck, the sun was a blazing white star in a wide open sky, though still no match for a raw spring morning. The cure for cold weather in the Yukon is called July and it was still a month away. I zipped up my windbreaker, walked over to the jetty, and sauntered down its gray wood planks toward my plane.

It had been moved to fuel it and was now moored directly in front of me, tethered dead center along the low floating dock, bracketed on either side by newer and sleeker looking planes, all sporting slick paint jobs and shiny prop cones.

None, though, were a match for mine.

That's because mine is the one and only, the DHC-2, better known as the DeHavilland Beaver, the *'flying half ton truck'*, the world famous legend of frontier aviation, and the plane that opened the north. I stopped to admire it, the way it towered over the other planes, mounted high on a lattice of ladders and struts over great big floats, looking clumsy and ungainly with its short pug nose, flat square windows, split front windshield, weathered aluminum, bulbous rivets, long thick wings, and a prop the size of a windmill.

Call it what you want—goofy, antiquated, ugly—but not since the last one was built in 1967 has anyone produced a better bush plane.

I turned left at the end of the jetty, walked past the nose, then turned around for a good view of my new windshields. They were crystal clear, spotless, perfectly installed. Every screw had been sunk flush to the frame and not a speck of sealer showed at the seams. I stepped on the float and unlocked the pilot's door, climbed up the ladder, got in and sat down. The floor and console were clean as a whistle. A cursory inspection revealed the job had been done inside with the same care and attention to detail as out. I was more than impressed and would have to congratulate the boys. I turned on the master switch. The fuel gauge showed three full tanks. I hit the starter button and the prop spun with gusto. My good old plane was ready to fly.

But was I?

The idea of doing a short sightseeing circuit was tempting but then I thought about my shoulder. It felt markedly better than yesterday but you need all four limbs to fly a Beaver, and so I thought, better check it out too.

With my right hand I reached down for the flap lever between the seats and gave it a pump. No problem. I gingerly raised the same hand to the center of the console and curled a finger around the throttle lever. A little pain, but not too bad. Then I raised my arm up some more, very slowly, toward the ceiling where the trim wheels for the elevator and rudder are located. And didn't get close. A stab of pain stopped me dead.

Damn.

There'd be no flying today, or tomorrow for that matter, not unless things improved a lot. Maybe another physio session at the Thurson Ames staff house was in order.

I almost forgot to get my phone charger out of the door pocket, but didn't, got out, locked the door, rubbed my shoulder, and went down to see Tim and Jim. They had the cowl off the nose of the little plane they were working on and were standing tiptoe on its floats, leaning into the motor from opposite sides with their toolboxes anchored securely between their feet.

They didn't see me coming, completely absorbed in their work, and I shouted through the wind from twenty feet away.

"Hey boys!"

They both turned their heads in unison and shouted back, "Hey, Brody!"

"Great job on the windshields, guys. Thanks."

"That was easy," said Tim, or Jim.

"Yeah, real easy," said Jim, or Tim.

"Well I'm impressed, thanks again."

I was about to leave when one of them said, "Hey Brody, some woman was down here looking for you."

"What woman?"

One of them said, "I dunno, some woman. She came down a couple of days ago, said she wanted to talk to you."

"Two days ago? Who was she?"

They both shrugged and looked at each other. One of them said, "Don't know."

"You didn't get her name?"

They stared at each other for a while, then shook their heads.

"What did she look like?"

"Kind of fat," said one of them.

"Yeah, kind of ugly too," said the other one.

"How old was she?"

"Young, like twenties," said one of them.

"No, old, like thirties," said the other one.

"Why didn't you tell me this yesterday?"

"Yesterday?"

"Yes, yesterday. At the hangar."

"At the hangar?"

"At the hangar. I was there, remember? You were eating lunch with Amanda."

"Right," they said in unison, nodding at each other.

Then one of them said, "Hey Brody, you see them puppies on Amanda? You can tell the temperature just by lookin' at 'em."

"I gotta go, boys. Thanks again."

"Later," said Tim, or Jim.

"Yeah, later," said Jim, or Tim.

* * *

I got into Mike's truck, plugged in my phone charger, and wondered about the fat ugly woman in her twenties or thirties looking for me. Who was she? Not Jennifer or Sarah or Leah, they weren't fat and ugly. Then I wondered why Tim and Jim, two otherwise intelligent men with such remarkable mechanical aptitude, could be so utterly, socially inept.

Go figure.

When I turned left off onto Fourth Avenue, I decided to prioritize my 'to do' list on the basis of where I was, which at the moment happened to be at the north end of town. Maggie's B&B was only a block away and I could stop to get my other boxers and T-shirt, in case my next physio session went all night. Like last night. You never know.

I parked Mike's truck in the gravel lot behind the house and walked a wide circle around to the front, keeping a wary eye out for a woman in black clothes with a tattoo on her neck. Based on events last night, Sarah Marsalis might still be on the warpath. There were two ripe bruises on my shins where she'd kicked me, and as far I was concerned, two was enough.

I went in the front door, snuck up to my room, and found my underwear neatly folded on a corner of the bed. They were dry and inviting.

A glance in the bathroom mirror told me I was due for some personal maintenance. I took time for a quick hot shower which is the only place I ever shave. Before I got out, I also washed my other boxers and T-shirt with the shampoo of the day. This time it was chamomile—whatever that is. I left the damp towel in a crumpled mess on the floor. The room was paid for through tomorrow and it was my way of assuring management their room was occupied. Based on what they charged for a night, it was the most expensive shower I'd ever taken. I opened the window, hung up my wet boxers and T-shirt on hangers, and was out of there.

I never did see Sarah, which was no great surprise, notwithstanding my concerns about running into her. On reflection I realized it was unlikely she'd be hanging around her room in the middle of the day anyway, and even if she was, so what? Were I to have to seen her, I would have simply ignored her—or made a beeline for the truck at a full gallop. Still, I was curious why she was back in the Yukon. Surely it had nothing to do with me, not with the new makeover she was sporting which could hardly be construed as guy bait. And finding and locating Tommy Kay in the Yukon was the responsibility of the Canadian cops, not the Americans, and Sarah was an American cop, so that couldn't be it. It was a fair assumption she might be one of the '*out-of-towners*' whom I was to meet in Robson's office this afternoon. More cops with more questions. Maybe then I'd find out why she was back. Whatever the reason, I doubted it had anything to do with our Mexican holiday. But I was still checking over my shoulder when I got back to Mike's truck.

Damn woman.

I drove out of the lot and decided my next stop was that stockbroker I met yesterday. Dave. Dave aka Clark Kent. Dave aka drunk Clark Kent. I hoped he'd made it into work.

The specter of easy money has always made me nervous. I'd been fretting about the five grand I'd parted with yesterday to buy something I knew nothing about, and wanted out. Sell my shares, get my money back, and close my account. I'd got this far investing in myself and intended to stick with the strategy. Never again would I make an impulsive investment.

On the three block trip over to Dave's office, I called the Café. She sang it like a chorus line.

"Minto Café!"

"Minnie, you call?"

"Brody! How's Jack?"

"He's fine, but..."

"But what?"

I figured everyone would know soon enough and it was as good a time as any to tell her the bad news.

After a long deep breath, I said, "They had to remove his leg, Minnie, to get rid of the infection."

A pregnant pause, then, "Oh, no. I'm real sorry to hear that, Brody. Poor Jack. That's just terrible. Everyone here is wondering who shot him."

"I am too. Probably something to do with that girl who was murdered."

"Right," she said.

That girl who was murdered.

We let that float between us for a moment while I drove slowly down Second Avenue, the only vehicle travelling north. I passed an RCMP cruiser waiting to pull out from a side street. Seconds later it was on my bumper with every blue light flashing.

Me?

I was less than a block from Dave's office and pulled into an angled parking spot. The cruiser stopped behind me.

With an eye on the cop in the rearview mirror, I said, "So Minnie, you called?"

"Damn right I did. There's some woman who keeps calling here for you. She's a real pest and it's getting tiresome."

"What woman?"

"Don't know. Leah says she called here twice yesterday and three times the day before. And she just called me for the second time this morning. I think she said her name is Ellen. You need to tell her to stop calling the Café or next time I'll give her your cell number, and I know you don't want me to do that."

"No, I definitely don't want you to do that. What's her number?"

"Hang on, got it here somewhere."

A knuckle rapped on my window. I held a finger up to the uniform at my door. A plethora of background noises were in my ear—people talking, plates clattering, a phone ringing, a cash register closing. There was another rap on the window, this one harder. I looked to my left and caught a fierce glare from a female officer.

"I gotta go, Minnie. If that woman calls again, tell her to call the shop. I'll be home Saturday."

I closed my phone and hit the window button. Of course the window didn't work so I cracked open the door. The cop stepped to the side and I opened it all the way.

"What can I do for you, officer?"

"Licence, registration and proof of insurance, sir."

She was a sturdy specimen, thick through the middle, late twenties, maybe five-eight with a broad flat face and the dead pan stare of a cop. Her bulky nylon coat was unzipped to reveal a Kevlar vest. The name tag on her lapel said 'E. Saunders'. She had a whole bunch of cop equipment dangling from her big brown belt—gun, handcuffs, pepper spray, taser, flashlight, nightstick, keys, radio—and that was just the front. You could hang a campstove, a few pots and pans, and a step ladder on the back when she wasn't looking, and I doubt if she'd notice.

"What's this about?" I asked, digging out my wallet.

"Use of a hand held cellular phone while operating a motor vehicle."

"Is that illegal?"

"Very."

"Huh, didn't know that."

"Now you do. Documents, sir."

"How do you know I was using a cell phone?"

"Because you drove right by me holding one to your ear."

"Maybe I was using it to scratch my neck."

"And talking to yourself while you were scratching?"

I found Mike's registration and insurance docs in a dusty envelope in the glove box. It was a good five minutes before she returned.

With a ticket.

"Two hundred and fifty dollars!"

"That's right, sir. Distracted driving is a serious violation. It's a major cause of accidents and injury."

"Wow. Next thing you know they'll ban two way radios in planes and cop cars."

"You have a good day, sir. And put away the phone when you're driving."

She started toward her car and I said, "Hey, officer?"

She turned and said, "Yes, sir."

"Your first name's not Ellen by any chance?"

"Why?"

"Just wondering. Hey, did you find Tommy Kay?"

"Who's Tommy Kay?"

"A murderer. But don't worry about it. Probably above your pay grade."

She stiffened and glared, poised to take a step toward me. While she was thinking about it, I jumped out of the truck and hightailed it to the sidewalk. And didn't dare look back.

* * *

What else could go wrong?

In the last four days someone had set a fire in the village, my plane had been sabotaged, my dog shot, and a woman murdered at my cabin. I'd been assaulted and injured, ripped off by a tire shop, besmirched by a reporter, and kicked in the shins by an ex-lover. And everywhere I went there was a cop in my face.

Just before noon I opened the door to the cubby hole for an office of Trans-Pacific Securities, and almost tripped over a pair of legs belonging to the same old timer sitting in the same chair as yesterday.

"Sorry," I said.

He lowered his newspaper, inspected his feet, and looked up at me with a crooked smile.

"No harm, no foul," he said with a chuckle.

Dave Sorenson had survived the night and was sitting at his desk. He motioned me into his office with a weak wave. With my back pressed against the wall, I sidestepped over a second set of legs belonging to the same old timer who'd been sitting in the other chair yesterday.

I was about to enter Dave's office when a voice behind me croaked, "Say Mister, is this you?"

The old fellow nearest the door was holding up his newspaper, pointing at the front page.

"Yes, sir," I said. "You showed me that picture yesterday. I told you it was me."

"But this here's today's paper."

THIRTY NINE

I reached out and snatched it from his hands.

It was me alright, pictured dead center on the front page of today's morning paper.

Come on. Again?

The photo was sprawled across the top of the page and showed me standing over the man who'd attacked me yesterday. I remembered when it was taken. I'd been nudging the guy with the toe of my boot, seeing if he was alive. But the picture told a different story. With the way I was leaning back on one leg, and with the other leg extended straight out, it looked like I was delivering a good kick to the ribs of a helpless man on the ground.

Terrific.

Of course I knew who had taken the picture, it had to be that chubby jogger with the cell phone. And now, after reading the headline, I knew her name.

Ellen Burke.

MURDER SUSPECT ASSAULTS JOGGER
Special to the Yukon Times
By Ellen Burke

The prime suspect for the murder of a woman in Minto this week is now also suspected of committing a serious assault in Whitehorse yesterday.

According to an RCMP police spokesperson, Lance Corporal Aaron Vanderbilt, a 29 year old U.S. Marine Raider currently stationed in Camp LeJeune, North Carolina, was jogging at the north end of the Whitehorse Waterfront Path yesterday morning when he was clubbed over the head with a tree branch, and sustained a serious head injury.

This reporter arrived at the scene seconds after Vanderbilt had been assaulted, and photographed C.E. Brody of Minto kicking the injured man as he lay unconscious on the path. Mr. Brody then fled the scene, leaving the man lying where he was, without calling for help.

The RCMP has confirmed that Lance Corporal Vanderbilt is the brother of the late Amy Vanderbilt of Haines, Alaska, a 26 year old woman found murdered last Monday at Brody's home in Minto.

Police say Lance Corporal Vanderbilt arrived in Whitehorse on Tuesday to accompany the body of his deceased sister back to their parents' home in Raleigh, North Carolina. After this reporter called 911, Mr. Vanderbilt was immediately taken to Whitehorse General Hospital by ambulance, where he is currently listed in fair condition.

No charges have been laid for the murder of Amy Vanderbilt on Monday, or the attack yesterday on her brother, or the murder of a man in Dawson last weekend. An RCMP spokesperson said it is too early to tell if the three crimes are connected. The spokesperson said a team of detectives is aggressively working on a number of

leads in their investigation of all three
crimes, and are asking the public for its
assistance. Anyone with information on
any of these crimes is asked to call the
RCMP in Whitehorse.

Mr. Brody was questioned by police
yesterday afternoon but was released
without charges being laid. He could not
be reached for comment. It remains unclear
what personal relationship he may have
had with any of the victims. The RCMP
said he has been ordered not to leave
the Yukon, pending completion of their
investigations.

I was dumbfounded, gawking at the paper in my hands, hardly
believing what I'd just read.

"Ellen Burke," said a voice.

"Huh?"

Dave Sorenson was standing behind me, reading over my
shoulder. I could smell the hangover on his breath.

"Ellen Burke. She's a total witch," he said.

"You know her?"

"Unfortunately. Went to high school with her right here in town.
The guys in our graduating class voted her least likely to get laid at
the prom. She's the most obnoxious person I've ever met. Probably
on account of her face."

Dave went back to his desk.

"Her face?"

"We used to call her the halibut."

"The halibut."

"Yeah, her eyes aren't in the middle of her face. They're like...
off center."

"I don't get it. Halibut?"

"A halibut, like the fish, right? When it's little, its eyes are on
either side of its head like a normal fish. But as it grows, one of its

eyes migrates over the top of its nose to join the other one. Then it can swim on its side along the bottom and look up with both eyes. Know what I mean?"

"You're saying Ellen's eyes are on one side of her head?"

"Well, kind of, yeah. Anyway, she's totally butt ugly. And I wouldn't worry about anything she wrote about you. She's mean and full of shit and everyone knows it. You could be in Hawaii when there was a hit and run in Whitehorse, and she'd put you behind the wheel. Both her parents were lawyers so she must get it from them. So what brings you in, Mr. Brody?"

"Say Mister, can I have my paper back?"

The old-timer had his hand out.

"Of course, sir, thank you."

I handed him his paper.

"So is it you?" he asked, tapping the front page with a crooked finger.

"Yeah, it's me."

"Huh," he said.

* * *

"I want to sell my stock, Dave."

"Sell it? You just bought it. And doubled your money in a day, case you didn't know."

"It doubled? In a day?"

"Yup. Your timing was perfect. You bought it yesterday at thirteen cents and now it's twenty-six cents. Pretty good return so far, I'd say."

"Yeah, I'd say so, too. But I still want to sell it."

"I wouldn't advise you do that, not now anyway. It's too soon. It's up to you of course, but this thing is just starting. Why not think about it? Wait a week or so."

"No, Dave, I want to sell now. Easy money makes me nervous."

"Spends the same as the hard earned kind."

"I know, but it still makes me nervous. I don't have a clue about this Thistle Creek deal, let alone the mining business."

Dave pursed his lips and said, "You know Mike Giguere, right?"

"Yeah, so?"

"Well why not talk to him first? He's the guy who knows what's going on, he'll give you the real story, not like the company president I talked to yesterday. I learned absolutely nothing from her, by the way. But Mike's the guy in the know and he can be trusted. Why not talk to him before you sell?"

"Did you say 'her'?"

"Yeah, some woman named Lynn Chan is the president of Thistle Creek Resources. I called her about their press release. She kept me on hold for five minutes, then all she gave me was some spiel. She sounded bored, talked like she was reading from a script. I doubt if she has a clue about the exploration business, let alone their project up here." He smiled and said, "But she did invite me to a party."

"A party."

"Yup. Thistle Creek Resources is having a big bash for brokers in Dawson. I think she said it was in a couple of weeks. It'll be another one of those deals with wild women, free booze, a trip to the property, and a whole bunch of bullshit with no real information. She put me on the guest list but I probably won't go. Those things are a waste of time. Been there, done it. But if you can track down Mike, well now he's the man to talk to, he'll give you the lowdown on the project. Think you'll be seeing him soon?"

"As a matter of fact, I'll be seeing him tomorrow."

"Well, there you go. He's a hard guy to pin down these days, came and left this morning like the building was on fire. When you see him, ask him everything you can about his Thistle Creek project, then decide if you should sell your stock. He might just change your mind. And could you ask him to give me a call?"

I nodded and thought about Lynn Chan.

Chan was the president?

"Okay, I'll ask him to give you a call."

Dave Sorenson was one smooth talker and a hell of a salesman. For the second day in a row he'd convinced me to do something against my better judgement. When I walked out of his office, I was still a shareholder in Thistle Creek Resources.

I sidestepped over four legs and made it past the old guys without tripping or knocking the television off the wall. When I reached the door, the one in the far corner cleared his throat and asked, "Sir, is this really you?"

Both men lowered their papers to their laps and leaned forward with their mouths open, awaiting the moment of truth.

I turned and said, "Yes, sir, it's really me."

"Huh," they said in unison, eyeing each other as I walked out.

FORTY

Lynn Chan was pacing, waiting for the elevator, holding her phone to her ear.

She was about to hang up when he answered on the fifth ring.

"Hello...Lynn."

He'd almost said 'baby' but caught himself.

"Tippy, what the hell are you doing? Why did I just get a pile of documents for a financing? I don't recall approving a financing, we don't need a financing, and we're not doing a financing. Any questions?"

Tippy let out a long slow breath.

"Lynn, it's something we have to do. You want this to work, don't you? We're about to make a lot of money. But it won't happen without the brokers. The brokers have the buyers and this financing will put stock in their hands." Tippy paused to let her absorb that, then said, "Look, it's all very simple. The brokers give us cash, we give them stock, they promote the stock, we sell our stock. It's how we make our money. I've done this before, Lynn, it's how the game is played. Now please, just sign the papers."

"And what if I don't, Tippy? Then what?"

Then what? You stupid bitch, you disappear, that's what. You go up in smoke...you...

Tippy took a deep breath. He knew an angry man was an ineffective one, but it was all he could do to control his temper.

"Lynn...please. Think about what I said. We absolutely have to do this financing. Now sign the papers and send them to the lawyers. Right now, okay? And you have a party in Dawson to organize. We can talk about that tonight. I'll call you later."

He hung up on her.

You arrogant bastard! Hang up on me?

Lynn was fuming when the elevator doors opened. She waved a fob at a keypad, entered a code, and pressed the penthouse button. Two minutes later she walked into her suite, slammed the door, kicked off her shoes, and glared up at the ceiling.

That thing is out of here.

* * *

Four blocks west of Trans-Pacific, a few minutes before one, I was lying low in one of the numerous niche restaurants in Whitehorse. This one had four tables crammed into a tiny alcove at the back of a health food store.

The Green Planet Café is a great place to eat lunch if you're not hungry, which was probably the best explanation why I was the only one in the place. The fare is, you guessed it, entirely organic and strictly vegan—salads and soups, gluten-free breads, and a variety of green teas and fair trade coffee—all served at outrageous prices with none of it that'll stick to your ribs.

I picked a table where I could keep an eye on the front door. It was fifty feet away at the end of a long aisle bordered with oak barrels brimming with rice, beans, and grains. Above the barrels were sagging wood shelves loaded with huge glass jars full of nuts and seeds.

A veritable bird buffet.

I was served by a pale gray woman in a long gray skirt with long gray hair. She was skinnier than a rake and and looked like she could use a cheeseburger and a handful of iron supplements. I declined her recommendation of the daily special—tofu stew with kale and green onions—and ordered a veggie sandwich with lots of butter. She said they didn't have butter so I went with the olive oil. I asked her if they had cheese. Sorry. She asked me what I wanted to drink and I told her a glass of organic tap water. She responded with a tiny weak smile of tiny gray teeth and shuffled off in a saffron daze.

I thought about the farmhouse breakfast I had this morning.

Jennifer would starve in here.

As happenstance would have it, she called that instant. I opened my phone and noted the battery was low. Again.

"Hello?"

"Brody?"

No *'Hey, guess what?'*

"Hey, Jennifer."

Silence.

"Hello? Jennifer? You there?"

"Brody, have you seen today's paper?"

"Yes, and it's bullshit."

"It's not true? You didn't beat up that guy on the path?"

"No, I did not beat up that guy on the path."

"But there's a picture of you kicking him."

"I wasn't kicking him. I was nudging him with the toe of my boot."

"Why didn't you call for help?"

I rubbed my forehead and exhaled with exasperation.

"Look, Jennifer, there's a very good explanation for everything. But all you need to know is I didn't attack the guy. In fact, he attacked me."

"He attacked you? Is that how you hurt your arm?"

"Yes."

"Oh."

Another long silence.

Then she said, "Look, I really don't know what's going on, or how to say this, but I don't think it's a good idea for you stay here tonight. I'm really sorry, Brody, but the cops came by about an hour ago and told me I shouldn't let you sleep here."

"The cops came by again?"

"Yes. That cop that was here yesterday? Well he just left. He asked me a lot of questions about what you'd been up to lately. Then he asked me if you'd been staying here at night and I said yes and he said that wasn't a good idea."

Monahan. The moron who'd been casing me at Dorval's clinic. The one I'd embarrassed in front of Robson.

"He's probably right, Jennifer, maybe it's not such a good idea."

"Is there somewhere else you can stay?"

"I guess."

Like the B & B. The proverbial frying pan to the fire.

"Great, maybe we can still get together this evening, you know, go out for something to eat, then work on your shoulder some more."

"Well..."

* * *

Lynn Chan was feeling a lot better.

She'd showered and shampooed and the stench from Earl was down the drain. She put on a pair of skinny jeans with lots of bling on the butt, a tight sleeveless blouse, and a pair of brand new heels.

Always heels for business.

Jeremy had called and said the guy from the security company would arrive at one, the locksmith at two. That gave her time to call California for a weekly update on her massage business. At least that was going well.

Last week's net was a little over fifty thousand, not a bad living for a single gal, she thought. The man she'd spoken to said they were low on girls or the number could be higher. He told Lynn he knew where he could get some fresh young ones, right off the boat, for five thousand a piece. She told him she'd think about it. Keeping girls was always the problem, the way they ran off.

When Lynn opened her front door, the guy from Stealth

Solutions & Security was holding a finger to his lips. He turned and beckoned her to follow him. They walked to the end of the hallway where he pointed at something high on the wall.

"It's not transmitting anymore but there's a camera in that thing up there," he whispered. "You've been under surveillance."

Lynn felt a sickening thud in her gut and her legs went rubbery. She gawked up at the thing, breathless.

Under surveillance?

It didn't look like a camera, more like a smoke detector with two tiny holes, one pointing at the elevator behind them, the other at the door to her suite at the other end of the hall. The guy unfolded a short aluminum ladder, stepped up, and pried the device off with a scraper. He scanned it with what looked like a small black cell phone with an aerial.

"Dead as a doornail," he said, popping the back off with a screwdriver and removing a couple of batteries. "This one's a cheap unit, a peel n' stick, transmits to a phone, uses batteries so it has a limited run time. It might have worked for a week or so. Whoever put it up there didn't need it for long."

"How long has it been there?" whispered Lynn.

"No way to know but at least it's not transmitting anymore. No audio in it either, always good to know."

The guy was speaking in a normal tone of voice again. He had a mischievous grin, like a kid with a secret, just having a great old time while his client was on pins and needles. He was young, probably had never shaved in his life, and looked fresh out of high school.

"But who...?" Lynn said, and didn't finish her question. The kid would have no idea.

"Always the first thing people ask. Seems everyone likes to watch everyone else these days. RF cameras are cheap and available everywhere."

"RF?"

"Radio Frequency. The radio signal from this camera was transmitting straight to a phone, but the better ones transmit to a receiver in a DVR or computer and the images are sent out over the internet. You can buy an RF camera on EBay for fifty bucks and watch anyone from anywhere in the world, anytime you want."

Lynn thought about that and nodded, still stunned.

"Can you check out my suite?"

"Sure thing," said the kid. He pulled the hood of his sweatshirt over his head and arranged it into a narrow snorkel around his face. Then he put on a pair of bugeye sunglasses. "Don't like my face to show when I'm looking into surveillance cameras," he said with another grin. "Wait here. Back in five."

He trundled down the hallway with his bag and the ladder, and the little black thing with the aerial, and disappeared into Lynn's suite.

* * *

Lynn had been stewing and pacing for all of five minutes when the door to her suite finally opened and the kid waved at her.

"Okay," he said, leading the way in, but stopping just short of the dining room table with an arm held out. "So this is a weird one. There's good news and bad news. I swept the bedrooms, bathrooms, kitchen and living areas, and did find a camera—but just the one—and it's live. Usually there's more than one, which is why it's weird. Anyway, the camera is up there in that chandelier and it's pointed directly at the desk in front of those windows. I guess whoever's spying on you is only interested in watching you when you're at your desk."

"Is that the good news or the bad news?"

The kid grinned and said, "Well, both I guess. It's bad news that you're being spied on, that's for sure, and also that the camera is wired into the power supply for the chandelier, which means it won't stop working unless you do something about it. But the good news is that the camera is transmiting to a receiver-recorder right here in your suite. I already found it, it's plugged into the back of your router."

"Why is that good news?"

"Because there's memory in it. It's got a flash drive."

"Memory? Flash drive? So what?"

"Well, you want whoever's watching you to stop watching you, right?"

"Right."

"Well you could just put a piece of tape over the camera lens. That would work but then whoever's watching you would know you'd found their camera."

"Go on."

"Well, then they'd know you were onto them, and who knows what they might do then? But there's another way to stop them from watching you. And they don't have to know about it."

"Oh, and what's that?"

"A little trick. We replace the live feed with a recording from the flash drive in the receiver. That way they'll think their camera is still working."

"You can do that?"

"Sure, it's easy. I'll use the memory stored in the flash drive to create a video loop for the last three days and broadcast that to them. That way they'll think they're watching live feed when actually all they'll be watching is a recording. Hopefully it will take them a while to catch on, if ever."

Lynn was impressed.

"So you're saying you can stop the live feed, replace it with stuff that's previously been recorded, and it will still look to live to them?"

"You got it."

"And then I can do whatever I want with my chandelier?"

The kid shrugged his shoulders.

"Why not? As soon as I do my thing, you can throw it away for all it matters, including their camera."

Lynn folded her arms and looked at him with admiration. She felt like hugging him.

"What's your name?" she asked.

"Danny."

"Okay, Danny. Do it."

FORTY ONE

Time flies in a library so that's where I went.

I'd been sitting in the Green Planet Café sipping tap water and burping bean sprouts when a bunch of young women walked in. Each was holding a suckling baby to a breast and I was more than happy to yield my table to the local chapter of the La Leche League.

While there were plenty of ways to kill an hour before my appointment with the cops, I'd gotten a compulsive urge to a little research. On the second floor of a new and airy two story building, I asked a young woman where I could find information on Yukon churches. She'd given me a knowing look and directed me to a large table with a great view of the Yukon River. She disappeared but soon returned with a cart heaped with books and pamphlets. In no time I knew why Minnie didn't want to talk about an old burned down church in Minto.

The reading was compelling and it was only pure luck that I happened to look up and check the time when I did. I left the library with three books due in five weeks, and while keeping a wary eye out for Tommy Kay on the way over, walked into the RCMP building at exactly one minute before three.

Right on time.

Ninja secretary greeted me on the third floor with her hands on

her hips and a fierce scowl. Today she was wearing a bright red
dress with a spider web pattern.

Spider-Woman Secretary.

She muttered something about the time of day and led me down
the hall to Robson's conference room. It was standing room only
inside.

The table in Staff Sergeant Robson's boardroom was packed
with cops—eight of them in all—sitting shoulder to shoulder, all
casting somber stares my way. I stopped behind the only vacant
chair, my usual one at the end of table, lowered what was now a
heavy backpack to the floor, and still on my feet, rested my hands
on the backrest.

"I guess you're wondering why I called you in here today," I
said with a stern look.

No response. No sense of humor. Cops.

The same five cops were there as yesterday, with Robson planted
in his usual spot at the other end of the table. Staff Sergeant Daniel
Munroe sat in the chair immediately to his left, with Constable
Monahan and his two buddies on the opposite side. On Munroe's
left was a tall skinny guy I'd never seen before, then an FBI guy
I knew, then the one and only Sarah Marsalis. The new guy was
about forty and looked too genteel to be a cop. He was pale and
frail, fortyish, immaculately dressed in a dark suit, crisp white
shirt, and a red silk tie. He had wire frame glasses and a little
goatee—and a shiny bald head full of hair plugs. Reminded me of
the cheap landscaping they put on highway medians.

Chia Pet.

I looked at all the faces sizing me up from both sides of the
table, then met Robson's glare.

"Well? Did you find him?" I asked.

"You're late!" he bellowed. "Now shut up and sit down!"

I looked at the clock on the wall.

"Late? You call four minutes *late*? Come on, Staff Sergeant,
this is the Yukon. Four minutes is not *late*."

"I said sit down, Mr. Brody!"

"Not beside her," I said, pointing at Sarah who was seated in the chair to my right.

"You have a problem sitting beside Special Agent Marsalis?" he asked in a sarcastic tone.

"Yeah, she kicks."

Sarah Marsalis—aka Rita Sorano, aka president of the Lisbeth Salander fan club—had her arms folded and was glowering at me with a clenched jaw. She still had the tattoos, the racoon makeup, the black T-shirt and jeans, but was lighter by a few piercings today. I couldn't see her feet so didn't know if she was wearing those evil pointed boots, but wasn't about to take any chances. I didn't want to be near her, even if she was still the best looking cop I've ever laid eyes on.

On her right sat the only cop I've ever liked from the get-go. Special Agent David Owen of the FBI was wearing an open collar white shirt, a navy blue blazer, and a big grin. He rolled back his chair, stood and leaned toward me with his hand out.

We shook hands with my elbow in Sarah's face.

"Mr. Brody, good to see you again," he said with a broad smile.

"Special Agent," I said.

"Actually, these days it's Special Agent in Charge, but please call me David."

"In charge, huh? What did they put you in charge of, David?"

With genuine humility he said, "Oh, you know, just a bunch more cop stuff."

"Might have guessed."

Owen tapped Sarah on the shoulder, smiled at her, and they switched chairs. She was seething about the move, but orders were orders. She glowered at me.

"Happy now, Mr. Brody?"

Robson again. The dark cloud in the room.

"Me? Happy? Always. Hey, can you fix a ticket for me?"

"No, I cannot fix a ticket for you. Now sit down or I'll cuff you down," he said with menace rising in his voice.

"Wait, gotta check something first."

I dropped to a knee and ducked my head under the table, then got up and brushed a bunch of invisible dirt off my jeans.

"What the hell was that about?" yelled Robson.

His face was turning a nice shade of red.

"Oh, just making sure Tommy Kay wasn't hiding under the table, case you guys hadn't checked there. But he's got to be in here somewhere, right? It's the only place you guys seem to be looking for him."

Shouldn't have said it. Robson stood up. Monahan did too. So did Owen who raised a hand at Robson. Monahan looked at Robson. Owen leaned toward me.

With a nod and a wink he whispered, "Best sit down, Mr. Brody."

I did. Robson waved Monahan to sit down. He did. Robson sat down and so did Owen. Things were quiet for a moment. Every eye in the room was flitting back and forth from me to Robson.

Robson gathered himself and finally broke the silence with, "One more smart ass stunt out of you and we'll finish this downstairs. We'll put you in a cage and our special guests can ask their questions through bars."

"And I won't answer them. You lock me up and I'm not talking to anybody, and that includes *special guests*."

"Excuse me?"

"You heard me. Lock me up and I'm not talking to anyone. I've had it with your threats, Staff Sergeant. My dog's been shot, my plane's been vandalized, I've been attacked by a stranger, a woman was murdered at my home, and all you do is call meetings. I'm front and center on the first page of the paper because you can't find the man responsible for this fiasco. So ask your questions here and now if you want answers. And make it fast, I've got better things to do than talk to a bunch of feckless cops."

No one pulled a gun but I'm sure Robson felt like it. He definitely won the staring contest and my eyes drifted to Sarah and Owen. She had her head in her hands and was rubbing her temples with her thumbs. Owen had his hands clasped together on the table in front of him, studying his fingers like he'd never seen them before. You could hear a pin drop until Robson rose to his feet again.

"He's all yours," he growled.

Robson jutted his chin at the three uniforms and they followed him into his office with their belts and holsters creaking and squeaking. The last one in line closed the door behind them.

* * *

Empty chairs were rolled away and everyone but me moved for some more elbow room. Landry moved to the other side of the table. Staff Sergeant Munroe took Robson's chair. Evidently he was now in charge.

"This shouldn't take long," said Munroe, "provided of course that everyone remains civilized." He gave me a stern look and continued. "Mr. Brody, we appreciate you coming in. I believe you already know Special Agent Marsalis and Special Agent in Charge Owen. On my right is Mr. Eric Landry, Executive Director of Compliance for the British Columbia Securities Commission. Mr. Landry and the BCSC are working together with the FBI and the RCMP on a joint US-Canada task force. All three agencies are investigating the criminal activities of two individuals, a man named Cheng Li, better known as Tippy Li, and his partner, a woman named Lynn Chan. As I alluded to a few days ago in Minto, Li and Chan are the promoters of a dubious exploration project run by a company called Thistle Creek Resources, a company which you are already familiar with.

"But Li and Chan are also complicit in other far more nefarious endeavors, including money laundering, human trafficking, smuggling, narcotics, and last but not least, murder. These two are as bad as they get, they belong behind bars, and that's our mission. It's why we're here."

"Excuse me, it's not why I'm here," I said.

"Actually, we were hoping you might be interested in...assisting us in their apprehension."

"Assist you? Why the hell would I do that? You told me Monday that testifying against Li is a death sentence. Thanks but no thanks. Now can I go?"

Munroe looked at David Owen, then at Sarah Marsalis, then at Eric Landry. There were subtle nods and winks all round.

Munroe spoke again.

"Why not hear us out, Mr. Brody? It won't take a minute. If you're not interested, fine, you'll be free to go. But I think it will be worth your while to listen to what we have to say."

I leaned back, folded my arms, and wondered how that could be so.

What do they say about curiosity?

"Okay," I said. "I'll listen. But only for a minute."

FORTY TWO

"Did you know there are only three Northern White Rhinos left on the planet?"

"I did not," I said to Special Agent in Charge, David Owen.

"Sad but true," he said, leaning back in his chair, apparently in no hurry. "It's a disgusting and dire situation. A great animal like that, been around for seven million years and in the span of a century we wipe it off the face of the earth. All because some people think rhino horn can cure a fever."

"That *is* disgusting," I said, wondering where Owen was going.

He sighed, paused a moment, then carried on.

"You know, a few years ago when the White Rhino was getting scarce in the wild, and the price of its horns reached twenty-five thousand dollars a pound, some asshole actually broke into a French zoo and shot one in its cage. Can you believe that?"

I had no idea what Owen was talking about and didn't answer his question. He had my attention though. Owen certainly knew how to control a meeting. The room was dead quiet and I could hear street traffic below us.

"Elephants," he said.

"Elephants," I said.

"A hundred years ago there were four or five million of them roaming the planet, now there are only four hundred thousand left."

"Okay..."

Owen had a hard look in his eyes, a look I'd seen a year ago when he was talking about something else.

"Know why?" he asked.

"Killed for their tusks?"

"Massacred is more like it. We're talking about millions of animals, Mr. Brody. Millions and millions of magnificent animals killed for ivory. And unfortunately the killing continues, as senseless as it is, and these days it's more ruthless and barbaric than ever. Elephants are now hunted at night from helicopters. The poachers have night vision scopes and shoot them from the air. They land, saw off their tusks, and in minutes are gone with the bounty. Often they leave an animal that's still alive to die in agony—no point in drawing more attention to yourself with a kill shot. It's the ultimate smash and grab, very lucrative, fast and easy. A pair of tusks can easily fetch a hundred grand. Most of them are shipped to China where carvers eagerly await more raw material. Obviously a lot of people still covet what they produce, trinkets and ornaments and sculptures for bedrooms and living rooms and offices. It's not something I'll ever understand. If you ask me, anything made from ivory is just a sick animal trophy."

"All animal trophies are sick," I said.

Owen nodded in apparent agreement and held my gaze for a moment. With his sharp calm eyes and a confidence that comes from know-how, he reminded me of a pilot I know in Dawson.

"Ever heard of fentanyl?"

"Yeah, it's a drug, right?"

"That's right, a narcotic, like heroin. Only fentanyl is a synthetic drug, cheap to manufacture in a lab and a lot more potent. Almost fifty times more potent. Which is the problem. Because fentanyl provides a lot more bang for the buck, heroin dealers mix it into their street product for bigger profits. But unlike heroin, a small overdose of fentanyl can be deadly. Two years ago in North America, twenty-five thousand people died from a fentanyl overdose. This year we expect the number to climb to over forty thousand."

"Hey, David?"

"Yes, Mr. Brody."

"Your minute is up."

He managed a weak smile and said, "Sorry, I do get carried away. I could go on and on, but I won't tell you about the trade in pangolins, another sick enterprise. Maybe some other time. So here's the deal..."

"Pangolins. What are pangolins?"

"They're like an anteater with big bony scales, about the size of a cat, and live in Africa and India. Currently they're the most trafficked animal in the world and Li's right in the middle of that wretched business too. But let's move on. The atrocities I've just described—killing rhinos and elephants for their horns and tusks, and pangolins for their scales—and selling fentanyl to heroin addicts, are only a few of the illegal enterprises commanded by Tippy Li. But what distinguishes these crimes from most is that they all carry a heavy cost for society, be it death or misery for thousands of people, or the eradication of animal species. Li's evil activities affect everyone in this world and it's why he needs to be put away."

"So why don't you?"

"Good question. We could arrest and charge him for all kinds of things, but at this point it would be a waste of time. We simply don't have the watertight evidence required for a conviction. Mr. Li is a very clever operator and knows how to keep his hands clean. With just a nod and a wink, he has other people do his dirty work."

"Is he here in the Yukon?"

"No."

"So why are you here?"

"Another good question, Mr. Brody,"

"Thanks. Now what's the answer?"

Owen hesitated and turned to Munroe. Munroe gave him a nod of approval.

"We're here to gather evidence."

"What kind of evidence?"

"Evidence as relates to a mining scam."

"A mining scam."

"That's right, a mining scam."

"Dave, can we just cut to the chase?"

Owen rubbed his chin.

"Alright," he said. "Let's do that. Let's cut to the chase. We'd like to charter your plane."

"Oh yeah? Where do you want to go?"

"Back and forth from Dawson to Thistle Creek."

"Back and forth?"

"Back and forth."

* * *

At the other end of the table, Staff Sergeant Daniel Munroe cleared his throat.

"Every single criminal, no matter how cunning or careful he or she may be, has at least one weakness to exploit," he said. "In the case of Mr. Li, that weakness is gambling. His favorite game is betting on gold exploration projects, and he always wins. He wins because he bets solely on his own deals and he wins because he cheats. Right now he's promoting a new scam called Thistle Creek Resources."

"Thistle Creek Resources is a scam?"

"Judging by every promotion Li's run in the past, and the press release that came out yesterday, yes, it's almost a certainty," said Munroe.

"You can tell he's cheating from a press release?"

Munroe looked to his right and said, "Mr. Landry?"

Eric Landry was evidently caught off guard and shuffled some papers to buy time. I looked at Sarah. She still had her arms folded and knew damn well I was looking at her, but chose to ignore me by gazing out a window. I supposed she'd heard it all before and was as eager to get out of there as I was. Unlike her, though, I didn't have a clue what these cops were up to, or why they 'needed' to charter my plane.

Now that, I wanted to know.

"Ever heard of a company called Bre-X?" asked Landry.

His baritone voice boomed off the walls and I almost jumped out of my chair. The guy had pipes like a ringmaster.

"Bre-X? Ah, no, I haven't," I said.

"The biggest fraud in mining history. In 1993 an Indonesian geologist assembled a land package in Borneo to explore for gold. He brought the deal to a Canadian promoter for financing. A penny stock called Bre-X was formed and its shares were listed on an over-the-counter stock exchange in Alberta, Canada. When drilling started in 1994, Bre-X stock was trading at ten cents a share. Two years later Bre-X was a six billion dollar company, listed on the Toronto and NASDAQ exchanges, and trading over two hundred dollars a share. Estimates that their Borneo property hosted as much as two hundred million ounces had all the big mining companies in a bidding frenzy for control of the greatest gold discovery in history. Every mutual fund had to own Bre-X. The Government of Indonesia wanted a piece of the action. Lehman Brothers and JP Morgan were clamoring to finance the world's newest mega mine.

"But then one of the big mining companies decided to check out what they were bargaining for. They went over to Indonesia and drilled some of their own holes. And guess what?"

"What?"

"No gold. Nothing. Nada."

"Nothing? How could that be?"

"That was everyone's question as they watched Bre-X stock crash back to a dime, then disappear forever. The whole world had been duped out of billions of dollars while Bre-X insiders made a cool hundred million. Yet not a single fraud conviction was ever won for the biggest ripoff in mining history."

I now had a sense what the meeting was about but was so damn interested in Landry's story, wanted to know more.

"How come?" I asked.

"There are plenty of books and movies about Bre-X, each offering its own version of events, including the usual set of convoluted conspiracy theories. In the end, though, the most plausible explanation is the simplest one: the con was due solely to the devious work of one man, and one man only."

"One man? And who was that?"

"The Indonesian geologist who'd brought the deal to Bre-X. He'd been given unfettered control over its exploration program and he took full advantage. For two years, without any oversight whatsoever, he was able to salt the drill samples before they were shipped for assaying. It's well established that he started with shavings from his own wedding ring, and when that was gone, proceeded to use gold he'd buy from local hand miners. So one man was able to con thousands of investors out of billions of dollars, simply by sprinkling gold dust on samples."

"So why wasn't he charged and convicted?"

Landry flashed a wry smile.

"He killed himself, just after his scam was revealed. He jumped out of a helicopter over a Borneo jungle."

I leaned back in my chair and said, "That's a hell of a story."

"A true one," said Landry.

"So to answer my question, how can you tell if someone is running a scam just by reading a press release?"

"We start with the good old sniff test. We ask ourselves if the assays are too good to be true. Everyone knows that gold is rare, but most people don't appreciate how rare. Mother Nature is very stingy in how she distributes it, and so it doesn't matter where in the world you look, gold is generally found in such low concentrations it can rarely be seen with the naked eye. So if you're lucky enough to find it, even at a grade of just a gram a ton, you might just have found yourself a mine. Think about it, that's all you need, one gram of gold per ton, one part in a million, like a drop of water in a bathtub. Anyway, when we read the press release Thistle Creek put out yesterday, and the incredible results they're announcing, well we certainly have our reasons to be suspicious. The grades are simply too high, and so are the intervals."

"Intervals?"

"The lengths of the areas tested that purportedly contain gold. It's one thing to encounter high grades over a few feet of a test area, but over a half mile? Possible of course, but not likely."

"So you think the Thistle Creek samples are being salted."

"Possibly. At this point we can't be sure why the reported grades are so high, not until we complete our investigations. Which is why we're here. There are other ways to falsify assays besides salting samples in the field and we're looking at all of them."

"What are the other ways?"

"Well, one other way—and the easiest one—is simply to lie. Draft a press release out of thin air and concoct the numbers. But without any documentation to back them up, or a geologist to sign off on them, that ruse is easy to expose and prosecute. Then there's..."

Landry hesitated. He looked at Owen. Owen nodded.

"What?" I said.

"Infiltrate the assay lab," said Landry. "Have someone inside the lab work the con—a lab employee who can salt the samples before they're assayed—or miscalibrate instruments used in the assay process, or falsify data like weights and volumes used in calculations."

I thought about Jennifer in her shop the other day, turning dials on some fancy instrument. Was she up to no good? It seemed hard to fathom. Jennifer seemed so natural and comfortable in her own skin. Then I thought about Mike. Was it in him to salt exploration samples? After all those years plying his trade in the Yukon wilderness? I dismissed both scenarios as implausible. Jennifer and Mike were confident and competent professionals who clearly took pride in their crafts, and besides, they both seemed to be such decent people. Cheating to make a buck wasn't in their DNA, at least I didn't think so. Then I thought about Sarah and her new 'job' at Thurson Ames. Now I knew what she was up to.

"So, Mr. Brody, about your plane," said Owen.

"What about it?"

"Well, we've done business before, last summer as you'll recall."

"Of course I recall. You paid me but never went flying."

"Right, but this time we intend to. We'd like to charter your plane for the next two months, on a standby basis."

"Who is *we*? And standby for *who*?"

"A company called Rockhound Consulting."

"Rockhound Consulting, huh? By any chance is Rockhound Consulting affiliated with the FBI?"

Owen didn't have to answer the question. Instead he said, "You may have noticed that Special Agent Marsalis has somewhat changed her appearance."

I chuckled and looked at Sarah.

"Yeah, I did notice a change. Something with the hair, maybe. Hey Sarah, did you do something with your hair?"

She ignored me again with the same vacant stare out the window, clearly not amused, trying hard to contain herself.

Owen sensed the tension and changed the subject.

"I understand from Special Agent Marsalis that you already know she has a job at Thurson Ames. And based on what Mr. Landry explained about salting, I assume you can guess why. That knowledge, and the purpose of her work at Thurson Ames, must stay in this room. Lives will depend on it."

You mean her life will depend on it.

Owen gave me a stern look.

I could see where this was going. Do a deal with Rockhound, do a little flying, keep my mouth shut, make a little money.

But definitely not worth it. Not after what happened last year. Not with the predicament I was in now. And definitely not if it involved Sarah Marsalis.

"Look, Special Agent...."

"It's Special Agent in Charge, or SAC, but as I said before, please call me David."

I sighed and said, "Right. Sorry. David. So David, this deal with

Rockhound Consulting, does it have anything to do with Tommy Kay?"

"No."

"No? No you're not looking for him? You don't think he might turn up in the middle of this Thistle Creek thing?"

"The answer to your first question is no, we are not looking for Tommy Kay. We're after Tippy Li. The answer to your second question is we have no way of knowing when or where Kay might turn up, if ever. But our investigation has nothing to do with him and we don't expect him to walk into our arms."

"That's nuts," I said.

I leaned back in my chair and folded my arms with my eyes on Sarah. She still wouldn't look at me.

"Mr. Brody, all we're asking you to do is pick up Special Agent Marsalis when she calls and fly her to where she wants to go. Just pick her up and drop her off. That's it. Nothing more. She'll be working in Dawson and will want to fly to Thistle Creek occasionally, or vice versa. I don't expect there will be many flights, and you won't have to leave the territory. Finding Kay in the Yukon is the responsibility of the RCMP, not of this task force. Kay has absolutely nothing to do with our investigation, or any business we happen to do with you."

I leaned forward and put my hands on the table.

"Come on, *David*. You know damn well Kay's out to get me, and maybe her too." I pointed at Sarah and said, "Last year she looked the guy right in the eyes and threatened to shoot him. Kay knows my plane, and disguise or no disguise, if he sees her with me, he'll know who she is. Then we're both dead. Find yourself another pilot."

I was almost to my feet when a hand went up.

"This meeting's not over, Mr. Brody," said Staff Sergeant Munroe. "I'll let you know when it is. Please sit down."

Please.

The good cop.

I huffed loud enough to let everyone know I wasn't happy,

but sat down anyway. Whatever these cops were selling, I wasn't buying. I'd had it with their skulduggery. Been there, done that, and it had almost got me killed last year. There were other planes and pilots who could fly Sarah around. This was a sucker bet. These cops didn't want me for my plane, they wanted bait to catch Kay.

And I was the bait.

Screw you. No thanks.

I was fuming when Owen reached down to the floor and picked up his briefcase. He placed it in his lap, dug around inside, and pulled out a three page document. He held it up, gave it a once over, then with great ceremony placed it on the table in front of him.

"This is the contract we're proposing," he said, tapping it with a finger. "I'd appreciate you giving it a quick read, before you make your final decision."

Owen slid it in front of me. We stared at each other for a moment. I blinked first. I scanned the first page, turned to the second one, and put a finger on a number halfway down. I spun the document around and shoved it back under his nose.

"Is this right?" I asked.

"Yes," said Owen.

"You sure?"

"I'm sure."

"I think you can do better than that."

FORTY THREE

I left the RCMP building with four things I didn't have when I walked in.

A contract, a satellite phone, a serious case of anxiety, and a check for twenty-five grand.

Twenty-five thousand dollars.

I needed my head read. What is it about money? I didn't do the deal to help people, or to save rhinos or elephants, or to rub shoulders with Sarah Marsalis again.

Pure and simple, I did it for the money.

Rockhound Consulting—for all intents and purposes the FBI— had just hired me to fly one of their employees around the Yukon. The contract called for seventy-five hours of flying time. As if that was going to happen.

The time I would actually spend flying Sarah Marsalis back and forth from Dawson to Thistle Creek might amount to ten hours, and even that would be a stretch. But I convinced Owen that Tommy Kay presented a real danger to me, that he was still out there lurking in the weeds, and was hell-bent on revenge. I also made it clear that I wasn't going to risk my plane, let alone my neck, for what he was offering. After negotiating with our best poker faces, Owen finally acquiesced and agreed to overstate the hours to bump the fee. As it turned out, the amount we settled on just happened to be what

I owed on my shop. Fifty thousand dollars. Half today, the rest in two months. More or less what I needed to pay off my mortgage. What a relief that would be, to be free and clear of debt.

The question was, would I live to see the day?

According to Owen, yes.

Me? I wasn't so sure.

Hence the anxiety.

I headed to the bank to deposit my check.

* * *

"Mr. Brody!"

I was about to exit the bank and had a hand on the door. The voice came from behind, shrill and urgent, and somehow familiar. I turned around to see whose it was.

No...

My nemesis. The chubby jogger. The Halibut. Ellen Burke.

"I have nothing to say to you, leave me alone," I barked, blasting out the door, marching off to Mike's truck.

Ellen Burke accelerated past me, spun around, and stopped me dead in my tracks by shoving her phone under my chin.

We were face to face and it was damn scary.

Dave Sorenson was right. Her eyes *were* off to one side. But he never told me they couldn't focus on the same thing. Or that the rest of her face needed warranty work. Her page boy haircut framed a face made entirely from substandard parts. Of course there were the eyes, they were definitely weird, but so was everything else. Her nose was too short, her mouth too wide, one ear stuck out, and she had no chin. Her upper lip was thicker on one side than the other and didn't line up with the one underneath. She was short and wide with a flat chest and had it all stuffed into a skin-tight spandex outfit. Over that she wore a quilted ski jacket two sizes too big, fully unzipped to reveal a roll of fat encircling her waist.

Those things aside, Ellen Burke could sure talk.

"Mr. Brody, are you aware the man you attacked on the Whitehorse Walking Path has regained consciousness?"

"I didn't attack anybody."

"The police are interviewing him right now. Are you concerned?"

"Concerned about what?"

"About what he might tell them."

"No."

"Why were you in the RCMP building this afternoon?"

"They've got great coffee."

I stepped to my left and she matched it with a quick sidestep to block my escape. A couple of boy scouts stopped to watch the man in the street interview. Two more joined them. It would be a wolf pack soon.

"Were the police interrogating you about the murder of Amy Vanderbilt?" she asked.

I ignored her question and walked the other way. In an instant she caught me and was at my side. Ellen Burke was like a junkyard dog, only more aggressive—and meaner.

"Who are you?" I asked.

"Ellen Burke, freelance reporter for the Yukon Times."

"Ellen Burke, huh? Know what Ellen? You're full of shit."

"Thanks for the quote, asshole."

"It's a good one, use it. It'll be the first accurate thing you've written all week. You don't have a clue what responsible reporting is. All you do is make up stories. I'm so fed up with your bullshit I'm about to call a real reporter and give him an exclusive on the biggest story in the Yukon for years. Have a nice day."

That seemed to do the trick because she let me go. But the wheels must have been turning and ten seconds later she was at my side again.

"So what's this big story?" she asked, panting and struggling to keep up.

"As if I'd give it to you."

"Do you want money?"

"No, I don't want money. What I want is fair and honest reporting, something you're not capable of. Now for the last time, leave me alone."

I was headed the wrong way to get to Mike's truck and darted across Main Street to go back the other way, disrupting two lanes of turtle speed traffic. One driver gave me a disapproving frown when I walked in front of his car.

Ellen stayed hot on my heels.

She'd taken the bait.

"I'm listening, Mr. Brody. What do you want for your story?"

"From you, nothing. You're not getting it."

"Why not? I'm the number one crime reporter in this city. Or didn't you know?"

"Whoever gets this story will be the *new* number one."

I was striding briskly down the other sidewalk with Ellen still beside me. She was breathing heavily, having a hard time keeping up, dodging parking meters and garbage cans. When she'd finally had enough, she grabbed my right arm and yanked me to a halt. I felt a sharp pang in my shoulder.

I glared at her hand and said, "Let go. And put that damn phone away."

She did.

"So what's this story?" she asked, huffing and puffing with her hands on her hips.

Time to set the hook. I tried looking her in the eyes but it made me dizzy. I wasn't sure which one her brain was using, the one focused on my nose or the one staring at my left ear.

"It has to do with the Yukon," I said.

"The Yukon."

"And mining."

"Mining too, huh? Mining and the Yukon, now there's a scoop."

"And murder."

"Well we've had a couple of those. How are they related to mining in the Yukon?"

I needed something else. If I couldn't get her to bite then tomorrow's front page would be another disaster. Then I had a brainwave. Every reporter's dream—a conspiracy—a cloak and dagger plot that would bring powerful people to their knees. The nirvana of the press.

With as much melodrama as I could muster, I leaned in close to her face and whispered, "Those murders? They're all connected. They're part and parcel of an international conspiracy."

"Oh, an international conspiracy."

"Shhh! That's right. And it runs through the highest levels of government, all over the world, including the Yukon's."

Well at least she didn't leave. While she was considering my bullshit, I needed to come up with more fodder.

"And what other governments are in this conspiracy?" she asked.

"China, the US, Russia, lots of others too. They all want control of something here in the Yukon. And they'll stop at nothing to get it."

"And what is this *something*?"

I gazed across the street at a souvenir shop called 'Rare and Collectible', then looked around nervously and in a hushed voice said, "Ever heard of rare earths?"

"Rare earths?"

"Shhh! Yes, rare earths. Find out everything you can about them. They're critical elements used to manufacture every electronic device there is, from televisions and cell phones to satellites and missile guidance systems. There are only a few rare earth mines in the whole world. The Chinese control eighty percent of the world's supply and they want to keep it that way. But there's been a huge new discovery in the Yukon. Right now everything's on the q.t., but whoever ends up controlling the deposit will control the future."

"And exactly how do you fit into this conspiracy?"

"Let's just say I'm an accidental player who wants out."

"Explain."

"Not here, not now."

"Then when?"

"When you get off my case. After you publish an article that makes it clear to everyone I'm not a suspect for the murder of Amy

Vanderbilt, the murder of Ralph Braun, or that so-called assault on that jogger."

"But you *are* a suspect."

"No, I'm not. Now do some research. Dig a little. Talk to the cops. If I was a suspect, I wouldn't be walking in and out of the RCMP building like I work there. The police and I are talking, but not about what you think. We're talking about something else."

"Like what?"

"Write that article and maybe I'll tell you. You can reach me at my shop in Minto. I'll be there Sunday. And quit calling the Café or there's no deal. And no more meetings in the street, I'm being watched. And keep this to yourself."

She looked around and I left Ellen Burke standing on the sidewalk with her face twisted in knots, wondering what the hell I was talking about.

So was I.

FORTY FOUR

I felt guilty for not once thinking about Jack all afternoon.

'Out of sight, out of mind' was no excuse. Time to go see him.

My phone rang twice on the three block walk over to Mike's truck but I didn't answer it. There were more important things to do than stop and chat on the phone—like avoiding an ambush by Tommy Kay. The whole way I stayed extra vigilant, scanning my surroundings, avoiding alleys, making wide passes around corners and cars, and looking over my shoulder a lot.

How had my life come to this?

As usual Mike's truck was hard to start but I got it going and joined the city's five o'clock exodus, driving north on Second Avenue. The phone rang again but no way I was answering it now, not if I didn't want another two hundred and fifty dollar ticket. When I parked in front of John Dorval's animal clinic, it rang again. Someone was being very persistent.

By the time I'd emptied my backpack of its books and pamphlets, assay forms, aeronautical maps, an FBI contract, my knife, a satellite phone, bank slips, a check book, a letter from the government, and a wad of cash—and finally located the damn thing wedged in a corner at the bottom—it stopped ringing. I flipped it open. No missed calls.

Strange.

Then I remembered a trick I'd learned last year. Press 'SEND' and it would dial the last missed call.

I am too smart sometimes.

After five rings, "Yes?"

She sounded distracted.

"Hey, Jennifer. You call?"

"No. I was going to but have been absolutely slammed with a rush job. Mike just sent some samples down with one of my techs from Dawson, said he needs the results tonight. I don't see why he couldn't wait until tomorrow morning and give them to you then, but it's his money. You're still going to Thistle Creek in the morning, right?"

"That's the plan. You're sure you didn't just call?"

"I said no, Brody. Why?"

"Nothing. Someone's been calling me but I don't know who."

After a short pause she said, "You hungry?"

"I could eat. And I could sure use another session on my shoulder too, if you have the time."

"I'll make the time if you bring me dinner."

"Sounds like a deal. What do you want?"

"Anything. I am famished."

Go figure.

* * *

When Jack saw me walk in, he popped up on his three legs and wagged his tail so hard he almost fell over. There was a new Bandage around his rump and he still had the clear plastic lampshade around his neck. I dropped to my knees and opened the wire screen door. He hopped out, put his front paws on my thighs, licked my face, then nestled his head in my lap.

"How is he?" I asked Evelyn Dorval who was standing behind me.

"Much better," she said. "Right now he's kind of dopey from the pain killers, a little confused and lonely too. But remember what I said, he'll be fine. He ate a little bit an hour ago and will have a lot more energy in a couple of days. The best news is the infection is gone."

I scratched his neck with both hands and whispered a few things in his ear. When he heard the word 'steak', he rolled his eyes up at me and I thought I might cry.

"I can still take him home Saturday?"

"Come by at noon," she said.

* * *

Deciding on dinner was easy. At the other end of the plaza was a Greek take-out joint. I ordered three souvlakis, two orders of spanakopita, and a stack of pita bread with tzatziki. If that wasn't enough, Jennifer could always eat one of the cushions on her couch.

While waiting for my order I played with my phone. I was still wondering who had called four times in the past hour. I spent ten minutes searching for the answer, delving deep into the esoteric world of push button menus with their nebulous names and nomenclature, exploring things like 'My Stuff', 'My Phone', and 'TTY'—whatever that is. After navigating down countless paths, and having to retreat again and again, never finding what I wanted and eventually becoming totally frustrated, I did what I always do. I turned the damn thing off and put it back in my pack.

* * *

When I walked into the Tire King, Rick Granger was standing behind the counter, smoking a cigarette as usual. He looked up from his paperwork, coughed, took a long drag, and stubbed it out in an overflowing ashtray.

"About to close up here, Brody. Hope it can wait 'til tomorrow. We open at seven."

"A check is all I need, Rick."

"A check for what?"

"For those tires I paid you for a couple of days ago. You billed the insurance company for them too, no need to get paid twice."

"Who says I billed the insurance company?"

"Jennifer Kovalchuk, the owner of the truck."

"I have no idea where she'd get that idea."

Rick reached into his shirt pocket for another cigarette.

"Huh," I said. "I must be mistaken. But I could swear she said you got her to sign some authorization form, so you could bill her insurance company directly. No problem, though, I'll just tell her to contact them for the reimbursement."

I opened the door to leave.

"Wait," he said.

Busted.

* * *

A full-size Toyota pickup was parked in the yard behind Jennifer's house. It was metallic blue with Yukon plates, almost new, and sparkled like it had just been washed.

I parked Mike's old truck beside it and walked into the Thurson Ames building through an open door. The air was ten degrees warmer inside. Jennifer was alone, working at the far end of her shop, standing in front of a roaring furnace. Its door was open and the radiation cast a rosy red glow on her face. She was wearing safety glasses, a white lab coat, big silver mitts on her hands, and had a firm two-handed grip on a pair of steel tongs. I watched her use the tongs to lift a cup size crucible from the furnace. It was full of molten rock and she set it down carefully on a steel table, then returned the tongs to the furnace. She hadn't noticed me yet and I watched her remove another crucible, and set it down beside the first one. While I waited for her to finish, I surveyed her operation.

Instruments on white benches ran along the wall to my left, sinks and shelves with chemicals spanned the end wall, and the furnace and several rock crushing machines were set against the wall to my right. Behind me was a caged-in area with hundreds of cloth bags inside. They had irregular shapes and I assumed they contained rocks to be assayed. I couldn't help but notice a large open padlock hanging on the cage door.

Jennifer didn't smile when our eyes met. She closed the furnace door, tossed her mitts aside, and turned off the fuel supply. When she walked past me without a word, I pointed at my face. She rolled her eyes, yanked off her safety glasses, and shoved them into the pocket of her lab coat. She closed the cage door, locked it with the padlock, and stomped outside with her coattails flying.

Oh, oh...

Jennifer had nothing to say until she'd inhaled a beer and was well into her second entrée. Then she pointed her fork at me and said, "So, what's new with you, *Mr.* Brody?"

"Not much. What's new with you, *Ms.* Kovalchuk?"

"I am royally pissed, that's what's new."

"Oh, yeah? Want to tell me why?"

"Well, as usual, it has to do with the company of the men I keep."

"Does that include my company?"

"Damn right."

"Well then, let me have it."

She leaned forward with her knife and fork held upright in clenched fists and said, "Well first of all, you won't tell me your first name. That's got to be a red flag if there ever was. Two, I ask you what's new and you say 'not much'. Three, the cops come by at noon and tell me I shouldn't let you stay here because you're dangerous. Four, according to the newspaper, you're a murderer and a thug. Five, some reporter just called here and asked me what I know about some conspiracy to corner the world's supply of rare earths. And according to this reporter, you're part of this conspiracy. Then she asks me if Thurson is doing the assays and if they're any good. Like, what the hell, Brody? Want to hear more?"

"Ah, Jennifer?"

"What?"

"Can I have that last piece of spanakopita?"

When she said nothing, I reached for the plate. She dropped her fork and grabbed my wrist.

"Did you hear a word I just said?"

"I did. Now what's the real reason you're upset?"

"That's not enough?"

"It is, but that's not what's bothering you. There's something else. That truck out back, who owns it?"

She let go of my wrist and leaned back in her chair. We tried staring each other down. No one blinked. I took the last piece of spanakopita and put it on my plate.

"Guess," she said.

"Where is he now?"

"Probably getting drunk and chatting up some floozy to bring back here tonight."

"Hmm..."

"Hmm...what?"

"There's a way to prevent that, you know."

"There is?"

"I'll tell you after you work on my shoulder."

* * *

A mile north of Jennifer's house, I turned into the Walmart and headed toward a cluster of campers and RV's parked well away from the building. Jennifer followed me in and stopped beside me.

For a cheating scumbag, Tony sure was a trusting soul. He'd left the keys to his truck in his trailer. By the time Jennifer came out of her house with a bag full of his clothes, I was all hooked up and ready to roll. Ten minutes later, Tony's home away from home was sitting in the biggest parking lot in the Yukon, which also happened to be the cheapest place in town to park an RV.

Can't beat free.

We got out of the trucks and looked around. My right shoulder was still burning from my physio and I rubbed it, then with a rueful smile said, "Think he'll like it here?"

Jennifer had her hands on her hips and was appraising our stark surroundings—a sheet of pavement decorated with light poles, a lot of dirt and dust, and paper wrappers skittering by us like tumbleweed.

"If he doesn't, he can always go somewhere else."

She didn't sound very sure of herself.

"Something wrong?"

She bit her upper lip and said, "I'd better call him, tell him where he can find his truck and trailer."

We marveled at the sprawl of concrete boxes where you could get everything from groceries and housewares to car repairs and garden supplies. The place was busy.

"I wouldn't call him."

"Well, I'm going to. It's the right thing to do."

I nodded and looked at the big red sign over the main entrance.

"You got a camera in that fancy phone of yours?"

"Course, why?"

"Send him a picture instead. A picture's worth a thousand words."

* * *

Not a word was spoken on the short drive to the corner of Fourth and Main. What do you say when there's nothing to be said?

Jennifer had just officially ended a long relationship with a man she didn't trust. But I could tell she was done with me too.

For a moment I wondered if I'd simply come along at the wrong time, or perhaps wasn't her type, or maybe she simply needed time to get over Tony. But who was I kidding?

She didn't trust me either.

Two days ago when Jennifer Kovalchuk picked me up at the the lake, she knew I was implicated for a murder in Minto. On the say-so of Mike Giguere, a man she *did* trust, she gave me a pass. But after two front page stories alleging I'd threatened reporters and attacked a jogger, then having her tires slashed, then learning my dog had been shot, then with the cops warning her off, and now a reporter asking her about some conspiracy I was supposedly mixed up in...well...who could blame her?

I'd dump me too.

I didn't tell her where I'd be staying the night, she hadn't asked and it would serve no purpose for her to know anyway.

She pulled her truck into a parking spot in front of the Gold Rush Inn, but didn't turn off the engine, and stared straight ahead with both hands on the wheel.

I cracked my door open and said as casually as possible, "See you tomorrow. The lake at three. Okay?"

"I'm sending Rita," she replied in a faraway voice. "Maybe Tony too. There'll be close to a thousand pounds to unload."

"Jennifer, whatever you do, please do not send Tony. Rita and I will be fine."

Rita.

I got out and stepped onto the sidewalk, then remembered something and walked around to her door. She lowered the window and I handed her the check from the Tire King.

"What's this?" she asked.

"Tire rebate."

"Five hundred dollars?"

"Hell of a deal."

* * *

I walked into the hotel lobby and waited for Jennifer to leave. A minute later I peeked out the window and she was still there, sitting exactly as I'd left her, still staring out the windshield. It was another full minute before she backed out into the quiet street, rolled down to the intersection, and turned left toward home.

I wondered when I'd see her again.

If ever.

My shoulder ached from my session, my backpack was heavy with books, and the specter that Tommy Kay might be skulking around town was a reality. Taking a cab to Maggie's B&B was easy to rationalize. I found a lone taxi out front with an eye-watering odor of ammonia inside, so much so I had to roll the window down. The driver didn't seem pleased that my destination was only four blocks away, so I told him to put an extra half mile on the meter by circling the B&B block a few times, then make a slow pass through the parking lot out back. When I was certain the coast was clear, I got out and he drove off happy with a twenty for his trouble.

My clean boxers and T-shirt lay neatly folded on one corner of the bed. It was the only area not covered by cushions and I wondered what purpose they served. I counted them. There were thirteen in all—*thirteen*—propped up like dominoes, no two the same, each one a different color and size. I stacked them up like sandbags along a wall. After a long hot shower I got into bed, opened one of my library books, couldn't concentrate, got up and went to the window, and gazed out at the city's rooftops with a lot on my mind.

The knock on the door was almost imperceptible, but I whirled around on high alert.

Could it be...?

I opened the window and looked down. It was ten o'clock at night but it might have been noon for all the light outside, and I had no trouble seeing the ground twenty feet below. But even if I hung from the windowsill before letting go, I was still bound to break something. I crept over to my backpack and found my knife.

Now what do I do?

Another knock.

I held my breath, tiptoed to the door, and pressed my ear against it.

"Who is it?"

"Open up."

A whisper, a woman, and a surge of relief.

Sarah Marsalis.

I set my knife down on the night stand and opened the door.

My legs went weak at the sight of her. The tattoos were still there, and so was the crazy hair and nose ring, but the makeup was gone. I was mesmerized by her clear brown eyes, high cheek bones, full sultry lips, and a complexion too smooth to be real. She was wearing a chic trench coat buttoned to the knees and I couldn't help but notice the silk pajamas and hotel slippers. She had her hands in her pockets.

She raised her eyebrows, tilted her head, and with the hint of a smile said, " Mind if I come in?"

"I don't know, Sarah, maybe that's not such a great idea, I..."

She took a step forward, backed me up with her nose an inch from mine, and closed the door with a foot. I was drowning in her eyes and could barely breathe.

"Sarah, really, I don't think this is the best..."

She hooked a foot behind one of mine and gave me a mighty shove in the chest. I stumbled backwards and she rode me to the floor. With her knees on either side of my chest, she grabbed my wrists and stretched my arms over my head.

"Don't move," she hissed, glaring down at me.

"I won't," I said.

Why would I? She had me pinned down, straddling me with her butt firmly planted on my belly. Other than the seering pain in my shoulder, it felt great. She let go of my wrists, sat up straight, dug something out of her pocket, and waved it in my face.

"Know what this is?"

"Ah, a phone?"

"That's right, a phone. A satellite phone. I've got one and you've got one. The FBI just gave you twenty-five grand to answer yours when it rings. I called you four times this afternoon and guess what? As usual you don't answer. So what else is new, huh Brody? But from now on things are going to be different. Because from now on you're going to answer yours everytime it rings. And you're going to hear it ring because you're going to have it with you everywhere you go. You go to the bathroom, you have it with you. You eat dinner, you have it with you. You go to bed, you have it with you. Even when you go flying, you have it with you. Got that?"

"Yeah, sure. Hey, Sarah? Can I get up now? My shoulder, it's a little..."

"Oh," she said, lowering her face into mine. "Thanks for

reminding me." She made a gun with her hand and pressed two fingers between my eyes. "If you call me Sarah again, I'm going to kill you. Click. Bang. You're dead. Just like that. Understand? My name is 'Rita' and you're going to call me 'Rita'—and nothing else. Are we clear on that too?"

I gulped and nodded.

"I didn't hear you," she said.

"Yes."

"Yes... *who?*"

"Yes...*Rita.*"

"Good. Don't forget."

She sat back and glowered at me for a moment, then stood up, put a foot on my belly, and gave it a jiggle.

"Getting enough to eat these days?" she asked with a sardonic smile.

She opened the door and walked out.

I struggled to my feet and closed it.

"Rita," I muttered to myself with a grin.

What a woman.

FORTY FIVE

For the second time in ten minutes, Tippy Li had to get to his feet and watch Lynn Chan walk out of the bar.

She was off to powder her nose again.

Women and their noses.

A waiter placed another glass of wine in front of him. He was drinking alone while she had yet to touch her sparkling water. Obviously her rotten attitude hadn't changed. For something to do he reached for his phone and brought up the website Sanders had emailed him last week. When the site came up, he entered a password. Seconds later a grainy image appeared. He brought the phone in close to his face.

Lynn's living room.

Amazing.

Her suite was dark but he could make out the lights in the building across the street, and the silhouette of her desk against the tall windows. He waited and watched but no one was home—which made perfect sense—Lynn was with him in a bar three blocks away. But what mattered was the camera in the chandelier was still working. He wondered when she'd take it down. When and if she did, he'd have to install another camera in something else. Of all his enemies, Lynn Chan had to be monitored as closely as any, until that is, her usefulness came to an end.

Tippy wondered when the time came, and if that ugly chandelier was still hanging over her dining room table, whether he'd use the phone number in his briefcase. Would he dare make the call that would blow her to bits?

Probably not.

Of course it would give him great pleasure, but he knew an explosion was always front page news and would garner an army of cops. So no, he'd use the tried and true method, the one that had worked so well ever since he'd gotten into the garbage business. A double tap in the back of the head, the body rolled up in a carpet, then dumped into a garbage truck, and shipped south of the border for *disposal*. Or was it dispersion?

The local papers would naturally report the mysterious disappearance of a wealthy young woman from Vancouver.

"Chan was last seen yesterday afternoon carrying a purse and a shopping bag, getting into a dark late model car near the corner of...."

And that would be it. End of story. She'd vanish without a trace. Neither the cops or the press would ever know what had happened to Lynn Chan, and in particular, that the next day she'd be blowing in the wind somewhere over Montana.

Tippy rose again when Lynn reappeared. She had on a short leather skirt and matching jacket, both as bright red as the fresh lipstick she'd just applied. He waited as she slid her world class derriere into the other side of the booth. She didn't say a word and was gazing around at everything but him.

"Lynn."

"Tippy."

"Everything okay?"

"Just peachy."

"Good. Can we talk?"

"You called the meeting, you talk."

Tippy clenched his fists under the table but managed to eke out a weak smile.

"Okay, I have some questions."

"Well, ask them."

He had to bite his tongue before saying, "The papers for the financing, did you sign them?"

"Signed, sealed, and delivered this afternoon. The exchange faxed me the approval just before five."

Tippy beamed and said, "Excellent, Lynn, that's just excellent. Tomorrow we'll put out a press release to announce the good news."

"We?"

"Okay, I'll do it. It's standard stuff anyway, you don't have to do a thing."

"Good," she said.

"See the close today?" he asked.

"No," she said with boredom written all over her face.

"Forty cents. And it would have closed a lot higher if I hadn't brought in some selling."

"You brought in selling?"

"Don't ever let a stock rise too fast without news, Lynn. Exchanges don't like it, sometimes they even halt trading and demand an explanation."

"Who were the sellers?"

"People you don't know, brokers who got cheap shares and warrants in the financing. Like I told you before, you need brokers to play this game. But never mind that, we're all set now. You and I start selling after the party in Dawson. By then two drills will be turning 24/7 and we'll be churning out press releases every second day. The brokers will be all over TCR and the stock will soar. Which reminds me, your assistant..."

"Jeremy."

"Of course, Jeremy. Has he...?"

"Yes. *He* has. He's organized everything and taken care of every detail—hotels, planes, buses, lunches—all looked after. I'll tell him you said thank you."

Lynn was glaring at him with blatant disdain. It was all Tippy could do to contain himself. He drained his wine and took a deep breath, trying to stay composed, looking around the room and acknowledging his henchmen.

"So, Dawson," he said. "The weekend after next."

"The weekend after next. Your broker buddies have to be in Whitehorse on the Friday before. Their charter flight to Dawson leaves late in the afternoon. We've sent them the schedule, so no excuses if they're late. Anything else? Are we done?"

Tippy leaned back and rubbed the scar on his lip. It would always be there, like the day it had happened.

It was twenty years ago. One of his girls in Hong Kong was complaining about what she was getting paid. An argument ensued and Tippy had slapped her. In a fury she swung her purse at him and the buckle caught him flush in the mouth. The cut was deep and had bled profusely. He vividly remembered watching the life drain from her eyes as he crushed her throat with his bare hands. In those days, Tippy did his own disposals. He remembered wrapping her body in a rusty old chain, and rolling it off the back of a fishing boat into the Hong Kong harbor.

Those were the good old days, he reminisced. Everything was so easy back then.

He looked at Lynn again. She was deep in thought, daydreaming at something over his shoulder.

Then she said, "So Tippy, are you going to answer or not? Are we done?"

"No," he said. "We're not done."

"Well, then, what else?"

"This property trip to Dawson, as the president of Thistle Creek Resources you are expected to attend. I will be going as well. I hope there is room on the plane for the two of us, and of course a few of my men."

"There will be room on the plane for you and your men. But I will not be joining you. I am not going on a junket to the Yukon with a bunch of stock brokers. Sorry, not going to happen."

Tippy nodded and appraised the woman before him. He wondered why he'd fallen so hard. Was it the exotic eyes? The sensual lips? The flawless white skin? Or the finest ass he'd ever laid hands on? He studied the nape of her smooth delicate neck. Whatever it was, perhaps she didn't deserve a bullet in the brain. Perhaps something else. With a different scenario now in mind, he clasped his hands together and wrung them under the table.

"Actually, Lynn, it is going to happen. In the next thirty days you are going to make ten million dollars selling stock you acquired for nothing. Think about it, ten million dollars for nothing. So when I say you are expected to attend this trip, it means you are going to attend this trip."

"Oh, is that so? And if I refuse?"

"Refusal is not an option, Lynn."

Tippy got up and walked out.

FORTY SIX

At 7:05 the next morning I shoved my good old plane off the dock, climbed inside, started the engine, and pointed it north at the power dam.

The big motor was barely turning over as I idled toward my target, a line of warning buoys half a mile away, strung across the north end of Schwatka Lake. There I would turn around and take off into a light south wind.

The sun was already high but the early morning air had a mean bite. It was barely forty degrees and I had the cabin heat turned on, but also the cockpit door opened a crack as a final attempt to clear some lingering cobwebs. I'd slept in fits and starts and had barely managed to drag myself out of bed. If I could get through the day then tonight a good sleep would be mine, back in my cabin, alone in my bed, with nothing around but my buddy, Russ, the wind in the trees, and the sounds of the river.

Through my crystal clear new windshields I glimpsed the same pair of shiny black ducks who'd got in my way the other day. They were fifty feet ahead, quacking up a storm, glaring at the great winged monster bearing down on them. When I got too close for comfort, they flapped their wings and ran across the water, then stopped, turned, and let me have it with an earful of duck profanities. They were still glaring daggers when my plane rumbled by and I tipped my hat in contrition. They started quacking again, evidently still very upset with me.

Story of my life, guys.

It would be another five minutes until the engine was warm enough for flight, so I reached into my pack and fished out my phone. I had to make a quick stop in Minto on my way to Thistle Creek. There was just enough battery left to call Reggie. When he picked up, I told him what I needed. He said he'd be waiting at the lake in Minto when I arrived. No man has a better friend than I do in Reggie.

I turned off the phone and put it away, then decided to check out the FBI's satellite phone. It looked kind of like a real phone, only heftier and heavier, all black, with a stubby aerial sticking out on top.

It was on so I pressed SEND.

About the fifth ring there was a hiss and a click.

"This better be good."

"Well, good morning to you too, Sar...Rita."

"You woke me up. What do you want?"

"Sorry, thought you had a real job to go to."

"I asked you what you want."

"Actually, I just wanted to see if this thing works."

"Of course it works, you idiot. Now goodbye."

'Idiot'?

"And goodbye to you too, *Rita*. You have yourself a wonderful day. See you this afternoon."

"What?"

"Don't forget your work gloves."

"What work gloves?"

When I started to laugh, she hung up.

* * *

The DeHavilland Beaver is the undisputed king of bush planes.

A world-renowned icon for frontier aviation, it was the first all metal STOL—an acronym for 'Short TakeOff and Landing'—and a godsend for bush pilots who had long been asking for just such an aircraft to get them in and out of impossible places in uncharted wilderness. Designed and built in Canada for that very purpose, the first Beaver flew in 1947 and in only a few years was an international hit. With long thick wings and gobs of power, the rugged new plane had no rival for takeoff performance—either loaded or empty—and *'the flying half ton pickup'* was soon hauling cargo and people across the fringes of civilization to the ends of every continent. The Beaver has landed at both poles, the base camp of Everest, and every outpost, lake, ocean, glacier, and island you can name. I know of no other machine that to this day remains the best in the business, seventy years after the first one was built.

A hundred feet from the buoys I turned mine around, checked the oil temperature, then every other gauge and setting one last time, raised the rudders, closed the door, and pushed the throttle lever ahead. My shoulder ached when I did, but that didn't matter. The roar of the engine was euphoric. A tingle went down my spine when I pulled back the yoke and the floats left the water.

I was flying again.

I took off south but had to go north and banked the plane east, made a long climbing turn through a hundred and eighty degrees, finished the turn at four thousand feet, flew through a narrow saddle on the west side of Gray Mountain, and emerged over the Yukon River pointed at Minto. With a few grunts and groans, I raised my right hand to the ceiling and trimmed the elevator for level flight.

Piece of cake.

The City of Whitehorse was drifting by on my left and I was happy to leave it behind, though admittedly it had been good to me on at least one count. Buying Thistle Creek stock had made me some easy money and it struck me then why people live in cities.

They didn't have to work.

I thought about Dave Sorenson, and Ninja Secretary, and all the cops I'd been talking to, and the women in the bank, and Rick Granger at the tire store—the scoundrel—and then Ellen Burke from the newspaper. For doing little more than talking and typing, they were all making a living. Of course there are other advantages to city life, like pretty girls and good food, and never underestimate shopping and cable TV to kill time. But even so, the three days I'd spent in Whitehorse felt like three months.

Ten minutes later Whitehorse was behind me and I was approaching the junction where the Alaska Highway veers west, and the Klondike Highway starts north. Navigating to Minto from Whitehorse on a clear day is easy, you simply follow the Klondike Highway north. It's as straight a shot as there is.

I scanned the gauges, surveyed the sky for other planes—there were none—and settled in for an hour of boredom. I looked out to my right at Lake LaBerge.

Like all big lakes in the southern Yukon, LaBerge is long and skinny, oriented north-south in the same direction as the ebb and flow of the massive glaciers that excavated them. Today the big lake was solemn and foreboding, its surface as gray and vacant as a sheet of slate. I tried to imagine how it might have appeared on this very day back in June of 1898.

It would have been a sight to behold.

* * *

The Klondike Gold Rush was the biggest and greatest in history, and the last great mass adventure for humanity. In the early spring of 1898 as many as a hundred thousand men—and a few hardy if not incredibly shrewd women—descended on the Yukon to seek their fortune.

There were several different ways to reach the goldfields of Dawson, and thirty thousand of the hopefuls chose the route that originated at the Pacific port of Skagway on the Alaska panhandle.

The Skagway route began with a dangerous ascent into the Coastal Mountains, a thirty-five hundred foot climb of fifteen miles, where the 98er's battled ice and snow, traversed creeks and crevices, and navigated over boulders and cliffs before reaching the summit of the Chilkoot Pass. With half their arduous trek behind them, they headed inland for Bennett Lake, another seventeen miles ahead, where an even bigger challenge awaited them.

The Yukon River.

With dogged determination the '98er's felled every tree in sight and built every kind of scow, barge and raft imaginable. Once done, all they could do was wait in the snow and cold for the ice on Bennett lake to break up, and hope their rudimentary vessels would keep them afloat all the way to Dawson, another five hundred river miles north.

When the ice on the lake finally broke up at the end of May, the first vessel was launched, leading an endless flotilla—by some estimates eight thousand vessels—sailing north to Carcross, then east across Tagish Lake, then north down Marsh lake, through Miles Canyon, through the White Horse Rapids, past the current City of Whitehorse, and out into Lake LaBerge.

For those who didn't drown, there were now four hundred and fifty river miles to go before they reached Dawson. From my seat high in the sky, it would have looked like a regatta down there.

I often think about why they did it. Only a few broke even, fewer still got rich, and all too many died on the adventure of a lifetime. Their motivation to leave behind familiar surroundings for an unknown fate in an unforgiving land has long been one of the great mysteries of the Klondike Gold Rush. Of course a great many 98er's were unemployed at the time—thanks to the bankers who had just created yet another recession—so that might explain part of it. But there were also thousands of others from all over the world who abandoned secure jobs and lives to join the stampede. So why did they go? Why would mayors and ex-governors, doctors and professors, let alone half of Seattle's street car drivers, just pick up and leave to join a mass exodus north? Was it the gold? Or something else?

Stretched across the horizon ahead of me lay the vast blue and green land known as the Yukon, as mystical and alluring as ever, strong and silent with its snow capped mountains, wide open valleys, powerful rivers, and infinite skies. The view from my seat had barely changed in a hundred and twenty years and I thought about the confines of a city with its slack-jawed overweight denizens, sleep walking through their daily routines, exhausted by noise and traffic, living lives they hadn't bargained for.

I realized then it may not have been the pursuit of gold why the 98'ers went north, so much as it had been a great escape. An escape from the boredom and banality of so-called civilization. Maybe the 98'ers were simply running from their lives. Or maybe they just wanted a greater legacy.

This world could use another gold rush, I thought to myself.

* * *

Sixty miles ahead a shiny black disc appeared on the horizon.

Two Spirit Lake has been home to my plane for over six decades. Five years ago I bought it from the estate of the man who'd flown it up to the Yukon in 1957. He'd landed on the little lake and it had been stationed there ever since. Hopefully it would still be stationed there in another sixty years. I needed a plan for that.

Half an hour later I checked the gauges, reduced power and pitch, pumped down the flaps, and started a gentle descent in a long semicircle for a southwest landing.

Which is when I saw the boat.

Two Spirit Lake is less than two miles wide between any two points, nothing more than a puddle left behind by a glacier. The fishing's not great—the water's too shallow—it isn't connected to anything, and there's nowhere to go in a motorboat. Occasionally a tourist will launch a canoe or kayak from the campground and go out for an evening paddle, but that's about it. So to see a boat in the middle of the lake is rare. It's what makes Two Spirit Lake such a great waterdrome, there's hardly ever any 'conflicting traffic'.

I continued my descent and straightened out for landing, aiming well right of the little boat which was barely moving. So long as it didn't take off like a rocket, there was plenty of margin for safety. When I cleared the trees and was over the water, I knew it wasn't going to take off like a rocket.

For one thing, it was a row boat. For another thing, the person rowing it was Old Hank.

Hank Sturmer had come north in the early fifties to work on the Klondike Highway. He was a young man then, a carpenter by trade, and had been hired to build camps for the construction crews. But he didn't like camp life, especially the drinking and incessant fighting, and he'd often disappear for days. No one knew where he would go, only that he would ramble off into the bush somewhere around Two Spirit Lake.

Hank picked the spot to build his log cabin five miles from the highway, a couple of hundred feet in from the shoreline of Two Spirit Lake, where no one on the water could see it. Other than a few things he'd liberated from his employer—a door, a window, some nails and spikes, and a pail of cement for the footings—everything else came from the land, including the earth for the grass roof.

Two years later Hank had finished his new home on a piece of land he didn't own. At the time it might have belonged to the Canadian Government, but who knew? And regardless, who cared? Hank's cabin was thirty-five hundred miles from Ottawa and the Queen's subjects had bigger fish to fry. Thirty years hence, well after the Canadian Government finally settled the land claim filed by the Minto First Nation, Hank became a squatter on their land. The natives didn't seem to care either.

Old Hank was just a harmless old recluse who was rarely seen and never bothered anyone. Today, after sixty years living in the Yukon bush, I doubt if he's ever heard of the Beatles or knows that man has walked on the moon.

Live and let live.

The floats settled into the water and I idled into the path of his tiny plywood boat, then turned off the engine. Hank was rowing hard with his back to me, barely making any progress, but holding a steady course toward my plane. He still hadn't looked around and I wondered if he even knew I was there. Had he not heard me? I hadn't seen him for a couple of years, perhaps he was deaf now. I got out and climbed down to the float to wait for the imminent collision. I was shocked to see that he was stark naked. It was cold on the lake with a mean wind blowing.

As expected, a moment later he ran into my plane with a gentle bump against the float. He let go of the oars and managed to turn his head, just enough to see what he'd run into, then looked back out over the stern again. I crouched down and grabbed the blunt-nosed bow.

"Hey, Hank, how's it goin?"

"No place," he said, keeping his back to me.

Now I knew he had a hearing problem.

"Aren't you cold?" I yelled.

"Yep."

"Then what are you doing out here with no clothes on?"

"Laundry."

"Laundry?"

"Yep, laundry."

He leaned forward, grabbed a rope at the stern, and began yarding it in. Every few feet there was a piece of clothing tied to the rope. First a pair of longjohn's, then a sweater, a pair of pants, a sock.

'Laundry'.

"Okay, Hank. I get it."

He tossed the clothes back in the water and sat down again. He was white as sheet, skinny as a rope, and I could count the ribs in his back. He had a full head of white hair and a long bushy beard, like an anorexic Santa Claus.

"Say, Hank, you getting enough to eat these days?"

"Yep," he said, studying his clothes floating behind the boat.

"You sure?"

"Yep."

He was sagging between the oars and his chin was low. I didn't believe him.

"Hey, Hank. What do say we tow this boat of yours over to the dock and give your clothes a real good cleaning? You can wring them out when we get there, then you can row back with the wind."

"You fix the leak?"

"What leak?"

"The leak in that float," he said, swinging a long sinewy arm around and pointing in the vicinity of my feet.

"How do you know it had a leak?"

"'Cuz there was so many of ya's pumping it out last week."

"You saw that? How could you see that? Where were you?"

"Over yonder," he said, pointing at the shoreline near his cabin. "I got me a telescope, you know. I could see you guys pumpin' out your plane."

I tilted my head and said, "Is that so? Who did you see pumping?"

"Well, there was you, and there was Reggie, and a guy with a beard too."

"A guy with a beard, huh? What did he look like, Hank?"

He shrugged and said, "Like you, I reckon. But with a beard. He had a red truck."

Now I knew. It was Dan Sanders who had filled the float with water.

Another mystery solved.

Hank was shaking like a leaf.

"Come on, Hank. Get in the plane."

* * *

Reggie had Hank's boat tied up to the other side of the dock before I'd even turned off the engine. I climbed out and took care of my own rope work, then looked at Reggie. He gave me a quizzical look as if to say, "Where is he?"

I jutted my chin at the plane and he opened the cargo door. Hank climbed down the ladder and stepped onto the dock. He was wearing a brand new snowmobile suit.

My brand new snowmobile suit.

I'd bought it last fall and had it stowed in the back of my plane for a 'just in case' situation. I guess this was a 'just in case' situation. Hank seemed very pleased with the fit and was checking

out all the pockets. I knew it was as good as his now. At least he'd
be warm rowing home.

"Did you bring it, Reg?"

"In my truck."

"Thanks. Twenty-five gallons in the center tank should do it,
then I can be on my way."

We both walked down the dock to a barrel of fuel and rolled it
up beside the plane. Reggie crouched down and effortlessly lifted it
upright. If you think you're strong, try standing a full barrel of gas
up on end—without a grunt. I left him to fill the tank and walked
over to his tow truck parked on the beach. On the passenger seat lay
a brown paper bag, and something rolled up in an old sweatshirt. I
took them both back to the plane and set them down on the cargo
floor behind my seat. As requested, inside the paper bag were two
coffees and two sandwiches. I looked at my breakfast, then at Hank.

He was sitting cross-legged in his boat, hauling in his laundry,
wringing out each article as it came over the stern, tossing them
behind him onto a growing pile. He must have had eyes in the back
of his head.

"You pumpin' gas there, Reg?"

"Yes, sir."

"Don't you spill no gas. Don't want no gas in my laundry."

"No, sir."

I took the bag over to Hank.

"Say Hank, can you help me with these sandwiches? There's
way too much food here for one man."

He looked up at me, then at the bacon and egg sandwich in my
hand. I was glad when he took it and it was gone in a hurry. I was
glad when he took the other one too. I left a coffee on the dock
beside him and walked back to Reggie.

"He's not getting enough to eat, Reg."

Reggie was lifting the pump out of the barrel and said, "He'll
never come in, Brody. He's too proud. He'll never come in."

"Well, could you put a box of things together for him? Get it out
to him today? Some coffee, some sugar, some eggs, oh and some

cheese, and flour and pasta too, and some fruit and vegetables, and a gallon of kerosene for his lamp...and if you know what kind of gun he's got, a box of shells, and..."

Reggie raised a hand.

"I'll handle it."

I nodded. Reggie had known Hank forever and would know exactly what he'd need.

"Right," I muttered, sipping my coffee, staring out at the lake.

The water was black and choppy, the sky pale and empty.

"Hey Reg?"

"What?"

"How's Russ?"

"Good."

"Reg?"

"What?"

"Thanks for rounding up my dogs."

"Sure."

"Hey, Reg?"

"What?"

"What's goin' on with the arena?"

"New load of plywood's comin' in today."

"Great, that's great. Say, maybe you ought to hire a guard to..."

"We did."

"Right."

I crushed my coffee cup, handed it to him, and got into my plane.

Ten minutes later I was airborne, heading for Thistle Creek, feeling depressed.

FORTY SEVEN

Roberta Klinger was feeling pleased with herself.

Though barely eighteen years old, she'd just backed up a thirty ton tanker truck down a narrow lane in a thick forest, without brushing a mirror.

Her Dad would be proud.

While her high school classmates were preparing for university in the fall, Roberta wanted nothing to do with that academic crap. All she had ever aspired for was a real job doing real work. It had been hers for the asking.

Twenty-five years ago her father had started Klinger Septic Service with a single truck. Now he had ten trucks and this year the family business would gross five million. A decade from now Roberta and her older brother would take over the reigns. As her father liked to say, *"as long as people are eating, you'll have shit to pump"*.

Roberta set the air brakes on the big Kenworth, left it idling, and climbed down from the cab. She went to the back, put on a pair of huge rubber gloves, flipped a few levers, and grabbed the vacuum wand.

Ladies first.

The suction hose played out behind her as she hauled the wand over to the outhouse. She opened the door, stepped inside, raised the toilet lid, and lowered the pipe through the hole. When it hit bottom, she turned a lever on the wand and the putrid slurry below began flowing out to the truck. But then it stopped. The pipe had contacted something—something heavy—something that shouldn't be there. Whatever it was, it wouldn't move. The wand was stuck on it and she couldn't lift it up. She closed the valve, took out her flashlight, and shone it down into the rank darkness below.

Five hundred feet away, Reggie McCormack heard her screams.

* * *

Lynn Chan was scared.

Ever since her meeting with Tippy last night, she'd been living with angst. Tippy's message had been loud and clear. Attend the party in Dawson, or else.

"Refusal is not an option."

In other words, do or die.

Lynn knew Tippy was a dangerous man whose enemies had a way of disappearing She had no intention of joining them. Like it or not, she'd have to attend his Yukon party.

Only now with a plan.

She wanted her life back and skulduggery was the only way out of this nightmare. The plan would either work, or it wouldn't. Que será, será. She had no other choice but to try. The alternative was no alternative at all.

This morning she'd had coffee with Danny, her favorite new IT guy. They'd met at a Starbucks a block from her condo and he'd handed her two burner phones, the kind with the large screens. With one of them he'd demonstrated how she could monitor last week's recorded surveillance of her desk—the same video loop being broadcast to Tippy's website. Whatever Tippy was watching on his phone, she could now watch on hers, courtesy of Danny's chicanery. Knowing at any particular time whether the broadcast showed her seated at her desk, or not, should ensure she'd never be caught in a lie.

Danny had also given her a short lesson for an untraceable

email account he'd installed in the other phone. She was impressed how unaffected he seemed whenever she asked for assurances about all this clandestine stuff. While he had to know she was up to something perverse, and for all he knew highly illegal, he had no qualms whatsoever about supplying her with the tools. It was just a game to him, and one for which he would be well paid.

Both phones, he assured her, would work in Dawson.

That was important.

So now for that ugly chandelier.

Lynn looked above her dining table at the bare wires hanging down from the hole in the ceiling. This afternoon Earl had taken it down and stowed it in a hall closet. What she had to figure out was how to exchange it for the one she'd bought, which according to Earl, was sitting in Tippy's hangar out at the airport. The question was, how to make the swap without Tippy finding out?

For that, she had an idea.

FORTY EIGHT

I took off from Minto with full fuel—over ninety gallons in three tanks—enough for the hundred mile trip up to Thistle Creek flying empty, and then the two hundred and twenty mile trip back down to Whitehorse loaded with rocks. I leveled off at two thousand feet and headed for the Yukon River. It would lead me to where I wanted to go.

A few miles northwest of Minto is the confluence of two mighty rivers, the Pelly flowing in from the east, and the Yukon flowing up from the south. Just downstream from where the rivers merge, I flew over the historic site of Fort Sekirk, long uninhabited but never to be forgotten.

Before the era of airports and highways in the Yukon, rivers were the prime infrastructure for inland trade, and there were few better spots to do business than Fort Selkirk. In 1848 the Hudson Bay Company established a trading post there, and business was great from the get-go.

But not without its problems.

The thing was, the natives had been conducting the very same business in the very same spot for eight thousand years. Understandably they weren't happy with the interlopers and as usual when dealing with the white man, their protests got them nowhere. By 1852 the natives had had enough with diplomacy and decided to take matters into their own hands. So they burned down all the white man's buildings, though to their credit, they did take great care not to hurt anyone. The white guys got the message and didn't come back for forty years, and this time with a different attitude.

This time all they did was build a general store and an Anglican church.

The Yukon River veers sharply west at Fort Selkirk. I followed it for fifty miles, then turned north and flew inland for ten miles, then turned west again at the top of the Thistle Creek valley and flew down the creek.

The scene below was remarkably different than a year ago. Gone were all but one of the bulldozers, all the loaders and excavators, and all the ore processing equipment. The camp near the river was still there, consisting of several personnel trailers and a large maintenance building, but what was new were the drills—a small one and two enormous ones—with an assortment of trucks surrounding each one. Men with yellow hard hats were bustling around the drills and looked up when I made a low pass to announce my arrival.

I left the creek valley and flew west across the Yukon River, then banked the plane steeply to the north and held a long tight right hand turn through a hundred and eighty degrees, and landed south into the wind and current.

Mike Giguere was waiting for me.

* * *

I swung open the cockpit door and shouted through the prop wash, "Hey Mike!"

"Hey, Brody! Right on time!"

I killed the engine twenty feet upstream of a wide floating dock and let the current carry me the rest of the way in. Moored to the other side of the dock was a good-sized motorboat covered in a canvas tarpaulin. With a five mile an hour current and a brisk wind, there was no time to waste securing the plane. Just before it bumped into the tires, Mike reached into the water and grabbed a wet rope trailing from the front float cleat. He ran it through a dock ring at his feet and quickly tied a knot. By the time I'd turned off all the switches, he had the rear float tied fast too.

"How was your flight?" he asked, wiping his wet hands on his jeans.

"Same old," was the best I could come up with. "How are things with you?"

"Can't complain," he said with a shrug.

I wasn't so sure about that. Mike was wearing sunglasses but they didn't conceal the purple under his eyes. He still had the splint taped on his nose.

"What happened to your face, Mike?"

He smiled and said, "You should see the other guy."

One of his pickup trucks was backed up to the dock with its tailgate down. The bed was full of cloth bags. My cargo of rock samples. An empty wheelbarrow sat at the ready. A man was seated in the driver's seat with his back to me.

Not Tommy Kay.

"Ready to load?" Mike asked.

"Let's do it," I said, stepping down to the dock, happy to stretch my legs. I glanced at his rope work and approved. He'd left some slack in the ropes because the plane was about to get a lot heavier and sink lower in the water. He knew what he was doing and knew his knots too.

I filed that information away and opened the cargo door, grabbed a two by eight plank, and laid it across the floor against the seat frames. It would stop things from sliding forward. Hard to steer a plane with rocks under the pedals.

The man in the pickup truck got out and slammed the door.

Well, what do you know?

Dan Sanders in person.

I'd have to keep an eye on the bastard.

Mike was halfway to the truck when I shouted, "Hey, Mike?"

He turned and said, "What?"

"I have this paperwork from Jennifer. Where and when do we fill it out?"

"All done. It's in the truck. I'll bring it out. You check off the bags when we bring them to you."

I watched him say a few words to Sanders when he got to the truck. They were pointing here and there and at the bags full of rocks. Mike shrugged his shoulders, shook his head, went to the passenger door and opened it. Once again, something didn't seem right. The way the two related didn't give me the impression that Mike was in charge. A moment later the two men arrived at the plane, Mike with a clipboard in his hand, Sanders pushing the wheelbarrow loaded with bags.

"Brody, you remember Dan from the Café?"

Sanders lowered the wheelbarrow and gave me a cold stare.

"Sure do," I said. "How's it goin', Dan?"

Nothing. The strong silent type. In fact with his shirt sleeves rolled up, I could tell from his bulging forearms and large thick hands that he was strong. Stronger than I'd thought. He didn't meet my eyes and was studying the inside of my plane through the cockpit door. I caught him dwelling on the windshields.

"You fly?" I asked.

With a deadpan gaze he said, "Nope."

It was the first time I'd heard his voice. It was deep and gutteral.

"Smart," I said. "Planes are nothing but trouble. Would you believe I just had to install new windshields in this one because some asshole took a hammer to them? And last week someone pumped water into one of the floats. Took me a day to figure out it didn't have a leak. Had to hire a guard to make sure it doesn't happen again."

Sanders didn't blink and looked down at the river running under our feet.

"Someone smashed your windshields with a hammer?" Mike asked with an incredulous look on his face.

"Hard to believe, huh? Looks like we've got a grade 'A' asshole running around here this summer."

I looked at Sanders for a tell, waiting to see if he had anything to say. He didn't. I caught Mike give him a fleeting glance. Sanders was ignoring us.

Mike broke an uncomfortable silence with, "Well, are we going to load these damn rocks or not?"

He handed me the clipboard.

The whole exercise went smoothly.

Sanders would unload the wheelbarrow on the dock beside my plane, and Mike would heave the bags up to the cargo bay. I sat inside and took them from him, and matched the tag numbers on the bags with the numbers on Mike's sample logs. I checked every bag carefully, looking for any tampering of the seal, and when satisfied all was right, initialed the corresponding number on Mike's paperwork and stowed the bags securely. Every time Sanders returned with another load of bags, Mike and I were ready for the next batch. When we were finished—it took about half an hour—every square inch of the cargo floor was spoken for. The total number of bags was sixty-two, and though I didn't know what they weighed, it was obvious by looking at the floats the plane was heavy.

Maybe too heavy.

"Think it'll fly?" Mike asked with a sheepish grin, studying the floats with me, both of us appreciating how low they were sitting in the water.

"We'll find out soon enough," I mumbled with a grimace. "At least there's a nice long runway to try."

"If I know one thing about a Beaver, it'll fly," he said. "They always do."

We stood in silence for what seemed like a long time, catching our breaths, considering the possibilities. I'd never seen the floats on my plane so low in the water. Dan Sanders was fifty feet away, leaning against the pickup. The wheelbarrow was already in the back with the tailgate up. He was smoking a cigarette, watching and waiting with overt impatience.

"We need to talk, Mike, and we don't have much time."

"About what?"

"About not getting killed. So while we're talking, we're going to put on a little show for Dan over there. We're going to have a discussion about this paperwork here. Okay?"

I tapped the clipboard in my hand with a finger and he gave me a perplexed look.

"That's perfect, you're a natural," I said. "Now then, that big Chinese guy you say is looking for me. His name is Tommy Kay, am I right?"

I pulled a pen out of my shirt, tapped the clipboard again, and held it out to him. He took it, flipped a page, and while shaking his head said, "How did you know that?" When I didn't answer, he said, "You're right, his name is Kay. But I don't think he's around anymore, I watched a plane pick him up on the Stewart River on Tuesday. Think he's gone."

"He'll be back, count on that. Did you get the tail letters?"

"No, but I'm pretty sure it was a Super Cub, red or orange I think, and it had a US registration. Couldn't see much of it, though, I was doubled over in the back of Dan's camper. Kay had just punched me in the stomach. It was his way of saying goodby."

"He broke your nose too."

Mike nodded and flipped a few more pages, pointing his pen at something irrelevant, then handed the clipboard back to me.

"Yeah, the son of a bitch. He cold cocked me flush in the face in my own home, last Monday night in Whitehorse." Mike sighed and looked around. "I'm putting my life in your hands by telling you this, but there's this guy at Thistle Creek Resources making me falsify assays for their damn press releases. If I don't play along, or if he finds out I've been talking to the cops, he said Kay would kill my daughter. I really don't know what to do."

"What's this guy's name?"

"Li."

I nodded and said, "What you do is just play along, Mike, so everyone including your daughter stays alive. Do exactly what you're told and everything will be fine. The police are all over this. Help is on the way. Where do I sign?"

He pointed to the obvious place.

"How do you know?" he asked with a look of shock.

"I just know, okay? Leave it at that. The cops hired me to help them. That's why I'm talking to you about this jam you're in."

"They hired you?"

"Well, me and my plane anyway."

He shook his head again.

"This whole deal is totally outrageous," he said, then after a pause, "Know what I don't understand?"

"What's that?" I said, dropping to a knee to sign the documents.

He bent over with his hands on his knees, pointed at the clipboard in my hand, and whispered in my ear, "Well, just about everything about this project, including that guy over there by the truck. I think he's working for Kay but I don't think he likes him any more than I do. Even so, I'm supposed to be in charge here, not him, but he never leaves me alone. He's always on my case, always telling me what to do, always takes the wheel when we go anywhere. And then there are the assays. Thistle Creek is an incredible property, Brody, the best I've ever seen. The geology is to dream for. I sent a few of the first drill samples to Thurson yesterday and the assays came back over the top. The results speak for themselves, just the way they are. But the brass in Vancouver is making me double all the numbers for their press releases. It's totally unneccessary, let alone illegal, and now my reputation is ruined forever. The con they're running is ridiculous and totally outrageous. No one with a brain in their head will believe the numbers they're forcing me to put out. So why do they bother?"

"Because they're stupid, Mike. They're liars and cheaters and don't know what they're doing. They underestimate everyone else's intelligence and that's what makes them criminals. And it's how we're going to bust them."

I stood up and Mike took the clipboard from me. He separated the pages and handed me my two copies.

"You sound pretty sure of yourself," he said with a glare. "I hope you're right. I'm in a hell of a jam here."

"I know, Mike. But remember, me and a whole bunch of cops have got your back. Just hang in and play along. Like I said, you'll be okay. The cavalry is on its way. Oh, almost forgot, Dave Sorenson wants you to call him."

"About what?"

"Don't know."

"Well tell him I'll try. If he doesn't hear from me, tell him to track me down at the party in Dawson."

"You going to that?"

"Have to. I'm supposed to give a presentation to a bunch of brokers and mining analysts. Not looking forward to it, I mean, lying about assays. And the company brass will be there, they say they want to meet me even if I don't want to meet them. Rumor has it they're closing the whole camp for the weekend so the drillers can go to the party, too."

He walked off to his pickup without another word. I'd be upset too. Mike had been all but kidnapped. My stomach growled as he climbed into the passenger side. I yelled at him and jogged up to his door. He rolled the window down. There was a banana sitting on the dash.

Beside a revolver.

"Hey, got anything to eat in there?" I asked.

Mike handed me the banana.

"Just this, but the best restaurant in the Yukon is up at camp if you want a real meal."

"This'll do. Say, you expecting trouble?"

I pointed at the gun. It was a stainless steel Ruger Redhawk, a .44 Magnum, just your basic everyday handheld cannon.

"Oh, that," he said. "Mine. I figured out in my old age that one of those beats climbing a tree when a bear's chasing you. Got a lot of them around here this year. Someone sees one almost everyday up at the dump. Couple of days ago a big one broke into one of the drillers' pickups to get at a bag of chips. Least we think he's big, you should see the inside of the truck. The steering wheel is bent so bad you can't even drive it. The bear broke every window in the cab and tore the interior to pieces. There's blood everywhere so he must be cut up real bad. He'll be madder than hell right now. You know there's nothing more dangerous than a wounded bear. The conservation guy was out yesterday and set up a couple of traps, but until it's caught, I don't go anywhere without protection. Whatever you do, don't walk up to camp unless you're armed."

"I'll keep that in mind," I said.

Dan Sanders leaned forward with his hands on the wheel and glared at me. Time to go. I gave Mike a pat on the shoulder and jogged back to the dock with breakfast and lunch in one hand. The truck roared off. I watched it climb a steep hill and disappear over the top into a dusty forest.

I was alone again, cocooned in an eerie silence that had descended like some transcendental force. For a moment I watched the river. It was wide and dark and vacant. An uprooted tree that had to be fifty feet long sailed past the dock, moving as fast as the current. Up and down the shoreline chunks of dirty ice and snow lay amongst the rocks and driftwood, hiding in the shadows cast by tall cliffs that rose virtually straight up. Not a mile downstream I'd found two murdered men in a plane last year. I turned toward the forest and wondered if a bear might be lurking. Suddenly I felt vulnerable.

I climbed into the plane, reached under the passenger seat, and pulled out the rolled up sweatshirt Reggie had delivered to me in Minto. I laid it across my legs, reached inside, and wrapped my fingers around the cold steel barrel of a vicious weapon.

I despise guns.

The only thing they're made for is to kill. People say they're good defense but that's nonsense. What defense? Guns are all about offense. Whoever shoots first, wins. At least if you use the one I had in my hands.

It's the ultimate street sweeper, a sawed-off shotgun with a pistol grip, a twelve gauge Remington 870, black and shiny, loaded with slugs, highly illegal at only two feet long, and the best winner-take-all personal firearm if you're serious about winning an argument. Mike's gun was a toy in comparison. Shoot anything at short range with a twelve gauge shotgun and it'll drop like a rock. Game, set and match with the pull of a trigger. There's never a flesh wound left by a twelve gauge slug, just a big hole in something's that dead.

I didn't buy the damn thing, I found it. An accidental discovery as it were.

I remembered when. It was on a warm spring day five years ago and I was climbing around the rafters of my shop, armed with a broom, trying to shoo a young hawk out of the building. The gun was lying on top of a wide beam, completely out of sight of anyone on the floor, twenty feet below. The building was sixty years old at the time and whoever had left it there, or why, well who knew? I'd considered it mine ever since.

Finders, keepers.

I remember taking it down, going outside, and firing a round at a pretty good-sized poplar tree. It cut it almost in half and my ears were still ringing when I put my new toy back on the beam. It had been there ever since, until this morning. Reggie is the only other person who knows it exists, where it's kept, and that for the first time in five years, it was traveling with me today.

By the way, the tree died.

With no sign of a bear or Tommy Kay, I wrapped the evil thing in the sweatshirt and put it back under the passenger seat, then untied my plane and ran it down the dock out into the fast moving river. By the time I started the engine and had the nose pointed in the right direction—into the wind and against the current—I was drifting backwards at five miles an hour.

I pulled the yoke back, shoved the throttle ahead, and wondered if my good old plane would take off.

FORTY NINE

It wouldn't.

At least not against a five mile an hour current and a ten mile an hour wind.

After five minutes of trying everything I knew, all I accomplished was to overheat the engine and get a couple of miles closer to Whitehorse. I backed off the throttle to let the cylinders cool down, and used the time to do some serious thinking, with a bit of risk analysis too.

In order to take off a float plane, the first thing you need to do is get the floats on top of the water—up on the steps as they say—so it can plane like a motor boat. Only then can you accelerate to a speed fast enough for flight. Which was the problem. The plane was so overloaded the floats were mushing through the water like they were stuck in the mud. I simply couldn't get going fast enough to get them up on the surface. Time to try something else.

I turned around and pointed the nose downstream. Hopefully with the wind behind the prop, the boost in thrust would increase my water speed. It worked. At about thirty miles an hour the floats stopped mushing and finally rose up on the surface. Now I was planing and could accelerate to takeoff speed. Problem was, I was going the wrong direction. I needed to take off into the wind.

Now for the tricky part.

Turn around while staying up on the steps.

The river was almost half a mile wide when I started a gentle turn out from the east bank, heading west toward the other side, planing over the choppy black water at thirty-five miles an hour. For what seemed to take forever, I nursed the plane through a long arc, most of it broadside to the wind and current, using a lot of left aileron to keep the wings flat, working the throttle to keep it up on the steps, steering with the rudder to maintain the turn, all the while keeping an eye out for floating trees, chunks of ice, and 'conflicting traffic'.

Not much chance of the latter in the middle of nowhere.

I finished the turn just short of the west bank, still planing, now headed into the wind. I added a little throttle, pumped the flaps down a notch, increased the prop pitch until the manifold pressure reached thirty-six inches—as much as I dared for the old engine—then pushed the throttle lever all the way forward.

With a turn of the wheel I lifted one float off the water, then the other, and finally—finally—was airborne.

Piece of cake.

But with everything at the limit—engine RPM, the throttle wide open, cylinder temperatures in the red, manifold pressure at thirty-six inches, and the flaps almost all the way down—my plane was flying like a wounded bird, wobbling all over the sky, barely climbing at the anemic rate of two hundred feet a minute. I backed everything off a bit and raised the flaps a little to give the engine a break. To my relief, the plane held its altitude, though it immediately stopped climbing and was a handful to fly.

The situation was absolutely ridiculous.

For the second time in a week I'd made a terrible error in judgement and was tempting fate again. Pure and simple I was overweight, one of the most common recipes for disaster in aviation. Was I stupid or what? Or maybe just stubborn. Or maybe both.

Whatever.

The river was three hundred feet below me and I would need to keep it there. Cold air is dense and provides greater lift than warm air, and the coldest air around was over the water. It was a little past noon and I wasn't going to take any shortcuts over a rapidly warming landscape. So long as my plane was flying like a pig, I would follow the Yukon all the way to Whitehorse.

Low and slow it would have to be.

* * *

I was almost out of fuel when I pointed the nose into the sun and prepared to land on Schwatka Lake.

At least my plane was airworthy again, having burned seven hundred pounds of gasoline in the last three and a half hours, and I had no trouble clearing the power lines and the dam with plenty of room to spare. Just before three o'clock in the afternoon I made a picture perfect landing on a picture perfect day in Whitehorse.

The cockpit thermometer said it was sixty degrees outside, and for all the distractions on the flight down, I'd hardly noticed a vast improvement in the weather. With the lake glittering like shattered glass, I dropped the rudders and squinted over the nose to find the dock. I lowered the bill on my cap and tried to discern the scene ahead. It seemed there was a lot of activity with a crowd milling about and the parking lot full of vehicles.

Now what?

The same two ducks from this morning appeared out of nowhere. They'd probably been submerged all day, lying in wait like Navy Seals, poised for another attack. They were twenty feet in front of me, paddling as fast as they could, quacking up a storm as usual. My shoulder ached, I was hungry and tired, and definitely not in the mood to make a detour around them.

I opened the cockpit door and yelled at them.

"Get the hell out of the way!"

They kept quacking and held their course.

"Move or you'll get run over!"

They quacked some more and at the last second, skittered off to one side. The big one hissed and glared when I puttered by.

"Screw you, pal! It's my lake too!"

"Quack, quack, quack."
Staff Sergeant Allan Robson was waiting for me.
And so it seemed, was everyone else in town.

* * *

Robson, the quintessential killjoy, was standing alone on the dock. He had his arms folded across his massive chest with his big shiny shoes splayed wide apart. The hat on his head was tilted low over his brow and he was wearing a pair of those mirrorized sunglasses that made him look like some bad ass southern sheriff. Fifty feet behind him, at the top of the jetty, stood the lady cop who'd given me a ticket for using my cell phone in Jennifer's truck.

She had her arms held out at her sides, keeping half a dozen hyperactive reporters at bay. They were jostling for position behind her, holding their cell phones over their heads, taking pictures of me. Ellen Burke was one of them. She was easy to spot, dressed head to toe in spandex, all red today, including a fully unzipped ski jacket fluttering like a flag.

Nice outfit, Ellen.

Behind the trick or treaters were two cop cars parked front and center, then a bunch more cars and trucks, and two pickup trucks I recognized. One was Jennifer's Dodge with the Thurson Ames logo on the door. The other one was a new, blue Toyota.

No.

I climbed out of the plane, tied it to the dock, then with the heat of Robson's glare burning into the back of my neck, opened the cargo bay door.

I turned to face him and asked, "So did you get him?" He just kept on glaring but said nothing. "No, huh? Oh well, no big deal. Maybe you'll get him tomorrow. So what can I do for you this time, Staff Sergeant? And what are all those reporters doing up there?"

I jutted my chin at the crowd behind him.

He took a deep breath and with great deliberation removed his sunglasses, folded them carefully, and slipped them into his shirt pocket. For a long time he stared at me with his cold blue eyes. The silence would have been deafening had it not been for the quacking behind me. The ducks had arrived, still hell-bent on ridding the lake of my plane.

"Hey," I said. "The questions get harder as we go along. What do you want?"

After a loud harrumph, he said, "It just follows you around, doesn't it, Mr. Brody? It goes on and on and on. You gotta wonder if it'll ever end."

"What the hell are you talking about?"

He reached into his coat pocket and pulled out a folded piece of paper, studied it long enough to irritate me, then shoved it in my face. I grabbed it out of his hand and unfolded it. Yet another photograph.

"Know him?" he asked.

It was a driver's licence photo of a Chinese man.

"No. Should I?"

"You sure?"

"Of course I'm sure. Who is he?"

"His name is Adrian Woo and he's dead."

"Lots of people are dead, so what?"

"Mr. Woo's body was found this morning by a young woman at the Minto Campground. He'd been stuffed down the ladies' toilet and was lying at the bottom of the holding tank. The chemicals had eaten him up pretty bad and the only reason we could identify him is that whoever put him in there was kind enough to leave his wallet in his pants pocket."

"And this was at the Minto Campground?"

"That's right. Not far from where you keep your plane. According to your buddy, that big kid..."

"Reggie McCormack."

"Right, McCormack. According to Mr. McCormack, Woo's body was discovered just minutes after you took off from Minto today. Now what can you tell me about what happened to Mr. Woo?"

"Not a damn thing. Never seen him before and don't know him.

And I wasn't even in the Minto Campground today. All I did was land and fuel up on the lake."

Robson nodded and looked at my plane.

"What's in the bags?"

"Toys for the kids at the mission."

He nodded, paused, then said, "Know what, Mr. Brody? That man you say you didn't assault on Tuesday? The one we carted off to Whitehorse General in a coma? Well he woke up yesterday. I just talked to his parents who came all the way up from South Carolina to see him. Right now he's just staring at the ceiling gurgling like a baby. But when he can talk again, and the doctors say he will, and he tells me what happened on the Whitehorse Walking Path, well then I'm gonna bust your ass."

Robson put on his sunglasses, turned to leave, then whirled around.

"And another thing," he growled, pointing a menacing finger at me. "Remember what I said, don't even think about leaving the territory."

He stomped up the jetty. I crumpled up the photograph and threw it in the plane.

Next...

* * *

They came running down the jetty like a gang of Black Friday shoppers. In an instant they had me hemmed in with an array of cell phones stuck under my chin.

"Mr. Brody, did you know the murdered man found in Minto today?"

"Was he murdered?"

"What was he doing in the Minto Campground?"

"Camping would be my guess."

"Why was he found in the ladies' toilet?"

"It's cleaner than the men's."

"Mr. Brody, what did that police officer just ask you?"

"He wanted to know what's in the bags in my plane."

"What's in the bags?"

"Leverite."

"What's leverite?"

"Leave 'er right there."

"Did he say you were a suspect for the man's murder?"

That one I didn't answer and looked up at the parking lot. Sarah was standing beside a man and two rubber wheeled wagons. I wondered if the man was Tony. He was tall and slim, wearing workboots, jeans, and a jean jacket. Sarah had on a black baseball cap to match her tight black jeans. She was holding a pair of work gloves in her hands. The two were fixated on me. So was Robson. He seemed to be enjoying the scene, leaning against his cruiser with a smirk on his face. It was time to put an end to this nonsense.

"Alright, ladies," I said with my hands in the air, "I have a brief statement to make, then you have to go." They all shut up and leaned in for the quote of the day. "Listen carefully, I'm only going to say this once." They leaned in closer. Ellen Burke was right under my nose. "I am not going to answer any more of your questions because I don't have any answers. It's the RCMP you should be talking to, they know who's responsible for these recent murders in the Yukon, and they damn well know it isn't me. They also know that all these murders are part and parcel of a much bigger story, a conspiracy to defraud the people of the Yukon. So I suggest you stop hassling innocent people like me and direct your inquiries to them. They're the ones who know what's really going on. And don't waste your time talking to that Staff Sergeant up there, he's one of the ringleaders and will be sure to deny everything. That's all I have to say. Now if you don't mind, there are people waiting to unload this plane and we need room to do that."

For a while they just stared with their mouths open, trying to absorb my earth shattering revelation. Ellen Burke sneered, gave me an angry look, then bolted up the jetty. The rest of the trick-or-treaters charged after her. As hoped, they descended on Robson like bees on a bear. He was waving his hands over their heads, trying to calm them down.

Told you he'd deny everything.

FIFTY

I figured Robson had two choices.

Either come back down to the dock and arrest me, which would save him face though not without some inconvenience, or simply leave.

Fortunately he decided on the latter, roaring off with his tires spinning, but not before wagging an admonishing finger in my direction. Or maybe it was a finger gun. Whatever it was, somehow I got the feeling he wasn't finished with me.

Sarah and the man she was with waited for the reporters to leave, who were dashing off to their vehicles to chase Robson. When the cloud of dust dissipated, the pair from Thurson Ames came down to the plane, pulling their little red industrial-grade wagons.

Sarah was all business and barely gave me a glance. 'Elvira, Mistress of the Dark' was sporting black lipstick today.

"Brody, meet Larry Brookes," she said in a deadpan tone. "Larry is working in Thurson's Whitehorse lab for a couple of days. He'll be returning to our Dawson branch on Sunday. Larry, meet Brody."

We shook hands without a word said but I picked up a definite vibe that Larry knew all about me and Jennifer. Still, I was relieved to know his name wasn't Tony, a man I didn't need to meet.

It took the three of us half an hour to unload the plane. I sat in the cargo bay and slid the bags out to Larry who had one foot on a float and the other on the dock. He'd transfer the bags into the wagons while Sarah inspected and checked off tag numbers against her paperwork. Each time the wagons were filled, we'd move them up to the parking lot and load them into the back of Jennifer's pickup. Evidently Tony's truck was not available for hauling rocks, being so new and all.

Sarah's boots had poor traction and I was more than happy to come to her rescue, pushing while she pulled her wagon up the jetty, providing me with an up-close and gratuitous view of poetry in motion. We made six trips in all and I enjoyed every one. She would have to know what I had my eyes on—what woman wouldn't—but hey, life's about weaving memories, right?

Which includes poetry as far as I'm concerned.

After we loaded the last bag into Jennifer's pickup, I closed the tailgate and dusted off my hands on my jeans. The little truck was sitting low on the axles. Larry drove away in Tony's Toyota. At least he was kind enough to take the little red wagons with him. It was now just Sarah and I left standing in silence in the parking lot. Fortunately we didn't need anything to say, not with the magnificent view before us. For a moment we admired the lake glittering under a bright warm sun with the pastel mountains of spring rising from the far shoreline. I was pleased to see my plane floating high in the water again.

After a long silence she said, "I need a copy of your paperwork from Mike Giguere."

"In the plane," I said.

She followed me down the jetty and I was instantly self-conscious. I'd been wearing the same jeans and shirt for four days and must have looked as raunchy as I felt. If Sarah's backside was poetry in motion, then mine was fingernails on a blackboard.

"So," she said.

"So," I said.

We were standing face to face beside the cockpit door. My duck buddies were paddling in circles between the floats, enjoying the shade of the fuselage, casting me dirty looks. One of them started cackling and hissing.

"Those two have really got it in for me," I said.

"No kidding. We could hear you yelling at them when you came in."

"You could?"

"Loud and clear." Then with her eyebrows raised she said, "Brody?"

"Yes?"

"The paperwork from Mike?"

"Right," I said.

I climbed in the plane and grabbed my backpack, removed the library books, then got out and locked the doors. I knelt down on the dock, and after a few seconds of digging around, found what she wanted. She separated the copies and gave me mine.

"Don't lose those," she said.

"I won't," I said, stuffing them in my pack.

"Got your satphone in there?"

"Yup."

"Good, remember what I told you. Keep it handy."

"How could I forget?" I said with my best smile.

"And charged up."

"Roger that, *Rita*."

I gave her a salute and she walked off without saying goodbye. I followed her like a puppy. Halfway up the jetty she stopped and turned around. I'd been concentrating so hard on her poetry again, I almost bumped into her.

"What are you doing?" she asked.

"Going to town."

"Not with me you're not."

"Did I ask you for a ride?"

She said nothing and resumed her march to Jennifer's truck. Once again I followed her, but only to the top of the jetty where I stopped and sat down on a log curb to face the lake. Her footsteps were fading behind me, crunching over the gravel. Then they stopped. Silence.

"What are you doing?" she asked.

"Waiting for the fuel guy," I said over my shoulder. "After he fills my plane, I'll hitch a ride in with him."

A pause.

"Why do you want to go to town?"

"Well for one thing, I'm really hungry."

Another pause.

"Oh, get in."

* * *

The truck was heavy and rode like a Cadillac. Sarah was driving it slower than a hearse and a line of traffic was building behind us. It was quiet in the cab with neither of us speaking. I rested my head against the passenger window and watched a flock of snow geese land on the river.

"So," I said.

"So..." she said.

"So, I solved the case."

"And what case is that?"

I laughed and looked at her.

"What case is that? Are you kidding? The case that has you up here. The case that has you dressed like Elisabeth Salander driving a pickup full of rocks around Whitehorse. That case."

"And how did you solve *the* case?"

"Well remember that guy with the hair plugs in the meeting the other day? What he said about falsifying assays?"

"His name is Eric Landry and I remember what he said."

"Good. Then you'll remember he said one of the easiest ways to cheat is to overstate numbers in press releases. And that's what they're doing. They're doubling the assays they get from the lab. The case is solved."

"Who is 'they'?"

"Who else? Those scoundrels running that Thistle Creek company, Li and Chan."

"And how do you know they're overstating the numbers?"

"Because Mike Giguere just told me they are. He says they're making him double the numbers."

"He told you that?"

"Yup, today at Thistle Creek, when I picked up the rocks. That's exactly what he said. And he's trusting me and you cops not to screw up because they threatened to kill his daughter if he didn't play along. So make sure you don't, okay? This is serious shit, Sarrr...Rita. Mike's neck and his family's necks are on the line here."

"Who exactly threatened him?"

I sighed and gazed out at the river again. The geese were getting organized for a lazy afternoon on the water. I wondered if I'd said too much. Or told the wrong person what I knew. Maybe I should have got some assurances about Mike's safety, *before* opening my big mouth.

"Guess," I mumbled, watching the geese in the mirror.

Sarah slowed the truck, if that was possible, and turned left on Fourth Avenue. The line of cars behind us accelerated back to a reasonable speed and continued on their way. She signaled and pulled over to the side of the road, put the truck in park, sat back with her arms folded, then glared at me with those gorgeous brown eyes.

"Was it Kay who threatened Giguere?"

"Hey, can you not drive and ask questions at the same time? I'm starving here."

"Did you tell Robson about this?"

"No. He was too busy grilling me about some dead guy they found in an outhouse, and how he was going to bust me for assaulting someone I didn't assault."

"Brody, you have to tell him."

"Why don't you tell him? As if it'll make any difference. That

guy is on permanent administrative leave. He likes sitting on his
ass too much to go out and chase bad guys."

She put her hands on top of the steering wheel, laid her forehead
on them, and closed her eyes.

"You are incorrigible," she whispered.

"What's that mean?"

"It means you can't be changed."

"Well that's good, right?"

She shook her head and pulled out into traffic again.

"If I only knew," she said.

* * *

Sarah stopped the truck a block north of Fourth and Main. I got
out and with a hand on the door asked, "Hey, do me a favor?"

"What?"

"Ask Jennifer to give me the total weight of those bags in the
back, when she can."

Sarah gave me a curious look, or maybe it was a suspicious one,
and nodded.

"Thanks, and thanks for the ride," I said.

I was about to close the door when she said, "Brody?"

"What?"

I was almost out of patience when she said, "How's Jack?"

"Okay, I guess. He lost a leg, you know. Someone shot him."

"I know. Where is he now?"

"At the vet's."

"When do you take him home?"

"Tomorrow. Why?"

* * *

It was beyond me why Sarah would volunteer to pick up Jack
and deliver him to Minto.

She knew him well enough, having spent time with him last
year, and he adored her. So I had no reservations that he'd be in

good hands. But Sarah Marsalis and I were hardly pals anymore, not since Christmas in Mexico anyway, and I had to wonder what she was up to.

She told me she'd be driving one of the Thurson trucks up to Dawson on Saturday, but by herself, not with Jennifer as previously planned. Whatever the reason for the change, I could live without an explanation, more than happy not to spend half my Saturday driving down to Whitehorse and back.

Still, a mystery if there ever was.

FIFTY ONE

With just a few things to do before I flew back to Minto, the priority was the ache in my belly.

It took me five minutes to walk over to the same restaurant where two days ago I'd picked up that giant pizza for Jennifer. The same young lady who'd carried it out to the truck greeted me with a big smile, probably because she remembered me as the guy who'd poured a pile of coins into her hands when he left. You've got to pay attention to coins in Canada. The smallest bill is a five and a handful of coins can amount to a car payment. I wondered how much I'd given her.

"Welcome back, sir. My name is Shelly and I'll be your server. How many will be dining?"

"Ah, just me will be dining. But I'd like a booth, if that's okay."

Shelly looked like she'd just been hatched. Her blonde hair was cut sassy short and she had on a pair of squeaky tight white jeans that would be illegal in a lot of countries. I followed them over to a booth at the front window and sat down on a comfy vinyl bench with a great view of Main Street.

She was still all smiles when she said, "Our special of the day..."

I raised a hand and said, "Here's what I want, Shelly. Three of the biggest steaks you've got, well done, wrap them up, I'll take them with me. And for the table, the biggest pizza you've got, double veggies. And a caesar salad with lots of bread. And two big glasses of water. Fast as you can, okay?"

Her mouth dropped open like I'd just ordered a barbequed cat but she said nothing, nodded, and hurried off.

There was time to catch up on some personal administration and I put my pack on the table, then took out the things I despised—my cell phone, my cell phone ticket, and the letter from the Yukon Water Board.

The phone display said I had nine missed calls—*nine*—and the low battery warning was flashing. Apparently my phone didn't charge itself. I cursed myself for forgetting that little detail. Again.

Damn thing.

When Shelly came back with my water, I handed her the phone with the charging cord.

"Hey Shelly, can you plug this in for me?"

"What is it?"

"A phone."

She took it from me and inspected it from every angle, turning it over in her hands like an archeologist pondering some stone age tool, then walked away without a word.

Just hatched.

I was signing a check for two hundred and fifty dollars, payable to the Clerk of the Court, whoever that is, when I glimpsed a familiar face walk past the window. I jumped out of the booth and dashed out the front door.

"Hey, Dave!"

Dave Sorenson turned around and reciprocated with, "Hey, Mr. Brody!" He walked back to me with a big smile and said, "See what Thistle Creek did today?"

"No. Say, got a minute?"

"Hours if there's beer in there."

We went inside. Dave removed his suit jacket and laid it carefully over the back of his seat. We sat down facing each other and he loosened his tie. Shelly arrived with my salad. Dave gawked at her.

"You hungry?" I asked him.

"Hi, Shelly," said Dave, ignoring me.

"Hello, Mr. Sorenson. Would you like a menu?"

"No, but you can bring me a Moosehead."

I dug into my salad and chawed off a hunk of bread.

Dave leaned out of the booth to watch Shelly leave and I thought he might fall off the end of the bench. He almost did the next time she left after delivering his beer. He inhaled half the bottle and wiped his mouth.

"Shelly Mavis," he said. "Man, did she turn out."

"I want to sell my stock, Dave. First thing Monday morning, okay? All of it."

That brought him back to earth.

"Gee, Mr. Brody, I really wish you'd take the weekend to think it over. This afternoon I called that woman president again and she told me they have another press release coming out on Monday. They'll be announcing the first drill assays and she said they'll be great. Why not wait a little while longer?"

"I've made my decision, Dave."

Dave scratched his chin and said, "She's hot, you know."

"Who's hot?"

"The president of Thistle Creek Resources."

"You met her?"

"No, but I talked to her on the phone. I can tell."

"You can tell a woman's hot just by talking to her on the phone?"

I wasn't going to tell Dave his hunch was right, that Lynn Chan was as hot as they came.

"Well, yeah," he said, giving me a bewildered look, as if to say, 'who doesn't know that?' Then he drained the other half of his beer, belched, and said, "Guess I'll have to go to that party in Dawson after all, to check her out. Hey, talk to Mike?"

He belched again and wiped his mouth. His eyes were glazed. Mine would be too. I don't think I've ever seen a bottle of beer consumed so fast.

"I did," I said. "Today. I told him to call you. He said if he doesn't call you, then you can catch him in Dawson next weekend. And between you and me, he also said the Thistle Creek project is the best he's ever seen. But I still want to sell my stock, Dave, so make sure you do."

Dave held up his empty bottle at Shelly when she whizzed by to greet more customers. The place was starting to fill up and getting Friday night loud.

"Well, at least you made *some* money," he said with an overt tone of disappointment. "TCR closed at sixty-two cents today."

"Did you say sixty-two?"

"That's right. Sixty-two cents a share. And you paid thirteen. So you're up a cool twenty grand in four days. Not a bad week, huh?"

"Not a bad week is right," I said, suddenly feeling guilty about my gratuitous good fortune.

Dave turned his head toward the bar, searching for a sign that his second beer was coming. Shelly appeared out of nowhere, standing beside us like a baby forklift with an enormous tray spanning her forearms. I pulled my pack off the table and swept my paperwork to the side. When she leaned over and lowered the tray to the table, my eyes locked on the biggest pizza I'd ever seen. Dave's were on her bosom.

"Hungry, Dave? There's plenty."

"No thanks. Just beer for me."

"Be right back with that, Mr. Sorenson."

"Hey Shelly, call me Dave," he said, looking up at her with a sloppy grin.

She flashed him an '*in your dreams*' kind of smile and left with the tray.

Dave drank and I ate. He was halfway through his third beer and I was halfway through my third piece of pizza when he asked, "So Mr. Brody, what do you know that I don't know about TCR?"

I shrugged with my mouth full and reached for a napkin.

"Nothing. But I'm glad I bought TCR stock and now I'm glad I'm selling it."

Dave's eyes narrowed and he leaned forward.

"Know what?" he said. "I think you know more than nothing. You're selling when everyone else is buying. Now why would you do that?" He leaned back with a smile of amusement and wagged his finger at me. "Come on, you know something, don't you?"

I downed a glass of water to buy some time and he took the opportunity to drain his beer.

"I don't," I said.

Dave knew I was lying. He knew because I wouldn't look at him. He held up his empty bottle until he got a nod from the bartender.

"Uh-uh," he said. "You know something."

He wagged his finger again, grinning ear to ear, confident and enjoying himself. I didn't like where this was going. I was in a jam and needed to throw him a bone.

"Look, Dave, it's real simple. I ran into Mike last week in Minto. He told me he was working at Thistle Creek and seemed enthusiastic about his new project. He told me I ought to buy some TCR so I did, through you. Then someone told me the promoter behind TCR was a shyster with a bad reputation. When I heard that, well, that's why I've decided to sell."

"Who told you TCR's promoter's a shyster?"

"Who?"

"Yeah, who?"

The question made me uneasy because I couldn't give him an honest answer, even if I'd felt like it.

"Does it matter?" I said.

"It does if it was the police."

"The police?"

"It seems you've been talking to them a lot lately, least based on what I read in the paper, and after talking to..."

"Who?"

"You know, your favorite reporter. The halibut. Ellen whats-her-name. She called me last night, you know. Asked me all sorts of questions about rare earths. She kept going on and on about them, like what they were used for, were they really rare, where to look for them, were there any in the Yukon. I told her rare earths could be found in every patch of dirt on earth, which is true, and she got mad and hung up. What a head case, huh? Anyway, she also asked me if I knew why you spend so much time talking to the cops, which I hadn't really thought about. Course I didn't have an answer, what could I say? But then I got to thinking..."

"Thinking about what, Dave? Isn't it obvious why I've been talking to the cops? They've been grilling me about murders I didn't commit and people I didn't assault."

He looked away and said, "Yeah, I guess, but..."

"But what?"

I was almost out of patience with Dave. Shelly had just arrived with his fourth beer and she looked at my pizza. Three quarters of it was left and I'd stopped eating. My appetite was gone, as if I could finish it anyway.

I shrugged with humility and said, "Shelly, would you please put the rest of this delicious pizza into small boxes for me. Stack them up, put the steaks on top, and see if you can get everything in one bag. Okay?"

"Yes, sir," she said.

Shelly walked off. Dave drank his beer. I sat and fidgeted.

A quiet minute went by which was much appreciated.

Then, "So here's the thing, Mr. Brody."

"What's the thing, Dave?"

He straightened up, worked out a burp, then slumped forward with his elbows out and his chin propped on top of his beer bottle.

"Stocks go up on bullshit and they go down on reality. But whichever way they go, you can always make money, provided you bet in the right direction."

"How can you make money if the price goes down?"

"By shorting the stock."

"What's that?" I asked.

"The opposite of what you did. You were long. You bought your shares low, the price went up, now you're gonna sell high. Short selling is really the same thing only the order of the transactions is reversed. First you sell the shares when they're high, then you wait for the price to go down, then you buy them back low. In the end it's the same deal, a purchase and a sale with the same spread and profit, only everything's done 'bass ackwards'."

"How can you sell shares you don't own?"

"Borrow them."

"From who?"

"Your broker. Brokerage houses keep pools of stock to lend to short sellers."

"And this is legal?"

"Of course it's legal. You've heard of Bulls and Bears? Bulls buy stock in a rising market, Bears short stock in a declining market. Short selling has been around for centuries."

"Sounds sleazy to me."

"Well it's not, it's totally legitimate, it's part and parcel of trading stocks. Short selling makes for a more efficient market." He stifled a hiccup, drained the last of his beer, and waved the empty bottle at me. "So now for the big question, Mr. Brody."

"And what's that, Dave?"

"Is TCR a short?"

He studied me for a long time but got nothing back but a blank stare.

Is TCR a short?

Dave slid across the bench and stood up.

"I gotta pee," he said.

FIFTY TWO

I was counting out twenties to pay my bill when I heard Dave gasp behind me.

"Shit," he said.

He reached over my shoulder, grabbed his jacket, and hightailed it toward the rear of the restaurant, presumably to escape out the back door.

I looked up to see what the problem was.

The problem was the halibut. Ellen Burke was stomping toward me with her red ski jacket flapping and steam belching from her ears.

"You bastard, we had a deal," she hissed, plopping her butt down across from me and sweeping my giant doggie bag and backpack aside to the end of the table.

"Whoa, Ellen! Nice to see you too! What the hell are you talking about?"

"I'm talking about that statement you just gave out at the lake. You just gave away my exclusive to every reporter in town."

"What exclusive is that?"

"Does the word conspiracy jog your memory?"

"Oh, *that* exclusive. Well first of all, you don't have an exclusive until you print that piece exonerating me as a suspect for three murders and an assault."

"That's Monday," she said.

"Monday? What happened to today or tomorrow?"

"Well in case you hadn't heard, another body was found in Minto today. That kind of took priority. And there's no paper on Saturday."

"So you're saying if there are no more murders this weekend, your article to take me off the hook will be in Monday's paper?"

"Provided no other reporter in town latches onto this so-called conspiracy theory of yours."

"How could they? They don't have a clue. You're the only one who knows anything about it, thanks to me. I guess the Staff Sergeant denied all knowledge, am I right?"

"He not only denied it, he was furious when I asked him if the RCMP had something to hide. And he got even madder when I asked him why no arrests had been made yet."

"Well that doesn't surprise me. The police have lots to hide and lots to lose."

"Says you. But no one I've interviewed has a clue about this conspiracy theory of yours, let alone a rare earth mine."

"Well if they did, they're certainly not going to talk to you about it, now are they? Otherwise it wouldn't be much of a conspiracy, right?"

Ellen had a glare going, at least I think it was a glare, with one eye fixed on my left ear and the other wandering around my nose. It was beyond me why she didn't need glasses.

"So help me, God," she snarled, "If you're jerking me around I'll dig up every sordid detail about your past and spoon feed it to the people of this city, one day at a time, for the rest of your life."

I held up my hands and said, "Know what, Ellen? This isn't working. Forget our deal. Find yourself another story. This whole thing is about to blow up anyway. I can live with some notoriety for a few more days."

I grabbed my pack and bag of food.

"Wait," she said.

"No."

I got up and walked over to the cash register. No one was there. Shelly was serving a table of new arrivals and acknowledged me with a just-a-sec wave.

Ellen got in my face and said, "What do you mean blow up? What's going to blow up? When? How? You owe me something, give me something."

I looked at her said, "What planet are you from, Ellen? The only thing I owe you is a lawsuit."

"Come on, one thing and you'll get your article on Monday."

"One thing?"

"One."

"Okay, one thing. But it's off the record."

"Off the record for a week," she said.

"Ten days," I said.

"Okay," she said. "Ten days."

"Make sure it is ten days or I'll give the story to another reporter. And you got this from an unnamed source, right?"

"Right. Now talk."

I looked around our space which at the moment was empty, then gave her the scoop of the century.

"Okay, those bags in my plane? They're full of rock samples that I picked up this afternoon at a property owned by Thistle Creek Resources. They're supposed to be tested for gold by the local assayer here in town, but I doubt there's much gold in them. What they actually contain are rare earths, and maybe a lot. The Thistle Creek project is being financed with Chinese money and a delegation will be visiting Dawson next weekend to check in on their investment. If I was you, I'd make sure I was there. There's a rumor that something big is about to break, so if you go up, you might end up witnessing Yukon history. Try to get an interview with anyone Chinese, they should all speak English. Shake the trees a bit, see what falls out. Now I've already said too much. Go write that article for Monday's paper. And remember, not a word to anyone for ten days."

Ellen's eyes wobbled and wiggled for a second, then she said, "Who was the dead man found in Minto today?"

"The cops didn't say?"

"No, not until notification of kin and all that crap."

"Right," I said, nodding my head.

"So do you know who he was?"

"Who says it was a 'he'?"

She gave me a look of disgust and said, "Ah, everyone?"

"Look, Ellen, I've said enough."

"So who was he? Did you know him?"

"I told you, I've said enough. You'll find out soon enough from the cops."

"Come on, if you know who he was, tell me."

I drew in a long breath and exhaled with feigned exasperation.

"Not a chance, my life's in enough danger." I paused with my mouth open and let her squirm for a few seconds, then said, "Look, I can't tell you his name...but..."

"But what?"

"Off the record?"

"Off the record."

"Ten days?"

"Ten days."

"He could be Russian. One of the competition. Now that's it. Go."

I pointed at the door.

"Russian?"

"I told you before, Ellen, every country wants a rare earth mine. The stakes are high, especially for this one."

"I'll call you Sunday," she said.

"No you won't. Call me Tuesday, after you publish that article on Monday about what a great guy I am."

She pulled what looked like a pen from her collar, admired it, and pressed the end.

"I've recorded this conversation, Mr. Brody." She gave me a

look of satisfaction, apparently pleased to convey that news. "Don't forget, in case you decide to deny anything later on."

"Fine, Ellen. And don't you forget about waiting ten days."

I watched her leave, wondering if she actually would wait ten days before spinning out her 'exclusive'. I might have felt guilty for the nonsense I'd just fed her, but didn't. Ellen's one and only objective was to get her name on the front page. She was brash, amoral, and unscrupulous. Credible reporting was not her brand of journalism. My guess was she'd cherry pick a few of the nebulous facts I'd fed her, work them into some convoluted yarn about rare earths—and a rumored mining conspiracy—and use vague innuendos to lead her readers down the garden path.

More or less what I'd just done.

Knock yourself out, Ellen.

All I really wanted was for Ellen to turn up in Dawson for the Thistle Creek party. If TCR's sham was about to be exposed by the cops, she'd be in the right place to break the story. And if those feckless cops were still biding their time, which wouldn't surprise me, then at least she could light a fire under their asses. Ellen Burke could screw up a church picnic and I couldn't think of a better candidate for the job. I also couldn't wait for her to interview Lynn Chan and Tippy Li about their rare earth mine.

"Sir?"

"Huh?"

Shelly.

"Would you like to pay your check now?"

"Oh, sure."

I plucked the check out of my shirt pocket. She'd decorated it with two flowers, a smiley face, and a 'Thank You' written in a large flourishing scroll. She was working me for all it was worth with a sloppy smile and had her head tilted over like a puppy. She knew a live one when she saw one. I tipped her a twenty.

"You have my phone?" I asked.

She handed it to me and said, "Sir?"

"Yes?"

"Are you that man who's always on the front page?"

Always?

FIFTY THREE

Two doors down from the restaurant, I walked into the drugstore, bought some envelopes and a sheet of stamps, and addressed my letter to the Clerk of the Court.

The woman who served me said there was a mailbox on the corner and I passed a rack of newspapers on the way out the door. I dropped the letter in the mailbox, then was overcome with a strange feeling. Had I forgotten something?

Money? Wallet? Backpack? My pizza and steaks? What?

None of the above.

I'd just seen my picture in the paper.

I went back to the drugstore and stared at today's front page.

The photo was taken yesterday and showed me walking out of the RCMP building. It was small, like the article underneath it, a single column in the top left corner, probably squeezed in just before deadline.

I took a paper and went outside to read it.

Breaking news.

ANOTHER MURDER IN MINTO
Special to the Yukon Times
By Ellen Burke

The partially decomposed body of a man was discovered late this morning in the Minto Campground, lying at the bottom of an outhouse holding tank.

Roberta Klinger, an employee of Klinger Septic Services of Whitehorse, made the grisly discovery while servicing the tank.

In a telephone interview early this afternoon, Constable Daryl Pageau of the RCMP Minto detachment told the Yukon Times that police had removed the body from the outhouse, as well as a small caliber hand gun found with it. Both the body and gun were sent to Whitehorse for forensic analysis. Constable Pageau said foul play is suspected and an autopsy will be conducted this weekend. He refused to provide any further information about the identity of the man or the cause of death.

It is the second time this week RCMP officers have been called to Minto to investigate a suspicious death. On Monday police were called to the home of C.E. Brody (pictured above) where they discovered the body of twenty-six year old Amy Vanderbilt of Haines, Alaska. The RCMP have ruled her death a homicide.

The Minto Campground is located five miles north of the Minto First Nation and provides vehicle access to the west shore of Two Spirit Lake. The lake is homebase for a charter float plane business owned and operated by Brody.

According to police, Brody was last seen this morning taking off in his plane from Two Spirit Lake, just minutes before the body in the outhouse was discovered.

"Taking off in his plane..."

The Yukon Times had just charged, tried, and convicted me for another murder.

With my head down I headed for the hotel to grab a cab, trying to walk and read at the same time, cursing Ellen Burke under my breath. Someone passed me and stopped.

"Sir?"

It was the woman who'd served me in the drugstore. I almost ran into her. She was blocking my way with her hands on her hips.

"Yes?"

"You didn't pay for your paper."

"Oh, sorry. Here, don't want it."

I held it out and she snatched it from my hand.

Said I was sorry.

Another fifty feet down the sidewalk, "Sir?"

I turned around and this time it was Shelly. She had on a jean jacket with a purse slung over her shoulder. In her hand was an envelope.

"Is this yours? It was under your table."

The letter from The Yukon Water Board. It must have fallen to the floor when Ellen Burke sat down and swept everything aside with one of her big fat arms.

I lowered my bag of food to the sidewalk and took it from her.

"Thanks," I said.

She smiled and stayed put while I slipped the envelope into my pack. Maybe this weekend I'd open it. Shelly was staring at me with a look of anticipation, as though she might be due another tip.

"Are you going to your plane now?" she asked.

"Ah, yeah, actually, I am. How did you know?"

"I'm going to the lake, too. Want a ride?"

She was bouncing on her toes like a kid who'd just got a pony for Christmas. I looked down the street at the lone taxi parked in front of the hotel.

The ammonia chamber.

"Why are you going to the lake?" I asked.

"To pick up my boyfriend."

"Oh, yeah? Who's that?"

"Tim Crothers. He works on planes up there. He's says he

knows you and he works on yours. He says you didn't do any of that stuff, like, well... like what they said in the paper."

"Well that's nice of him. So Tim is your boyfriend, huh?"

"Well, hello! Like, yeah!"

She kept her hands planted on her skinny hips until I said, "Okay, Shelly, I believe you. And I'll take the ride. Thanks."

She had on white sneakers to match her white jeans and I could barely keep up with her. She led me halfway down the block, then ducked down an alley. We emerged in a small parking lot behind the restaurant. She pressed a button on her key fob and the doors on a brand new Nissan Sentra unlocked with a honk and flashing lights. Seems everyone has a new vehicle but me.

Serves me right for taking care of mine.

Shelly was a talker. It was a two mile drive to Schwatka Lake and by the end of the first mile, I knew she was twenty, had no idea what she wanted to do with her life, hated winter, had issues with her mother, and wasn't sure what to buy Tim for his birthday. I tuned her out for the second mile and admired the river. The geese were gone.

When we got to the lake, Shelly said she'd wait in her car for Tim. I thanked her and left her playing with her phone. Tim, or maybe it was Jim, was closing the engine cowl on a Cessna 206. His twin brother was gathering tools and loading them into a wagon. As usual they were wearing identical coveralls, today with short sleeves. They both gave me a wave as I walked toward them and I gave them a wave back. My duck buddies were nowhere to be seen when I stopped beside my plane. I unlocked the doors, got in, and flipped the master switch. All three tanks had been filled and I was good to go.

"Hey, Brody, got something for you."

I was halfway through my preflight check with the cockpit door wide open and looked down at Tim, or Jim, standing on the dock beside me.

"What?"

He was holding up a large brown envelope with my name on it.

"Some real hot babe left this for you," he said.

"A hot babe?"

"I'll say. Tall, nothing but legs, tight pants, tight T-shirt, nice chest. She was driving a pickup. Know her?"

"Maybe."

Jennifer.

"So Shelly gave you a ride, huh?" he said, gazing at her car in the parking lot, shaking his head.

"She did. She says she's your girlfriend. That true?"

"No, but she thinks she's Tim's"

Now I knew who I was talking to.

"Thinks?"

"She's a psycho hose beast, Brody. She texts him nude photos and comes down here everyday at lunch with a pizza. Tim listens to her yack so he can eat for free. The girl never shuts up."

I nodded and wondered what I'd do if I was getting nude photos and free pizza everyday from a hot young woman who never shuts up.

Tough call.

"Hey Jim, could you check the oil for me?"

~~I got out, and while he did~~ that, walked to the end of the dock and opened the envelope. Inside was a stapled set of sample control logs and a handwritten note.

Brody, use these from now on. Do not use Mike's! Next pickup is next Friday at Thistle Creek. 10:00 am sharp!

I couldn't imagine why it was such a big deal to not use Mike's paperwork, it was exactly the same as the forms in the envelope. But all that mattered to me was the where and when of the next pickup.

A week today. Next Friday. No problem.

Jim leaned out of the cockpit and shouted, "Needs some!"

"Do it!"

While I waited for him to fetch the oil, I dug out my phone and turned it on. It was half charged.

After six long rings, "Minto Café."

"Hi, Leah."

"Brody! Where are you? Did you hear what happened here?"

"I'm in Whitehorse and yeah, I heard."

"That girl who found the guy? She's been out back in one of the cabins all afternoon. Mom says she's like totally freaked out and just lays on the bed staring at the ceiling. Her Dad's coming up to get her. Reggie said Daryl puked when he saw the guy's face. He says it was like all melted away. And they found a gun too."

I sighed and said, "Bizarre stuff, Leah. And it's lies."

"It's lies?"

"Yes. You said she lays on the bed, you should say she lies on the bed."

"Whatever. Hey, Mom's really mad at you."

"Oh, yeah? How come?"

It dawned on me then that every woman I knew was mad at me.

"That reporter from Whitehorse called here three times this morning. Mom said she got so fed up she gave her your cell phone number."

"Can't blame her, Leah, I'd do the same," I said with resignation, now with a pretty good idea who was responsible for my nine missed calls. "So Leah, who called me from the Café?"

"Not me. Probably Mom. Or maybe Reggie. He wanted to talk to you about something."

"What?"

"I don't know. Wait, he just walked in."

"Leah, do me a favor and take a flight note. Whitehorse to Two Spirit Lake, direct. Okay? ETA tonight at eight."

"Got it, here's Reggie."

"Hello."

"Hey, Reg, how's it going?"

"Good."

"Ah, Reg?"

"Yeah?"

"Could you drop Russ off at my place tonight? About eight-thirty?"

"Okay."

"Thanks. And don't feed him too much for dinner."

"Okay."

"Take care of Hank?"

"Yup."

"How is he?"

"Good."

"Plywood come in?"

"Yup."

"Great. Hey, did you want to ask me something?"

"Yeah."

"What?"

"Mrs. Deerchild is coming to visit. She wants a ride in your plane."

"Mrs. Deerchild wants a ride in my plane?"

"Yup."

"When?"

"Sunday."

"Okay, we can do that."

Silence.

Guess we were all caught up.

"Anything else, Reg?"

"No."

"Okay. See you tonight."

"Okay."

Click.

Mrs. Deerchild.

I wanted to talk to her.

FIFTY FOUR

Lynn Chan made two calls at noon.

Tippy was certain to kill her if he knew what she'd done, but he was probably going to kill her anyway. At least now she had a plan to save her life.

After two glasses of wine, and using one of the two phones Danny had given her, the first call she made was to her bank in the Caymans. When Lynn told her account manager she wanted to sell all her Thistle Creek shares, he was shocked.

"Why sell when the stock is on fire?" he'd asked.

"That's personal," she'd said.

When she told him she didn't want anyone to know which brokerage house was dumping millions of shares of Thistle Creek Resources into the market—an easy clue for Tippy to track down the culprit—she'd been transferred to the trading desk. A young man named Arturo answered and explained he could distribute her shares to at least ten different houses who would jointly execute the sale. That way, he explained, the selling would appear to be coming from all over the place. When Arturo asked what price she wanted to sell the shares, Lynn told him whatever he could get.

"So to be clear, you want to sell all your shares in Thistle Creek Resources, at the market, just hit the bid, whatever it is,

no minimum price, no daily limit. Are those your instructions?"
Arturo had asked.

"Those are my instructions," she'd said. "Just blow them out."

Being a Friday afternoon, Arturo said it would take him a couple
of business days to set things up, and the selling wouldn't start until
the next Wednesday. Lynn said that was fine. Arturo also told her
it might take a few days to sell her entire position—all ten million
shares—and she said that was fine too. Whatever she ended up
with—two, three, four, maybe even five million dollars—it would
still be a lot more than she'd paid for them, and net her a nice tidy
profit. Offshore and tax free to boot.

The second call she made with Danny's phone was to the British
Columbia Securities Commission. She refused to provide her name,
saying only that she was a whistleblower and had incriminating
information about a certain stock promoter. She was asked to hold
and waited five minutes until a man named Eric Landry took her
call. She made an appointment to meet him, also next Wednesday,
at her lawyer's office.

When she finished the second call, she went into the kitchen
with Danny's phone. She found a hammer in a drawer, wrapped the
phone in some newspaper, smashed it to bits, then put the mess in
a bag and dropped it down the garbage chute.

Now for that damn chandelier.

* * *

Her desk phone was ringing when she walked back into her
suite. Instinctively she ran and picked it up.

"Thistle Creek Resources."

"Lynn."

She stifled a gasp and said, "Hello, Tippy."

"Surprised to hear from me? Where have you been?"

She'd been ignoring his calls since their meeting last night. She
hadn't checked the caller ID when she'd picked up.

Stupid. So where had she been?

She faked a coughing fit and picked up the other phone Danny had given her. She touched an icon on the screen and coughed again to buy more time. Seconds later the video feed of her suite appeared, the same feed that Tippy could well be watching with her. The feed showed her sitting at her desk with her back to the camera, but *not* with a phone to her ear. If Tippy was watching the feed, he might wonder why that was.

She coughed again and said, "Let me put you on speaker, Tippy."

Lynn breathed a sigh of relief. The video feed showed her at her desk using both hands to do paperwork. But now there was no reason for Tippy to suspect she wasn't on the phone with him.

"Are you okay?" he asked.

"I'm fine, swallowed something the wrong way, sorry. I've been around, in and out, you know me, always busy. I'm at my desk now. So what's up?"

Lynn was trying to sound as upbeat as possible though she was shaking like a leaf, praying the video didn't reveal another inconsistency. She could hear the clatter and conversation of a bar in the background. Tippy was holding court in his favorite watering hole. It was a little after one o'clock on a Friday afternoon and the markets had just closed.

"See what we closed at today?" he asked.

"Not yet, been swamped."

"Sixty-two cents and nothing but bids chasing the stock. Wait until Monday, Lynn, we have another press release coming out and we'll be trading a dollar by noon."

Lynn was fixated on her cell phone, terrified that the video might show her leaving her desk. She had to end the call but would risk a question.

"That's fantastic, Tippy, congratulations," she said with as much gusto as she could muster. Then, "Oh, almost forgot. I'm missing an earring. You didn't find one at your place by any chance? A pearl stud?"

"No, but I wouldn't be worrying about a lost earring. In a couple of weeks you can buy all the earrings you want."

"I know, but they were a gift from my grandmother, sentimental value and all that. I'd really like to find it. Maybe it's in your plane. Are you flying tomorrow?"

Tippy paused, knowing she could well be right. The last time they flew together was coming back from the Caymans, and with nothing else to do on the eight hour flight, had played some rough games in the back.

"Not going anywhere until we leave for the Yukon," he said, recalling the best flight of his life, keenly aware of a stirring in his loins.

"Would you mind if I went out and took a look?"

"Go ahead. But call the hangar first, make sure someone's there to let you in." Then he said, "So, Lynn, the reason I called…"

"Yes?"

"What are you doing for dinner?"

Did she have a choice?

* * *

He could tell you the name of the place—Chicken, Alaska— but had no idea where it was. The pilot who'd flown him in from Fairbanks said Dawson was eighty miles east, about an hour's flight, which was probably the reason Mr. Li had sent him here. He hoped Mr. Li would call soon with instructions.

Before he lost his mind.

Tommy Kay walked out of the dreary guest cabin he'd been cooped up in and surveyed his surroundings. Nothing had changed, it was always the same, just dust and dirt and trees. Trees in the yard, trees on the hills, trees on the mountains. Even the light never changed, always bright, all day long, all night long. It was a little past noon Alaska time and the mosquitoes would be out soon.

He closed the cabin door and three huskies chained to a post in the center of the yard raised their heads. They did every time he emerged from the cabin. They stared at him for a few seconds, then dropped their heads on the dirt and went back to sleep.

They were as bored as he was.

Kay looked across the yard at the pilot's house. The pilot hadn't been around since dropping him off, but his wife was home. He could see her fussing in the kitchen and she would be bringing out his lunch any minute. He could eat in the house if he wanted, maybe even watch some television, but the pilot's wife was a witch. She had this shrill scratchy voice that reminded him of a parrot. He didn't like her nosy questions either and had put a quick end to them with a long menacing stare. She hadn't had much to say since then.

Kay sat down on a rickety wood bench and took out his phone. There was no cell phone service in Chicken but he could always play solitaire. Anything to kill time. It was times like this he wished he knew how to read. When the back door to the house opened, both he and the dogs looked up. The pilot's wife was waving at him with a phone in her hand.

"Phone call," she screeched from across the yard.

That voice.

He lumbered toward her with his muscle bound arms swinging like wings, advancing his feet by rotating his thick torso one way, then the other. When he passed the dogs, one of them got to its feet and growled. He turned to face it. The dog cowered and lay down.

"Don't be takin' too long, this thing's three dollars a minute," the witch screeched, holding out a satellite phone from behind the screen door.

Kay grabbed her wrist and yanked her out into the yard. He could have broken her arm with a press of his thumb, but didn't.

"Wait out here," he said, taking the phone from her and walking into the kitchen.

* * *

Tippy Li put his phone down on the table, reached for his Scotch, and wondered why all of a sudden Lynn was being so pleasant. What was she up to?

"So a date with the president, huh?" asked Gerry Feldman who was seated at the other end of the booth, grinning ear to ear as usual.

The two rent-a-dates wedged between them giggled. The men had been ignoring them like they were part of the decor, which they were.

"Just business," said Tippy, giving his drink a swirl and contemplating its amber glow.

"Business my ass," said Gerry. "I met her you know. She came into the office yesterday to sign some papers. She was wearing this tight yellow leather skirt and stopped the whole show. Man, has she got a caboose on her. Half my brokers followed her out to the hall to watch her walk to the elevator."

Tippy gazed around the room, counted his henchman, then waved his hand at Gerry.

"I need to make a call," he said.

Gerry downed the rest of his Teachers and winked at the women beside him.

"Mind if I take these with me?"

"All yours."

The women giggled and slid down the leather bench after Gerry. Gerry was all smiles while he waited for them to adjust their skirts and bosoms.

"When's the next press release?" Gerry asked with his eyes undressing the talent.

"Monday. It'll be the best one yet. Make sure you buy early. We'll be a dollar by noon."

"Oh, we'll be buying early," said Gerry. "Count on that."

Tippy waited for Gerry and his new toys to leave, then reached into his suit pocket and pulled out a slip of paper. He dialed a number and waited.

A moment later he said, "Mr. Kay, please," and a moment after that, "Be in Dawson next Friday."

FIFTY FIVE

It's not everyday you find a dead man in an outhouse.

Which explained why the Café parking lot was full. The booze and bullshit would be flowing all night.

I drove by and a few miles later slowed and turned for the dirt lane leading down to my cabin, an event that invariably stirs my sense of independence. I was almost home, to the hallowed shelter I'd built with my own two hands, a place where I could reunite with my dogs and enjoy some peace and quiet. Of course one dog wouldn't be there, Jack was still in Whitehorse, but Russ would be and I couldn't wait to see him.

For most of the flight up from Whitehorse I'd been daydreaming about my first evening home in a week. The first thing I'd do was spoil Russ with a nice piece of steak, then treat myself to a long hot shower, then put on some comfy clothes and head out to the deck for some R&R.

Kick back, relax, pat the dog, open a cool one, soak up the scenery under a warm spring sun. But when I stopped at the river, my reverie was crushed by a surge of despair.

What the hell?

There was garbage everywhere.

Someone had paid me a visit since the cops had left. The long strands of yellow police tape had been breeched and pieces of it were fluttering from the trees on either side of the lane. I grabbed my gun and got out to investigate. The closer I got to my cabin, the more garbage there was. I climbed the last five stairs to the deck and knew what had happened.

Bottles, jars, cans, plastic wrappers and paper were scattered all over the place. My little grill lay on its side with the lid torn off. The aluminum screen door to the porch was a twisted mess, hanging askew from a single hinge. The front door was wide open. I pumped a round into the chamber, tiptoed through the mess, and stepped inside.

The difference between a bear and a bomb is that a bomb doesn't eat your food.

I stared aghast at what had been my clean and efficient little kitchen. Now it was in shambles. The fridge was all but destroyed with the interior ripped out and its broken bins and shelves strewn all over the floor. The oven door had been used as a step stool and was broken off clean. Cupboards had been pulled off the wall and torn apart. Pots, pans, dishes and cutlery were everywhere. The only clue that a bomb hadn't gone off was that every food container had tooth and claw marks. My two steaks had been devoured, as had my peas, potatoes, lettuce, tomatoes, grapes, crackers, cheese, eggs, soup, beans, spices, sugar—and based on the shredded remains of a large paper bag—twenty pounds of dog food.

Only a bear.

Evidently he didn't watch TV and had spared the living room of his wrath. I walked through a cloud of flies into the bedroom to see if he'd gone in there. He hadn't, but the cops sure had. I could tell by all the patches of white residue where they'd lifted a million fingerprints. They'd leaned the bed up against the wall, pulled all my clothes out of the closet, and left them in a heap in a corner with the concrete block.

I walked into the bathroom where there were even more fingerprint patches. Gone was every bottle and bar of soap, all the towels, and all of Amy's lotions and potions, probably taken for forensic analysis.

I noticed the toilet seat was up and the water in the bowl sitting at the rim. Obviously it was royally plugged up.

If you didn't eat it, don't flush it.

Whoever was responsible, and I doubted it was the bear, had taken the top off the tank and left it in the shower. As if the problem was in the tank.

Morons.

I went outside, sat down on the edge of the deck, gazed out at the river, and pondered life. Live long enough and sooner or later you're going to hit your funny bone, stub a toe, bite your tongue, break a nail, get a tooth ache. While some people say it's okay for a grown man to cry, I thought about those poor folks who in seconds lose everything to a tornado. Everyone's life is a dream come true—at least for someone—and mine could be a lot worse. I was alive and healthy, could afford a new kitchen, and had the whole next week to rebuild it. All I had to do was accept fate and get to work. I sighed and got to my feet again.

Never liked those kitchen cabinets anyway.

* * *

With my shotgun across my knees, I was sitting on the throne in the leaky outhouse behind my cabin, swatting mosquitoes, thinking about kitchen cabinets, a plugged toilet, and why the front door to my cabin had no damage. Obviously it had been left open. After dealing with the minor nuisance of an aluminum screen door, the bear had just walked in. Not that I blamed him, it was his nature to follow his nose, and his nose had led him to a couple of steaks festering on the counter.

But bear security is food security and in the previous five years I'd never had one attempt an entry. So did the cops not know any better than to leave food lying around? Why hadn't they put those steaks in the fridge? And why hadn't they closed the front door when they left? Had it simply been oversight? Or not.

Before my suspicious imagination got the better of me, the

bucket of bolts that was Reggie's old tow truck came rattling and rumbling down the lane.

Russ.

The dented driver's door opened with a pop and a screech. Russ jumped out into a cloud of dust and charged me at full throttle. He leapt high in the air, bounced four paws off my chest, ran back into the woods, and came roaring out to do it again. This time I was ready for him and caught him in my arms, and received a major face wash for it.

"Okay, enough," I said with a stern look.

He stopped with the tongue and we studied each other, eye to eye, nose to nose. He still had some swelling in his face from his night in the woods with Jack, but didn't look the worse for wear. My little hero started with the licking again and I put him down. While I was wiping my face with the sleeves of my shirt, he blasted up the path to the cabin, probably hoping to find Jack.

Reggie looked at the gun in my hands and said, "Need it?"

I shook my head and said, "Nope."

He nodded with his hands in his pockets, appraising the mess around us.

"Bear," he said.

"How do you know?"

He pointed at the ground in front us and said, "That."

I took a step forward to where he'd pointed and he swung out an arm. Stopped me like a steel beam.

"See?" he said, pointing again.

I followed his finger down to what might be a paw print in the dirt, and though not entirely sure what I was looking at, said, "Big bear, huh?"

He shrugged and said, "Maybe little bear, big feet."

"Well he ate two steaks and a whole bag of dog food."

Reggie shrugged again and said, "Bears eat a lot."

* * *

It was Saturday morning and felt like one of those magical

moments from childhood, the kind where you wake up in an absolutely breathless world where the air's so still you can hear forever. I was lying in bed with my eyes glued shut, trying my best to stay asleep, deciphering the far away sounds drifting through the window—the drone of a plane, a vehicle on the highway, a songbird chirping, a car door slamming—each one so clear and distinct as to seem surreal.

A car door slamming?

I forced my eyes open and was greeted by a high wood ceiling and for a moment wondered where I was. Russ was lying between my feet and was on high alert with his ears up and a gutteral growl growing deep in his throat. We looked at each other with the same question.

Who the hell is that?

Leah wasn't expected until ten, at least that's what I'd told Reggie to tell her when he left last night. I grabbed my gun, followed Russ down the stairs, and stopped at the side door to my shop.

"Who is it?"

"Duh."

Leah.

If she was on time, I'd slept for ten hours.

I put the gun on a shelf and opened the door.

"Were you still in bed?" she asked with disgust, blowing past me toward the back of the shop.

"Hey, I was tired, okay?"

Standing in front of me was a young girl from the village. I told Reggie that Leah could bring a helper, and what do you know, she brought Tonya. Tonya was maybe fourteen, short for her age, skinny as a rake, and lately had been following Leah everywhere she went. Knowing her circumstance, Tonya could use a hero, having to live with a single mother who didn't do much else other than spend the majority of her time and money in the Café bar, looking for 'Mr. Right'.

"Hi, Tonya."

"Hi, Mr. Brody. Leah said…like…well maybe I could help."

"You sure can. Ready to go to work?"

"Yes."

"Good, we've got a big job to do."

Leah came back carrying a vacuum cleaner with its hose coiled around her neck, clutching two brooms, a dust pan, a roll of paper towels, and a box of garbage bags.

"Well, are you going to help us or not?" she snarled on her way out the door.

Guess it was early for her too.

* * *

Leah took charge.

In twenty minutes the three of us had emptied my little cabin of everything that needed to be washed or thrown out, which was just about everything we could pick up. Tonya was assigned laundry duty and I drove her up to the shop with a truck load of clothes, bedding, four bulging garbage bags, and of course, Russ. I told him to stay in the shop and guard Tonya but when I left, he followed me back down to the cabin. He spent the rest of the morning patrolling the property, sniffing everything that could be sniffed, all the while keeping a sharp eye on me while doing a stellar job of killing time.

Meanwhile, Leah and I had work to do. She had already begun to sweep, vacuum and wipe while I—low man on the crew—had been assigned the dirty work. Like unplugging the toilet and gutting the kitchen.

But first things first.

I opened the closet at the back of my cabin to check my wind powered electric system. It had to be the calmest morning in a year, and without a breath of wind, the charging gauges read zero. No surprise there, but the bank of batteries at my feet held a healthy thirteen volts, plenty to run the vacuum cleaner all morning. Russ joined me behind the cabin and we took a moment to stare up at the windmill, frozen perfectly still against an empty blue sky, mounted high atop a tall steel pole. I went over to the big propane tank and closed the valve.

As predicted, my little propane fridge was a write-off, but the stove could be repaired with a new door and hinges. I disconnected the gas line and dragged the fridge out of the way, then with a crowbar, sledge and portable drill had the whole kitchen dismantled in an hour—cupboards and cabinets, drawers and countertops, plumbing and sink. Not long after I had the whole works stacked in a pile out on the deck. I removed the twisted screen door and added it to the pile, then the grill, and got Leah to help me wheel out the fridge.

A few minutes before noon I was lubricating the hinges on a perfectly good front door when Leah confronted me. She had a rag in one hand and a spray bottle in the other.

"I'm hungry," she said, wiping her brow with the back of a hand.

"Girl's gotta eat," I said.

We closed all the windows and I left a mosquitoe coil smoldering on the coffee table. Anything in my cabin with wings was about to meet its maker.

Up at the shop I rummaged around for an ancient Coleman camp stove while Leah helped Tonya finish the laundry. The 'to do' pile was gone and I was pleased to see two stacks of neatly folded clothes sitting on top of the dryer.

One of life's great luxuries has to be air dried bedding. But when I told the girls to hang my sheets on the clothes line outside, they weren't pleased. Leah was grumbling about a perfectly good dryer when they walked outside with two baskets full of damp sheets.

I found the Coleman, took it out to the picnic table, and fired it up. I went to the fridge, took out last night's pizza, wrapped the pieces in aluminum foil, and laid them on the stove.

While lunch was heating up, I made two phone calls. The first was to the only wildlife officer I know who doesn't like the outdoors.

"Yukon Conservation, Carmacks. Officer Zaagman."

"Melvyn, Brody here."

"Well speak of the devil, me and the boys were just talking about you. Kill anybody today?"

"No, Melvyn, I didn't kill anybody today."

"If you say so. What can I do for you?"

"A bear broke into my cabin yesterday and tore it up. He had lots to eat and he'll be back. I need a trap up here."

"That cabin of yours, it's on First Nation land, right?"

"Yeah, so?"

"So you're not First Nation. Someone from the Minto Band has to put in the request. And it has to go through the Whitehorse office. They open Monday morning."

"I'm not waiting until Monday morning, Melvyn. How about you leave the trap at my shop. It's not on First Nation land and I'll tow the trap down to the river myself."

"No can do, Brody, rules are rules."

"Tell you what, Melvyn. How about I shoot the bear and leave him in the middle of the Klondike Highway. Expect a call from the cops tonight to pick up a bear blocking traffic."

"Now you watch yourself, Mister. Threatening a Yukon Conservation Officer is a criminal offence."

"I'm not threatening you, Melvyn. I'm saying what I'll do if you don't do your job. Now bring me a trap."

"I'll make some calls," he grumbled.

The second call went better. The guy at the propane store in Whitehorse was more than happy to sell me a brand new fridge. He told me it would be exactly the same model he'd sold me five years ago, only new and improved. I wondered how you can improve a fridge. He said he'd be happy to install it and would take away the old one at no charge. I told him I'd be happy to let him take it away if he gave me two hundred dollars. We settled on a hundred. He said he had a used door and hinges for my stove, and would be up next Wednesday to install everything. I told him to make it Friday.

Russ was giving me the hungry eye when I hung up the phone.

I had half a bag of dog food in the shop and added some chopped steak to his usual ration. His lunch was gone before I'd stowed the bag. So was he.

The girls and I went outside and we ate our pizza at the picnic table. They sat facing each other at one end of the table, whispering, giggling and generally ignoring me, except when they had a question about the dead guy in the outhouse. When they got tired of the same answer every time—a shrug of my shoulders—they tuned me out and left me to my thoughts.

My thoughts were that my shoulder still hurt, Jack would be arriving soon, and so would Sarah Marsalis.

FIFTY SIX

At four o'clock there was still no sign of Sarah and Jack, and I was beginning to get antsy. Maybe she was driving slowly because of Jack, or maybe she was just driving slowly. No way she could get lost. You can't get lost on the Yukon highway system, there are only two main highways.

After Leah and Tonya left I went back down to my cabin and fixed the leg on the bed, tidied up the bedroom, put clean sheets on the bed, and restocked the bathroom with stuff I'd hijacked from the apartment over my shop. After a well deserved shower, I sat down on the deck and was just starting to sketch out a plan for my new kitchen when I heard a racket coming down the lane. The rattling and clanging couldn't be Sarah, I know a trailer when I hear one.

I grabbed my shotgun and instantly resented my new habit of reaching for it every time a stranger approached. The sooner Tommy Kay was arrested, the sooner I could return the damn thing to where it belonged, on a rafter high in my shop. I walked to the edge of the deck and took a cautious look down from behind the pile of junk that used to be my kitchen. When I saw my visitor, I hid the gun in the porch.

The guy in the pickup towing the bear trap was named Blake. Blake was a tall gangly kid with eyeglasses, buck teeth, and a perpetual smile. He wore a drab green, department-issued shirt with yellow badges, blue jeans, and boots. On one hip he was packing a pistol concealed in a holster, on the other hip a canister that looked like a small fire extinguisher. He told me he'd just graduated from college with a major in bear habitat. I guess that qualified him to set bear traps. Evidently they didn't teach him how to back up a trailer in bear college, it took him three tries to park it straight.

Blake cranked down a leg at each corner of the trailer, then disconnected it from the truck. After he moved the truck out of the way, I walked around the trap. It was basically a corrugated steel tube, like a culvert, mounted horizontally, painted white, about ten feet long and four feet in diameter, decorated with black and yellow signs portraying a bear in silhouette, plastered with warnings like 'DANGER STAY BACK', and 'LIVE BEAR TRAP'.

One end of the tube was closed off with a round steel cap welded in place, the other end had a steel mesh gate mounted in a frame. The gate was square and rode up and down between two vertical rails. Blake grunted when he raised the heavy gate up and locked it in place with a pin. He went back to his truck, opened a cardboard box, and came back with a bunch of bananas.

"Bananas?" I asked.

"Bears love bananas," he said, "especially when they're as rotten as these ones."

I watched him slide another pin into the gate frame, attach a cable to the pin, run the cable along the top of the trap, loop it over a pulley, and drop it through a hole that looked like a chimney. Then he crab-walked into the trap with his bananas and hooked them to the cable hanging down inside. After making a few adjustments to take the slack out of the cable, he backed himself out and removed the first pin he'd inserted.

It was a simple design. The bear walks into the tube, grabs the bananas, which pulls the cable, which pulls the pin, and the gate drops down behind him.

Gotcha.

Blake handed me his card and said, "Okay, sir, you're all set.

Call me anytime day or night the instant you get a prisoner." He pointed at Russ who was studying the strange new contraption. "Keep him inside at night. That's usually when bears turn up. A dog can spook them."

If you only knew.

"Say, Blake," I said, pointing at the canister on his hip, "is that bear spray?"

"Sure is."

"I've heard about that, does it work?"

"Most of the time. Unless they're real mad. Which is why we carry a gun."

"Right. Well, thanks for coming out so fast."

"Yeah, you were real lucky there. This trap came available the minute the Carmacks office called. We've been bringing bears down from Dawson steady and I was just releasing one about thirty miles north of here."

"I hear there are a lot of them up there this year."

"I'll say. Most of them are grizzly cubs recently chased off by their mothers. It's mating season and Mama bear knows she can't have her cubs around for that. She knows if a male approaches her to mate, he'll kill her cubs if they're with her."

"Really?"

"As savage as it seems. A male wants only his offspring to survive, another male's offspring is competition."

"That *is* savage."

"Law of the jungle," Blake said with a shrug.

"So you think it could have been a grizzly that tore up my kitchen?"

"Doubt it. With all the forest around here, I'd say it was probably a black bear. Probably a young one, just chased off and looking to establish its own territory. It hit the jackpot with your cabin."

I nodded but thought it unlikely a young bear could do so much damage.

"A little bear could destroy my kitchen?"

Blake shrugged again and said, "No problem. Any size bear can wreck a kitchen. They're incredibly strong. A hundred pound bear can kill any man on the planet."

"But it ate twenty pounds of dog food."

"Bears eat a lot," he said.

*　*　*

They arrived just before five.

When I heard Mike's truck, I dashed down the path to greet them. Through the windshield I could see Sarah had a fierce stare going. I waited in the middle of the lane and for an instant wondered if she was going to run me over, but she stopped a few feet short of my chest and turned off the engine. Jack was sitting in her lap and when he saw me through the steering wheel, darted over to the passenger door. He put two paws up on the armrest with his tale wagging like crazy, and squealed with delight when I opened the door.

The large plastic cone encircling his head made him look like a sunflower. The bandage was gone from his rump. A jagged line of sutures marked the incision where his leg had been removed. If it wasn't official before, it was now. Jack was a three legged dog and would be for the rest of his life. In a bittersweet moment, I leaned in and gave him a hug. That was good enough for him. He was home. Russ jumped into the truck to join the lick fest. The three bachelors were reunited and ecstatic about it.

"How are you, Sar...sorry...Rita?" I asked, grinning at her through a frenzy of lapping tongues and wagging tails.

She didn't look at me, fixated on the bear trap in front of her. No response.

"How was the drive up?" I asked.

Still no response.

"Are you...?"

"Do you have a gun handy?" she asked.

"A gun? Why do you want a...?"

"Because I need to shoot you."

"Shoot me?"

Shit.

"Damn you, Brody, I called you twice and you didn't answer. What is wrong with you? We're paying you fifty grand to be on standby 24/7 and you can't be bothered to answer a phone?" She turned to me and said, "My life is at stake here, do you not understand that?"

I grimaced and hunched my shoulders. I'd forgotten all about the satellite phone. It had been in my pack, sitting on the couch all day. Between the noise of a vacuum cleaner, and all the trips to the shop, I'd missed her calls. I was so accustomed to living in a phone-free zone at my cabin, it had never crossed my mind to carry the damn thing with me. But it was no excuse, I'd screwed up and was ashamed.

"I'm really sorry," I said. "I will not let you down again."

"We can cancel the contract if you want."

"No, Sarah. I said I will not let you down again, and I mean it."

She studied me for a moment, then pointed a finger over the steering wheel.

"What is that?"

"A bear trap."

"Why do you have a bear trap?"

"Long story."

"Well I've got lots of time. And we need to talk."

Oh, oh.

She got out of the truck and walked up to the trap. Russ followed hot on her heels and I carried Jack over to watch the inspection. After a slow walk-around, she said, "Got anything to eat?"

* * *

It was déjà vu all over again.

Sort of.

Almost to the day a year ago, I'd baked a fresh caught salmon and served it with baby potatoes and a caesar salad, entertaining the lovely Sarah Marsalis at the very same table, sipping wine and watching the river go by. It was the day we'd met and the conversation had been courteous and careful, two perfect strangers saying all the right things, wondering where the evening might lead. But tonight there was no wine and little to be said. We ate Chinese food from the Café, talked mostly about the bear, stared out the window a lot, and avoided every potential landmine, including what had happened in Mexico. I didn't dare ask her about Tommy Kay.

The silent treatment was beginning to wear on me when she murmured, as though to herself, "It's so quiet here."

"One of life's great luxuries," I replied, wishing she'd look at me, tired of admiring her face in profile, wondering if the ink on her neck was permanent.

Jack and Russ were at her feet gawking up with awe. The woman seated across from me was the same woman they'd come to worship last year, only now she was sporting tattoos and piercings and plastered with jet black makeup. But the radical change in her appearance didn't seem to affect them, there was something about her they found mesmerizing.

She put down a plastic fork and finally looked me in the eyes.

"That was excellent," she said. "Thank you. By the way, how's Charlie?"

She was referring to the man at the Café who'd cooked our meal. If you ask me, Charlie Woo makes the best Chinese food in the territory. Last year he'd been the victim of a human smuggler, but after the demise of his scumbag handler, Sarah had played an instrumental role in getting Canadian immigration papers for him and his son.

"He's great, thanks to you," I said. "He's up from Whitehorse for the summer. Spent the winter there so Charlie Junior could go to Kindergarten. Everyone's thrilled to have them back."

"Say hi to them for me, would you?"

"I will. They often ask about you, you know."

With a hint of satisfaction she nodded and said, "That's good to know." Then after a pause, "So."

"So?"

"I wanted to explain why I was late. I was on my way to pick up Jack when an emergency meeting was called."

"Another meeting?"

She held up a hand and said, "Don't start with me, Brody."

"Sorry."

"This is for your ears only, alright?"

"Should the dogs leave?"

She shook her head and said, "So yesterday afternoon we got a call from Eric Landry at the BC Securities Commission…"

"The guy with the hairplugs?"

She rolled her eyes, slapped the table, and glared at me.

Shut up.

"As I was saying, Mr. Landry called to say he'd just received a very interesting phone call from an anonymous source. The source is a woman who claims to have incriminating information about a certain stock promoter, someone who just happens to be promoting Thistle Creek Resources. Mr. Landry thinks the caller was Lynn Chan, its president. A little detective work indicates the caller probably was Chan, so the timetable for our strategy has been moved up."

"Meaning?"

"Meaning we expect to make an arrest next weekend in Dawson."

"Who are you going to arrest?"

"None of your concern. Anyway, what we did was immediately solicit the help of your girlfriend. Those sample logs she delivered to you yesterday have invisible watermarks and will provide crucial evidence in a trial."

"She's not my girlfriend, Sarah, I mean *Rita*, or whatever your name is. And Jennifer gave them to a mechanic, not me."

"But you did get them, right?"

"Yes."

"Good. Make sure you use them next Friday when you load at Thistle Creek. It's critical Mike Giguere does not use his own logs, we need him to use the watermarked ones. Okay?"

"Okay. So why do you think it was Lynn Chan who called this Landry guy? And what did she say?"

"Also none of your concern. But what is your concern is that you carry that satellite phone on your person every hour of every day, until I tell you otherwise. Clear?"

"I already told you, I won't let you down."

"Good again. Now then, next Friday or Saturday I may need you to fly me to Thistle Creek on a moment's notice, so you and that plane of yours have to be on standby in Dawson the whole weekend. Is that also clear?"

I looked down at Russ and Jack and shrugged in apology.

"Sorry boys, another road trip."

They didn't seem to care.

"Brody?"

"What?"

"Did you hear me?"

"Yes. I'll be there."

"You better be. Don't mess up or…"

"I know, you'll shoot me."

"Okay, now that we have that out of the way, I need to tell you how to take care of Jack."

She picked up a tin plate with the last piece of Chicken Soo Guy and headed to the couch. Russ followed her with his tongue hanging out. Mine was too as I honed in on the back of her tight black jeans. Jack hopped and stopped, hopped and stopped, then turned around and looked up at me. Poor guy didn't know what was going on but he sure knew where he wanted to go. I picked him up and carried him the rest of the way over, sat down on the opposite end from Sarah, pulled a blanket off the back, and laid him down between us. Russ jumped up on the couch to make it a foursome. Jack may have had trouble walking, but he could still beg. The two of them were sitting on their haunches, shoulder to shoulder, panting and licking their chops in Sarah's face. With one arm holding them at bay, she held up a bottle of pills in her other hand and rattled them to get my attention.

"He's still in pain so you have to give him one of these every twelve hours for the next three days. Then half a pill every twelve hours for another three days. No running, jumping, or climbing for two weeks. Keep him inside, he needs to rest. Absolutely no games or playing. Walk him on a leash for his bathroom breaks. Keep your eye on the incision. It's normal if it's a little damp, but if it starts oozing, or gets red, call Doctor Dorval right away. You have to go see him in two weeks for post-op x-rays and to have the sutures removed. The collar stays on 'til then, no excuses. Everything you need to know is on a sheet of paper which I'll give you before I leave."

While trying to absorb all that I gazed out the window at the mountains.

"What time is it?" she asked.

"About eight, I guess."

"Oh, he's due for his next pill."

She opened the bottle, stuffed one in a large piece of chicken, and held it in front of his nose.

Gulp.

There was one for Russ too, then it was back and forth for a while with each offering getting smaller and smaller until the chicken was no more. She stood and lowered Jack to the floor. "No jumping," she commanded, wagging a finger at him and casting me a stern look as well. I watched her glide over to the kitchen in her stocking feet and stop in front of a tuft of pipes sticking out of the floor. With her hands on her hips she surveyed the scene and said, "This is too weird. No kitchen. You can't even make coffee."

"I can make coffee."

"How?"

"With coffee, water and a pot."

"You have those?"

"Yup. And a campstove, too."

"Hmm." She walked into the bedroom for ten seconds, came out and said, "Hey. Clean sheets."

"So?"

"So I don't have to be in Dawson until tomorrow evening."

"That's nice."

"Maybe I'll stay the night," she said with her first genuine smile of the evening. "If it's okay with you, that is."

"Ahh…well…I…"

"Would you like me to stay the night, Brody?"

"Ahh…well…"

"Okay, I'll stay. But you know what that means, don't you?"

"Look…I really don't…"

"It means you get the couch."

FIFTY SEVEN

'The couch'.

With the midnight sun pouring in the windows, I was semi-comfortable, lying under a sleeping bag, reading one of my library books, utterly absorbed in an appalling story about cultural genocide. It was a disgraceful and shameful saga in Canadian history and a tragedy I had been completely unaware of. No wonder Minnie didn't want to talk about the church that burned down.

When the British and French 'discovered' the vast land now known as Canada, they instantly appreciated its infinite potential. But there was a huge problem. People were already living there. So wherever the newcomers went, they had to negotiate a deal with each and every native tribe they encountered—deals they had no intention of honoring—written down on scrolls of parchment in a langauge the natives didn't understand. The deals the British and French drafted were called treaties.

For a couple of hundred years the treaties seemed to work. Relations between the two civilizations bumbled along with the white guys conducting their European import-export business however they wanted, using the land however they saw fit, and one way or the other winning all the arguments. But everything changed when Canada became a country in 1867.

The natives were still there, and so were the treaties. And you can't build railways and roads and ports and cities on someone else's land.

Fortunately for the new country, it had God on its side.

The Indian residential school system was concocted by the Federal Government of Canada to assimilate the country's aboriginal population into the new Euro-Canadian culture. The thinking of the imperial colonists was that if they could extinguish the existing language and culture of aboriginal children, then in a single generation every existing treaty would become redundant, and the land would be up for grabs. And what better way to convert a generation of kids than with religion?

So an insidious partnership was formed. The Canadian Government would build the schools and get the land, and the churches would run the schools and get the souls.

Under the dubious authority of the Indian Act of 1876, eighty so-called residential schools—a euphemism for kiddy penitentiaries—were built across the country with the Roman Catholic, Anglican, United, and Presbyterian churches franchised to run them. Throughout the next century, in spite of the best efforts of parents to resist mandatory attendance—which invariably involved trying to hide their kids—the cops and clergy managed to remove 150,000 aboriginal children from their families and ancestral lands, and ship them off to institutions hundreds of miles away for a good old fashioned brainwashing.

In all, as many as six thousand children died.

The 'students' in the so-called Indian residential schools were beaten if caught speaking their own langauge, poorly fed and clothed, and abused sexually and otherwise. In one school, a government scientist purposely malnourished a group of kids in a scientific experiment. Influenza and tuberculosis ran rampant and generally went untreated. If the kids attempted to escape, they were hunted down and taught hard lessons with corporal punishment and isolated detention. Parental visits and holidays at home were made virtually impossible by policy and procedure. For the thousands of Canadian aboriginal children who died under mysterious circumstances, documents and records conveniently went missing. Many of the dead were buried in unmarked graves, with parents never informed.

As to the education itself, well understandably it was heavy on religion and light on academics. But only half the day was reserved for classroom teaching anyway, the kids spent most of their time either cleaning the buildings or tending gardens in the overcrowded and underfunded institutions.

By the time the last Canadian residential school closed in 1990, the country had built its railways, ports, roads, and cities, and had occupied most of the land it wanted. Meantime, most Canadian aboriginals had long been corralled onto reserves.

In the early 2000's, well after the damage was done, Canada eventually found its moral conscience. Commissions and inquiries were conducted, checks issued, wreaths laid, ancient treaties dusted off, and numerous land claims settled.

No hard feelings.

As a final gesture for own their redemption, all but one perpetrator issued a profound and public apology to Canada's aboriginal people, including the Prime Minister of Canada, Provincial Premiers, the RCMP, and three of the four churches who had been running the show. The notable exception was the Roman Catholic Church who had operated more than half the schools. The Pope refused to apologize though he did issue a statement expressing his "sorrow". The Vatican must have had a tobacco industry lawyer.

With disgust I slammed the book shut and got up. Jack and Russ were in the bedroom and I gingerly opened the door. They were snoozing beside the bed, guarding queen bee who was buried under a mound of blankets.

"Pssst."

Their ears went up and they opened their eyes.

"Come on, let's go. Outside."

Their ears went down and they closed their eyes.

"Chicken."

The deception worked and out they came. I picked up Jack,

grabbed my gun on the way out of the porch, and carried him down the stairs to the path. After he'd relieved himself, I carried him back up the stairs and lowered him to the deck.

He and Russ looked up at me with big eyes, as if to ask, "So where's the chicken?"

I scratched Jack's ears and said, "You know, pal, I want to take that stupid thing off your neck as much as you do, but it's gotta stay on for another two weeks. Sorry."

He sighed but seemed happy to be home.

It was after midnight and getting colder by the minute, but I decided to walk out to the edge of the deck anyway. It's where I do my best thinking and there was plenty to think about. I sat down with my shotgun across my knees and my legs hanging over the edge. My best buddies snuggled up against my thighs.

The sun had sunk as low as it would go, now hiding behind a mountain, spreading a warm orange glow over the land. All was quiet except the sounds of the river below us. Together we watched a solitary hawk glide in from nowhere, make a long slow circle over the forest, and disappear into its green abyss. The world was at rest, preparing for another long hard day of evolution. Even the mosquitoes were taking a break.

Shivering in a sweatshirt and sweatpants, I began sorting through the clutter between my ears. There was nothing that could be resolved at the moment but perhaps some mental desk cleaning would alleviate my anxieties. Sort the issues into categories, stack them in piles, identify the problems, come up with the solutions, get a good night's sleep.

Threats first.

The biggest one had to be Tommy Kay. Unless the cops found him first he'd be sure to find me. But so long as I saw him coming, and with my shotgun at the ready, I should have the advantage. Simple problem, simple solution. Kill him.

Then there was that pyschotic from the newspaper, who if not by now, was about to ruin me with her fake news. Ellen Burke had granted me a temporary reprieve while she awaited the next installment about a conspiracy to control the world's supply of rare earths. For the next few days at least, I should be safe. The question was, what was the next installment? I had no idea and would have to come up with something.

Then there were the cops. Who knew what they were plotting and scheming? Robson had told me to my face that I was not a suspect for Amy's murder, but for some reason he seemed adamant on busting me for assaulting her brother. After a bit of thought I decided I had nothing to worry about. If I hadn't assaulted anyone, what evidence could he possibly have? All the same, sooner or later he was sure to pay me one of his surprise visits, and I'd have to remember to keep my shotgun out of sight.

Last but not least was that bear who'd wrecked my kitchen. There was no point in building a new one until he, or she, was caught and relocated. But a bigger concern was for my dogs. Two fearless Jack Russell Terriers will drive any bear crazy and run it off in no time. But if one of them had just lost a leg, well now that's a different story. I'd have to ask Reggie if he'd stay at my cabin and watch them while I was in Dawson next weekend. Meanwhile, the best I could hope for was the bear would return soon with a hankering for rotten bananas.

It dawned on me then that whatever threats Kay or Burke or Robson or even a bear might pose wasn't bothering me nearly as much as a cloud of emotional baggage, and a ton of guilt. My thoughts drifted to the people I actually cared about, it was they who were weighing on my mind. I was worried about letting them down.

Like Old Hank in his cabin on Two Spirit Lake, alone and isolated, spending another night with no power, no plumbing, and no way to communicate with the outside world. He'd survived like that for over sixty years and was the last of the 'colorful five percent', those remarkable and eccentric men who'd chosen to lead an ascetic life in the Yukon wilderness. But it was time for him to come in now, he was simply to old to fend for himself, and I wondered how to make that happen. For some reason I felt if I didn't do something, no one would. Maybe I could come up with a compelling incentive to get him in. But what? For the time being, all I could do was hope he'd be okay.

I thought about Jennifer Kovalchuk, young and beautiful, smart and competent, confident and kind, and an entrepreneur at that. Definitely a keeper if there ever was. It seemed to me the only thing she wasn't very good at was choosing men and I had to lament the irony of that honest impression. Just knowing me for two days had got her tires slashed and the cops buzzing around her life. Now they had her doing favors for them. I sighed and wondered why I never fell for women like Jennifer, why it was always the flawed ones that drew me in. Maybe it had something to do with natural selection, some kind of quality control feature in Nature to protect the good ones from the likes of me. I hoped she was okay, too.

I thought about Amy Vanderbilt who had breathed her last not fifteen feet behind me. Poor Amy, self-absorbed and unfocused, but totally harmless. She had the right to live her life searching for whatever it was that might make her happy, and someone had stolen that from her. Once again I had to wonder why anyone would kill her. And who. I really wasn't so sure anymore. Maybe it wasn't Kay after all. Maybe it was the dead guy in the outhouse, the guy Robson said was named Woo. But who killed Woo and why? And whoever did kill Woo, why leave a gun with his body? Was that the gun used to shoot Jack? Did Woo shoot Jack *and* kill Amy?

My head was spinning with too many questions and not an answer to be had. I decided to give them a rest. One thing was for sure, though, Amy's death was on me and the guilt was oozing from every pore. I couldn't blame her brother for thinking her death was my doing, and wanting revenge for it. Hopefully he'd recover from the blow to his head.

Which got me to thinking about Ray and what he was up to. He'd saved my life and I wondered how and if I could ever repay him. I hoped he was okay, too, and that I'd see him again soon.

I thought about Leah and Reggie, two native kids who were the first generation of Canadian aboriginals to finally have their own land and nation enshrined in Federal law. I admired them for their generosity and sense of community, for accepting an outsider like me into their fold, and for not ever once mentioning the raw deal their ancestors got. Reggie had spent hours looking for Jack, Leah had taken him to town, and together they'd saved his life. How could I possibly repay them? As far as I was concerned, Reggie and Leah were true champions, as well as great friends, and I felt lucky to have them in my life.

I thought about my day tomorrow and all the things that needed to be done: clean my deck, clean my shop, tend to Jack, spec out a new kitchen, draft a shopping list, and take Mrs. Deerchild for a plane ride.

I wondered who she was and why Reggie said she was the one to ask about a church that burned down in Minto over sixty years ago. I also wondered what she could tell me about the Canadian Government's residential schools. Maybe she was a victim. I'd find out soon enough.

The hawk appeared again, rising out of the trees, climbing high over the forest with a piercing scream, its wings beating hard as it headed our way. When it reached the river, it relaxed and veered north, transformed its wings into two perfect airfoils, and soared off on a cushion of air. No aircraft can match the aerodynamic diversity of a bird. Nothing we've ever made comes close.

I wondered if it was one of the pair I'd seen last year. Maybe the male, off to fetch food for a mate sitting on a nest, incubating a clutch of eggs. It would be nice to have a family of hawks flying around this fall.

The front door opened and closed. Russ and Jack turned their heads but I couldn't be bothered. I knew who it was because my boys would have let me known otherwise. They were on their feet with their tails flapping. She sat down next to me, close enough to touch. I held a steady gaze across the river, determined to ignore her, but couldn't help notice she was bundled up in my sleeping bag.

Home sweet home.

A bear wrecks my kitchen, a woman takes my bed, and now helps herself to my sleeping bag. Which reminded me, I needed to buy a new snowmobile suit.

I wasn't going to say anything, content to enjoy the aura of the midnight sun, but she'd evidently come out to talk.

"Is that a gun?"

"Yup."

"Is it yours?"

"I guess."

"You guess?"

"That's what I said."

"Where did you get it?"

"I found it."

"Found it where?"

"In my shop"

"Is it registered?"

"My shop?"

"No...the gun."

"Doubt it."

"Well don't let the RCMP catch you with it."

"They won't if you don't tell them."

"I won't tell them"

"Good."

Now that we had that out of the way, I wondered why she'd really come outside to sit in the cold with me.

"Brody?"

"Yes?"

After a long pause, "Do you ever think about...?"

This time the pause was so long I had to look at her. She'd removed all her makeup and most of the metal trinkets, and looked exquisite.

"Think about what?" I heard myself ask, turning back to the scenery.

"Oh, never mind."

"Never mind what?"

Another long pause.

"Us."

Curiosity killed the cat and perhaps now, a pilot.

Idiot. Why did you have to press her for an answer?

Now I was at the bottom of a deep pit, standing on a bed of alligators.

"Ah...sure...I guess so...sometimes."

"And?"

"And what?"

"And what do you think, when you think about us?"

The alligators were beginning to stir.

"Ah...well..."

"Look, I wanted you to understand something about me, and about what happened in Mexico. It was all my fault, it was the drinking. My drinking. I have a problem and have had for a long time. And I also wanted to tell you that I am really, really sorry about what happened down there."

"I'm sorry too, Sarah. I shouldn't have left."

"Maybe," she said. "But I deserved to be left and don't blame you for doing it. I probably would have done the same. Obviously I have issues and they bubbled up the minute we got there. Everything was just so damn perfect—too perfect—just you and me and the sun and that beach, holding hands in those hammocks under the trees. I was so damn happy, Brody, I just couldn't stand it. Which has always been my problem. Every time I've ever been happy, I get overwhelmed with this incredible sense of guilt, as if I have no right to feel that way. I don't expect you to understand, I never have, it's just the way it is. So I dealt with it the only way I know how, which was to go out and get drunk. It had always worked before, and when it didn't work the first time, I did it again, and again, and again. That's why I ran off and got drunk four days in a row, as absurd as that might seem to you. I just wanted you to understand why I did what I did. And I wanted to tell you that I've never been happier than when I was down there with you."

She stopped to wipe away a tear. My mouth was too dry to say anything and I turned away.

Then she said, "I've stopped you know, the drinking I mean. I'll never have another one. And I've been getting help. I'm getting better, slowly."

I cleared my throat and said, "That's good, Sarah, really good."

We watched the river for a while, then she asked, "Do you ever get drunk, Brody?"

"Drunk? You mean like have one too many? Or do you mean like wake up on a picnic table in a State Park beside a naked girl I don't know?"

"That happened to you?"

I turned to face her again, smiled, and shook my head.

"No."

She gave me a friendly punch in the shoulder, leaned hers against mine, and moved her face in close to mine. I could smell my soap on her. She was searching my eyes and I made the mistake of searching back, becoming instantly lost in hers, frozen in a rapture.

Damn woman.

"So," she said.

"So," I said.

"So thanks for listening, I've been wanting to tell you that for a long time."

"Glad you did."

"Brody?"

"Yes?"

"Your cabin is kind of cold."

"I'll light a fire."

* * *

About six o'clock in the morning there was a thunderous crash outside. Through the haze of sleep it sounded like steel colliding with steel, like a car accident.

Naturally it set off Jack and Russ who came running out to the living room making a raucous racket, followed close behind by a tall slim woman wearing candy cane striped, silk pajamas. I sensed them walk past me, and for the second morning in a row, needed a moment to figure out where I was. Were it not for the frenetic barking, I could have been dreaming.

With a crick in my neck, I carefully raised my head off the armrest and squinted at the three of them. They were standing in front of the window at the end of the couch. Sarah was bent over with her hands on her knees, face pressed up against the glass, peering sideways at something outside. On either side of her, Jack and Russ had their front paws up on the window sill, woofing and growling, looking in the same direction.

For a second I studied Jack and admired his ability to balance on one rear leg, then admired Sarah's candy cane pajamas, then dropped my head back to the armrest and closed my eyes.

"We got him, Brody! We got him! Come look!"

We?

I pulled the sleeping bag over my head, groaned, and thought about taking a holiday.

"Brody?"

FIFTY EIGHT

On a cool and overcast Sunday morning in Vancouver, Lynn Chan was shivering in the back seat of her own car. She knew she was inadequately dressed for the weather, but there are times when a girl has to do, what a girl has to do.

She'd gotten up early for a long hard workout, then taken a hot bath to shave and oil her legs—smooth and shiny legs were the key to the mission—applied a heavy layer of makeup and a lot of red lipstick, and squeezed into a pair of tight white shorts, a skin tight top, and the tallest most uncomfortable heels she owned. She'd skipped the bra, that would have been counterproductive. Because whatever it took, today was the day she was getting her chandelier back.

She caught the driver's eyes in the rear view mirror.

"Earl, take your eyes of my tits and get them back on the road. If I catch you looking again, you're fired. And turn up the damn heat."

Jolted from his trance, Earl stiffened and closed his mouth, tilted the mirror down, and focused on the empty street ahead. He looked every bit the part he was about to play—the quintessential chauffeur—cleanly shaven with a fresh haircut, decked out in a conservative black suit, white shirt, black tie, and requisite driving cap. Last week, after a predictable and protracted tantrum, Jeremy finally acquiesced to Lynn's order and took Earl out to buy his new uniform. Earl had been surprised at the sensation of power a suit gave him, he'd never owned one before, and couldn't wait to wear it at his daughter's wedding in the fall, provided of course he lived that long.

He patted its inside chest pocket for the third time since they'd left Lynn's building, just to make sure. Inside was his phone and a small piece of wood required to start the job. In the trunk of Lynn's Lexus was the chandelier he'd taken down the other day, and a power drill to complete the swap. He could only hope Ms. Chan knew what she was doing. She sure liked to live dangerously, he thought, putting her life on the line for a ceiling light.

While Earl was checking his suit jacket pocket, Lynn was fondling a tiny round lump wedged under the hem of her tight white shorts.

The missing pearl earring.

Yesterday she'd called the hangar and Tippy's copilot had answered. She'd met him once before, the time she and Tippy had flown to the Caymans. His name was Jin. Jin was young, from Hong Kong, not particularily good looking but professionally turned out, and as Lynn had been quick to appreciate, a real crotch watcher.

Your lucky day, Jin.

Jin said he'd been expecting her call. Mr. Li had mentioned she might be out sometime soon to search for a missing earring. Jin told Lynn he'd be at the hangar on Sunday morning and would be happy to be of assistance, though he doubted she'd have any luck. He said the cleaners always conducted a very thorough search for any forgotten items before they vacummed, and would have found it. But she was welcome to come out anyway.

Twenty minutes later they were the only car on an empty service road skirting the airport. When Lynn spotted the New Horizons hangar, she ordered Earl to pull in. He stopped the big Lexus in front of a tall wire gate, lowered his window, and pressed the call button on an intercom box.

The gate rolled open.

Like most aircraft hangars, the New Horizons building was large, tall, and featureless, basically a big steel box with a corrugated steel roof and a name on the side.

"That's the one we went in," said Earl, pointing at the lone exit door at the back of the hangar as they crawled past, staring at it in silence. It was as smooth as a board and the only way to open it would be from the inside. They turned left at the corner and drove down the side of the building to the office at the front.

Earl stopped Lynn's Lexus behind the only car in sight, a black Porsche 911 parked in front of a plain blue door with a small glass window. Lynn might have guessed Jin would drive a Porsche, the best panty remover on the planet.

"Don't screw up," she snarled at Earl. "And remember, look mean and keep your mouth shut. And stay in touch, I need to know what's happening. You've got ten minutes, no more."

"Ten minutes will be plenty," he said with a sigh.

The blue door swung open and Jin came running out. He had a hand on Lynn's door before Earl could even open his own.

"Good morning, Miss Chan," said Jin in his clipped Cantonese accent, beaming a broad smile, holding her door open. He was dressed for flight in a pressed white shirt with gold epaulets, navy blue pants with razor sharp creases, and black shoes with thick rubber soles. Even so, he was no taller than Lynn.

"Good morning, Jin. How are you?"

"I am wonderful, Miss Chan, thank you. And you?"

"Fine, a little cold, but fine."

A little cold.

Her nipples looked like door bells.

Lynn smiled coyly at him and swung a stilletto out of the car with a sweeping arc to the pavement. Then she turned her back to him and fussed in her purse for her phone. She knew where his eyes were now and could have been loading a pistol for all he'd notice.

They walked single file into the small office with Lynn leading the way and Jin close behind. Earl was all but forgotten at the back of the line, and while Jin worked a keypad to open an interior door,

Lynn glanced back at the help. Earl was doing his best to appear tough and mean but came across more like someone with a belly ache.

Tippy's jet was a spectacular sight. The Dassault Falcon 8X sat dead center in the middle of a vast slab of painted gray concrete, the only aircraft in the cavernous building, its silver wings and white fuselage gleaming perfection under the bright overhead lights. It had been backed in and was pointed at the huge hangar door, now closed, but looked poised and ready for flight.

Lynn admired Tippy's prized possession and had to concede it was indeed a majestic machine. He said it cost him fifty million and she had no reason to doubt it. She noted the front cabin door was open and the stairs were down, awaiting her inspection.

She glanced around but there was little else to see, other than on the far wall where an electric tug to ferry the plane in and out of the hangar was parked beside a luggage cart. A few electrical service boxes with neatly coiled cables were mounted on the wall above the tug. And that was about it, until her eyes drifted to the back of the building and found the exit door a hundred feet away. There it was, right beside the door, the wooden box, the one Jeremy had been gushing about, covered in a blanket like a Christmas present.

Her chandelier.

She looked at Earl who nodded once.

"Wait outside," she snapped at him, then to Jin in a soothing voice with a soft smile, "Would you mind helping me, Jin? It shouldn't take long. As I explained on the phone, I'm looking for a small earring, a pearl stud. It was a gift from my grandmother, something very special to me."

"Of course, Miss Chan, I'd be happy to help you look for your earring. Please, after you," he said with a deferential tilt of his head and an exaggerated sweep of the hand.

Lynn stopped at the foot of the stairs, put a hand on the railing, and removed her shoes. Jin stood close behind her, poised to catch her should she fall. Such a gentleman. She walked up the stairs with him breathing up her butt.

Earl watched them disappear into the plane, then per instructions, counted to ten and hustled to the back of the hangar. He went out the exit door but left it wedged open with the block of wood from his pocket. He walked along the back of the building, turned left at the corner, and went down to Lynn's Lexus. He drove it back to the exit door, got out, opened the trunk, and slipped inside the hangar with the power drill. Two minutes later he'd removed all twenty screws securing the top of the wooden box. He lifted it off.

It was to be the riskiest part of the mission. Earl could not be seen by Jin at the back of the hangar. Time for Lynn to put on her show.

The instant she entered the plane, she wasted no time dropping down on all fours, and with her butt raised high in the air, began crawling down the aisle on her knees and elbows, scanning the floor on either side for an earring that wasn't there. Her performance worked perfectly. Jin was so fixated on the rear end of his VIP guest, he wouldn't have noticed a marching band go by outside. When Lynn peaked back between her legs, he was following her like a puppy, crawling on his knees and elbows, too. When they reached the rear of the plane, Lynn jumped to her feet, stepped over him, and started digging her hands into seat crevices. Taking the cue, Jin got up and mimicked her search on the other side of the aisle. No luck. No earring.

Not yet.

Lynn put her hands on her hips, heaved a sigh, and with feigned dismay said, "Well, Jin, it's obviously not up here. Let's take a quick look in the suite, shall we? Then I won't waste any more of your time."

"My time is all yours, Miss Chan. You are not wasting my time."

He opened the door to the suite and beckoned her in with another sweep of his hand. Lynn smiled and squeezed past him, eye to eye, with a two breasted brush across his chest. Jin immediately thrust his hands into his pockets. Her cellphone buzzed. She pulled it out of her back pocket and looked at the screen.

'ok'

The hardest part had been getting the old chandelier into the wooden box. Earl had to shove the chains and most of the dangling junk up against sides, then bend the wheel out of shape—crush it for all intents and purposes—to make it fit. He heard a few light bulbs pop when he screwed down the top, but who cared at this point? He put the blanket over the box and walked out to the car with Miss Chan's new chandelier.

After he was parked behind the Porsche again, Earl sent the text to Lynn, as per instructions. He left the motor running and turned up the heat. Maybe heat would stop the shaking in his hands.

Lynn was ecstatic. Mission accomplished! Now for the happy ending.

She opened the door to her left and stepped into the spacious lavatory, took a moment to poke around the spotless compartment, then crossed the aisle and stepped into the shower. Leaving its door open for Jin's viewing pleasure, she did a couple of slow pirouttes, stopped with her backside to him, curled her fingers under the hem of her shorts, pulled out the earring, and clasped it tightly in her fist.

"Definitely not in here," she said, emerging with a glum look, moving toward the bed, shaking her head in dismay with her hands on her hips. She paused for a moment to appraise it. Satin sheets. How could she forget?

Time for the finale.

She spent the next full minute on all fours, crawling and slithering around the slippery bed, treating Jin to every lascivious pose she could come up with while digging under the mattress. Things were so quiet she could hear him breathing. When she'd worked the charade for all it was worth, she plunged her clenched hand into a space between the mattress and the wall, and froze.

"Found it!" she squealed.

She bounced off the bed and held it out to him. By now Jin's eyes were glazed, his mouth agape, with beads of sweat glistening on his forehead. He gawked at the earring with his hands still buried in his pockets, speechless. She wrapped her arms around him, gave him a squeeze and a pelvic thrust, then dashed down the aisle to the front of the plane, skipped down the stairs, picked up her shoes, and ran barefoot out to the car.

Earl jumped when she opened the door.

"Step on it, Earl. I need a shower real bad."

FIFTY NINE

Mrs. Deerchild was standing on the dock, beside my plane, waving a prayer bag, muttering away.

I stopped my truck and gave Reggie a look. He held up a hand. *Leave her be.*

I got the message, turned off the engine, stayed put behind the wheel, and lowered my window. A gentle breeze filled the cab with the sweet scent of spring. Reggie walked over from his tow truck and leaned against my door. We watched Mrs. Deerchild for a while. Now she had her hands over her head and was swaying back and forth.

"She's removing its evil spirits," said Reggie.

"Oh," I said, wondering what evil spirits might be dwelling in my plane, then thinking it was probably a good idea anyway. You just never know about evil spirits.

Reggie had opened the cockpit and cargo doors and we waited while she continued her ritual to rid the old plane of its demons. She sat down and looked almost child-sized in one of Reggie's aluminum deck chairs, with her toes barely reaching the dock. From a hundred feet away it was easy to tell she was an elderly aboriginal woman, probably in her late seventies or early eighties. She wore her long white hair braided in two ropes that cascaded down to her lap over an ankle length dress, and was bundled up in a

heavy wool shawl that dwarfed her tiny frame. She stood up again
and did a little dance that made the frills on her moccasins flutter.
Then she sat down for the final time, kneaded her prayer bag with
both hands, muttered a few more things, and relaxed and looked
out at the lake.

"You can go out now," said Reggie.

Evidently the exorcism was over.

I headed for the dock, stopping on the way to grab another chair
off the back of Reggie's truck.

With my best smile I said, "Good morning, Mrs. Deerchild. My
name is Brody and I'm your pilot. Ready to go flying?"

"This is the one," she said, pointing at the cargo bay. "This is
the plane that took my boy away."

She had yet to meet my eyes which gave me a chance to study
her. She was missing her front teeth and her face was dark and
wrinkled from a lifetime of dry cold weather. I guessed she'd
probably spent most of it outside. There was something odd about
her eyes though I wasn't sure what. Reggie's deck chair screeched
when I unfolded it. Like everything else he owns, it could use a few
shots of WD40.

I sat down beside her and leaned forward with my elbows on
my knees.

"How do you know it's the same plane, Mrs. Deerchild?"

"See that?"

She was pointing at a barely discernible dimple in the fuselage,
almost out of sight below the cargo door. It had been there when I
acquired the plane five years ago. It was beyond me how anyone
would notice it—let alone remember it after so many years—but
obviously she had.

"Amazing you'd remember that," I said. "So where did my
plane take your boy?"

"To Whitehorse. It was a long time ago but I remember it like it
was yesterday. Two men came into the village and took him away,
and three other boys, and four girls too. And then they flew them
away in this here plane. I remember the date, it was August twenty-

seven, 1960. I heard later what they were doing, why they were taking such young children. They called it the 'Sixties Scoop'." She paused for a moment, then said, "He was only five years old, you know." She dropped her chin and looked at her hands. "I never saw him again."

"Never?"

"No," she said, shaking her head. "Never."

"What happened to him?"

She turned toward the lake and I barely heard her say, "I don't know."

My chest tightened in revulsion with the revelation that my plane had been used as an instrument in a crime. It certainly explained the evil spirits.

"Who took him, Mrs. Deerchild?"

"The priest from our church, and a policeman, too. They came to our cabin and said they had to take my boy to a school in Whitehorse. I told them he was only five years old and didn't have to go to school for another year, but they said he had to go right away. They made us get into the back of a pickup truck with the other mothers and kids, then they drove us out here, to this very same spot, to this very same plane. They put the children in the back and the policeman climbed in with the pilot up front, and then they flew away."

With the morning sun behind us, the cargo bay was bathed in a bleak bright light. I was stunned, trying to imagine all those confused and scared little faces back there, staring out at their mothers, wondering why they were being taken away, and to where. The image was so damn depressing I felt like calling it a day and going home. Could I ever think about my pride and joy the same way? But I still wanted to know more, in particular about what had happened to the church in Minto.

I gathered myself together and asked, "Mrs. Deerchild, the church in the village, do you remember what happened to it?"

She was quiet for so long I wondered if she had any intention of telling me. She was still clutching her prayer bag in her hands, massaging it with her thumbs.

Finally she said, "It burned down."

"That's what I heard. Was it an accident or do you think someone might have...burned it down on purpose?"

Again she stayed quiet. There was no point in pushing her, she'd answer if she wanted. I folded my arms, dropped my head back, and stared up at an infinite empty sky, thinking about those poor kids and the dastardly things people do to each other. What is it about humans that drives them to dominate other people?

A train of Canada Geese appeared to the south, three or four thousand feet above us, strung out in a long, ragged 'V', flying north at forty miles an hour, with the faint sounds of their honking trailing behind them, permeating the uncomfortable silence. I often wonder why geese waste energy making noise while exerting themselves to the limit.

"It was one of the men in the village."

The voice seemed to have come out of nowhere.

"Which man in the village?"

"I don't know, it doesn't matter now, they're all gone. But any one of them might have done it. They were all working down the highway when the priest and the policeman came and took our children. The government had just finished building the bridges over the rivers and the men in the village were hired to paint them. They lived in road camps and worked ten days on and four days off. When my husband came home a few days later, he asked me where our son was. I told him what had happened and he stormed out. He and some of the other fathers went off to Whitehorse to get our children back. But they got thrown in jail and didn't come back for weeks—without our children. One night, a few days after they came back, the church burned down. It was a very hot fire and it burned right to the ground. The only thing left was the bell sitting in the ashes. The next morning my husband and his friends took the bell out on the river and dropped it in the water."

"So the police never found out who set the fire?"

"No, no one would talk to them, so they never did. But it didn't matter, I don't think anyone, even our policeman, was sad to see that priest leave. There were rumors he was doing evil things to some of the young boys, so when he drove away in his great big car the next morning, no one was sorry to see him go. We never asked to have that church built on our land, and we sure weren't going to ask anyone to build another one."

Go figure.

She got up, and with me following close behind, took five careful steps to the end of the dock. We stood there for a long time, side by side, absorbed in our thoughts. Below me a small fish darted out from under the dock, took a quick look around, and retreated back to safety. She raised an arm and pointed to the right.

"Over there, on the other side of the lake, that's where Hank lives," she said.

"You know Hank?"

"Everyone knows Hank." She swung her arm over to the left and said, "And there's the point. When we were teenagers, me and my friends used to walk out there on hot summer nights and go skinny dipping. It was never long before we'd see Hank rowing his little boat toward us. He must have been watching us with his telescope. We would laugh and run away before he got too close."

I had to smile and said, "I think he still has that telescope."

"How is he?"

"Fine, I guess."

"Would you hold my hand, Mr. Brody?"

I was surprised at the question but took hers in mine.

"You're a good man," she said.

"Think so?"

"Yes. I can tell by your hand. And Reggie says so, too."

I wasn't so sure they were right.

"Do you want to go flying now?" I asked.

"No, I'm tired and need to rest. And there's nothing for me to see anymore."

"Maybe some other time. Just ask Reggie, I'll take you up

anytime you want, Mrs. Deerchild. And actually, at this time of year, there's lots to see. As you know, the land is beautiful in the spring, the mountains are white, and the lakes are blue, and everything in between is green."

"But there's nothing for *me* to see, Mr. Brody. I'm blind, you know."

* * *

The bear trap was gone. Hopefully it had been towed away with the right bear in it. I didn't want another demolished kitchen.

I parked beside Mike's truck and headed up the path with my shotgun and Sarah's satphone, carrying a huge cardboard box full of food and ice from the Café. It was all I could manage not to drop it and couldn't see where I was going.

When I'd left for the lake, Sarah said she'd wait for Blake and take care of Jack until I got back. She said she'd be leaving at two, I said I'd be back at one, and it was only noon. She was standing on the deck with Jack in her arms, plastered in a fresh coat of war paint, watching me stagger up the path with Russ jumping up and down beside me, trying to see what was in the box.

"You're early," she said in a cheery voice with a wide smile, looking down at me as I started up the stairs.

With a grunt of exertion I made the last step onto the deck and said, "Sarah? The door?"

"Right," she said. She put Jack down and opened it for me. "So how was your flight? Did that lady enjoy it?"

"We didn't go," I said, lowering the box to the kitchen floor beside an ancient steel cooler.

"How come?"

"She didn't want to."

"Why not?"

"I don't know. She just didn't."

"Is that why you're grumpy?"

"I'm not grumpy. How 'bout we eat, okay?"

"Oh-kay," she said.

I put the ice in the cooler, threw my groceries on top, and headed to the couch with what was left in the box.

"Who ordered their burgers with just tomatoes?"

Burgers.

Russ and Jack put their front paws up on the coffee table and I put their lunches in front of them. They made off with them like bandits.

"Do we have to have that thing on the table?"

"What thing?"

"The shotgun."

"Safety's on."

"Would you mind putting it somewhere else? Please?"

I was watching Jack. He seemed a little dopey but was hungry enough to eat the pattie. Then he lay down in front of us and sighed. It broke my heart to see what he was going through. Russ followed me when I went out to stow the gun in the porch, scooted past me, and took off for another adventure.

When I sat down again, Sarah said, "You haven't asked me what the bear guy had to say."

"I was going to," I said between a bite of burger and mouthful of fries.

"He said it was a black bear, a male, three or four years old, about a hundred and fifty pounds. He left you a canister of bear spray. It's out in the porch. He said the instructions are on the can but he showed me how to use it. I'll show you after lunch."

"No need."

"No?"

"Not if the instructions are on the can."

I lost the next five minutes of my life in a daze, daydreaming out the window, my mind saturated with depressing thoughts, hardly tasting my food. The cabin was deathly quiet with Sarah in a shut down mood of her own.

She startled me when she got up and left for the bathroom. She'd hardly touched her food. A moment later she reappeared with a small daypack slung from a shoulder.

"I'm leaving now. Please don't get up. Thanks for lunch and putting me up. It was really nice to spend a night in your cabin again, Brody, even if it doesn't have a kitchen." She smiled at that and walked over to Jack, knelt down beside him and rubbed his head. He flapped his tail and gave her an adoring look. "Don't forget to give him his pills, next one's tonight at seven, okay?"

"Why are you leaving? You've still got an hour. I thought we could talk."

"Talk? Brody, you're not even here. You're somewhere else. I'll leave you alone to sort it out. See you Friday in Dawson. And please, please, please…keep that phone handy. Next weekend will be a dangerous one for me. I'll probably want to fly to Thistle Creek on Friday night, so be ready to go. And whatever you do…"

"I know. Don't call you Sarah."

She smiled and said, "Bye, Brody."

"Bye, Rita."

"Next weekend will be a dangerous one for me."

The instant the door closed, I missed her.

SIXTY

By Wednesday afternoon, things were looking up.

For one thing, no more bear. At least I hadn't seen one, and what I couldn't see with my own eyes, my boys would have seen with their noses. It looked more and more like the culprit who wrecked my kitchen was the one captured in the trap. By now he'd be scrounging his next meal miles away in a new stomping ground.

Another good thing was Jack's steady progress. He was sleeping most of the time because of the painkillers, but whenever he was up, seemed to be adapting well to life on three legs. It was inspiring to have him hop around after me whenever he was hungry. Which lately had been often. With his appetite back to normal, I knew he was going to be fine. I'd have to let Evelyn Dorval know she'd been right. Life does go on, even for a dog.

One more good thing, after a long morning of hard work, was that my shop was clean again. And so was the small collection of dishes, glasses, mugs, cookware and cutlery drying on a towel on the washing machine. I'd just finished cleaning all the bear germs off my kitchen stuff, thrown out the chipped and damaged pieces, and was assessing what was left: two plates, a glass, two coffee mugs, a bowl, a pot, a frying pan, a roasting pan, and enough utensils to cook just about anything. What else does a single guy need?

I scratched 'new kitchen stuff' off my shopping list.

Which left three items.

Screen Door, Grill, Kitchen.

As for the last item on the list, I'd taped an outline of the new and improved version on the floor of my cabin, measured everything twice, and knew the exact specifications of what to order—cabinets and cupboards, a counter top, a double sink and a fancy faucet. And since we were well into the twenty-first century, I thought it was high time I owned a microwave. The built-in kind. Problem was, I really didn't want to go back down to Whitehorse to get any of it. As far as I was concerned, the place was nothing but trouble. Which got me to thinking. The propane guy was coming up on Friday to deliver my new fridge. Maybe he had room in his truck to bring up a kitchen. No harm in asking.

I was reaching for the phone over the bench when it started ringing. I stepped back and stared at it.

Now who could that be?

Robson? Doubtful. Cops don't call to make appointments. They break down doors, barge in, and interrupt people's lives.

Sarah? Also doubtful. If she wanted to talk she'd call me on the satphone, which was now firmly affixed to my belt.

Ellen Burke? Now that was a possibility. Ellen would have no qualms about calling me, even if she had yet to print the article saying I wasn't a murderer. I'd eaten breakfast at the Café this morning and checked both Monday's and Tuesday's papers, and she hadn't come through with her end of the deal. To hell with her, I thought. Until she published that article, she wasn't getting her next installment of total nonsense. *Sorry Ellen, no ticky, no laundry.* I would not be afraid. I would fear no evil. I'd tell her like it is.

I picked up on the seventh ring.

"What!"

"Mr. Brody! You're hard to get a hold of!"

That's what they all say.

Dave Sorenson.

"Hello, Dave. Sell my TCR?"

"Sure did. All forty thousand shares, as ordered."

"Great, how much did I end up with?"

"After commissions, a little under thirty-six thousand dollars."

"Thirty-six thousand dollars? You're telling me there's thirty-six thousand dollars in my account?"

"That's right. You made a profit of thirty thousand dollars. You know, for a while there I thought you'd made a big mistake and were selling too soon. Thistle Creek Resources put out this incredible press release on Monday morning with gold assays like I've never seen or heard of before. I sold all your shares twenty minutes later at ninety cents, but by noon they were up another twenty cents and trading a buck-ten."

"A buck-ten? Holy cow. What are they trading at now?"

"Well, that's why I called."

"Oh?"

"Remember me explaining short selling to you?"

"I do."

"And how you can make money short selling a stock if it's going down?"

"Yes, Dave, I remember. And it's not something I'm ever going to do."

"Hear me out, Mr. Brody."

I sighed. Dave Sorenson had made me over thirty grand in a week and I wasn't going to hang up on him. He was enthusiastic, intelligent and affable, and while hardly my kind of guy for all the drinking, I couldn't help but like him. "Okay, Dave, I'm listening. Go ahead. But I'm not short selling any stock."

"Okay," he said. "So on Monday, the day the press release came out, Thistle Creek Resources shot up forty-two cents and closed at a dollar-four with two million shares changing hands. Yesterday, Tuesday, the stock backed off a little and closed at ninety-seven cents, with about the same number of shares changing hands. A small drop was to be expected, there's always a bit of profit taking after a big rise on news.

"But then today, the market for TCR just fell apart. In fact I thought it was going to tank. It was an absolute bloodbath out there. This morning four million shares got dumped in three hours. There was so much selling coming in from all over the place, it's a wonder the stock only fell twenty-five cents. At one point it was trading as low as fifty cents, then someone came in at the end of the day and bid it up again. So to answer your question, Thistle Creek Resources closed at seventy-two cents."

"Wow, guess I was lucky to sell when I did. My timing was perfect."

"Lucky? I don't think so, Mr. Brody. Perfect timing in the stock market is never luck. Perfect timing only happens if you have perfect information." He let that hang between us for a moment, then said, "So once again, I have to ask you, what do you know that I don't know about TCR?"

"Nothing. I told you already, Dave. Other than hearing the Thistle Creek promoter is a crook, nothing."

I heard him take a deep breath. We both knew I was lying. But for all kinds of reasons there was no way I could tell him what I knew.

"Look," he said. "Here's the deal. Junior exploration stocks are just bets. But if it ever comes out there's a hint of fraud, or criminal activity going on behind the scenes, especially after the Bre-X debacle, then all bets are off. The Exchange will suspend trading and if the shares ever do trade again, no one wants them anymore. They become worthless overnight.

"So, Mr. Brody, you bet and you won. You've cashed out and taken all your profits. But me and my clients, including Mike Giguere, well we haven't. So without telling me precisely what you know about Thistle Creek Resources, I'll know what to do in the morning if you tell me just one thing."

"And what's that, Dave?"

"Whether you're going to short Thistle Creek Resources."

* * *

Tippy Li was seething.

Never, ever, had he seen a day like this.

The markets had just closed and he was at his usual station, a booth in the corner with a view of the bar, sitting between two new girls from the agency. These ones he'd never met before and he thought the one named Dahla was kind of cute. He doubted she was old enough to drink but that was okay.

The room was crowded for a Wednesday afternoon and markedly louder than usual. Tippy caught numerous looks being cast his way but no broker in his right mind would dare approach him, not today, even with the mouthwatering eye candy on display. TCR had been the market's biggest loser, falling twenty-five percent, and the grim look on his face said it all.

Stay away.

Everyone was a suspect and everyone knew it. Best they all keep their distance until Tippy figured out who'd been messing with his stock.

And he always did.

He reached for his phone and touched a number.

"Yeah, Tippy."

"Where the hell are you, Gerry?"

"End of the bar with a hot one."

"Get over here."

Tippy ended the call and reached for his drink. The mellow burn of Chivas didn't help. He'd just parted with three million dollars to prevent TCR from sinking into oblivion and was furious about it. The question was, what would tomorrow bring? Another avalanche of selling? He had to be ready and knew what to do, though it could get expensive.

Gerry Feldman shouldered between two of Tippy's henchmen on a beeline for Dahla.

"Other side," said Tippy, pointing at the second best looking woman in the place.

Gerry couldn't hide his disappointment but changed direction and went where he'd been told, sliding in beside the one who might have been old enough to drink. He put his hand on her bare thigh. She smiled at him.

"Tell me, Gerry."

"We've been analyzing the selling all day, Tippy, ever since it started this morning. Whoever's dumping TCR knows what they're doing. The selling's coming out of eleven houses from Sidney to London, but there's no telling who the asshole is. All we know is that no one's borrowing from the pools, so it doesn't look like it's the work of a short. My guess is someone's dumping a huge position, so there can't be many candidates. If I was you, I'd look inside."

Inside.

Tippy clenched his jaw. Gerry was right, the selling had to be coming from 'inside'. He leaned back, folded his arms, and shook his head.

After all he'd done for her.

A waiter arrived with a platter of drinks. Teachers for Gerry, Chivas for Tippy, Neopolitans for the ladies. The drinks were served and the waiter left. Tippy noticed Dahla's eyes were already glazed and she had a glow on. He decided she actually was kind of cute.

"I need buyers, Gerry."

Gerry took a long drink and said, "We have you covered, Tippy, but not above fifty cents. There's a million dollars standing by if it goes that low, but that's the best we can do. Sorry. Our clients just bought ten million shares at a quarter, they're hardly motivated to pay more than that, especially after what happened today. This shit has everyone real nervous. The phones were ringing off the hook all day and it was all we could do to keep them from selling and running away."

Tippy nodded. He'd have to do this himself. Stock markets hate uncertainty and the only cure for uncertainty is buying. If he had to, he'd buy every damn share in the company with his own money, whatever the cost.

"Alright, Gerry. We're done. I need to make some calls."

Gerry slid down the bench, got to his feet, and downed the rest of his drink. He looked at the girls and said, "Mind if I take these with me?"

"Just the one you handled."

Gerry frowned. His date of the day slid out after him.

Tippy watched them walk out of the bar, arm in arm. When they were gone, he picked up his phone and logged onto his new favorite website.

Lynn wasn't at her desk. No surprise there, she hadn't been at her desk for four days. And she hadn't been answering the company phone either. Where the hell was she? He dialed a number in Alaska. It rang for a long time. He asked for Mr. Kay.

"Yes."

"I have a job for you in Dawson."

Tippy hung up and looked at Dahla.

"Ever been to the Yukon, Dahla?"

"Is that a club?"

* * *

Lynn Chan was doubting herself.

How had she got herself into this mess? All she wanted was her life back.

There were four men in the next room discussing her future, trying to hash out a deal. But what kind of a deal? Her lawyer said he'd come to get her, if and when she was needed. Needed? Why wouldn't she be needed? The meeting had been her idea, not theirs. But there she was sequestered, sitting alone at a table in a small adjoining office. Not what she'd had in mind.

All she'd envisioned was a simple meeting with her lawyer and the man from the BC Securities Commission, the one named Landry whom she'd talked to on the phone last week. She was prepared to tell him all about Tippy's skulduggery, and in return, he'd let her off the hook for the company's deceipt. Tippy would go to jail, she'd resign with impunity, end of story. Of course she sure as hell wasn't going to testify against Tippy, that was a no-brainer. But so long as he didn't find out she'd squealed on him, or that she'd sold her Thistle Creek shares, all would be fine. Lynn could lie with the best of them and Tippy never had to know who'd sunk his boat. Going to bed with him a few more times should allay his suspicions.

But Landry had turned up for the meeting with two other men, and both of them had cop written all over them. So what was this meeting really all about?

It was cause for concern but there was no reason to panic, not yet anyway, not with everything else going so well. She picked up one of the phones Danny had given her and held it in both hands. She needed to delete the email on the screen but wanted to take one more look, just to make sure it was real. When she'd read it for the first time an hour ago, it had made her giddy.

Sold 3.68M, Avg .67, Net $2.4M, Bal 6.32M, A.

'A' for Arturo, 'M' for millions, $ for dollars.

Arturo had started selling her TCR.

He'd sold 3.68 million shares at an average price of sixty-seven cents and she was up a cool 2.4 million dollars. And there was more to come with another six million shares to sell. Outstanding, she thought. She deleted the email and hoped Danny was right about his fancy program, that the message from Arturo would be erased from sender through server, and be gone forever.

Danny.

The kid was a genius.

Lynn's phone conversation with Tippy last week had almost been her demise. She realized then she couldn't have Tippy watching an empty desk when she was talking to him on the company phone, nor could she be shown sitting at her desk when she wasn't home. How stupid had she been to have not considered those impossible scenarios?

Enter Danny.

The day before Lynn went to the airport to swap chandeliers, he'd turned up at her door with a little black box. It had taken him a few days to copy, splice and edit all the previously recorded video to create two seamless versions—one with her sitting at her desk, the other showing it vacant. Now Lynn had a choice of two videos to stream to Tippy's website. With the flick of a switch on Danny's little black box, she could broadcast either one, depending on the deception she wanted to convey.

She could be at her desk—or not. She could be in—or out.

Right now, she was *out*.

The door opened.

"Miss Chan?"

SIXTY ONE

Friday morning was a gorgeous spring day with clear blue skies and just a tickle of wind, but I didn't feel like flying.

At least not to Thistle Creek to pick up rocks, or to Dawson to pick up a cop, even if the cop happened to be Sarah Marsalis.

But there I was in my good old plane, idling across Two Spirit Lake with a full load of fuel, heading for the far side, about to turn around and take off. I'd completed all my preflight checks and there was nothing else to do but contemplate the weekend ahead, and all its ominous trappings.

A deal's a deal and I'd be more than well paid for the mission ahead, which is why I was prepared to leave my dogs and home for a whole three days. But the prospect that a killer named Kay might be waiting in ambush was a daunting and distinct possibility. He'd know where I was headed and when to expect me. He'd know from talking to Dan Sanders, who'd know from talking to Mike Giguere.

Thistle Creek at ten, Dawson at noon.

So were Kay and I about to meet again?

The sawed off shotgun under the passenger seat provided some degree of comfort, as did the can of bear spray in my backpack. If I didn't have the nerve to shoot Kay, maybe a shot of chili pepper in the face would stop him long enough for me to call the cops with Sarah's phone.

The best laid plans of mice and men.

* * *

When I flew down the Thistle Creek valley, there wasn't a soul in sight. The operation was all but abandoned—no drills turning, no equipment moving, no men working.

The only vehicles in sight were two pickups parked side by side in front of an industrial size black and yellow trailer. I assumed the trailer must be the camp kitchen based on the wire cage out back stuffed with garbage bags, an incinerator beside it, and not far away, two bear traps parked at the edge of the clearing.

One of the vehicles was a yellow pickup loaded with sample bags, the other a red pickup with a white camper. I pushed the wheel forward and swooped down to the trucks, then pulled the wheel back and applied full power to let Mike know I'd arrived.

And Dan Sanders, too.

And anyone else within a mile.

Five minutes later I touched down on the Yukon River—against the current, parallel to the shoreline—and did a double take at a blur of orange that whizzed by on my left.

I let the floats settle into the water, opened the cockpit door, and looked back. Mike's truck was at the end of the dock with Sanders sitting on its open tailgate. An empty wheel barrow stood at the ready in front of him. Mike was standing in the middle of the dock waiting for me. He gave me a wave and I waved back. But what had my attention was the plane.

Last week there'd been a motorboat tied to the other side of the dock, now the boat was gone and in its place sat an orange Piper Super Cub on floats. It had a US registration on the side of its fuselage. Could it be the same plane Mike saw last week on the Stewart River? The one that picked up Kay?

And if so, did that mean Kay was here?

Every instinct and premonition told me to run, just shove the throttle ahead, take off for Dawson, tell the cops what I'd seen, and be done with Thistle Creek.

But I couldn't.

I wasn't going to abandon Mike, not under any circumstance, especially this one. He'd endured enough pain and anguish—alone. Without any of the brave men and women of law enforcement to have come to his rescue, someone else had to step up to the plate. Might as well be me, I was there. But then I thought, *wait a minute*, if Kay was about to ambush me, why would he wave a red flag and leave a strange airplane sitting out in plain sight? I decided he couldn't be that stupid, that there was no way he was around. There had to be another explanation for the plane. I stood on a rudder pedal, turned around, and headed for the dock.

From there, my day went downhill in a hurry.

* * *

"Hey, Brody."

"Hey, Mike."

"Great day for flying."

"Not a bump in the sky."

He nodded without looking at me, got down on his knees, and plucked the front float rope out of the water before the plane bumped into the dock. Mike was wearing sunglasses and still had the splint on his nose. I could see the dark bruising under his eyes had changed to a yellowish green, a sure sign of healing. Before asking the obvious question, I said, "How's the nose, Mike?"

"Ah, you know, getting better I guess. Can't wait to breathe through it again. Haven't tasted a thing for a week," he said with a forced chuckle.

He walked past me on his way to tie up the rear but kept his eyes down, doing a lousy job of trying not to look nervous. I sensed his apprehension, stepped down to the float, and did a quick scan of my surroundings. Sanders was on his way with a wheelbarrow heaped with canvas bags full of rock samples.

"Say, Mike, whose plane?"

"Oh, a friend of Dan's from Alaska. Think he's leaving tomorrow," and then with a weak smile and a little too quickly,

"Not the one I saw last week on the Stewart, least I don't think so, case you were wondering."

"Right."

But I knew it had to be. Mike was either naive or a lousy liar. There was no point in asking where the boat had gone, or who'd taken it.

I gave the little plane a quick appraisal. It appeared to be clean and in good condition. Like the Beaver, the Piper Super Cub is an ubiquitous part of the northern landscape, a venerable bush plane that's popular in Alaska for its simplicity and convertibility from wheels to floats to skis. But with less than half the load capacity and horsepower of mine, and not nearly as rugged with its pipe frame and fabric skin, its biggest advantage is affordability. I was about to walk over for a closer look when Sanders stopped his wheelbarrow in front of me.

"No time for that," he said, jutting his chin at my plane. "This is a rush job. Open the door."

I glared at him and said, "A rush job? No one told me anything about a rush job. I don't do rush jobs. Now if you'll excuse me."

I moved to my left to step around the wheelbarrow and he sidestepped to his right and put a hand on my chest. I grabbed his shirt sleeve and gave it a twist and a tug.

"Get your hand off me," I barked with more bravado than I thought was in me.

He moved it up to my neck and grabbed my collar. An instant later we each had our hands on the other guy's collar and were jerking each other back and forth in a clumsy tango.

Sanders was a formidable man, thick and strong through the middle, and though an inch shorter than me, probably twenty pounds heavier. But I had a longer reach and better footwork. We danced around the middle of the dock for a few seconds.

Stalemate.

"I said this is a rush job," he said.

"And I said I don't do rush jobs," I said, breathing harder than I wanted him to see, hoping our jostling match didn't end up in the river for a drowning contest. If something didn't end this soon, there'd be fisticuffs.

Mike stepped between us and tried to intervene with his best effort to untangle us.

"Hey, guys, chill!" he shouted, now part of the fray.

Three grown men.

Sanders blinked first and released his grip. I was more than happy to let him go because my right shoulder was on fire. The two of us stood face to face, glaring at each other, panting like race horses, trying to straighten ourselves out without looking at what we were doing. Sanders reached his hands behind his back and might have been tucking in his shirt, but when one of his hands came back, it was holding a gun.

Mike's gun. The .44 Magnum. Sanders waved it in my face.

I must have gasped when I stared down the barrel of the most powerful handgun in the world, wondering if it was to be my last image of life. If Sanders pulled the trigger, I'd never hear a sound, never see a flash, never feel a thing. There's no faster way to die.

He waved the gun over my shoulder and said, "Open that door and get in the plane, now!"

His hand was shaking and he had a crazed look in his eyes.

"Jesus, Dan! What the hell are you doing? Put that thing away!" Mike exclaimed.

I raised my hands and took a step back.

Sanders waved the gun at the cargo bay door again.

"Shut up, Mike," and then to me, "I said open that door and get in. We've got rocks to ship. Now move!"

"Okay, okay, I'm moving, I'm getting in."

He backed me up to the edge of the dock where I turned around, stepped onto the float, swung open the cargo door, and climbed into the back, shaking like a leaf. Sanders stepped onto the float in front of the pilot's door, took a step up the ladder, and surveyed the cockpit.

"Got a gun in there?"

By the time I opened my mouth to say something, he'd already found it. He pulled it out from under the passenger seat, stepped down to the dock, and unwrapped it from the sweatshirt.

After a careful inspection he looked me up and down and said, "What the hell are you doing with a street sweeper?"

"Found it," was the best I could come up with.

"Is that a satellite phone?" he asked, pointing the gun at my hip.

"Yeah."

"Throw it on the dock."

I sighed, unclipped it from my belt, and tossed it at his feet. He gave me a menacing glare, picked it up, then went to the end of the dock and hurled it into the river.

Ker-splash.

If Sanders didn't kill me, Sarah was certain to now.

"That a knife?" he asked, waving the gun at my belt.

"Yeah."

"I'll take that too," he said. "Throw it on the dock."

I did.

Sanders shoved the six-gun under his belt behind his back, picked up the knife, carried it and my shotgun up to Mike's pickup, and tossed them both in the cab. He came back to us and said, "Alright, let's do this. And you guys keep your mouths shut. No talking."

The three of us had loaded my plane before and knew what to do. Mike handed me a clipboard with his paperwork and I waited for Sanders to leave with the empty wheel barrow to get another load.

As soon as he did, I whispered, "Is that guy crazy?"

Mike shook his head and whispered back, "He's a mean son of a bitch, Brody. Best do what he says."

I took a deep breath and tried once more to stop shaking.

"Jennifer gave me some forms, Mike. She says they're the exact same as yours, but the cops wants us to use them."

I opened my backpack and pulled them out. He took them from me, looked them over, shrugged and nodded like he didn't care. I slipped them into the clipboard over his. Mike started handing me bags and I entered the info from the tags and arranged the bags where I wanted them. I didn't inspect the seals because I no longer cared either. At least not about the chain of custody for sample bags. It just didn't matter any more. Whether the samples had been tampered with or not, I already knew the scam. The assays were simply being falsified.

When Sanders left for his third trip to the truck, I whispered, "Where is he, Mike? Where's Kay?"

His eyes flitted about and he whispered, "I have no idea."

"Come on, it's me asking, where is he?"

"I said I don't know, Brody. Haven't seen him since last week on the Stewart."

"Is that the plane that picked him up?"

"I told you already, I don't know. I never got a good look. Super Cubs are all the same to me."

"So where's the pilot?"

"Up at camp."

"He's here?"

"Yes. He landed about an hour ago. Flew right over us when he came in, just like you did. Dan went down to get him and the two were back in ten minutes."

"But just the two of them."

"Yes."

"So where's the boat, Mike? Who took it?"

Sanders reappeared and we both shut up while he unloaded another pile of bags. I peeked at Mike's pickup and was surprised to see it was almost empty. We were almost done. Two more trips for Sanders and that would be it. The shipment would be smaller and lighter this time.

When Sanders left again, Mike said, "I don't know. Maybe they set it adrift, no one ever uses it anyway. When I came down with Dan to meet you, the plane was there and the boat was gone."

As usual there were more questions than answers. The biggest one was whether Kay had just flown in and left Thistle Creek in the boat. But one thing was for sure, another pilot was here. If he knew how to fly a Beaver, then my assumption that I'd be leaving with another load of rocks was now in doubt. The only certain way out of this jam was to take out Sanders. But how?

I dug into my pack and found the canister of bear spray.

SIXTY TWO

"Hurry up, we haven't got all day!"

Dan Sanders had his hands on his hips and was standing on the dock like a man in charge. He was ten feet from the cargo door watching me arrange and rearrange bags in the back of my plane. I'd been doing it for a while to draw him in and it was working.

"What the hell are you doing?" he asked, taking a step forward.

"Almost done," I said, crawling up to the front of the cargo bay, now within reach of Blake's bear spray which was sitting against the fuselage, behind the pilot's seat, out of his line of sight.

"You're done when I say so you're done, and you're done. Hear me? Enough with the bags, let's go!"

He took another step closer.

I almost had him where I wanted. For five minutes he'd been watching me perform a seemingly pointless exercise of swapping and shuffling bags around the cargo bay floor. I knew I had him because he'd been concentrating on the bags—not me—trying to make sense of what I was doing.

"Shouldn't be long," I said, shuffling and switching two more bags behind the seats.

When he'd finally had enough of my nonsense and stepped onto to the float, I grabbed the canister, swung it up in front of him, and squeezed the trigger. There was a great roar of expanding gas and his head disappeared in a blast of chili pepper. With both hands clutching his face, he staggered back onto the dock and let out a blood curdling squeal. Then, in an orange cloud of capsaicin— that's what the instructions said was inside—he sunk to his knees and began whimpering like a child. He couldn't breathe, see, taste or smell, and I had to wonder if he could even hear. I leapt out of the plane, yanked the gun out of his belt, and instantly appreciated what he was going through.

With my eyes, nose and throat burning, I made a mad dash up to Mike's truck to escape the acrid mist. Mike was seated on the passenger side with his window up, oblivious to what had just happened behind him. Coughing, wheezing and gasping, I was yelling before I got there.

"Water, Mike! Water, water, water!"

He jumped when I opened his door and I pulled him out by the arm.

"What the hell Brody, what's wrong with you?" Then he looked down at the dock and said, "What's Dan doing in the river?"

After pouring a bottle of water over my head, and dousing my face with another, we went down to the dock and hauled Dan Sanders out of the river, and walked him back to the truck with his eyes glued shut.

* * *

Mike was behind the wheel, I was jammed up against the passenger door, and Dan Sanders sat between us with the barrel of a Ruger Redhawk pressed against his ribcage.

"You move, I pull," I said. "Hear me?"

He barely nodded but I was certain he wasn't going to try anything. Let alone having a gun in his armpit, he was soaking wet, shivering with cold, wheezing in short gasps, and constantly rubbing his eyes. It would be a while before he could open them.

"Water," he murmured.

"Maybe later, if you're good," I said.

The road to the camp began as a steep narrow notch cut through the cliffs. Mike had his foot to the floor as we roared up the hill to reach the plateau on top. From there we weaved for half a mile through a tall spruce forest along the north side of the creek valley. When we emerged from the trees, Mike braked and stopped in front of the black and yellow trailer. We both got out but left the doors wide open, leaving Sanders inside. I walked around to the driver's side with my shotgun. Sanders was five feet away when I jacked a round into the chamber.

Click-Clack.

Nothing else in the world makes that sound.

It's the catch-all, international command for "freeze", "hands up", "drop your gun", and "don't even think about it". Not that I thought Dan Sanders was about to attempt an escape, he could barely breathe and was as good as blind with his eyes welded shut.

I handed the shotgun to Mike and in earshot of Sanders said, "If he gets out, shoot him. I'll be right back."

I walked into the trailer and found a wiry old man sitting by himself at a long mess table. He was drinking coffee and gave me a casual up and down appraisal.

"Howdy," he said, looking back at the television mounted high on the wall at the end of the room. CNN was on.

He was in his sixties and had the appearance of an authentic Alaskan or Yukon bush man—frayed ball cap, lumberjack shirt, jean jacket and jeans, a straggly gray beard, unkempt gray hair, a ruddy dry complexion, and a pair of strong hands that could probably do just about anything. His eyes were the giveaway, I know a pilot when I see one.

"What's your name?" I asked.

He looked at me and said, "Pete. What's yours?"

"Brody. You alone, Pete?"

"Yep, just me and the TV here. I'm told the whole crew's in town."

I looked around the empty kitchen and saw a nest of wires on a shelf where a two-way radio probably sat not too long ago.

"You belong to that Cub down on the river?" I asked.

"Yep. You the Beaver pilot?"

"That's right. You know how to fly a Beaver?"

"Been a while."

"How long's a while?"

"Ten years."

"How many hours on a Beaver?"

He stroked his beard and said, "Couple of thousand, I reckon, why?"

"All I needed to know. Come with me."

"How come?"

"Because I say so."

He skidded his chair back, stood up and asked, "Who are you?"

"A guy with a .44 Magnum."

I lifted my shirt to prove it.

"Where to?" he asked.

"Jail," I said.

* * *

I picked up a bunch of bananas from a bowl on the table, and on the way out of the kitchen, stopped and opened the door to a large pantry. Just about everything on the shelves was in a container the size of a paint can—baked beans, soup, spaghetti sauce, mayonaisse, salad dressing, peanut butter, jam, ketchup—you name it. I loaded up Pete with a pallet of water bottles and two cans of peanuts, and followed him out with the bananas in one hand and the Ruger in the other. Always keep your prisoners well fed and hydrated, you never know when you might need to march them somewhere.

We went out to the truck and I dropped the tailgate. Pete loaded the pallett of water and peanuts. Mike was leaning against the driver's door watching Sanders. Sanders was in the cab rubbing his eyes.

I closed the tailgate and said, "You carrying, Pete?"

"Nope."

"Turn around," I said.

He did and I frisked him like they do on TV. He was 'clean' as they say, and I nodded at Mike and tucked the Ruger under my belt.

"You taking us to town?" Pete asked.

"Nope. We've got a jail right here."

He turned around to face me again and said, "You do?"

"Sort of. So Pete, who took the boat?"

"That son of a bitch I just flew in here, that's who took the boat."

"This son of a bitch have a name?"

"I didn't ask and he didn't say."

"But you don't like him."

"Damn right I don't like him. I let him stay at my place and he killed one of my dogs."

"Really?"

"Yes, really. The bastard kicked him to death in front of my wife. Bruno was just a good old dog who never hurt anyone. The Missus told me about it on the radio this morning, just before I picked up the guy. I still can't believe he did it."

"So what's this guy look like?"

"Real big, strong, Chinese. Mean lookin' too. Could hardly fit him in the plane. And he hardly ever says a word."

I nodded and said, "So Pete, if this Chinese guy took off in the boat, why are you still here?"

"'Cuz he told me to wait for him. Said he'd be back tonight. Said if I wasn't here when he got back, he knew where I lived and would come lookin' for me."

"Did he go upriver or downriver?"

"Down."

Dawson.

I pointed at Dan Sanders in the cab.

"Know him?" I asked.

"Sure, that's Dan. He got me this job. What's wrong with him?"

"I think he has something in his eyes. How do you know him?"

"He was a friend of my boy. Why's he all wet?"

"He fell in the river. You say he was a friend?"

"The two of them were in the same company. They did two tours in Afghanistan together." Then after a long pause, "My boy died over there, you know. It was eight years ago next month. Came home in a box."

I nodded and said, "Real sorry to hear that."

We leaned against the tailgate and looked at the trees for a while. I decided there was something I liked about Pete. There didn't seem to be any lying in him.

"So Pete, did Dan ask you to fly that Chinese guy here?"

"Yep. I went and picked up the asshole last week on the Stewart and flew him to Fairbanks. Then the next day I picked him up in Fairbanks and flew him to my place in Chicken. Then I flew him back here this morning. It was just supposed to be a simple three leg charter and a week of room and board. But he wasn't supposed to kill my dog. And I thought the job was done when I dropped him off here this morning. Dan never said nothin' about waiting around another day to fly the guy somewhere else. That wasn't part of the deal."

"Chicken, Alaska? You live in Chicken, Alaska?"

"Is there another Chicken?"

I stifled a chuckle and asked, "So what are they paying you?"

"Nothin' so far, but I'm supposed to get five grand."

"Five grand, huh? Sounds like one of those cross-border trips without a customs stop, Pete."

"Screw customs. You go back far enough and we all crawled out of the ocean. Borders are just lines on a map drawn up by a bunch of politicians. If you can walk or take a boat to where you're goin', and you're not smugglin', might as well fly Air Pete. Lot faster."

Pete was obviously a rebel and lived in a world with ragged edges. But it was clear he didn't have a clue what he was mixed up in. The sooner I got him out of this mess, the better. Especially since Kay would be as likely to kill him as pay him when he'd served his purpose.

"Okay, Pete, I gotta put Dan in jail now. Wait for me here, I won't be long. Then you can go home."

"Why are you putting Dan in jail?"

"Because he deserves it."

* * *

Five minutes later, two hundred feet behind the kitchen trailer, at the edge of a spruce forest, I was sitting on the open tailgate of Mike's pickup truck, staring at Dan Sanders through a wire mesh gate.

It had taken a little coaxing and prodding to get him in, but given he was as good as blind—and under threat of another shot of bear spray—he eventually cooperated and crawled in on his own. I'd bound the gate shut with all five feet of the trip wire and doubted an engineer could open it.

Even a mechanic might take a few minutes.

The Thistle Creek jail had its first inmate.

"Okay, Dan, I know you can't see very well, but I'm sitting beside a number of things you could use in there. Let's see, what have we got, there's bottled water, peanuts, bananas, mosquito repellant, and oh—look at this, Dan—some Benadryl for your runny nose and Visine for your eyes. And lookee here, a really nice, thick, wool blanket, just the thing for a cold night in a bear trap. But before I part with any of these items, I need you to answer some questions."

"What kind of questions?"

"The same questions the cops will ask when they get here, provided of course Kay doesn't turn up first, in which case he'll just kill you and you won't be answering any questions. But let's look on the bright side, Dan. Maybe you live through the weekend. The important thing for you to realize is that your gig with Thistle Creek Resources is over. It's time to start covering your ass. Okay? Hello? Dan?"

After a while he said, "I'm not saying a thing."

"Come on. You've done a lot of bad things and you're in a ton of trouble. You're sitting in a bear trap in soaking wet clothes with your eyes glued shut. It's time to start singing, get it all out, cut yourself some slack. Think about all this cold clean water five feet away. It can be yours for a song. So my first question is, where's Tommy Kay?"

"Fuck you," he said.

"Wrong answer, Dan. That just cost you a bottle of water. You're down to five now. Keep in mind it'll be a while before anyone turns up to let you out of there, and I'm sure you know how miserable life can be without water."

"Leave me alone."

"Let me explain again the major predicament you're in, Dan. You're looking at two scenarios, and only two. If the cops get here first, you live. But if Kay gets here first, you die. Think about it, it's that simple. You either survive the weekend or you don't, depending on who gets here first. However…"

"However what?"

"However I might have just the thing to give you a fighting chance against Kay, if he gets here before the cops do, that is."

"What's the thing?"

"First you have to answer my questions."

"Why should I trust you?"

"Do you have a choice?"

He was sitting in profile with his back curled against the curvature of the tube, constantly rubbing his eyes. Silence. I decided to try again.

"Where is he, Dan?"

He heaved a sigh and said, "He said he was going to Dawson, that's all I know."

"Did he say if he was coming back?"

"Tonight, late."

"To fly off somewhere in that Super Cub."

"Good thinking, Sherlock."

"Did he leave with full tanks?"

"What do you think?"

I did some quick and rough calculations. If Kay had left Thistle Creek for Dawson with full tanks in a twenty-five foot motorboat, then with a five mile an hour current at his back, he'd have the range and speed to travel the hundred odd miles to Dawson in about four hours.

If he left two hours ago, then two hours from now.

But for Kay to return to Thistle Creek against the current would take him at least six hours. And he'd need to fuel up to make it back. The cops would know by then to be on the lookout for a large man fueling a twenty-five motorboat because I was going to tell them to be on the lookout. The more I thought about it, the clearer it became that Kay was unlikely to return in a boat. Too much hassle, too much time, too much risk. He'd want to fly back for his rendezvous with Pete. And who better to fly him back than me? It had to be what he had in mind. Which officially made me a marked man.

Might have guessed.

"Okay, Dan, next question. Who torched that lumber in Minto?"

He ignored me, consumed with rubbing his eyes.

"Come on, you're wasting my time," I said. "Do you want to live or not? Who set those fires?"

He took a deep breath and said, "I think it was Kay and some Chinese guy named Adrian. I heard them talking about setting a fire when they came up here last week to get my truck."

"Okay, now we're getting somewhere. So who killed Amy Vanderbilt?"

He turned to me with his eyes closed and said, "Who?"

"Amy Vanderbilt. The young woman who was killed at my cabin."

"I have no idea about that, only what I read in the papers. Sounds like you did it."

"Well I didn't."

"Then it must have been Kay or that Adrian guy."

"And how about my dog? Who shot him?"

"Your dog? How would I know who shot your dog?"

"Okay then, how about my plane? Someone pumped water into one of the floats. Was that you?"

It took him a while to respond.

"Yeah, that was me. Kay told me to do it. When he tells you to do something, you do it."

"And how about my windshields? Did you smash them?"

"Don't know anything about any smashed windshields."

"Alright, so who killed that Adrian guy?"

"He's dead?"

"Sure is. They found him at the bottom of an outhouse in the Minto campground."

Sanders shook his head and said, "Three guesses, first two don't count."

"Okay, last question. Who slashed Jennifer Kovalchuk's tires?"

"Who's Jennifer Kovalchuk?"

"The woman who owns Thurson Ames Assayers. Someone slashed the tires on her truck."

"I have no clue."

I was out of questions and hadn't learned much, other than Kay was probably on his way to Dawson and that Sanders was just another conscripted and reluctant member of Kay's support group. It seemed all the egregious crimes in the past week were either the work of Tommy Kay or Adrian Woo. With Woo dead, the prize remained Kay. At least now I knew where he was headed, and what he had in mind.

"All right, Dan. I guess you've earned your survival stuff."

I backed the truck up beside the trap and started dropping things in through the hole in the top. It reminded me of a little chimney and I felt like Santa Claus. The blanket took some time to get in, we had to work it back and forth until he could pull it through. The can of peanuts was too big to fit through the hole so I popped the top off and poured them in—to a litany of curses from the inmate.

When I started the truck, Dan's muffled voice bellowed from inside the trap.

"Hey! I answered your damn questions, now what about that thing to fight Kay?"

"Oh, right," I yelled back.

I pulled out Mike's gun, flipped out the cylinder, removed all but one bullet, wiped down the whole thing with a shirttail, got out of the truck, carried it to the trap by the trigger guard, and dropped it down the hole in the top of the trap. It landed inside with a resounding clank. I got back in Mike's pickup, but didn't start the engine, and waited for the predictable reaction.

"Hey, what the hell? One bullet?"

"How many do you need? It's a .44!"

I knew he wouldn't try to shoot me when I drove off. For one thing, he couldn't see. For another thing, why would he waste his one and only bullet on me if he couldn't get out of the trap?

Dan Sanders needed that bullet for Kay.

* * *

Pete was raiding the kitchen, Mike was packing his bags, and I was leaning on Pete's truck running out of patience. For something to do I rummaged around the cab for a tire iron, found one, and walked over to Dan Sanders' red pickup with the white camper and Alaska plates.

What goes around, comes around.

After a minute of hammering the front windshield on both sides, the whole thing resembled a sheet of shattered glass candy. I stepped back and admired my handywork, then thought something still didn't look quite right. I pulled the knife from the sheath on my belt and poked a neat hole into each tire's valve stem. Dan's truck was hissing at all four corners when Pete emerged from the kitchen carrying a heavy cardboard box.

"Why'd you do that?" he asked with a grunt, sliding the box into the back of Mike's truck.

"Sending a message," I said.

"To who?"

"To anyone who thinks they can mess with my plane."

We watched Sanders' truck slowly sink down to the rims.

Five minutes later Mike and I were standing on the end of the dock, watching Pete take off for Chicken with a cardboard box full of frozen steaks. I guess he figured if he wasn't going to get paid, then fifty pounds of meat was better than nothing.

"Think he'll call the cops?" Mike asked.

"No way," I said. "He'll lose his license if they find out he landed here without a customs clearance. But we can call them. Maybe they can intercept Kay before he gets to Dawson. Got your satphone handy?"

"No."

"No?"

"No."

"Where is it?"

He jutted his chin at the river.

"Same place as yours. With the camp radio."

Mike and I took off for Dawson with a plane load of rocks, four bananas, and a circus size can of peanuts.

Chasing Tommy Kay.

SIXTY THREE

When he cleared the last stand of trees at the end of the island, it appeared on his right.

Finally.

Dawson.

For a while he thought he might have missed it.

He'd been on the river for over four hours and could barely feel his hands. Even with the hunter's cap and canvas coat from the Mission of God, he was cold to his core. He looked over the bow at the houses and buildings and wondered why anyone would live up here. Nothing but cold water and cold air and skinny trees. Trees, trees, and more trees. They seemed to be everywhere and he was sick of looking at them. He'd hit two of them floating in the river and was lucky not to have put a hole in the boat.

Tommy Kay eased back the throttle, slowed the boat to a crawl, and turned off the motor. He surveyed the sky behind him but could neither hear or see a plane. But he knew it wouldn't be long. He reached into his gym bag, selected the phone he wanted, and pressed SEND.

Someone said, "Yes."

"I'm here."

"We see you. Stay on the left side. We're just past the ferry terminal."

The line went dead and Kay tossed the phone into the river. He reached into his bag and took out another phone. He pressed SEND on that one too, and waited again.

Someone said, "Are you there?"

"Yes."

"Good. Your package will be delivered tonight. Ten o'clock."

The line went dead.

He tossed that phone into the river too, then started the motor and pushed the throttle ahead.

* * *

The Dassault Falcon 8X had just finished its two mile taxi out from the New Horizons' hangar and had joined the queue for Runway 26R, third in line for takeoff. In less than two hours, its crew of three and two passengers would arrive in Whitehorse.

After ending the call from Dawson, Tippy daydreamed at the phone in his hand for a while, then looked up at the pretty young woman strapped in the jump seat at the front of the cabin. She was slim and attractive in a pressed blue uniform, and gave him a warm smile. He acknowledged her with a nod and gazed across the aisle at Lynn.

Of course there was no comparison. Lynn was in a league of her own, the perfect accessory for a private jet. Exotic and gorgeous with an aura of unattainability, today she was wearing tall suede boots, black leggings, a gold cable knit sweater, lots of red lipstick, and the latest Prada sunglasses on a cloudy day in Vancouver.

Very chic, very upper end, very expensive.

And very dead.

He marveled at how calm and composed she seemed, oozing self-confidence, idly flipping through the pages of a glossy magazine. He wondered how she'd behave were she to know she was the 'package', that by midnight tonight her lifeless body would be wrapped in chains, rolling along the bottom of the Yukon River.

A shame, really—he wished there was another way—but it was a fate she deserved. With almost total certainty, Tippy now knew it had been Lynn indiscriminately dumping TCR shares into the market. Ten million of them to be exact, the same the number of shares she'd deposited in her Cayman bank a month ago.

Gerry Feldman had called an hour ago to tell him the brokerage houses dumping TCR had abruptly stopped their selling. He said when his analysts went back and added up all the sales from those houses over the past three days, the number was a little over ten million shares. Gerry also said the total short sales position for TCR was less than half a million shares, a typical number at this stage of the game.

So Lynn was the culprit. She was the enemy.

And enemies must die.

* * *

She could feel his eyes burning into the side of her face but wasn't going to look at him. Of course by now he'd know what she'd done, and that was bad enough. But now he'd want to have sex with her, probably as soon as they took off. Tippy always wanted sex when they took off. She loathed the thought of it but sometimes a girl has to do, what a girl has to do. At least it would be for the last time.

She sighed and turned the page in her magazine and was presented with an article on Tuscany. Above the article was a large picture of an old stone villa covered in vines, surrounded with topiary and flowers, overlooking a majestic backdrop of bronze hills and green valleys in the Italian countryside.

Now that was a life she could go for.

Maybe she would when this was over. She certainly had the means now, with more cash than she could have hoped for, most of it sitting safe and sound in her bank in the Caymans. All she had to do was execute the plan her lawyer had negotiated with the cops and that man from the British Columbia Securities Commission.

The deal she'd made wasn't exactly what she'd had in mind, but it was still better than no deal, and simple to execute. By this time tomorrow she'd be free of Tippy and could live the life she wanted.

If he only knew what the night would bring.

She stifled a smirk and began reading the article.

Tuscany.

SIXTY FOUR

We never saw the boat.

For almost an hour we flew low and slow, heading north, winding our way down the middle of the river. Mike and I each took a side and searched every inch of its dark flat waters, including every nook and cranny along its banks, but saw nothing but a bear and a couple of moose.

The whole time since we'd left Thistle Creek, he'd been munching on peanuts and I was getting tired of the smell.

"Hey, you gonna eat all of those?" I asked with a nudge in his shoulder, pointing at the can in his lap.

Mike chuckled sheepishly and said, "Better stop, huh? The cook went to town yesterday with the rest of the crew and I am starving."

He put the top on the can and shoved it under his seat.

"There are bananas in my pack," I said.

"No thanks, I'll eat in town," he said, pointing over the nose at Dawson rising on the horizon. "Guess he beat us there."

I shared his disappointment with a nod. Kay was evidently adept at staying out of sight and was once again a step ahead of his pursuers. I backed off the throttle and prepared the plane to land beside the funkiest town on the planet.

Dawson was the epicenter of the richest gold rush in history.

Over twenty million ounces of gold have been mined out of the creeks and hills south of town since the bonanza discovery made back in 1896. By 1898, what had been a sleepy settlement at the confluence of the Klondike and Yukon Rivers, exploded into the continent's largest city west of Winnipeg, and north of Seattle.

But while thirty thousand brawling miners—and a few wild women—may not have been the best demographic to start a city, Dawson was regardless doomed from the start.

The Achilles heel for the new 'Paris of the North' was the ground it was built on.

Situated on top of a deep frozen mixture of silt and sand—essentially a block of ice known as permafrost—very few buildings built in early Dawson survived for very long. For one thing, as soon as the surface was disturbed the permafrost would begin to melt, and whatever was built on top would start sinking and fall apart.

That, and whenever someone knocked over a candle, it seemed the whole place would burn down.

Which is why the 'boom town in a bog' has barely grown in over a hundred years. Today, with a population of just thirteen hundred year-round residents, Dawson still has mud streets, wooden boardwalks, and a smattering of crooked old wood buildings that somehow survived the last century. Which is what makes the place so authentic—it's virtually the same place it was in 1898.

I called Dawson ATC and told them I was inbound and wanted to land at the Dawson Water Aerodrome. A woman in the tower approved my request—they always do—and in the lexicon of air speak told me what I already knew. The winds were light and variable out of the south, the sky was clear, and don't run into the car ferry. I prepared my heavy plane for landing and flew down the west side of the river, made a steep 180 degree turn to head back south, flew *over* the ferry, and descended down to the water along the east bank.

"Looks like we've got quite the welcoming committee," said Mike, pointing at the dock as the floats settled into the water.

I shook my head at the scene ahead. What was it about docks

lately? It seemed everywhere but Minto there was a crowd waiting for me.

I dropped the rudders and steered toward the foot of King Street.

* * *

Three pickup trucks and a small gray car were parked in the gravel lot above the jetty. Two men and two women were standing on the dock with two little red wagons ready to load.

The two women were Jennifer and Sarah. One of the men was Larry Brookes, the tall guy who'd helped Sarah and I unload my plane in Whitehorse last week. The other man I'd never seen before. He was also tall and kind of looked like Larry. I surmised the chances were pretty good his name was Tony, because one of the trucks was a new blue Toyota.

Great.

Still, I was glad to have the whole Thurson Ames gang in attendance. Tommy Kay was unlikely to confront me while in their midst.

Mike squeezed between the seats and got back into the cargo bay, and when the left float slid up against the dock, climbed out the cargo door to secure the rear cleat. I went out the cockpit door to tend to the front.

Jennifer's employees were giving the boss plenty of room. She was standing alone under the left wing with her hands on her hips, and a very intense look. When I returned to the cockpit ladder, she skipped the pleasantries.

"Got your paper work?" she asked in an all business tone of voice.

I smiled at her and said, "Nice to see you again too, Jennifer. Sorry we're late. Yeah, sure do."

I turned around, stepped down to the float, and pulled the clipboard out of a seatpocket. When I stepped back onto the dock, the tall guy I didn't know was standing beside her. He was a good looking guy with dark eyes. Never liked good looking guys with dark eyes. He too had a very intense look.

With a sigh of exasperation, Jennifer said, "Brody, this is Tony Brookes. Tony, meet Brody."

So Tony was Larry's brother. I might have guessed, they had the same build. There was a pregnant pause while I sized him up and tried to assess his attitude, but found myself extending my hand anyway.

"Nice to meet you, Tony."

Guess you know by now I slept with your fiancé. But hey, there's a perfectly good explanation. See… what happened was…

Tony's hand came up from his side, but not to shake my hand. It was clenched in a fist, sailing through the air in a long looping arc that caught me flush on the chin.

Pow!

His sucker punch had landed right on the money and spun me around. I went down with a knee crashing hard into the float and my head bouncing off the cockpit ladder. My ball cap came off and I watched my sunglasses sink into the Yukon River. In the next split second I decided I'd had enough of bullies twisting my arm, choking and grabbing me, waving guns in my face, and now coldcocking me in the face. In a rage I whirled around and launched myself at his knees, picked him up, and pile-drived him into the deck. The air came out of him with a whoosh and a grunt. Tony may have been good looking but he was also a wimp. I had him pinned under me and his only reaction was to cover his face with his hands. I was now in a perfect position to the deliver the punch of the century, one of those 'everything you've got' blows, straight down into his fine Roman nose. I raised my right hand to execute my revenge, about to rearrange his face, when a jolt of pain shot through my shoulder. My arm was caught on something and wouldn't move.

What?

Out of nowhere Jennifer's two big hands yanked me to my feet, turned me around, and with a mighty shove in the back, sent me stumbling down the dock, toward the jetty—and Ellen Burke.

"Don't hit me!" Burke screamed, holding her phone out like

a shield as she shuffled backwards to get out of my way. Today's lycra outfit was a shiny royal purple, worn under the usual unzipped red ski jacket.

"Hit you? Why would I hit you?" I shouted, rubbing my throbbing shoulder. I tasted blood and touched my lip. Ouch. I checked my teeth. All there. "What are you doing here, Ellen? What do you want?" I bent over and inspected my left knee, which also hurt. "Hey, you write that article yet?"

While waiting for the answers, I turned to check the scene behind me. Jennifer had my Tire King ball cap in one hand and was swinging it back and forth, shaking the water off it. She gave me a sheepish look and a shrug of her wide shoulders in a self-deprecating apology. Behind her Larry Brookes was standing over his still prone brother, lifting him up and down by his belt, trying to get him to breathe again. Mike had a concerned look because Tony was gulping like a fish. Sarah was standing at the far end of the dock with her back to everyone, obviously not interested in having her picture taken.

"No, Mr. Brody. I did not write that article and I'm not going to!"

Ellen again.

She was halfway up the jetty but still taking pictures.

"You lied to me," she shouted at the top of her lungs. "Everyone I talk to says there's no such thing as a conspiracy to corner the world's supply of rare earths. You're trying to make a fool of me. You're nothing but a liar and a thug!"

She ran off in a mad dash to the small gray car with her jacket flapping and her feet spinning like propellers. Once she got it started—which took a while—she floored the accelerator and backed up way too fast, lost control, and ran smack into the front bumper of Mike's other truck. There was a big crunch of sheet metal as her trunk lid crumpled in against its winch. It took another moment for her to find the gear she wanted, then she gave me the bird, spun the tires, and accelerated away. I shook my head and limped back to Jennifer.

"Thanks," I said, accepting my soaking wet ball cap from her.

"I'm really sorry, Brody."

"So he knows."

"Yeah, he knows."

"Who told him?"

"I did. He asked me and I told him."

"Why did you tell him?"

"Because when I told him we were through, he wanted to know why. I told him there was someone else and he wanted to know who. So I told him who. He promised to behave. He lied."

"Men lie, Jennifer."

"Tell me about it."

We held each others eyes for a while, reciprocating a tacit acknowledgement that there was nothing left between us. I put my wet hat on my head and said, "Let's get these rocks unloaded."

She stopped me with a hand and said, "We've got this, Brody. You need a doctor."

"A doctor? What for? I don't need a doctor."

"Yes, you do. You have a split lip and you need stitches. Rita!"

* * *

'Rita' was at the wheel of Jennifer's truck and we were on our way to Dawson's only medical clinic. She was driving just slightly faster than I could run and I was hoping we got there before I bled to death. I was holding a wad of Kleenex to my cut lip and kept inspecting it in the mirror, to see if the bleeding had stopped. No chance of that, it was a gusher.

To break the ice I said, "Hey, you guys find Tommy Kay yet?"

"Nope."

"Well, I'll give you a hint where to look for him. I think he's in Dawson, or at least real close."

"And why do you think that?"

"Because he left Thistle Creek for Dawson in a boat this morning."

"Says who?"

"Says me. And Mike Giguere will tell you the same thing."

"We'll be talking to Mr. Giguere this afternoon."

"Good. But in the meantime, take my word for it. Kay's here now. Tell the RCMP, okay?"

"I will." She looked over at me and said, "Hey, you are really bleeding. Does that hurt?"

"Yes it hurts. Hey, what about my keys and backpack? And I want my plane locked when that crew leaves."

"Jennifer will lock up your plane and put the keys in your pack. Is that where your satphone is?"

"Um, well...actually...no. I don't have it anymore. But there's a very good explanation for that. You wouldn't believe what just happened at..."

"Christ, Brody, I don't believe this!"

"Just listen, okay? You need to hear what happened."

"Spare me. I don't want to hear what happened. It doesn't matter now anyway. You won't be needing it."

"I won't? How come?"

"You just won't, okay?"

"Okay," I said. "But I still think you should hear what..."

"Brody, I said I don't care."

"Suit yourself," I said. "But you really ought to..."

"Brody, I said...I...don't...care." Then after a pause, she said, "I'll go get your keys and backpack after I drop you off at the clinic. Check with the front desk when you get to your hotel."

"I have a hotel?"

"Yes, courtesy of the FBI. It's all booked and paid for." She handed me a cardkey. "You're in room 201 at the Eldorado under the name of John T. Leonard. You're going to stay put in that room until exactly eleven-thirty tonight. No running around town, no going out to eat, no using the phone. You just stay inside in your room and wait."

"Wait for what?"

Her phone rang.

"Five minutes," she murmured, "Then he's all yours."

When she hung up, I said, "I'm all whose?"

"You'll see."

"Hey, what if I need to fuel my plane? Can I use the phone for that?"

"Do you need to fuel your plane?"

"Not really."

"That's what I thought. Now please don't use the phone."

"Can I watch TV?"

"Yes."

"Great. Do I get to eat?"

"Two meals will be delivered to your room, one at two o'clock, one at seven o'clock. And under no circumstance do you open your door unless you hear exactly five knocks and someone say, 'Room service for Mr. John T. Leonard'. Exactly like that. Got it?"

"John T. Leonard, huh? So what happens at eleven-thirty tonight?"

"We'll be picking you up, so be ready to go. Your room overlooks the alley at the back of the hotel. Be on the lookout for an unmarked police SUV. When you see it drive into the alley, you walk out of your room, walk down the stairs—do not use the elevator—and walk to the end of the hall immediately to your right. We'll be waiting outside the exit door. You walk out and get in."

"Who is *we*?"

Sarah exhaled and said, "Look, not that I should be telling you this, but by then we'll have made at least one arrest and an army of cops will be heading to Thistle Creek to seal off the camp. It needs to be secured before the techs start turning it upside down to do their forensic work. We need you to fly me and two SWAT guys down there tonight. Our job is to make sure no one comes in or out of that camp using the river before the main team arrives by road. They're expected at two a.m., which means we need to be there before then. I want to take off no later than midnight. That should be plenty of time, right?"

"Yeah, it's only an hour flight. You'll be there at one o'clock. So what do I do after I drop you off?"

"Nothing. You leave. You go home."

"That's it?"

"That's it."

"Is my contract over then?"

"Looks like it."

"Wow, hell of a deal." I thought about the second twenty-five grand payment I was due from the FBI. For a moment I felt guilty about how much I would make from them for doing so little. Then I thought about Dan Sanders waving a gun in my face and didn't feel so bad. "So you're absolutely sure you don't want to know what happened to my phone?" I asked.

"Later."

When she stopped in front of the clinic, I got out and said, "Thanks. And hey, when you get to Thistle Creek tonight, tell those SWAT cops to check out the bear traps."

"What bear traps? Why?"

I closed the door and went into the clinic.

* * *

Jennifer had been right. I needed stitches. Three of them.

I'd walked into the clinic without my backpack which meant I had no wallet, no ID, no insurance card, no money.

Lucky for me, Laura DeLaney was behind the counter. Laura did double duty as the Dawson health clinic's chief administrator as well as being a registered nurse. She was also the girlfriend the summer before a woman named Deb, who was the girlfriend the summer before Sarah. Two more long stories with the same sad endings.

"Well, well, look what the wind blew in. What happened to you?" she said.

"How are you, Laura? Slipped and fell on a ladder."

"This ladder have a fist?"

I smiled as best as I could and said, "You should see the other ladder."

"Follow me," she said. "The doctor's in."

Twenty minutes later I walked back out to reception with a frozen lower lip and a goofy looking mouth with stitchwork. Laura had an open file on the counter and a form for me to sign.

"Still the same billing information?" she asked, "Brody, Minto, Yukon?"

"That'll work," I said.

"Better put some ice on that jaw or you'll never kiss again. Three times a day until the swelling goes down."

"Good advice."

She slid the form at me and I noticed a big sparkler on her left hand.

"Hey, Laura. Did you go out and get married on me?" I asked with surprise while signing on the dotted line.

"I did, last winter in Hawaii."

"And?"

"And so far, so good. He's a great guy, Brody, you'd approve. But I gotta tell you…there are days I have to wonder why I did it. I'll never forget that line you told me about the three rings of marriage—the engagement ring, the wedding ring, and the suffer-ring."

I patted her hand and said, "Be nice to him, Laura, he's only a man."

When I turned around there was a cop in my face. She was the same one who'd given me the ticket in Whitehorse for using my cell phone while driving.

'E. Saunders'

"Ready to go, sir?"

"Go where?"

"Your hotel."

"I guess. You come all the way up to Dawson just to drive me to my hotel?"

"Busy weekend, sir."

I followed the garage sale hanging from her belt and we went out to her cruiser.

* * *

Constable Saunders drove past the front of the Eldorado Hotel, then turned left at the first intersection, then left again into the alley behind the building.

After a slow pass to let me reconnoiter the alley—seen one, seen 'em all—she turned left again and stopped her big blue car at the street.

"I'll let you out here," she said. "You have to enter through the front door."

"Thank you," I replied, looking around for a big mean guy. I got out and stepped onto a wavy wooden boardwalk in front of the two-story hotel and wondered if E. Saunders had any idea why she'd been told to give me a three hundred and sixty degree tour of its exterior. But to my benefit, I did locate my exit door.

No one had left my backpack at reception so I did what I'd been told to do and went up to my room. Ten minutes later I was flicking through channels on a lousy TV when there were five knocks on the door. I asked through the door who it was and a young woman's voice said, "Room service for Mr. John T. Leonard."

Whoever owned the voice was gone by the time I figured out how to open it and found a tray lying at my feet. It was the standard industrial-grade guy's lunch—burger, fries and a Coke—but with a bucket of ice as a second side.

Very thoughtful.

I managed to eat without chewing on my frozen lip, then went into the bathroom for a facecloth to wrap up some ice. The man in the mirror was only vaguely familiar with a bulging raw lip and a large mouse residing inside his left cheek. With time on my hands, I decided to do something I hadn't done for a long time.

Have a bath.

Maybe heat would limber up my sore shoulder and knee.

For the next half hour I lay soaking in a tub of hot water with a facecloth full of ice held to my jaw, analyzing the peeling wallpaper around the faucet, thinking about my midnight mission to Thistle Creek, but mostly wondering about Tommy Kay.

Where the hell was he?

SIXTY FIVE

It was nine-thirty and the party below was booming through the floor.

Not that the noise bothered me, I certainly didn't need any more sleep, having snoozed on and off all afternoon until my dinner arrived at seven.

Salisbury steak with another bucket of ice.

I got off the bed and limped over to the window, opened it up, stuck my head outside, and surveyed the alley below. It was empty save for a young couple walking by. They were holding hands, sharing a laugh about something, perhaps heading home after dinner or on their way to another bar on a Friday night out. The sun was well north of west, about to complete another day's long slow circle around the horizon, casting a peaceful orange glow that would last all night long.

Sarah Marsalis and her SWAT buddies were due in two hours. I turned and looked at the phone beside the bed and wondered for the umpteenth time why Sarah had told me not to use it. What difference could it make? Of course I also wasn't supposed to leave my room. My problem was I still hadn't been reunited with my backpack and had a serious separation anxiety building inside. I needed it back, if for no other reason than the keys to my plane would be inside. Surely a quick trip downstairs couldn't hurt, see if it had been left at the front desk. Just down and back.

Shouldn't take a minute.

Near the bottom of two flights of stairs I stopped for a quick scan of my environment, ever vigilant for a large hulking man on the prowl, though thinking it unlikely anyone wanted for murder would be hanging around such a crowded place. The lobby had a steady stream of revelers coming and going in all directions, with an uproarious din emanating from the bar at the far end. There was a small elevator to my left and I located the hallway to my right I was to use later. Only one receptionist was on duty. She was attending to a woman checking in. When they'd finished their business, I waited for a couple of fat guys to go by, then headed over to the counter.

The woman who'd just checked in was going the other way, pulling a small rolling suitcase. She gave me a double take.

You should see the other guy.

The receptionist was a young Filipino woman. She was barely five feet tall, nicely groomed, neatly dressed in a red skirt and white blouse, and all smiles. Her name tag said Reyna and she was poised for action with her hands hovering over a keyboard.

"Hello sir, pleased to meet you, sir. Welcome to the Eldorado, sir. Name please, sir."

"Hello, Reyna, my name is Bro...John Leonard. Did someone leave a backpack here for me?"

"Very sorry, Mr. Brojohn Leonard, no backpack for you."

"Are you sure?"

"Yes, Mr. Brojohn Leonard. No backpack for you, sir. Very sorry, sir."

"Are you sure? Wait, maybe it was left for Mr. C. E. Brody. Could you check please?"

She opened the door to a closet behind her and I could see it sitting on top of a suitcase. She looked at the tag on it, then closed the door and said, "Yes, a backpack for Mr. C.E. Brody, but not for you, sir."

"Um, actually, it is for me. I am Mr. C.E. Brody."

Reyna smiled.

"But you say you are Mr. Brojohn Leonard."

"Look, Reyna, I'm a guest here and that is my..."

I caught myself and stopped. I could see where this was going. She'd have another name to process if I gave her my room number and would probably call security if I didn't shut up. What to do?

Behind me came a familiar voice calling my name. Well an attempt, anyway.

"Mishta Brogee!"

Dave Sorenson.

Dave was already hammered but maybe he could help.

"Hey, Dave. You made it up."

"Yup, and am I ever glad I did. Did you see her? Hey, what happened to your face?"

"Fell on a ladder."

"A ladder, huh? So did you see her?"

"See who?"

"Lynn Chan. She's in the bar right now. Remember what I told ya'? I just knew she was hot, but man, she is smokin' hot. " Dave stopped for a burp. "Go check her out. She's at the first table on the right when you walk in."

"Ah, Dave, could you do me a favor and tell Reyna here my name?"

"Your name?" Dave spread his hands on the counter, tilted his head, and broke out a big smile. "Hello, Reyna. That's a very pretty name. Are you a model, Reyna?" When she smiled with embarrasment, he said, "You sure look like a model to me."

"Dave, just tell her my name, okay?"

From beside me someone else said, "Young lady, I can attest to this man's identity. He is Mr. C.E. Brody of Minto. He's a very well known man in the Yukon. Now please give him his backpack."

The voice was confident and commanding with an air of authority. It belonged to a professional looking woman in her fifties, the one who'd just checked in. She'd left but had come back and was now standing beside me. I took a look at her and had no idea of who she was. Reyna obediently opened the door behind her again, picked up my backpack, and put it on the counter. She pulled off the tag, slid it in front of me, and handed me a pen.

"Sign here, please, Mr. C.E. Brody."

I did and saw that Dave had given up on his seduction of Reyna. He was wobbling back to the bar, wagging a finger in the air.

"We need to talk," he said. "And check out Chan."

When I turned back to Reyna, the woman beside me was holding out a business card. I took it from her.

Marsha Price, CBC News North.

"Thanks for your help…Ms. Price. Do I know you?"

"You would if you've been listening to the radio up here for the last twenty years. Seems Reyna does. I host the morning show."

"Oh, well radio's not really my thing. In fact I don't listen to the radio. So how do you know me?"

"I read the papers."

"Well don't believe everything you read."

"I don't, especially anything by Ellen Burke. But her stuff does make for light entertainment. By the way, she just showed me the picture she's going to use in Monday's paper. I must say, it's very incriminating. You appear to be assaulting a man in front of your plane."

I groaned and rolled my eyes. "Thanks for your help," I said, starting toward the stairs.

Reporters.

She walked beside me pulling her little suitcase and said, "You know, Mr. Brody, you really ought to do some damage control before Ellen Burke runs you out of the territory."

"And how would I do that?"

After pushing the button for the elevator, she said, "The problem with a newspaper is that it only presents one side of a story. You get a slanted viewpoint because only the writer has the voice. If you want yours to be heard, you need to do a radio interview. Call me and we'll set one up."

My mouth must have fallen open when she said the word *interview*. Like that was going to happen. The elevator doors parted and Marsha Price stepped inside and was gone. I started up the stairs.

"There you are," he said with a smile. "I have been looking for you."

He was coming down from above and stopped in front of me on the landing, blocking my way. He was shorter than me, Asian, young and fit, wearing a tight black T-shirt under a beige windbreaker. I'd never seen him before.

"Who are you?" I asked, staring at him as his hand went to my elbow.

He smiled and said, "It is not important who I am. What is important is for you to come with me."

"No, thanks."

"Yes, please. This way, please." He swept his hand at the stairs below us and gave me a self-deprecating nod of encouragement.

"I said, *no thanks*."

"And I said *yes,* and *please*. You will come with me now."

And with that he gave my elbow a little squeeze and a bolt of lightning shot down my right forearm and out the ends of my fingers. I gasped and wondered if he'd broken a bone. He turned me around and led me down the stairs, then down the hall to the right, and opened the door to a men's room. I was still holding my arm when he pushed me inside and said, "It won't last long, Mr. Brody. But you will do as I say or I will do it to your neck. That is much worse. Do you understand?"

I was bent over, cradling my arm as though it might fall off, but managed a nod.

"What do you want?" I moaned.

"The keys to your plane."

"The keys to my plane?"

He put his hand on my neck.

"Okay, okay," I said, and dug them out of my pack.

What the hell? Who was this guy? The keys to my plane?

"Thank you. Now you will meet Mr. Li."

* * *

He dispatched me to the bar unattended. I looked back at him while crossing the lobby. He was ignoring me, calmly leaning against a wall fifty feet away, typing something into his phone. He knew I wasn't going to run away—I had boots on my feet and he had sneakers. I was as humiliated as anyone can be, having just been neutralized and pushed around by a man twenty years my junior, two inches shorter, and thirty pounds lighter. But I guessed that must be his specialty—coercing cooperation by inflicting pain. Some people's kids. I kept telling myself there was nothing I could have done to defend myself. My arm was on fire and I rubbed it. My fingers were tingling and I rubbed them too.

The bar was packed to overflowing with a boisterous crowd so loud I could hardly hear myself think. It was bulging out the door and there was no going in. Until, that is, another Asian guy emerged from the throng and beckoned me over with a finger. He jutted his chin in the direction I was to follow. My new handler was a little bigger, a little older, and a lot meaner than the last one. He pushed and shoved aside whoever was in his way, and cleared a path in front of us. We stopped in front of a table not far inside.

And there was the man himself.

Tippy Li was seated with a harem—two heavily painted teenagers wearing skimpy satin dresses to his left, and to his right one of the most exquisite women I've ever laid eyes.

Lynn Chan, no doubt. I was an instant fan, captivated by her exotic almond shaped eyes and porcelain smooth skin, ruby red lips and shimmering black hair, and tiny delicate hands working a gold telephone. Dave was right, she was smokin' hot. I wondered why Li would even bother with the other two. Maybe they were door prizes. The one sitting next to him looked too young to be in a bar.

Chan caught me gawking at her—and after a furtive glance at the stitches in my lip—gave me a dismissive look and went back to tapping her phone with her thumbs. The two young ladies were all smiles and couldn't take their eyes off me. The gorilla who had delivered me to the table stepped back, leaving Li and I to make our own introductions.

When Li noticed his new guest, he leaned back, folded his arms, and studied me up and down with curiosity. He was easily recognizable by the scar on his lip, which was even more conspicuous than in the photo I'd seen. It gave him an appearance of someone who was perpetually disgusted, but rightly or wrongly, I could only interpret it as unfettered disdain for the likes of me.

He was a small man, impeccably dressed and impeccably groomed, wearing a black blazer, a black silk shirt, and a wrist watch worth more than a house. His hands were small and delicate, perfectly manicured, and his face was shaven as smooth as glass. His glossy black hair matched his flat black eyes which were utterly lifeless and devoid of emotion, revealing nothing of what he might be thinking. Which didn't help me because I had no idea of why I was standing in front of him.

"Do you know who I am?" he asked with his cold eyes boring through mine.

"Ah, the shortest guy in the bar?"

The girls laughed and he backhanded the one closest to him. She yelped and threw her hands to her face. At the same time my handler delivered a short punch to my right kidney. I jerked up, gasped, and struggled to catch my breath in yet another bout of agony. Someone's hands grabbed the back of my jeans to prevent me from sinking to the floor until I could get my hands on the table to support myself.

"My name is Li," he said calmly, as if nothing had happened. "What is yours?"

"Brody," I gasped through clenched teeth with my head down and my eyes watering.

"I understand you are a pilot, Mr. Brody. Is that right?"

"Yes," I grimaced, learning to breathe again.

"Hmm. And you flew in here today from Thistle Creek, is that also right?"

"Yes."

"With the geologist who works there."

"Uh-huh," I grunted, now able to use my right hand to rub my lower back.

"This geologist, is he a friend of yours?"

"You might say."

Li nodded and asked, "And what has he told you about my business?"

"Your business?"

"My exploration business at Thistle Creek. What has your geologist friend told you about my business there?"

I was on thin ice. It seemed Li knew Mike had confided in me about what was going on at Thistle Creek. But how? Then something occurred to me. On the way to the clinic today, Sarah said the cops would be talking to Mike later in the afternoon. If Li's goons had been following Mike around town, maybe they'd seen him talking to the police. If that was the case, then maybe they'd had a chat with him and learned he'd also been talking to me. In which case, Mike's life was as good as over. And so was mine. It could well be that I was one of the last loose pieces that could implicate Li.

"Nothing," I lied. "I don't know anything about your exploration business. I'm just a pilot with a plane who was hired to fly rocks. All Mike told me was that the project is a good one."

Li gave me a cynical smile, then turned to the young woman he'd hit. She had become a distraction. She was bleeding from her nose, wailing away, and in spite of the best efforts of her friend to console her, wouldn't stop.

"Get her out of here," he scowled at her friend. "Clean her up and don't come back until she is quiet."

I caught Chan take a fleeting glance at the girls when they stood to leave. She had put away her phone and had her arms folded. She hadn't touched the drink in front of her and seemed anxious and apprehensive. Her eyes were flitting about the scene behind me, as though searching for something—or someone. But there couldn't be much for her to see other than an impervious wall of loud men drinking beer. The place was as packed and rowdy as ever.

Li took a deep breath, clasped his fingers together, and leaned forward with his elbows on the table. With the hint of a smile he said, "You are lying to me, Mr. Brody. Lying to me is always a painful mistake. But tonight you are fortunate because I need you to do a job for me. I need you to deliver a package."

"A package?"

He put his arm around Chan. The move surprised her and she turned away. He squeezed her shoulder, stroked her hair, ran a finger under her chin, and smiled at her. She reciprocated with a glare of pure unadulterated hatred. Li removed his arm and looked back at me.

"Yes. A package. It must be flown to Thistle Creek tonight." He looked at his watch and said, "You will deliver it now."

He downed his drink, and after a nod and a wink, two of his henchman sprang into action. The one behind me grabbed my arm and turned me toward the bar. Another one grabbed Lynn Chan by the wrist and hauled her to her feet.

Then two very bizarre things occurred.

The first was when Lynn Chan used her free hand to pick up her Bloody Mary and tossed the whole thing into Tippy Li's face. Everyone froze as he rose from his chair with his mouth agape, his arms splayed out at his sides, dripping tomato juice from head to crotch. To say the least, he was enraged. The audience was just as stunned and suddenly fell silent, awaiting his reaction. Retribution was sure to be swift and cruel. But at that very same instant, the second bizarre thing occurred.

Three giant cops—three RCMP officers in full uniform wearing bulletproof vests—emerged from the crowd and barged into the ring. I'd never seen any of them before. They were huge, six-five or more, nothing but muscle, and quick to establish the purpose of their visit.

"I'll take this from here, sir," said one of them with a dead calm glare, removing the hand around Lynn Chan's wrist. Li's henchman was more than happy to give way and quickly retreated out of sight. The big cop placed two island-sized hands on Chan's shoulders, turned her to face Li, and whispered something in her ear. She put her hands behind her back and he cuffed them. Li's eyes were as big as dinner plates and he sunk back into his chair aghast, now the only one seated at the table. His eyes were spitting venom at Chan but she denied him the pleasure of a response, content to stare at her feet.

Then my favorite new cop from Whitehorse, Constable E. Saunders, arrived on the scene. She proceeded to pat and squeeze every inch of Lynn Chan, from head to foot, up and down, in and out, taking her time to conduct a fastidious search of the prisoner for a concealed weapon. Saunders was especially thorough around Chan's butt, crotch and breasts, to the fascination of the beer-toting crowd, who if not before, were fixated.

Oh, to have been E. Saunders at that moment.

Then, as suddenly as they had appeared, the three huge cops disappeared into the crowd with their prisoner and Saunders in tow. The room quickly regained its moxie and the decibel level returned to its previous dull roar. I caught a glimpse of Dave Sorenson waving at me. He was grinning ear to ear, pumping a fist in the air.

In hindsight, if I'd been thinking on my feet, I might have grabbed one of the cops and begged him to take me with them. But for some reason I didn't, perhaps because I felt the danger was over. It wasn't.

Which explains why, after a signal from Li, someone grabbed my arm and whisked me away—toward the other end of the bar, through a swinging door, through a kitchen, through an exit door, and out into the alley—where I was summarily tossed into a camper van.

The guy behind the wheel of the van was the one who'd intercepted me on the stairs. The guy who tossed me into the van was the one who'd escorted me to Li's table. And the guy wrapped up in chains at the back of the van was Mike Giguere.

SIXTY SIX

The two ends of the chain had been wrapped around his neck, twisted into a spiral, run down to his crotch, wrapped around his legs, and returned back up to his neck where they were attached with a lock.

Houdini proof.

They probably weighed all of twenty-five pounds and there was no doubt why they were on him. He was lying motionless on the floor, in a heap at the rear of the camper.

"Mike, you okay?" I hissed, which earned me a love stomp in the ribs. I too was lying on the floor, with a foot on my neck.

"Shut up or I hurt you."

My handler.

To my relief, Mike moved. He resembled a rag doll with his arms and legs spread out in every direction, barely breathing, with every sign of someone who'd undergone a severe beating. His beard and clothes were stained with dried blood and several fingers on one hand looked broken. He was clearly a vanquished man and must have known his life was about to end. Deep inside me a visceral sensation of hate was building in waves.

These people are pure evil.

When the van slowed, I heard gravel crunching under the tires and knew where we were. Where else but the dock? The driver got out and slid open the side door. We were at the top of the jetty and I could see the nose of my plane.

It was a little after ten o'clock and the air was perfectly still. I could hear the river gurgling a hundred feet away. The man with his foot on my neck got up and stepped outside to talk to his partner. They were both wearing sunglasses, ball caps, and identical large black ski jackets. Clearly they knew what they were doing, it would be impossible to identify one from the other, let alone pick one out of a lineup. They exchanged a few words in Chinese and were scanning the scene while I rubbed my neck and considered my options.

There were no options.

One of the men walked out of sight and I heard his footsteps circling the van, probably making sure we were alone. Of course there wouldn't be any cops around, they'd be oiling their guns for the big Thistle Creek raid—or in another meeting.

When the man returned from his reconnaissance, he and his partner got back in the van. They had to step over me on their way to get to Mike, and one of them stomped on my ribs again, just for fun. They lifted Mike to his feet and zipped him into another large black ski jacket—exactly like their's—then a ball cap and a pair of sunglasses—exactly like theirs—and dragged him outside. Everytime he grunted or groaned, they'd punch him.

Mike could barely stand on his own two feet under the load of the chains, but one of the men got him moving in a drunken like stagger, led him down to the plane, opened the cockpit door, helped him up the ladder, and threw him in. He howled with pain when he landed on the passenger seat.

"Now you, " barked the other man, waving me out with a hand.

He walked behind me down the jetty, down the dock to the plane, told me to climb in, and slammed the cockpit door behind me.

Asshole. You don't slam doors on things that fly!

Before I could even get comfortable, the two had untied the floats and pushed us out into the river.

Idiots!

I'd never started the motor so fast, desperate for power before the current carried the plane down the shore and it ran into something.

The instant the prop began turning, I opened my door for a look behind. We were already below the dock, drifting backwards, picking up speed with the tail just feet from the shore and the nose swinging out into the river. I goosed the throttle and hoped the cold motor didn't stall. When I turned around for a look out the other side, his enormous face was in mine.

"Remember me?"

* * *

At that instant I fully appreciated the old metaphor about having your heart burst out of your chest. Mine was pounding so hard I thought it might explode. Before adrenalin killed me, I whipped around and stared dumbfounded at the console, trying to catch my breath, absolutely terrified and feeling terribly stupid at the same time.

In my haste and panic to save my plane, there'd been no time to ponder why two thugs would throw Mike and I inside and push us out into the river without supervision.

But with Tommy Kay on board, they had that little detail covered.

Duh.

So now what?

"Where's the girl!" he yelled.

The girl, the girl...Lynn Chan?

I was still too paralyzed with fear to speak. He grabbed my hair, twisted my head around, and gave it a shake. We were nose to nose again. "Where's the girl? And where's my money? I want my money!"

'My money'. The four hundred grand.

"What girl? What money?"

He slapped the right side of my face so hard little shiny stars began floating between us and my left ear was ringing like a gun had gone off.

"Where is she?" He was furious, shaking my head like a toy.

His head was the size of a basketball and his shoulders as wide as an ox. I'd had the same view of his face a year ago but something was different this time. He didn't look well. His eyes were bloodshot and watery, his skin was red and flushed, and he had a runny nose. Maybe he had a cold. I noticed something else different about him too, but didn't know what.

Summoning up every bit of courage, I yelled back, "The cops arrested her. And I don't know anything about your money. And don't hit me again or you'll have to fly this thing yourself!"

He slapped me again anyway, maybe not quite as hard as before, but the blow still stung like hell. My right ear was now on fire with an air raid siren wailing inside. He let go of my hair and sunk back to his heels. I turned to face the console again and rubbed my ear, jaw and neck. My hand felt damp and I looked at it. Blood. I touched my lip. It was split wide open again and bleeding buckets.

Damn.

I was scared. Of course I could easily fly scared—I can't count the number of times I've done that—but knew I had to calm down to think my way out of this jam. Or else die.

We were headed out into an empty river, save for the ferry which was loading vehicles a mile downstream on the other side. I added some power to hold us stationary against the current and pointed the nose south, toward Thistle Creek. The engine oil was heating up and in a few minutes we could take off. I took a peek to my left at the dock and the town. The van was gone and the streets were empty. No help to be had there.

I heard a clattering and a screech of metal and knew what Kay was doing. He had pulled one of Reggie's deck chairs out of the cargo net and was unfolding it. While he was making himself comfortable for his flight to Thistle Creek, I thought about Mrs. Deerchild and her attempt to exorcise my plane of its demons. So much for that exercise, there was evil on board and it was alive and well.

Mike was studying one of his hands, showing signs of life. I reached into my door pocket and pulled out a bottle of water and stealthily dropped it between his legs. After a feeble attempt at taking a drink, he stiffly nodded his thanks.

It was hard to look at him. Even with his complimentary sunglasses, I could see his nose was a mess again. His jaw was broken too, skewed well to one side, and he was breathing through an open mouth. The missing teeth were obvious. Both his eyes were purple and there were cuts and contusions all over his face. I could only imagine what they'd done to the rest of him. He tried to take another drink, barely able to hold the bottle to his mouth in his gnarled hands, but this time a tree trunk shot over his shoulder and snatched it away from him.

"Fly the plane! We are going to Thistle Creek!"

Attila the Hun was ready for his flight.

* * *

Li's henchmen had my backpack.

Inside was my knife and the bearspray. The flare gun at the back of the plane might as well be a million miles away. And when I felt under the seats for my shotgun, it wasn't there. Thistle Creek was an hour south and Sarah and the cops weren't even due at the dock before we'd get there.

Which left me with my brain and plane to neutralize Kay.

A bit of luck would be welcome, too.

I knew exactly how things would pan out if I didn't do something. As soon as we landed at Thistle Creek, Tommy Kay would see the Piper Cub was gone and know his ride had left without him. He'd toss Mike into the river and force me to fly him to Chicken. There he'd kill me, and Pete, and probably Pete's wife, too, and just for fun, probably every dog he could get his hands on.

So...one hour.

"Fly the plane!"

"Okay, okay, I'll fly the plane!"

* * *

There was no point in explaining to Tommy Kay the effects of oil temperature on its lubricating properties. But I needed another five minutes before making a full throttle takeoff.

I added a little power to give him the impression things were happening. The nose came up and the floats began plowing through the water, making waves with lots of foam. That seemed to calm him down. Then I proceeded to do everything that needed to be done—like raise the rudders, pump down the flaps, set the trim, the fuel mixture, and the prop pitch. With those things accomplished, and with a conspicuous flurry of hands, I then proceeded to waste time performing a series of entirely pointless things, like opening and closing vents, turning the carb heat on and off, and fiddling with wheels and dials.

Kay had to be running out of patience when I finally cinched my seatbelt tight, and Mike's too, pulled back the yoke, and pushed the throttle ahead. The motor roared and we were on our way.

Only minutes after the floats left the river, Kay sneezed. And sneezed again. And again, and again, and again.

They continued in a series of cannonading blasts that for a moment I feared might blow out a window. Even Mike lifted his head with a start. I was too busy pumping up the flaps to count them all, but there must have been eight or nine, one after the other. The monster behind me did indeed have a cold, and a doozy at that. It occurred to me what else was different about him. His voice. He was all stuffed up. Which gave me an idea, and though maybe not a great one, the only one I had.

Few people appreciate just how very little breathable atmosphere there is on our planet. It's actually only a wafer thin layer of air, clinging to the earth's surface like shrink wrap on a box, held in place by gravity. You need not climb very high above sea level before it—including the oxygen it contains—rapidly becomes less dense. Everyone needs oxygen—every second of every day—which explains why most people have difficulty functioning at altitudes over ten thousand feet, and why ninety-five percent of us live within five thousand feet of sea level. As I climbed toward thinner air, I thought Mr. Kay could use a practical lesson in atmospheric physics. Maybe if I got him up high enough he'd pass out, or at least become lethargic, though I wasn't quite sure what I'd do in either event.

But I had to try something. Anything to soften up the bastard.

All the way up to five thousand feet I could hear him struggling to breathe. At six thousand feet he started to wheeze, at eight thousand feet he was coughing, and at ten thousand feet he fell out of his chair with a clatter and a thump, choking and gagging.

Choking and gagging?

His physiological reaction to the higher altitude seemed pretty extreme, but hey, he did have a cold. And besides, not everyone reacts the same way to a change in air pressure. I wasn't going to analyze it, it was what it was, and the best result I could have hoped for.

I kept climbing, wondering how to take advantage of the stress he was in.

At twelve thousand feet, fully two thousand feet higher than you're allowed to fly without supplemental oxygen, there was a great commotion behind me. I leveled the plane out and took a peek behind me.

Kay was on his knees, frantically thrashing with his hands inside a small bag. With shock I noticed how his face had changed. In fact it looked downright grotesque. His eyes were completely swollen shut and his lips, cheeks and neck were all puffed up. He was in a panic, gulping for air like a fish out of water, blindly tossing things out of the bag. What the hell? We were only at twelve thousand feet. What could be wrong with him? What was he searching for? A knife? A gun?

In a rage he picked up the bag, held it upside down, and shook out its remaining contents. Clothes, toiletries, cellphones, sunglasses—everything went to the floor with most of it rolling around. What was he after? He started crawling on all fours, pawing at everything in the scattered mess, grabbing and tossing things aside, huffing and puffing like he was about to explode. I realized he was as good as blind, but equally aware that he could still kill me in a flash. He looked even bigger on his hands and knees—you could serve a party of four on his back. I surveyed the cabin for something to bonk him on the head with, but saw nothing. But I did spot what he was after.

It was an EpiPen. I knew what it was because a kid in high school had one, and he never went anywhere without it. It looks like a big magic marker but is actually a spring loaded syringe with a dose of adrenalin inside. You stab yourself in the thigh with it if you have an allergic reaction to something like a bee string, or latex, or shell fish, or nuts or...

Peanuts!

Of course! Why else would Kay have an EpiPen? He was allergic to peanuts.

Mike had been munching on them all morning on the flight from Thistle Creek to Dawson. Kay wasn't having difficulty with the altitude—or a cold—he was having an allergic reaction to peanuts! Ever since we took off from Dawson, he'd been locked in a chamber full of peanut dust.

I unclipped my seatbelt, spun around, kneeled on the seat, and reached down to grab the pen. It was lying on the cargo bay floor just feet below me, but try as I might, my outstretched fingers couldn't quite reach it.

Kay was still on his hands and knees, snorting like a pig, circling the cargo bay like a trapped animal, wheezing and coughing, sweeping his hands back and forth, pursuing the same thing I wanted. He was blind as a bat and I held my breath as he crawled past me, and to my great relief, missed the EpiPen by an inch as he started another circuit. Of course there was no way I was getting back into the cargo bay with him. Blind or not, he'd have no difficulty dealing with any competition.

Desperate times call for...

With my back still to the console, I reached behind me and found the wheel with my left hand, and shoved it forward. The nose dipped down and I watched the EpiPen. It wanted to roll toward me, but needed more of a hill. I pushed the wheel forward some more and the nose dropped some more. Still not enough. We were picking up speed and I found the throttle and pulled it back, still with my eyes on the prize. But the EpiPen simply wouldn't move.

Time to stop messing around.

I got comfortable in my seat again, hauled the wheel back to my chest, and held it there. The plane leveled out then started to climb. And climb. In no time the only thing to see out the front windshields was a sheet of pale blue sky as my weight shifted onto my back. I hadn't touched the throttle and watched the speed come down—ninety, eighty, seventy, sixty, fifty—and felt the controls become sloppy and soft as the airflow over the wings died away.

The instant before the plane stalled on its tail and fell out of the sky, I shoved the wheel all the way forward. Five seconds later we were going straight down at a hundred and twenty miles an hour and I hauled the wheel back and pulled out of the dive.

We'd just lost eight hundred feet in altitude.

"What...is...?"

Kay's voice tailed off and he couldn't finish the question.

I turned my head, and with my arm dangling over the seatback, studied him for a moment. He looked like death warmed over, sprawled out on his back, his head canted to one side, panting in shudders. The EpiPen was right under my hand and I reached down and picked it up.

"Nothing, just a little turbulence," I muttered, doubting he heard me and doubting he cared.

Kay was utterly incapacitated and needed to be kept that way. I reached under Mike's seat and found the can of peanuts he'd stowed there this morning. After giving it a shake, I popped the top off and poured them out onto the passenger seat floor. When I checked inside the can, all that was left was the good stuff—peanut dust. That I sprinkled over my shoulder—all over Kay's face.

I nudged Mike in the knee and held up a thumb. It took him a while to respond with a grimace and a thumbs-up of his own. I was relieved he was conscious but concerned about his condition. Clearly he was in a lot of pain and needed medical attention. The sooner the better.

The big question was, how long would Kay be out of it?

Turning around and going back to Dawson might otherwise make sense, except there was no guarantee Mike and I would survive it. Kay could recover any minute and would kill us the moment we landed there. Of course we could always land on the river, throw him out of the plane, and then proceed on to Dawson. But that would take some explaining after—cops, cops, and more cops. Been there, done that. And, I thought, it would be no easy task to throw a three hundred pound monster into the river anyway, especially if he put up any semblance of a fight. Besides, the last time I thought the frigid water of the Yukon River had been his demise…well…

We'd been in the air for forty-five minutes and were now only ten minutes from Thistle Creek. The cops would be there in three hours. I decided I'd rather have Kay spend the rest of his life in a nine-by-nine cell than do him the favor of drowning him. If I could somehow get him into one of those bear traps, then the authorities could deal with him.

So that was the plan.

I backed off the throttle and pushed the nose down.

SIXTY SEVEN

The challenge was how to move a three hundred pound block of solid muscle out of the plane and into a bear trap.

I'd just tied up to the Thistle Creek dock. Mike and Kay were still inside with the doors closed, immersed in a cloud of peanut dust. I figured as long as the cabin was polluted with allergens, Kay should remain semicomatose, and Mike should be safe for a while. But I had to move fast, I wanted him out of there before Kay woke up.

So how to do this?

I looked at the truck parked at the end of the dock. It had a winch on its front bumper. One problem solved. Now to get Mike out. He couldn't be in the plane when I was dealing with Kay.

I opened the cockpit door and was surprised to see Mike trying to get out on his own. He already had one foot up on the pilot's seat and was struggling to get the other one up too. He was paying a heavy price for his efforts with his face twisted in pain. I looked at Kay who was lying perfectly still, and could only hope he wasn't playing possum.

There was no need for talk, there was no other choice. Mike had to come out, even if it hurt. I reached over and grabbed a handful of his blue jeans at the ankle, lifted up his other leg, and put them together on the seat. He groaned when I did. I grabbed him by the chains, pulled him across the seats, and helped him down the ladder. We staggered arm in arm to the middle of the dock where he collapsed in a heap.

He was clutching his knee, and with a gasp and grimace said, "Neecah."

"Kneecap?"

He nodded and said, "Ashtard roke it."

"Which bastard was that?"

He jutted his chin at the back of the plane. Say no more.

My hatred for Kay was visceral, pulsating through my veins in waves. I would have to control my primeval urges if he was to survive as a prisoner.

"That winch on your truck work?"

Mike nodded, then he pointed at the plane. "Shawgun," he said.

I shook my head and said, "Gone."

"Loo in the flo."

"Look in the float?"

He nodded and waved at the plane again.

Loo in the flo.

I went over and opened the first storage compartment door at the front. Nothing but ropes. I opened the next one. My little gun in the sweatshirt was stuffed into the leg of a pair of hipwaders. I took it out and checked the magazine.

Full.

Game changer.

I walked back to Mike and said with a smile, "Know what, Mike? You're not just a pretty face." He gave me the bird and I handed him the gun. "Be right back. If the bastard gets out, shoot him."

* * *

I needed a bunch of things, and fast.

When I roared into the camp, the kitchen trailer had two visitors sitting out front. One of them had his nose buried in a can of ketchup, the other was tearing apart a box of frozen steaks.

I leaned on the horn and charged them. They both ran off—but not very far—stopped when I did, and turned around to check me out. The one with a steak in his mouth had strands of plastic wrap hanging from his teeth, the one with the ketchup had a sticky red face. They were both young grizzlies and more curious than scared of the intruder.

They had their eyes glued on me when I backed up and stopped next to the kitchen door. It was buckled in and the jam was a splintered mess.

Little bears.

At the top of my shopping list was the first aid kit I'd seen inside at noon but quickly decided against going in to get it, there might be another bear inside. I headed for the equipment maintenance building down the road. The two bears watched me leave, then returned to their meals.

All the doors were locked. No surprise there, they usually are when tools are at stake and the owner's not around. But I needed a chaincutter. I backed up on an angle and ran the corner of the bumper into a man door. It burst open with a bang. Even with no lights on inside, it didn't take long to find what I wanted. It was hanging on a wall, not far from a first aid kit the size of a suitcase. I scratched those things off my list and headed down the hill toward the two bear traps at the edge of the clearing. I needed one of them for Kay.

Unfortunately, both were occupied.

I had expected to see one with its gate in the closed position— the one with Dan Sanders in it—but the gate was down on the other one too. It was a hundred feet away and I drove over and stopped in front of it, and looked straight into the eyes of a very large grizzly bear.

I knew he was big because the hump between his shoulders was rubbing against the top of the tube. That, and his head was the size of a planet. He clearly wasn't happy about the situation, bouncing up and down on his paws, and snorting a lot. I bent over with my hands on my knees and peered in at him through the screen mesh gate, wondering how to get him out of there without getting myself killed. He took my stare as a personal affront, clicked his jaws a few times, took a step back, and charged me. I jumped a foot off the ground when his head hit the gate with a resounding crash of steel on steel.

"Hey! Simmer down! I'm going to let you out!"

He launched himself at the gate again with another crash of steel that echoed up and down the quiet valley. I caught the scent of bananas mixed in with some not so nice odors, and looked back at the trap Sanders was in. Both traps were identical, which got me to thinking...

I jumped into Mike's truck and backed it up to the other end of the trailer, and after a bit of back and forth, got the the tongue perfectly aligned over the ball on the rear bumper. Then I cranked up the support legs on all four corners, lowered the tongue onto the ball, and was ready to roll. It took me less than a minute to tow my new four hundred pound pal over to Dan Sanders.

I lined up the truck and trailer with the trap Sanders was in, and backed up until I heard a bang. Contact! The two traps were now aligned end-to-end, gate-to-gate, just inches apart. If Dan Sanders hadn't been awake before, he sure was now, suddenly face to face with a large agitated grizzly bear not a foot in front of him.

I got out of the truck and said, "Don't shoot him Dan. I've got some great news!"

"What the hell are you doing?" he screamed.

I ran back to Sanders' trap. The two traps were so close together that even if I opened both gates, neither the bear or Sanders could escape through the gap between them. Sanders couldn't see or shoot me, even though I was standing right beside him.

"So, you want to hear the good news or not?" I asked.

"Not 'til you get this monster out of my face!"

"No can do, Dan. I'm in a hurry and need a trap. An empty one."

"What for?"

"We're holding Tommy Kay at gunpoint down at the dock. I need a trap to put him, then we can leave."

"Who is we?"

"Me and Mike."

"So what's this good news?"

"The cops will be here soon. "

"That's good news?"

"For you."

"How do you know they're coming?"

"Never mind, but they are."

"So what are you doing here?"

The bear was snorting and moving around, rocking the trailer on its springs.

I heaved a sigh and said, "Well for one thing, I want Mike's gun back. You don't need it anymore and I don't think it'll do you any good to be arrested with it, especially since you stole it from him and were waving it in my face this morning. So how about you pass it out the top to me, grip end first, please."

"No thanks, I'm keeping it. We had a deal."

"Come on, Dan. It's Mike's gun and it's as good as gone when the cops take it from you. I just want to give it back to him, that's all."

"And what if I don't?"

"Well, seeing as I need a trap for Kay, if you don't give it to me I guess I could always open both gates on these two traps. Chances are you and this bear will end up together in one of them, and then I'll have an empty one to tow down to the river. We can do it that way."

"I'll shoot you."

"Shoot me? Through a steel mesh gate when you can't see me? You can try but you'll probably miss, and maybe even catch a ricochet. And remember, you only have one bullet."

"Then I'll shoot the bear," he said.

Now he was thinking out loud.

"Well, I guess you could do that. But as you can see, he's pretty

big, and he might take a while to die. I'd expect he'd be pretty
mad too, and if you do shoot him, then I'll definitely open up both
gates."

"You son of a bitch. Why don't you just leave and let him out
somewhere else? Then you can have your goddamn empty trap."

"Because if I open the gate somewhere else he can run me
down before I can get into the truck. Come on Dan, be smart about
this. With Kay locked in a trap down at the dock, you don't have
to worry about him. You'll be safe in your cage when I let the bear
out. And if you give me Mike's gun, then I don't have to mention
to the cops that you were waving it in my face this morning. You
might even walk out of jail tomorrow morning."

After a pause, he said, "What about Giguere?"

"I'm sure he'll go along. He just wants his life back. We all do."

Dan Sanders went quiet but the bear was getting restless,
huffing and puffing, running out of patience like me.

"Okay," he said. "I'll give you the gun. But Giguere says
nothing about what's been going on here."

"No, Dan. You give me the gun and Giguere says nothing about
what you did to me this morning. The rest is your problem."

Again he went quiet. Now I was out of patience.

"Screw this, I haven't got all night," I said.

I hoisted myself onto the top of Sanders' trap, crawled to the end,
reached across the gap, and heaved up the far gate. The bear poked
his enormous head out and shoved his nose up against Sanders'
gate, and started sniffing. *Peanuts?* I heard Sanders skedaddle to
the rear of his trap.

"Okay, okay, you can have your goddamn gun back!" he yelled.

The grip of the gun poked out of the chimney. I let go of the
gate which I hadn't pinned in place. It fell down onto the neck of
the bear. He bobbed his massive head up and down, and the gate
screeched as it moved up and down with it. But no way he was
backing up, he was looking for the exit doors. I grabbed the gun,
jumped to the ground, ran to the truck, got in and started it.

Then I tromped on the gas and blasted up the hill toward the camp, watching my outside mirror. Halfway up the bear fell out, did a couple of barrel rolls, and got to his feet in a cloud of dust. Last I saw of him, he was walking back down the hill toward Dan Sanders.

Peanuts.

* * *

Without bothering to check if it was locked, I backed up Mike's truck and rammed the bear trap into the door on one of the sleeper trailers, and blew it off its hinges. Once inside, I raided a small fridge and made off with three bottles of water, a family size Coke, and a bag of ice cubes. After tossing those in the cab, I went back in for what I came for. It took me two trips to drag out a single bed mattress and an armful of bedding and towels. I took off for the dock with the wheels spinning, the box full, and an empty bear trap in tow. The two little grizzlies looked up when I sped past the kitchen trailer, but they were too busy eating to wave goodby.

Tommy Kay was lying spread-eagled on his back, on the edge of the dock, in front of the open cargo bay door. Mike was exactly where I'd left him, in the middle of the dock, with the shotgun trained on the inert heap in front of him. For a split second I wondered if he'd shot Kay, but without a drop of blood anywhere, knew that wasn't the case. I would have heard it if he had. I turned around and backed up the truck and trailer in as straight a line as possible with Kay, and turned off the motor.

"Trade 'ya," I said, dangling Mike's six gun in front of him. He laid the shotgun down and took his revolver from me, coddling it like a baby bird in his broken hands. He had removed his sunglasses and looked worse than I could have imagined. One of his eyes was blood red and the bone around it was caved in at the eyebrow. It was clearly a fracture and put me in the perfect mood to deal with Kay.

"Anks," said Mike.

"When did he get out?"

"Ush affer you lef, ink ees deh."

"Dead?"

I picked up the shotgun and stepped toward Kay with a nervous finger on the trigger, wary of any sudden move he might make. I had no compunction about shooting him if he did.

"Hey, you dead?" I said, poking him in the belly with the barrel of the shotgun, then swinging it up to chest and holding it there. "Maybe I should shoot you just to make sure. What do you think?"

He snorted, but just once, and weakly. Obviously he wasn't dead but his skin had a deathly blue hue and he was breathing in short shallow gasps. His face was even more swollen than before, mottled with hives, and kind of reminded me of a four cheese pizza—with anchovies. The guy was in real trouble but I wasn't going to help him. I thought it both amazing and ironic that molecules—not muscle—had reduced him to this dire plight, but could summon no empathy for him. Tommy Kay was a cruel and evil man. Mike needed a hospital and the enemy had to be locked up.

On my way back to the truck, I passed the shotgun back to Mike and said, "Wait one. Remember, shoot him if he moves."

I put the winch in neutral, pulled out fifty feet of cable, ran it up and over the hood and roof of the cab, then over the box to the trap, and dropped the hook down the chimney on top. I had to raise the gate again, it had fallen shut after the bear jumped out, and this time I pinned it open. Then I went and got some things out of the cab.

After getting Mike to his feet and removing his ski jacket, I stood behind him and clamped the jaws of the chaincutter over the lock on his neck.

"Don't move," I said.

He didn't. I squeezed the long handles together and cut through the shackle as easily as cutting a piece of thread with a pair of scissors.

"Give me a lever long enough...and I shall move the world."

I wondered if Archimides owned a chaincutter.

Mike was rejuvenated when the chain fell to his feet and told me he felt light as a feather. I handed him a dry towel, and another one I'd just dunked in the river, and told him to clean himself up while I dealt with the prisoner.

"You move, you die," was all I said to Kay after dropping the pile of chain between his feet. I knelt down and wrapped four figure eights around his ankles, and after tying the ends into a loose knot, went back to the trap and pulled out the cable hanging down inside. Kay was licking his lips and fluttering his eyelids when I returned with the cable in my hands. I prayed he wasn't about to suddenly recover. As fast as I could, I hooked the cable hook onto the chain, then ran to the front of the truck, flicked a lever, pressed a switch, and the winch began to turn.

There was a screeching of steel on steel when the cable tightened and began sliding over the hood and roof of the truck, and through the chimney on top of the trap. Kay's feet came together and his arms went out to his sides as the winch began dragging the enormous man across the deck toward the trap.

By the time his feet reached the gate, his hands were over his head and his jacket and shirt were rolled up around his neck. I wondered how many splinters he'd picked up in his bare back, but wasn't going to check. When he was well inside the trap, and his feet started rising up to the chimney, I ran to the front of the truck and turned off the winch.

Gotcha.

Mike whooped and gave me a feeble fist bump when I walked past him on my way back to my plane. Inside the cargo bay I gathered up all of Kay's belongings, stuffed them into his bag, and carried them over to the trap. I tossed the bag onto his chest, but before closing the gate, remembered something. I reached into my shirt pocket, took out his EpiPen, studied it for a moment, and wondered what to do with it. After a long look at the river behind me, I decided he couldn't hurt me anymore.

I gave it a wipe and placed it in the open palm of his right hand.

I closed the gate and pinned it shut, then with the chaincutter made such a mess of one of the tracks that the only way to open the trap would be to cut a hole in the gate. I left the chaincutter where the cops would be sure to find it.

Mike and I spent the next five minutes lying on a blanket in the middle of the dock, poking around the first aid kit between us, tending to each others wounds—mostly his—though I did most of the whining, especially when I held my split lip together so he could tape it closed with a bandage. In contrast, there was barely a whimper out of him when I put a splint on his knee, three more on his fingers, taped up his nose, and bandaged the cut over his eye. I wrapped the bag of ice in a towel and told him to keep it on his knee. When I asked him if he'd ever been a hockey player, he gave me a crooked smile through his broken jaw and said, "Ow chuh know?"

We each took twice the recommended dosage of Aleve and chased it down with plenty of water, and then for good measure, Mike took a few long slugs from a bottle of cough syrup—the good stuff with codeine.

A few times we'd glanced over at the trap for a look at Kay, but it was too dark to see inside, and what he was doing. I briefly considered throwing a bucket of water on him to wake him up— like they used to do in the movies—but this wasn't the movies and I didn't have a bucket.

I dragged the mattress and the rest of the blankets from the truck to the plane, made a bed for Mike in the cargo bay, and then we did what every man does before taking off in a bush plane on the Yukon River—we pissed in it.

Which reminded me of the letter from the Yukon Water Board, which I hadn't opened, which was in my backpack, which I no longer had.

After making Mike as comfortable as possible, I closed the cargo door and took a final look around. It was after midnight but the sky was bright and the land glowed gold in the long flat rays of the sun. It was cold and getting colder, probably now in the forties, with the air as still and quiet as it would have been a thousand years ago. For a moment I indulged myself in the absolute silence of the wilderness, thinking about the last fourteen hours of my life—how incredibly lucky I'd been to have survived them—and to be finally free of Tommy Kay.

It felt good.

I also thought about Sarah Marsalis who at the moment was probably apoplectic, believing I'd stood her up, and in front of her RCMP colleagues at that. I felt badly for her. After all her work and preparation for a heroic raid on Thistle Creek, her pilot and plane hadn't shown up. Unfortunately there was no way for me to communicate with her to explain why not, but hopefully by the morning she'd know and would find a way to forgive me.

Back to the present and the question of the moment. Where to take the star witness for the prosecution? Dawson was only an hour north but Mike needed the kind of surgery you could only get in Whitehorse. If we went to Dawson, all they could do for him there was clean him up and fly him to Whitehorse. And not until the morning. I had enough fuel, a family-sized Coke to keep me awake, so Whitehorse it was.

I was thinking about Russ and Jack when we took off.

SIXTY EIGHT

The northern sunrise chased us all the way down to Whitehorse, catching the plane about two o'clock in the morning, plowing the night's shadow off the horizon like a great tsunami.

About twenty miles north of Whitehorse International, I called ATC and woke up a sleepy controller at the Yukon's only 24/7 airport.

"Whitehorse Tower, Papa Papa Alpha Golf, Beaver on floats, twenty miles north, heading 170, inbound for Schwatka, got a medevac on board, request an ambulance, over."

A minute later, "Papa Papa Alpha Golf, you are cleared to land, straight in, winds calm, pressure 30.1, visibility unlimited, no conflicting traffic. What is your medevac?"

"A guy who needs an ambulance."

"Injuries or illness?"

"Injuries."

"Alpha Golf, please describe his injuries."

"Ah, Whitehorse Tower? I'm flying a plane here. But they're bad."

"Copy that. Is he critical?"

"Don't know, I'm not a doctor. But don't send a cab, the guy needs an ambulance."

A pause, then, "Roger that, Alpha Golf, dispatching an ambulance."

* * *

Schwatka Lake was like a pool of mercury when I crossed the power dam and touched down on its glossy surface, sending long silver waves rolling toward the shore. It was just before three o'clock in the morning when I dropped the rudders and pointed the plane at a cluster of blue, red, and yellow flashing lights.

The last responders were waiting—an ambulance as requested— and a police cruiser that wasn't. There was also a small pickup truck parked in the shadows beyond them, with a tiny figure leaning against it. At least there was no sign of those obnoxious ducks.

"Hey Mike!" I yelled over my shoulder, "We're here. Next stop is Whitehorse General. How are you feeling?"

It took him a while to say, "Gooh."

"Hang in there, okay? In ten minutes you'll be surrounded by beautiful women catering to your every desire."

"Hah!"

Fifty feet from the dock I killed the motor and glided up to two big guys who looked like they lifted weights. They were standing at either end of a gurney. One of them held the wing strut while I limped down the ladder on a stiff left leg, tied up the floats, and opened the cargo door.

"Good evening, sir. What have we got?" asked one of them as his partner took a step up the ladder for a look inside.

"*What we have got* is a guy with a broken jaw, broken teeth, broken ribs, broken fingers, and probably a broken knee cap. He's pretty beat up but conscious, and oh, he has a lot of codeine and Aleve in him."

The guy nodded and asked, "How about his neck and spine? Has he complained about any loss of sensation or tingling in his limbs?"

"No."

"What happened?"

"Mining accident."

The guy nodded again and said, "Okay, we'll take it from here," and then, "Sir? You need stitches in that lip."

I left them to tend to Mike and took a few steps down the dock to get out of their way. A tall, young RCMP constable with a pen and notepad intercepted me. The name tag on his coat said R. Desmond.

"Good evening, sir," he said. "A few questions."

"What kind of questions?"

"Let's start with your name."

It was cold, I'd left my windbreaker in the hotel in Dawson, and all I had on was a shirt. I also didn't exactly feel great, not with all my aches and pains, including the one pulsating in my lip. The last thing I wanted to do was answer 'a few questions' on a cold dock on a cold lake in the middle of a cold Yukon night. There was a clatter behind us. The two EMS guys were loading a stretcher into the plane.

"My name is Brody. Will this take long?"

The cop's eyes lit up with recognition and he said, "C.E. Brody? Hey, I need to talk to you. Who's the guy in the plane?"

"His name is Mike Giguere."

"Where's he from?"

"Whitehorse."

"Okay. How about you tell me what happened? Start at the beginning."

"Hey, Officer Desmond? Between the RCMP and the FBI, you cops already know the beginning—and just about everything else that's happened since—right up until about eleven o'clock last night. And right now I need a doctor. So what do you say we do this later?"

"Watch your back, sir," he said, nudging me to the side.

The EMS guys squeezed by with Mike on a stretcher. Now I knew why they needed all those muscles. Carrying him up the jetty on a folded gurney was a lot easier than rolling it.

"Looks like my ride is leaving," I said to Desmond. "Gotta go. Come by the hospital in a couple of hours."

"Ah, sir? That's not your ride."

"Says who?"

"Says them. Only immediate family members can ride with a patient in an ambulance, and only if the patient is critical."

"Who came up with that stupid rule?"

He shrugged his shoulders and said, "Don't know, but it's the rule."

"So how do I get to the hospital? Can you give me a ride?"

"I can give you a ride," said a small voice behind him.

* * *

"Who are you?" I asked.

"Anaya Bakshi."

"Anaya, huh? Your parents know where you are, Anaya?"

"Very funny. I'm twenty-one years old."

She said it like she was used to saying it. She was tiny and looked too young to be twenty-one. She'd just stepped out from behind Desmond and didn't come up to his armpit. Anaya was wearing sneakers, jeans, and a blue anorak, which made me feel all the more cold. She had thick raven black hair, dark liquid eyes, and a dark olive complexion.

"What are you doing here?" I asked her.

Constable Desmond stayed quiet, towering over her, evidently as interested in her answer as much as I was.

"I'm a freelance reporter," she said. "I was monitoring ATC chat and heard about the medevac. Just curious."

"In the middle of the night?"

"Couldn't sleep."

"Right. Do you know who I am?" I asked.

"Yes."

"How?"

"You're Papa Papa Alpha Golf. You're C.E. Brody."

"Okay, then you must know I'm a crazy violent man and a murder suspect. Why offer me a drive to the hospital?"

"Because I know who you are and you're standing right in front of a police officer, who also knows who you are. I don't think you're any of the things that the paper says you are, and obviously neither does he. Now do you want a ride to the hospital or not?"

I shrugged, looked at Desmond, and with the sweep of a hand, said, "Alright, Anaya, lead the way."

She did. I followed her up the jetty with the big cop breathing down my neck, his shoes squeaking with every step.

When we got to Anaya's truck, Desmond said, "Ah, Mr. Brody, we're not quite finished yet. You can make a full statement later but I need to know if a crime was committed against either you or Mr.Giguere. Could you tell me briefly what happened to Mr. Giguere?"

Constable Desmond didn't seem like a bad guy and I decided there was time for a short explanation.

"Okay. Mr. Giguere and I were kidnapped last night in Dawson and we were both beaten up, obviously him worse than me. Then these two Chinese guys threw us into my plane, and a guy named Tommy Kay was waiting inside, and he forced me to fly him down to Thistle Creek where we…"

"Wait," said Desmond, scribbling frantically with his eyes as big as saucers, "You're saying a man named Tommy Kay was waiting inside your plane in Dawson? Was he a large Korean man with…?"

"You mean that thug every cop in the Yukon and half the continent has been looking for? The answer is *yes*. Anyway, so we flew him down to Thistle Creek, and then we incapacitated the bastard, and then we put him in a bear trap. You ought to call your Staff Sergeant Robson. I believe he's up there right now, strutting around Thistle Creek hoping to earn a medal. Tell him he'll find Kay in a bear trap down at the dock."

"A bear trap?"

"Yes."

"Tommy Kay is in a bear trap?"

"That's what I said."

"And you say you and Mr. Giguere incapacitated him. How did you do that?"

"Long story."

"And then you put him in a bear trap."

"That's right."

"Is he still in it?"

"I guess, unless someone let him out."

"How did you get him into a bear trap?"

"We winched him in."

"You winched him in?"

"Yup, we winched him in."

Anaya's mouth was still open when we got into her truck.

* * *

Halfway to the hospital, she said, "So, Mr. Brody, that's quite the story you just told that cop."

"Yeah, well it's all true," I said, admiring the fancy new scanner mounted under the dash of her truck, noting it was tuned to 118.3, now with no reason to believe she hadn't been monitoring Whitehorse ATC. "Are you going to do an article about it?"

"Well, it is a little far fetched. I certainly wouldn't put my name on something like that without first corroborating your version of events with Mr.Giguere's."

"Wow. You'd actually strive for an accurate account of what happened?"

She smiled wryly and said, "Serious journalists do."

"Are you a serious journalist?"

"I certainly am. You don't amount to much in this business without credibility. I just finished my BA and begin a Masters in Journalism this fall. I'm not going to jeopardize that investment by telling tall tales."

"Really."

"Really."

Whitehorse was sound asleep and the streets were empty. We drove past the SS Klondike, then turned right onto the Riverdale Bridge. It wasn't far to the hospital.

"So Anaya, if you're such a serious and ambitious journalist, what are you doing up here? Not much happening."

She smiled politely and said, "I was born and raised here. I like to spend my summers with my friends and parents. And I'm not really working as a journalist, my summer job is an assistant copy editor with the Times. Unless I come across one hell of story, I won't bother pursuing it. Stories up here rarely make it past the city limits."

"Did you say the Times? Isn't that where Ellen Burke works?"

Anaya took a deep breath and said, "Well, she's not actually an employee, she's a freelancer like me. But she does sell most of her stories to the Times."

The undertone in her voice was subtle but told me all I had to know. Anaya was not impressed with the body of work produced by Ellen Burke.

Seemed no one was.

Which is why I asked, "So Anaya, if you were to be offered an exclusive on the biggest mining scam in years, a Yukon story but of great international interest, would you be interested?"

She stayed quiet as we pulled in to the hospital parking lot and rolled to a stop at the emergency entrance. The boys in the ambulance were just leaving. It was a relief to know Mike was now in good hands.

Anaya tilted her head and looked at me.

"What kind of a mining scam?"

"The kind that will make it past the city limits. The kind with murder, kidnapping, extortion, international stock market fraud—stuff like that."

I knew I had her by the look on her face.

"Here? In the Yukon?"

"Come back at noon and I'll tell you all about it."

SIXTY NINE

Tippy Li was exhausted and maybe a tad car sick, too.

They'd been driving all night, and after seven hours lying on a bed in the back of a camper van, he hadn't slept a minute. How can you sleep when it never gets dark?

Ever since they'd left Dawson there'd been no cell phone service. He'd been checking his phone incessantly, fretting over whether there was something wrong with it. Then, after climbing a long rise on the Klondike Highway, two bars appeared on the screen. Finally.

Whitehorse must be close.

Civilization. If you could call it that.

At least the place had a runway long enough for his jet to take off.

Tippy was slowly coming to grips with what had happened last night in Dawson. He knew his latest promotion was as good as dead. Someone was out to get him and they'd succeeded. The theatrics of the police in a crowded bar had been well planned and orchestrated. Arresting and cuffing the president of Thistle Creek Resources in front of sixty brokers was no fluke, it was a show put on to ruin his game. There would be no brokers visiting the property today, they'd all be leaving Dawson just as soon as they could, feeling like suckers, never again to buy another share of

Thistle Creek Resources. The stock was doomed. On Monday the
securities commission would announce a slew of charges against
Lynn and the company, and the exchange would halt trading.

It was all over but the crying.

He'd had setbacks before and knew it was the price you paid for
taking risks. But this one stung. Last week he'd dumped over five
million dollars buying Lynn's shares, just to keep the game alive.
All that money—all for nothing.

He'd been screwed. And he knew by whom.

Women.

They might be weaker physically but evolution had leveled the
playing field by making them sexy and beautiful, and excellent at
lying and conniving. Never trust a woman. He'd always known it
but had done it anyway.

Stupid.

Tippy knew the first objective in business is to survive, and
survive he would. It was time to protect himself with some damage
control.

He looked at his phone again. Tommy hadn't called yet which
was a surprise. He should have finished the job hours ago and was
supposed to call when he got to Alaska. Perhaps he'd had phone
problems, too. Or maybe his flight out of Thistle Creek had been
delayed, bad weather or something. Tippy shook his head. What
a godforsaken place to do business in, he lamented. He'd check
again later.

Tippy's first call was to his pilots who were staying at a hotel in
Whitehorse. After eight rings, one of them picked up and said they
were ready to go. *Liar.* The guy was in bed and he'd woken him
up. They'd probably been partying all night and were hung over.
Pilots. Highly skilled and indispensable for brief assignments, but
otherwise absolute dead weight. Keeping pilots around was like
owning race horses, except race horses don't get drunk.

Next he called his lawyer in Vancouver and woke him up too.
Tippy told him what had happened in Dawson and summarized
his suspicions as to why the president of Thistle Creek Resources

might have been arrested. He asked for a meeting later in the day. His lawyer tried to allay his anxieties.

"You have nothing to be concerned about, Mr. Li. You are simply a shareholder, not management. You have no responsibility whatsoever for the reprehensible transgressions of this company. Its officers and directors and consultants are solely culpable for these duplicitous and fraudulent press releases. You must invoke your legal rights. We'll monitor the court proceedings against Chan and the company, and advise you when to commence an action. In the meantime, please try to relax. Drop by anytime and we'll discuss the lawsuit. I'll be home all weekend."

Consultants.

The geologist was a consultant and had posed the biggest threat to Tippy, and come to think of it, so had that smart-ass pilot friend of his. But Tommy had tended to both of them last night. So no worries there.

He thought about the idea of filing a lawsuit against Thistle Creek. He owned two thirds of the shares so he'd get two thirds of its assets. After the latest financing, Thistle Creek had over three million dollars in the bank. Two million dollars was nothing to sneeze about. He'd think about it.

He then thought about the man from the army they'd hired, the one named Sanders who had built the bomb in Lynn's chandelier. After some deliberation, he decided Sanders wasn't going to yap to the cops, not after installing a bomb to blow up her condo, let alone the role he'd played in babysitting the geologist. The guy was under Tommy's thumb anyway, and you don't talk to cops when you work for Tommy Kay.

Tippy gazed at the three men at the front of the van. They were young, dumb, and loyal. They'd come up with him from Vancouver and served him well in handling the geologist and the pilot. But now they were a liability. He couldn't keep them around. Fortunately they were easy to replace. He'd send them back to Hong Kong as soon as possible. There'd be plenty for them to do there.

Which left Lynn. Never before had he trusted a woman, so why this time? Had it been love? He thought about that for a moment, then realized no—plain and simple—it was her ass. He had to admit to himself that whenever he thought about her, it was the only image that came to mind. Not her eyes, not her smile, not even those sultry red lips of hers—just her ass. Of course a fine one it was, and it had overwhelmed him. But he realized there was nothing else about her that appealed to him. She was just another unhappy irritable bitch—a dime a dozen these days—though bedding this one had cost him way more than a dime.

Five million dollars of Tippy's money was now in Lynn Chan's bank account. It would take time and paperwork to get it back, and she would need to be kept alive throughout the process. Which could be days. Which meant more time for her to talk to the cops. Which was unacceptable. Lynn had to be eliminated and the sooner the better. He'd recover his money from her heirs.

He wondered how much she'd already told the cops, knowing well she'd eventually tell them everything anyway, once they dragged her into court and charged her with a bunch of things she didn't do. That would be on Monday in Vancouver. While Tippy desperately wanted to see her suffer—a splash of battery acid in the face, or a week in the country with a motorcycle gang—he knew what the priority had to be.

She had to be gone before Monday.

There'd be no time for payback.

Lucky Lynn and her grade 'A' ass. She would have to die fast.

* * *

After escorting her out of the bar, they'd whisked her down to Whitehorse on a very nice plane, put her up in a very nice hotel, and stationed a very nice cop outside her door. They'd even removed the handcuffs and carried her luggage up to her room, though they did confiscate all the sharp things like nail files and scissors.

Lynn had been too agitated to sleep. *This was really happening.* It was beginning to sink in and she'd tossed and turned all night. She'd actually been arrested and was about to be charged with securities fraud, income tax evasion, money laundering, and a litany of prostitution charges. She was in this up to her ears and knew her life was about to change.

The meeting at her lawyer's office last week had been a game changer. She'd gone into it thinking she was in control, but how wrong she'd been.

It was unbelievable what the cops knew about her. They'd had her under surveillance for months.

One cop from the FBI produced a stack of photographs—photographs of her coming and going from her bank in LA, accepting thick envelopes in massage parlors, passing a briefcase to Tippy at LAX, and on and on. Then the cop produced her last tax return, slid it in front of her, and with his eyebrows raised, tapped a finger on the bottom line.

Another cop from the RCMP produced another stack of photos. They showed her and Tippy together—walking arm in arm down the hallway of her penthouse, going in and out of restaurants and clubs, getting into elevators and limos—and the most damning ones, descending the stairs of his jet in the Caymans and kissing on the tarmac.

Shocked and speechless, her lawyer had raised a hand and asked her to leave the room so he could hash out a deal.

The one he negotiated was a simple one.

"Help the police bust Tippy Li and you don't go to jail."

Jail.

It was a no-brainer to take it. She could not go to jail. Tippy was sure to try to kill her anyway and the cops were promising to protect her, which was better than no protection at all. So why not cooperate? True, she would have to testify against Tippy and pay millions in penalties and fines—let alone the taxes she owed—which meant losing half her wealth. She would also have to close her massage parlors in California. But anything was better than going to jail, let alone dying.

And she'd still be rich.

In the next half hour they'd worked out the details, including when and how she was to be arrested in Dawson. She'd then be flown to Vancouver and taken directly to her condo. And there she would have to stay. Until Tippy had been tried, convicted, and incarcerated, she could not leave her building without a police escort. They would take her passport and she would not be allowed to leave the country. When she asked how long that would be, they said they didn't know.

But it could be years.

She and the two cops were the first to board the early morning flight from Whitehorse to Vancouver. Lynn was wearing a ball cap, sunglasses, a sweatshirt two sizes too big, jeans and sneakers. She hoped no one in the boarding area recognized her. A uniformed cop named Saunders escorted her down the jetway and into the plane, and pointed to the window seat in the first row of economy, right behind a bulkhead. Lynn took her seat as directed and the female officer sat down in the aisle seat beside her. An RCMP detective named Munroe took a seat in the row behind them. Not a word was spoken.

The cabin was only half full when the door closed and the plane was pushed back from the gate. Lynn rested her face against the cool window and scanned a gloomy gray sky as they started to taxi. She hoped it was sunny in Vancouver, she was depressed enough. She closed her eyes and thought about her chandelier. At least she was going home.

Had she been paying attention, she might have watched Tippy's jet barreling down the runway and take off with a roar.

It was eight o'clock in the morning.

* * *

The knock on the door woke him up.

"Mr. Li? We are in Vancouver," came a woman's voice through the door.

Tippy woke with a start, wondering for an instant where he was, until he recognized the familiar contour of the fuselage above him. It was a little after eleven o'clock in the morning and he had on a pair of fine silk pajamas. He was in bed in his plane. He'd been sound asleep for the last three hours. He lifted the window shade and looked outside. They were stopped in front of the New Horizons hangar. The engines were winding down. It was a sunny day and Tippy was tired.

He hurriedly dressed in fresh clothes from his en suite wardrobe, splashed some water on his face, brushed his teeth, threw on a clean jacket, and grabbed his phone. When he opened the door, the cabin was empty. Only one of his pilots was still in the cockpit, the other would be getting the tug to push the plane into the hangar. At the bottom of the stairs, the flight attendant greeted him with a smile and a nod of reverence. He ignored her. His three henchmen were huddled together at the corner of the building, smoking cigarettes. Tippy walked into the hangar and checked his phone.

He had one missed call and one text message, both from the same number, both about an hour ago. But neither was from Tommy. They were both were from Dan Sanders.

Tippy looked at his watch and felt a twinge of anxiety. Why hadn't Tommy called? He knew the answer when he read the text.

Police have TK call me Dan

He dialed the number.

"Hello."

"You called."

"Yeah, thought you should know a million cops raided the camp last night and took us to Dawson. They let me out of hospital about an hour ago."

"Hospital?"

"Had something in my eyes."

Tippy took a deep breath. Something was wrong.

"Where is Tommy?"

"I don't know. He doesn't answer his phone. Probably in jail."

"Jail? Why would he be in jail?"

"I don't know."

"When did this happen?"

"Last night."

"When last night?"

"After midnight, about three o'clock in the morning."

Tippy could feel the blood pounding through his temples.

"*What* happened?"

After a pause, "That fuckin' pilot is what happened. He locked us up in bear traps and took off. The cops let us out when they got to the camp. It took them a long time to get me out. You should have seen..."

"The pilot locked you in bear traps?"

"Not like leg traps, they're like a culvert with a trap door on the end. The bear walks in and..."

"Shh! Where is the geologist?"

"I don't know but I think he took off with the pilot."

"Took off for where?"

"Dawson or Whitehorse, be my guess."

"Find him!"

"I can't. Got no wheels. The pilot wrecked my truck."

"Then get some wheels! Find him!"

Tippy ground his teeth. *What a disaster*. The geologist was still alive. He looked at one of his henchmen and waved him over.

"Do not lie to me," said Tippy. "Did Tommy hurt the geologist?"

The man was nervous but dared not lie.

He nodded and said, "Yes."

"How bad?"

"Bad."

'Bad'.

If the geologist was injured, the pilot would be certain to take him to a hospital. The hospital would call the police. The police would ask questions.

For the first time in a long time, Tippy Li felt panicked. If either the geologist or the pilot started talking about Thistle Creek—and assays—he was doomed. The police would descend like buzzards. He had only hours, and perhaps only minutes. There was no other choice.

He had to flee.

Jin was coming out of the hangar with the tug. It looked like a huge lawnmower and the electric motor whined louder as he got closer. Tippy held up his hand.

"Stop! Put that back. We are going to Hong Kong."

"Yes, Mr. Li. But first we will need fuel and catering."

"Do it! And make it fast!"

"Yes, Mr. Li."

SEVENTY

Five minutes, ten minutes, twenty minutes...

What the hell was taking so long?

Tippy had been killing time by walking long slow circles around the inside of his empty hangar, stewing and constantly checking his phone, monitoring the video from Lynn's condo. Her desk was empty and the shades on the big windows were closed. Obviously she wasn't home and he wondered where she was. Sooner or later the cops had to ship her south. The question was when? He could hardly call to ask. Nothing to do but wait, watch, walk—and worry.

As to the waiting, he'd never been much good at that and went outside to see what was taking so long. The fuel truck was enormous. It had a big chrome tank and three axles, and had been filling the plane for what seemed like forever. His pilots were talking to the fuel guy and when they saw Tippy approaching, one of them held up a splayed hand.

Five minutes. Tippy sighed. At least the catering truck had come and gone.

He went back into the empty hangar and decided to do another lap around the cool and cavernous building. He was dead tired and couldn't wait to take off, go back to bed, catch up on the sleep he'd missed last night. In the meantime there was nothing else to do but get some more preflight exercise. A good idea considering the flight to Hong Kong was ten hours.

When he started walking again, he thought about his new life there. He'd be safe in Hong Kong—China had no extradition treaties with Canada or the US—and when he really thought about it, there wasn't a single thing he did in Vancouver that he couldn't do over there. He spoke the language, had businesses and friends, and owned a beautiful penthouse in a gorgeous new building, right on the ocean, with a breathtaking view of Victoria Harbor and the South China Sea. Still, he would miss the wide open spaces and clean cool air of Canada, not to mention its endless variety of women. There had always been a critical shortage of blondes in Hong Kong. He'd have to bring some in.

When he reached the rear of the building, he stopped in front of a boxlike object. It was sitting next to an exit door and was covered with a blanket. Every time he'd passed it in the last ten minutes, he'd wondered what it was. It was the only thing in the whole building that didn't seem to belong and it stuck out like a sore thumb. What was it? This time his casual curiosity got the better of him and he lifted a corner of the blanket for a peak underneath. It was a stout wooden box, a cube roughly three by three by four, with a lot of screws holding it together. He gave it a nudge with his knee. It didn't budge. Something was inside. He wondered what and removed the blanket.

The shipping label held the answer.

The box had been shipped from a company called Sherman Glashutte in Rattenberg, Austria—to the Lucky Star Trading Company in Vancouver, Canada—attn: L. Chan.

'Glashutte'.

As in *glass*.

As in *Lynn's chandelier*.

If there was one thing he knew about Lynn, she always had to have the best. He could use a nice chandelier, he thought, for his condo in Hong Kong, maybe hang it in the foyer. There was no point in leaving it behind, she certainly wouldn't be needing it.

He snapped his fingers. One of his henchman came running. "Put this in the plane," he said.

* * *

With thirty thousand pounds of fuel on board, the sleek little jet was as heavy as it would ever be, rolling slowly away from the New Horizons hangar, thumping over every seam in the pavement, heading toward the runways of Vancouver International Airport. The pilots had already filed their flight plan and the passenger manifest listed six souls on board, all of them holding Chinese passports— two pilots, a flight attendant, and three Hong Kong residents—the latter being Tippy's henchmen. But there was another passenger who was not listed on the manifest, a man currently in the bedroom at the back of the plane. Were anyone to ask his chauffeur, he would say he had picked up Mr. Li at his hangar after he arrived from Whitehorse, and driven him to his Vancouver residence.

Of course that wasn't true. In fact the only thing the chauffeur had picked up was Tippy's cell phone, in case the police were tracking its location. The chauffeur was told to leave the phone with Tippy's doorman, with clear instructions to keep it on and charged.

Once again, Tippy Li was about to disappear without a trace.

Now using the plane's satphone, he checked his voicemail again. Tommy hadn't called. Tippy sighed with exasperation, then with the onboard computer, logged onto his favorite website. He waited for the video feed to come up, keeping his eyes glued on the TV at the end of the bed. An image crystallized. Nothing had changed. The scene was still dark. She still wasn't home.

He left the website open, took a quick shower, got back into his pajamas, and before they took off, used the intercom to order a drink—a Chivas, a double, neat.

But even after a stiff drink, he was too wound up to fall asleep, tossing and turning for all of the twenty minute climb out of Vancouver. As much as he tried, the excitement of escaping imminent arrest was too much to overcome. Sleep would have to wait. He ordered another drink, rubbed his face, and stared at the ceiling some more.

The plane was eight miles above the ocean when he sensed a flicker of light at his feet. He thought it might have been a ray of sunlight flashing off a wing, but no, it was something else. He looked at the TV.

Something was different.

It was the windows.

The shades were open.

Lynn was home.

He swung his feet to the floor and stood up, transfixed by the grainy image of her desk silhouetted against the bank of bright windows. He sat down on the edge of the bed, sipped his drink, and felt its familiar warmth run down his throat. He watched and waited. A few moments later she walked into the frame, sat down, picked up the phone, and with her back to the camera, began talking. Probably to her lawyer, he thought. For a while he sat still as a statue, mesmerized, as though he was right there in the room with her, and not wanting her to know it. She got up once and disappeared for a moment, then returned with a drink of her own, and made another call. She seemed relaxed, more so than he might have expected.

He knew what he had to do. Ordering a contract hit was out of the question. With Lynn's arrest, the cops were now sure to be protecting their star witness with everything they had. They'd have men stationed all around her building, and probably outside her door too. She was inaccessible. There was only one way to do this.

Yet he found himself hesitant. A bomb going off in a downtown building was a big deal for the cops, especially if it killed one or more of their own. It would be all hands on deck for however long it took to find the perpetrator.

But Lynn had to die.

It was not an option.

He opened a drawer under the bed and took out his briefcase.

Inside he found the tiny piece of paper with the number Sanders had given him. He entered it into the satphone.

Tippy lifted his drink to the TV in a mock toast.

"So long, Lynn."

He drained his glass, took a deep breath, and pressed SEND.

* * *

The sea was calm, the air was warm, the skies were clear, and the fish were biting.

Two years ago—after a divorce he didn't want—Peter Van Oort had moved to Campbell River, a small city halfway up the east coast of Vancouver Island, to reinvent himself. He'd bought himself a little house, a little boat, and in no time life was worth living again. Most days he couldn't imagine his past, let alone ever moving back to the big smoke of Vancouver.

After a twenty minute fight, and what a fight it had been, he'd landed a thirty-five pound Chinook salmon that left his hands and arms aching. Time to relax and celebrate with a cool one. He leaned back in his seat, and with a cold beer resting on his belt buckle, gazed up at the clear blue sky.

It had always been where he belonged.

Pushing fifty, Van Oort was an airline pilot. Every second week he'd travel south to his old stomping ground to go to work. If you could call flying a 747 'going to work'. Making just two round trips a month to Tokyo made him a very good living, with plenty of time off to enjoy his new life.

He counted six contrails above him, long vapor trails left by the jets leaving Vancouver and Seattle, heading northwest on the great circle routes to distant places on the far side of the Pacific. Today the contrails were long and puffy, glowing snow white under a bright midday sun, hanging as motionless in the air as if someone had painted them there. Their length told him it was a great day to be flying eight miles high. And even higher.

One of the contrails was well above the rest, perhaps a mile or so, and Peter knew it belonged to an executive jet. He'd never flown one, let alone ever been in one, and wondered what it would be like compared to a '47. He'd have to try that someday and would add it to his bucket list.

With fascination he watched the tiny silver speck moving across the sky, ever so slowly gaining on the bigger planes below. Then something absolutely astonishing happened.

From where there was once a tiny silver speck came a brilliant white flash, a streak of orange, a long billow of black smoke, and a plume of debris raining to earth.

Before he even wondered what he'd seen, he knew.

It hadn't just come apart.

It had exploded!

Peter Van Oort reached for his radio and called the Coast Guard.

SEVENTY ONE

At noon sharp on Saturday, Anaya Bakshi walked into my room at Whitehorse General with Constable R. Desmond of the RCMP.

The shades were drawn and the room was dark. The nurse said not to open them because I was under 'concussion protocol'.

Seven hours earlier, when a doctor shone a light into my eyes, he said I might have a concussion. I told him that was ridiculous, that the only things wrong with me were a sore head, a ringing ear, a split lip, a sore jaw, a stiff shoulder, two sore ribs, a sore kidney, and three bruises—one on my knee and two on my shins. But a concussion?

Give me a break.

He insisted on admitting me anyway, *for observation* he said, which I agreed to on the condition he stitched my lip and let me get some sleep.

Constable Desmond wanted my formal statement about what had happened the previous night at Thistle Creek, and politely asked Anaya if she'd mind stepping out of the room. I told him she was my legal representative and would have to be present or there'd be no statement. He wasn't pleased but let her stay.

Desmond had a cell phone and Anaya had one of those tablet gizmos, and they stood on either side of my bed recording my account of events the night before—at least to the best of my recollection—being concussed and all. Desmond said I had to go to the RCMP building to sign my statement, the minute I was discharged. I told him the minute I was discharged, I was flying home to Minto, and to fax it to Daryl. He said okay.

After Desmond left, and with my statement recorded on her tablet, Anaya had plenty of fodder for a front page story. I advised her to write it fast and submit it in time for Monday's paper because she might have some competition. Ellen Burke would in all likelihood be submitting her own version of my visit to Dawson, and it would probably include a picture of me attacking a man on a dock. Anaya thanked me for my advice, said that's what she was intending to do anyway, and that she also had a picture of me on a dock.

I then gave her some insight into the past year of my life, including a little background on the Thistle Creek scam, though not enough details for an exposé, at least not to the standards of a 'serious reporter'. I told her if her first article was fair and accurate then the rest of the saga would be hers for the telling—exclusively—with plenty of material to write a three or four part series. The only condition was that Mike and I would henceforth be referred to as 'reliable sources'. That way, we could go about our lives without having to look over our shoulders. She said that was fine.

On her way out the door, Anaya stopped and asked if there was anything she could do for me. Poor girl should have known better. I hadn't seen my backpack since Dawson and had absolutely nothing with me. She left the room with my dirty clothes and a to-do list, which included picking up a submarine sandwich. She said she'd be back in a couple of hours.

In spite of my prejudice against reporters, I had to concede Anaya was a pretty good egg.

Not long after she left, Mike's wife walked into my room and introduced herself. Simone Giguere was about Mike's age, fifty something, nicely dressed and groomed, with a warm smile and the patient eyes of someone used to waiting. For as long and often as Mike's work took him from home, she must have known what she'd signed up for when she married a geologist.

Simone said they'd just wheeled him out of surgery and I could visit him in a couple of hours. It had taken the surgeons four hours to stitch, wire, and staple him back together—including one orbital socket, both sides of his jaw, three fingers, and a knee cap. She took my hand and thanked me for saving his life, and all I could do was nod and feel guilty for not flying him out of Thistle Creek the previous week—when I had the chance. She said he needed another operation on his eye in a couple of days and his recovery time would be approximately four months, provided he stayed still long enough to heal.

I was about to tell her that the whole Giguere family might still be in danger, but there was no need. Simone volunteered that they were all being kept under twenty-four hour police guard, and as soon as Mike was released from hospital, then she, Mike, and their daughter would be moving to another city. Which city she had no idea, the cops wouldn't or couldn't say. But the Gigueres could not return to their home in Whitehorse until the bad guys were convicted and locked up.

By four o'clock I was going stir crazy, pacing around the room, staring out the window at the sky and the river, desperate to get out of there and fly home. I was stranded and utterly helpless without my backpack. I didn't have a red cent, let alone a credit card, or a check, any ID, and now no clothes.

Where the hell was Anaya?

This time when I turned away from the window, my clothes were lying on the bed in a little pile, all freshly laundered. Things were looking up. Anaya was sitting in the guest chair, playing with her tablet, grinning ear to ear.

Hospital gowns.

I wondered how long she'd been sitting there and asked her what was so funny. She burst out laughing like a ten year old and didn't stop until I was dressed and ready to go. Then, in the elevator ride up to the third floor, she had another good laugh.

Very funny.

At the door to Mike's room, Constable Desmond raised a hand at us. He was standing beside Mike's bed, holding a phone to Mike's ear, and I could make out the sound of my voice. Desmond was replaying my statement. When the phone went quiet, he said something to Mike, who responded with a thumbs up. Satisfied he had what he needed, Desmond stowed his phone and came over to us, said he'd wait in the hall, that there was someone he wanted me to meet.

Anaya and I went over to see Mike.

He was in rough shape. They'd shaved off his beard and the exposed parts of his face were one solid bruise. The rest of his head was wrapped in bandages and there was a plastic cage on his face radiating pins and bolts and braces to hold his jaw and forehead together. It brought to mind Hannibal Lecter and made me feel squeamish. The rest of him wasn't much better with his leg in a full cast, but with the section around the knee left open. Half the fingers on one of his hands were bound in splints and he had stitches everywhere. But he could still smile with his eyes and feebly offered me his one good hand, if you could call it that, which I took in mine for a perfunctory though delicate handshake.

"So when are they going to operate on you?" I asked.

He closed his eyes and waved a hand at me, then beckoned to Simone who held her phone up in front of him. He obviously couldn't talk with his mouth wired shut, and slowly typed something on the screen. Simone held it out to me.

dont make me laf hurts

Mike pointed at Anaya.

"Reporter," I said. "A good one."

He looked her in the eyes, gestured at me, asked for the phone again, and typed something else. I caught what he'd typed when Simone passed the phone to Anaya.

hero

With a dismissive wave of my hand, I tried to smile and said, "Don't *you* make *me* laugh."

I left the room depressed. Anaya was behind me and we followed Constable Desmond to the elevator, went up to the fourth floor, walked down the hall to the end, and entered a lounge. It was a bright corner room with big windows affording nice views of the city and river, with plenty of chairs and couches and tables. There were all kinds inside, patients and visitors alike, young and old, many of them in wheelchairs. One young girl in a body cast was lying on a stretcher, sharing a laugh with a nurse.

They all had big eyes for the big cop.

Desmond led us to a corner table with three people sitting around it. The tall young guy in the middle was the person Desmond wanted me to meet. I knew who he was when he rose to his feet.

Lance Corporal Aaron Vanderbilt.

The woman sitting to his right had to be his mother. She stayed put in her chair with her chin glued in her hands, fixated on the window, and didn't give me a glance. The man to his left would be his father, definitely military, and he stood up with his son to analyze me.

Desmond said, "Mr. Brody, this is Lance Corporal Aaron Vanderbilt. He has something to say to you."

Aaron Vanderbilt extended his hand and for some reason I shook it.

His words were slow and deliberate, as if thoroughly rehearsed, and the focus of his eyes told me he wasn't quite right.

"I am very sorry for attacking you," he said. "I know now you did not kill my sister."

And that was it. He sat down like he needed a rest.

Desmond said, "Mr. Brody, there will be no charges laid against you in connection with the assaults last week on the Whitehorse Walking Path. Mr. Vanderbilt admits you did not assault him, and he has agreed not to press charges against you or anyone else.

"However, we cannot release Mr. Vanderbilt from the country until you waive your right to press charges against him. The Vanderbilt family would like to go home to bury their daughter.

Will you waive your rights, or do you wish to press charges against Mr. Vanderbilt?"

It was a complete turn of events. Robson was out of the picture and Ray was off the hook.

"Yeah, sure, I'll waive the charges. It never entered my mind to charge anyone, anyway." I looked at Vanderbilt senior and said, "I'm very sorry about what happened to your daughter, sir, it was completely senseless."

He said nothing but seemed relieved. I sensed he didn't think I murdered his daughter. His wife was a different story. She still wouldn't look at me. Her daughter was dead and it would probably be a long time before her son was normal again, if ever.

All my fault, of course

I'd refused to eat the prison food offered at breakfast and lunch, and was famished. On the way to Schwatka Lake, I attacked the submarine sandwich Anaya had got me in town while she asked questions about what had happened on the Whitehorse Walking Path. Mostly I gave her a lot of muffled one word answers, and whenever she got frustrated I'd say, "Next installment, Anaya."

When we got to the lake, we carried the boxes of groceries she'd bought down to my plane, and set them down on the dock. In one of the boxes I found a new pair of drugstore sunglasses, as requested. When I got into my plane and checked the fuel guages, I could have hugged her.

She'd called the fuel company.

"You are one good egg, Anaya. Thanks for everything. Hey, what do I owe you?"

"A hundred and twenty-two dollars and sixty cents, and two more stories."

"Deal. You'll get your money soon and let's make it three stories."

We smiled at each other, exchanged phone numbers, and she said she'd call me on Monday morning for her next installment. I watched her walk up the jetty with a bounce in her step, then remembered something.

"Hey, Anaya?"

She stopped and said, "Yes?"

"One more little favor, if you would."

"What?"

"There's a guy who hangs out in front of the post office, looks a bit rough around the edges, a big native man. His name is Ray. Give him a dollar if you see him. Tell him it's from Brody."

SEVENTY TWO

It was Sunday morning and for the first time in over a week, I woke up in my own bed—alone—thinking about Sarah Marsalis and kitchen cabinets.

Sarah was on my mind because I could smell her on the pillow. It was actually kind of nice to wake up with the scent of a woman in bed, without the woman.

Thanks to Reggie, the cabinets and cupboards for my new kitchen were out in the living room—stacked to the ceiling—along with a new screen door, a new gas grill, a new microwave oven, two new countertops, a new double sink, a new faucet, and bags and bags of hardware.

The guy from the propane company had installed a used door on the stove, which looked great, and there was a shiny new fridge cooling the groceries I'd brought up from Whitehorse. Last but not least, the pile of garbage on the deck that was my previous kitchen was gone. I had to assume Andy and Arlo had been dispatched by Reggie to come down with one of the highway department loaders to haul it all off to the dump. Their standard fee per load was a 'case of 24'—as in bottles of beer—and though I wasn't sure if the job had taken them one or two trips, I figured they each had a case coming.

As for Reggie, I still didn't have a clue how to repay him for all the favors he does for me, and the list keeps growing. Money means nothing to him and once again I thought I'd better come up with something—and soon.

The guy is pure gold.

With everything for the project now at hand, hopefully by the end of the day I'd have the kitchen finished. Tomorrow I'd install the screen door on the porch, and hopefully it wouldn't take too long to put the grill together. The box said 'some assembly required' which in fact means *a lot of assembly required*. I'd tackle that job out on the deck some evening, with a beer or two. Beer helps calm your nerves when you're searching for missing nuts and bolts.

With a full day of work ahead I got out of bed feeling sore all over, and limped into the living room to say good morning to my dogs. They were quiet. Jack was under the kitchen table and wouldn't look at me. Russ was on the carpet at the front door and wouldn't look at me either. Then I noticed one of my boots was lying on its side between them.

It was missing a lace.

* * *

The job took longer than expected—they always do—in the history of walls and floors no one's ever made a straight one.

But the result was worth the work and a sight to behold with every cabinet, cupboard, door and drawer—and countertop— plumb, square, and level.

My new kitchen was perfect.

I couldn't stop playing with the stick shift faucet and was looking forward to washing dishes with a pull out sprayer and twin stainless steel sinks. In the middle of nowhere on the Yukon River, I had a kitchen with hot and cold running water, a stove, a fridge, and could cook gourmet meals again.

Just one more thing to install before making myself a man-sized BLT.

It took less than a minute to get it out of the box, set it on the kitchen table, and another five minutes to take it apart. With all the panels removed, I started searching inside for the most obnoxious, redundant, and ridiculous thing ever installed on an appliance. The instant I located it, something set off my dogs.

It was five o'clock in the evening and they were hungry, which made them all the more wild, whirling around the cabin, bouncing off the windows, and barking up an earsplitting storm. I grabbed Jack and put him in the bedroom before he hurt himself. He was still barking after I closed the door.

There are only two things in this world that make them go that ballistic.

A bear or a cop.

Or two cops.

Daryll appeared through the window first, then Staff Sergeant Robson. Five hundred pounds of cop was standing outside in the middle of the deck, looking around like they were lost. Daryll had a large envelope in his hand. I squeezed out the front door holding Russ back with a foot, knowing if he got out he'd tear the pants off one of them—probably Daryll's. Russ hates Daryll.

"Hey boys, great to see you again. What can I do for you?"

The way they looked at me said it all. They were on serious business. But what? Robson glared at me with his steely blue eyes and jabbed a finger my way.

"You know, Mr. Brody, one of these days someone has got to make a movie about you."

"A movie about me? Why?"

"Because never have I seen or witnessed so much death and destruction caused by one man who's not in jail."

"Death and destruction?"

Robson held out his hand without taking his eyes from mine, and Daryll handed him the envelope.

"Somewhere we can sit and talk?" he asked.

* * *

Daryll wasn't invited to the powwow and went back down to his big blue jail on wheels. I got a couple of deck chairs out of the porch and set them down on the deck, spaced well apart, facing the river. I sat down in one but Robson picked up the other one and moved it around to face me, close enough so he could lean into my face, which gave him a great view of Russ in the window behind me, growling and baring his teeth at him.

After a long pause, and making a great show of flipping back and forth through the pages of the statement I'd given to Constable Desmond, Robson harrumphed and said, "So Mr. Brody, looks like you had a very busy day on Friday. Flying back and forth from Thistle Creek to Dawson, locking up people in bear traps, getting into a fight with a man on a dock, but then that's just another day at the office for you, right? And by the way, that was quite the mess you left at Thistle Creek."

"I left a mess?"

"Well someone sure did. The kitchen and a sleeper trailer were ransacked and robbed, a truck was vandalized, and the repair shop was broken into."

"Probably bears," I said.

"Right, bears," he said.

He looked down at my statement, flipped over a page, and read some more. He might have been trying to make me feel uneasy but I knew his game. I ignored him and looked across the river. No hawks. I waited him out.

"Tommy Kay," he said after a while.

"Yeah, what about him?"

Robson raised his eyebrows and asked, "Was he alive when you winched him into that bear trap?"

"Alive? Yeah, he was alive. Why?"

"You're absolutely sure about that that?"

I straightened up and put my hands on the armrests. "Of course I'm sure about that. I was there. Why are you asking me if he was alive?"

"Because he's dead."

"Dead? Tommy Kay is dead?"

"As a doornail. He was dead when we found him in the trap,

and he was still dead when they laid him out on a stainless steel table in Dawson yesterday morning."

"Holy shit!"

"Surprised?"

"Well, yeah, of course I'm surprised."

"So are we. It seems Mr. Kay died under a very unusual circumstance. I was hoping you could give me some insight into what happened to him. The coroner says he died of...let's see here..." Robson looked down at his paperwork. "Upper respiratory edema, triggered by an anaphylactic reaction to peanuts."

"An anaphyl...?"

"A severe allergic reaction, Mr. Brody. Seems Mr. Kay was allergic to peanuts. His throat and airways swelled up so much he couldn't breathe. He suffocated."

"From peanuts? No kidding."

"No kidding is right," he said. "Did you know Mr. Kay was allergic to peanuts?"

"Well, I kind of suspected it was something like that, after he started choking and coughing in the back of the plane."

"Were there peanuts in your plane?"

"Yeah, lots. Mike Giguere had a big can of them, he was munching them all morning when we flew up to Dawson. Peanuts are still allowed on Air Brody flights."

Robson gave me a long cold stare and said, "Did you open a window when you saw the stress Mr. Kay was under? I mean, he must have been under a lot of stress."

"Oh right, like I was gonna do that for a guy who beats us up, hijacks my plane, and is going to kill us as soon as we get to Thistle Creek? I don't think so, Staff Sergeant. So no, I wasn't going to open up a window for the asshole. And besides, there are no windows that you can open in my plane."

Robson nodded, sighed, stuffed his paperwork back in the envelope, and said, "Okay, Mr. Brody, that's all for now. I'd like to stay and chat but had better get going. Mr. Kay is currently lying on ice in the back of our plane, out at your fine little airport here.

Got to get back to Whitehorse before he thaws out. There'll be an official coroner's inquest into the cause of his death, probably in Whitehorse in the fall. I'm sure you'll be getting an invitation, so don't leave the territory without letting me know."

He got up, took a step, stopped and said, "Oh, almost forgot. You need to read and sign your statement about what happened Friday." He dug it out of the envelope and handed it to me. "You can read it tonight and take it up to Constable Pageau tomorrow. Please sign it in front of him."

This time he took two steps before stopping.

"Say, you hear about that plane crash yesterday?" he asked.

I exhaled with overt exasperation and said, "And what plane crash might that be?"

"One of those little corporate jets went down off the coast of British Columbia. It had just left Vancouver and was headed for Hong Kong. An eye witness said it was just flying along and blew up in midair. Apparently it came raining down in a million pieces all over the ocean. Weird, huh?"

"Yeah, that does sound weird. I'll have to read about it. Thanks for telling me."

"You're welcome. By the way, there was something else weird about that crash. We think Tippy Li might have been on board."

"Tippy Li? The guy who ran Thistle…?"

"Yeah, that Tippy Li. Turns out it was his plane. Got any ideas about who might want to blow up it up?"

"Ah, everyone?"

"Good answer," said Robson with a sardonic grin. He was almost to the stairs when he stopped again.

With a finger in the air, he turned around and said, "Oh, one more thing, Mr. Brody."

Columbo lives…

I was shaking my head when I stood up. The guy was driving me crazy.

"Yes, Staff Sergeant."

"Something I can't figure out, been racking my brain about it all weekend."

"And what's that?" I asked with my hands on my hips.

"Well, when we opened that bear trap to extricate Mr. Kay, he had an EpiPen in the palm of his hand. An EpiPen is a ..."

"I know what an EpiPen is."

"Oh, is that so? Anyway, obviously Mr. Kay carried one for a reason, like a personal emergency such as the one he was in. What I can't figure out is why he didn't use it. I mean all he had to do to save his own life was remove the cap and inject himself. Now why wouldn't he do that?"

All of a sudden Robson had his icy cop glare going again.

I shrugged my shoulders and said, "A mystery to me."

We held each others eyes for a long time, then he nodded, tipped his hat and said, "You have a nice evening, Mr. Brody."

* * *

There are times when a man can use a beer, and there are times when a man needs a beer. I *needed* a beer.

Jack was whimpering in the bedroom and I opened the door for him, then went over to my shiny new fridge, grabbed a cold Corona, and took it out to my project at the kitchen table. I may have had good reason to be upset, but there was no way I was going to let a suspicious cop ruin my day, let alone stop me from finishing my kitchen.

I'd just picked up a pair of wire cutters when my boys made a beeline for the living room window, put their paws up on the sill, and with their tails wagging in a blur, started whimpering and whining.

Two seconds later Sarah Marsalis walked in like she owned the place.

"Got something for you," she sang out, smiling ear to ear, holding up my backpack while Russ and Jack danced around her feet. She dropped it on the floor in front of me, turned toward the kitchen, and put her hands on her hips.

"Wow, ever nice!" she exclaimed.

Her tattoos were now faded shadows of what they'd been two days ago, and the piercings and metal junk were all gone. She was wearing tight black jeans, a tartan flannel shirt, sneakers, and a plastic watch on her wrist. Her hair was still jet black but I'd bet my plane it would be auburn again soon.

I wanted to reunite with my backpack but couldn't take my eyes off her. With my mouth still agape, I watched the magical movements of her jeans as she walked into the kitchen. She opened and closed every drawer and cabinet, then the stove, then the fridge. When her inspection was complete, she leaned on the counter with her hands wide apart, and said, "This is totally awesome, Brody."

No, Sarah, you're totally awesome.

"Thanks," I said, admiring the woman I once knew, preparing myself for the impending dressing-down for my no-show on Friday night.

She noticed what I was working on and asked with a frown, "What are you doing?"

"Replacing the Kitzenjammer valve."

She squinted at the shiny box and packaging strewn all over the floor, walked over to the table, and crossed her arms.

With the hint of sarcasm, she said, "I thought they stopped using Kitzenjammer valves in microwave ovens."

"The good ones still have them," I said. "So where did you find my pack?"

"It was stuffed in a trash can at a gas station in Dawson. Someone dropped it off at the police station. The cop at the desk read your ID and called me to see if it belonged to the same C.E. Brody that stood me up at the hotel. That's when we knew something was wrong. And don't worry, I didn't tell anyone what the 'C' stands for...*Cornelius*."

"I know, you wouldn't dare," I growled.

"Never," she said with a chuckle.

I shook my head and said, "So I guess you know all about what happened Friday night."

"Well I do now, after reading that statement you gave the cops in Whitehorse yesterday. Sounds like you had quite the adventure, and as usual were lucky to survive, on account of peanuts I'm told. I was scared for you, Brody."

I leaned back and looked up at her. She was standing right beside me, looking down into my eyes, and I was kind of thinking how nice it would be if she'd sit down in my lap.

Dream on.

When she didn't, I said, "Yeah, peanuts to the rescue. Hey, I'm really sorry about Friday night, Sarah. I screwed up. I should have just done what I was told. I shouldn't have left my room."

"Not the first time you haven't done what you were told," she said.

"Yeah...well..."

We smiled at each other and stared into each others eyes for a a long time, trying to read each other's minds. I gave up first and looked back at the task in front of me. If there's one thing I know about women, it's that there's no reading them. I picked up the wirecutter, snipped two wires, used a pair of pliers to pull out what I was after, and held it up like a surgeon inspecting a gall bladder.

"Is that the Kitzenjammer valve?"

"No, this is the dinger. The Kitzenjammer valve is on the other side."

"Why did you take out the dinger?"

"Because I don't need a fire alarm to tell me when my coffee's hot."

"Oh."

"Want it?"

"No thanks."

I tossed it into the box on the floor, leaned back, took a slug of beer, and looked up at her again. She was staring at my mouth with great concern.

"Does that hurt?" she asked.

"Does what hurt?"

"The cut on your lip."

"Only when I smile."

She leaned over, cupped my chin in her hand, and delicately brushed her thumb across the bandage. Her face was only inches away.

She scanned the rest of my face and said, "Your jaw is really swollen."

"I know."

"Does it hurt?"

"Not much."

"Brody?"

"Yes, Sarah."

"You need a haircut."

"I know."

"Brody?"

"What?"

"Did I tell you I'm moving to Seattle?"

"No."

"Well I am, at the beginning of September."

"That's nice."

"They're giving me a week off to move."

"That's nice, too," I said with my head spinning, completely absorbed in her eyes, breathing the scent from her hand, thinking about my pillow.

"So..." she said.

"So..." I said.

She took her hand away, straightened up, folded her arms, looked around and bit her lower lip. I could hear dog tails thumping on the floor.

"Well, since I'm going to be living in a sublet for a while, I hardly need a whole week to move. So I was thinking...maybe I'd go somewhere, take a little holiday."

"Oh, yeah? Where to?"

She took a deep breath.

"Well, I was thinking about here."

"The Yukon?"

"Uh-huh."

"Great idea, Sarah. The Yukon's a magical place in the fall, the colors are…"

"I mean here, Brody, as in right here," she said, tapping the table.

"Right here?"

"You're not making this easy for me, you know that?"

"Wait. Are you saying you want to visit *me*?"

"That's a perfect way of putting it."

"Gee, Sarah, that would be great. But you know there's not much to do around here."

"That's okay, I don't want to do much. I just want to hang out."

"Hang out."

"Yes, hang out. You know, read books, go for walks, watch the river go by, I might even do some cooking, if you let me."

"Now you're talkin'."

She smiled, put a hand on my shoulder, and gave it a little squeeze. I reciprocated by putting my hand on her hip, about as low as I dared, and gave it a little squeeze.

"One inch lower and I'll break your arm," she said with a glare.

"Darn," I said with a grin.

When the door closed behind her, Russ and Jack looked at me.

"Don't worry boys, she's comin' back."

They wagged their tails.

SEVENTY THREE

Never mind the calendar, summer was over.

It was a cold and sunny afternoon in early September and I was trying to stay warm, sitting outside in front of a crackling fire, sheltered from the wind in an amphitheater of tall white poplars cloaked in mops of gold. With every gust their leaves would shiver like sequins, and each time a few would fall off and flutter to earth. In another two weeks every branch would be bare.

I'd decided to use benches instead of log stumps for my new firegazing pit—stumps weren't the kind of seating for what I had in mind. Two people can't snuggle on a stump.

My hands were still buzzing from the chainsaw I'd had in my hands for the last two days, but there was now enough wood in the porch to keep me warm for a year. Though I've never been rich, there's nothing like a couple of cords of dry split firewood to make a man feel wealthy.

With my dogs at my side I gazed across the river at the first dusting of snow on the mountains. Russ and Jack were licking their chops, watching intently as I blew on a hot dog I'd just withdrawn from the fire. It was a little too black for my my liking, and besides, they'd been getting every second one and it was their turn. They had their front paws up on my thighs, and when the prize was cool enough to eat, I tossed a half to each one of them and they snapped them out of the air.

Gulp, gone, next please.

I still was marveling at Jack's miraculous recovery and his ability to function as if nothing had happened to him. He was a happy healthy dog again and could give Russ a run for his money at just about anything, save for a flat out run, and even then never finished far behind. It's remarkable to me how resilient animals are, how they simply accept fate and get on with their lives. Three legs, four legs, what's the difference?

Jack was my hero.

* * *

A few weeks ago two boys from the village had been out hunting grouse on the far side of Two Spirit Lake and dutifully stopped in to check in on Old Hank. They found him in his bed with the stove still warm.

He'd died in his sleep.

The next day Reggie and I borrowed a boat and crossed the lake to go through his things. Of course he didn't have much—two old rifles, an axe, a saw, a shovel, a few tools, a few pots and pans, and his so-called telescope—which was actually an ancient transit level he'd probably 'acquired' during the surveying of the Klondike Highway. Beneath his bed, under a floor board, we dug out an old coffee can.

The contents pretty well told the whole story.

There were thirty-four one dollar bills circa 1951, a few silver coins, a gold nugget, a tiny faded picture of a couple we guessed might have been his parents, his birth certificate from Germany dated October eleven, 1930, and two faded newspaper clippings.

One clipping was a wedding announcement for a young couple from Victoria, British Columbia—Ingrid Sophie Schulz and Heinrich Walter Sturmer—dated June the tenth, 1951. The other clipping was an obituary dated September the eighth, 1952—*Ingrid Sophie Sturmer, and child, together in childbirth...*

The weather forecast for Hank's service had called for pale and sad skies with a hundred percent chance of tears. The whole community came out to stand in a drizzle that surrounded us like a curtain, and there must have been a hundred people strung along the shore of Two Spirit Lake to bid farewell to a legend. With Mrs. Deerchild sitting in the bow, Reggie rowed Hank's old boat out a couple of hundred feet and we watched her stand and do her little dance. Then the two took turns pouring his ashes into the lake. Hank was now one with his wife and child.

Anaya Bakshi wrote three front page stories for the Yukon Times, one after the other, on the Monday, Tuesday and Wednesday following the demise of Tommy Kay. Twenty minutes after Staff Sergeant Robson informed me that Kay had died, Anaya received her first 'anonymous' tip from a 'reliable source'. She'd been waiting at the Whitehorse airport when the RCMP plane arrived and unloaded Kay's body. The photo she got told a thousand words.

Anaya's first article described the heroics of a Yukon bush pilot from Minto, who'd freed a kidnapped geologist from a man named Kay, who'd been on Canada's most wanted list. Her next article covered the arrest and arraignment of a Vancouver woman named Lynn Chan, who'd been arrested in Dawson and charged with multiple crimes, including conspiracy and intent to defraud investors in a Yukon gold exploration project. Her third article delved into the mysterious circumstances surrounding the crash of a corporate jet off the coast of British Columbia, which claimed the lives of everyone on board, including an organized crime boss named Tippy Li, who had ties to Kay, Chan, and the same Yukon gold exploration project.

Ellen Burke's story about the same Yukon bush pilot from Minto assaulting a man on a Dawson dock was never published. Anaya's story had already been chosen as the front page feature of the day, and Burke's story had been rejected as 'irrelevant'.

When I took Jack to Whitehorse to have his stitches removed, I called Anaya and we met for lunch. She told me Ellen Burke was no longer submitting stories to the Times, that she was now writing fake news for some alt-right wing Super PAC based out of Alaska. Apparently Ellen's new gig paid her three times as much.

After lunch I went to the post office and ran into Ray. We shook hands and he told me he got the buck I owed him from Anaya. After I picked up my mail, we went down to the sporting goods store. When we walked out twenty minutes later, he was wearing a brand new pair of boots and I was carrying a brand new snowmobile suit. Then we went over to the drugstore where I bought every leather lace they had. When I explained to Ray why I needed so many laces, he told me if I rubbed an onion on the next pair, my boys wouldn't eat them.

In my mail were two more letters from the Yukon Water Board—the second and third final notices—which followed the first final notice I'd been carrying around for a month, which I'd finally opened. The notices said I needed to purchase a license for the ten gallons of water I pumped out of the Yukon River everyday.

I figured I had better deal with the Water Board before they cut off the river on me, and found their offices on the top floor in a building on Main Street. If sitting is the new smoking then the staff in there was three packs a day. I stood at the counter for a good five minutes before one of them struggled to her feet to attend to the only customer in the place.

My water license cost a hundred dollars for a year and the large woman who served me was kind enough to waive all the fines and late penalties. She said she'd read all about my heroics and could appreciate why I was late coming in. I thanked her and asked her if I decided to collect water off the roof of my cabin—instead of pumping it out of the river—whether I'd need a license to take rain out of the sky. She said not according to current regulations.

On the way out of town I dropped in to see Mike and his wife. The Giguere family never did have to leave town—not after the deaths of Kay and Li—but were still under police protection. Constable E. Saunders stopped me in the driveway and asked to see my ID. She must have been bored.

Mike was lying on the couch in the living room with a leg

propped up, reading a book, and looked a whole lot better than the last time I saw him. He said he was pretty much pain free and would be back to work in no time. His wife Simone shook her head and said he wasn't going anywhere until she said so.

Mike told me he'd given the cops a comprehensive statement about our close call with Tommy Kay, as well as everything else about the assay scam orchestrated by Tippy Li. With Kay and Li out of the picture, and with Lynn Chan pleading guilty to all the charges against her, there was no longer a need for Mike to go to court. I was relieved for him.

One guy who *was* going to court was Dan Sanders. According to Mike, the cops had released Sanders from jail the morning after Kay had died, with clear instructions to leave the country. Sanders then returned to Thistle Creek to repair and retrieve his truck, but having never been paid for his work, decided to settle his account with barter. Before leaving for Fairbanks, he'd helped himself to forty thousand dollars worth of tools from the maintenance building. When customs checked inside his camper at the US-Canada border, and found it stuffed with industrial tools, they arrested him, seized his truck, and shipped him back to Dawson. He was currently in jail there, being held without bond, awaiting trial.

Speaking of money, Mike said neither he or Jennifer or anyone else they knew had been paid a single dollar by Thistle Creek Resources. When I told him I hadn't either, he scratched his head and said something wasn't right. The company supposedly had three million dollars in the bank, so what was the hold up? Mike said he was considering registering a lien on the claims.

On July the first, the draw for the Minto Arena Lottery took place during the Canada Day birthday bash at Two Spirit Lake. The winner of a brand new Dodge four-by-four pickup truck was a woman from Alberta. When Reggie and I matched the winning ticket number to the stub in the sales book, I had to smile. The five preceding tickets had been sold to none other than one Alan Robson of Whitehorse, Yukon.

Close, but no cigar, *Staff Sergeant.*

For the second year in a row, I was bestowed the honor of serving as Grand Marshall for Minto's big beach party. As usual there was controversy and I was required to make some tough decisions.

The first crisis arose after I disqualified Arlo and Andy from the canoe race. The race was scheduled to start at two o'clock in the afternoon, but long before that, they were too drunk to partake. This was the second year in a row they'd done this, and so I also banned them from ever entering again. They became very angry and threatened to file an official protest. On the condition they dropped the idea, I issued them a bunch of beer tickets.

The next one concerned the use of the men's outhouse. The men were complaining about long lineups because the women were using it too. After taking one of the women aside to find out why, she confided to me that the ladies didn't want to use their own outhouse because that's where Adrian Woo's body had been dumped. The solution was simple and it took me less than five minutes to swap the signs on the doors. The men didn't seem to mind the switch, so long as they didn't have to wait on the women.

My final decision of the day was to never, ever again serve as Grand Marshal.

The final steel panel for the new Minto Arena was bolted in place on August first. The exterior of the steel arch building was now complete and it resembled a giant, semi-submerged culvert. There was still plenty of interior work to do before anyone could play bingo or hockey, but the project was on schedule and under budget. Everyone in the village couldn't wait for the grand opening in October.

A few days later the ice making machine and a Zamboni arrived on two flat bed trucks. When Reggie told me that he and a pal would be going to Whitehorse for a week's course in how to operate them, I saw my chance to do *him* a favor. A phone call later, everything was arranged. I asked him to drop his truck off at my shop before he left, so I could fix its squeaky front door.

The day Reggie left for town, a guy from an auto body shop in Whitehorse pulled into my shop with a vehicle trailer, and hauled the old tow truck away. Five days later the same guy returned with the same old tow truck, and I barely recognized it. As instructed, the body shop had installed a new windshield, refurbished the seats, installed new mudflaps, completely restored the body, and painted it fire engine red with orange flames on the doors. When Reggie returned and walked into my shop, all he did was shake his head, get in, and drive away.

He liked it.

By mid-August I was beginning to wonder if Sarah was still intending to visit me. She had yet to call and I had to admit to myself I'd be disappointed if she didn't come up. Which explained why I was now in the habit of answering the shop phone every time it rang.

It seemed the more I answered it, the more it rang.

Go figure.

A couple of weeks ago my favorite stock broker called. Dave Sorenson was in a good mood because Thistle Creek Resources was trading again—at six cents a share. He asked me if I wanted to cover my position and I asked him what position that might be. He said my short position in TCR which was currently fifty thousand shares. "Damn right I want to cover my position!" I yelled at him and he put me on hold. When he came back on the line, he said it was done. When I asked him what the balance in my account was, he said approximately sixty-two thousand dollars. After a few deep breaths, and a very long pause, he asked me if I was okay. I told him I was and to cut me a check.

Sixty-two thousand dollars.

I could rationalize flying down to Whitehorse the next day as my old plane was due for a fifty hour inspection anyway—gotta follow the rules—but my prime objective was to do a little banking, and while there, maybe pick up my mail and get a haircut.

The haircut took ten minutes and then I went and picked up my mail. There was a letter from the US Treasury which contained the second twenty-five thousand dollar tranche for my FBI flying contract.

Still nothing from Thistle Creek Resources.

I called Mike and he said he was doing well. He said he hadn't received any money from Thistle Creek either, and neither had Jennifer. He asked me if I wanted to be included on the lien they were going to file on the Thistle Creek claims and I said sure. Speaking of Jennifer, Mike asked me if I was going to her wedding.

Her wedding?

Mike said Jennifer and Tony Brookes were getting married in the fall. I had to shake my head at the news and told him I had yet to receive an invitation. Somehow I doubted I would.

When I went into the bank to deposit the check for the twenty-five thousand dollars I hadn't earned, and the check for the sixty-two thousand dollars I also hadn't earned, I felt guilty. All that money for doing nothing. I thought about how stressful it must be to make a living without working. I deposited my checks, paid off my mortgage, then flew home, looking forward the whole way to chopping and splitting firewood.

* * *

The fire had died down to a bed of hot coals and I got to my feet and zipped up my jacket.

On the other side of the river three hawks were circling over the trees, two adults and a juvenile, the latter having appeared for the first time only a month ago. I wondered what had happened to its siblings, but it was nice to see the little family flying around together. One of them screeched, then they turned in unison and flew off toward the south. I watched them for as long as I could, until they merged into a single speck against an empty gray sky, and vanished from sight. It left me wondering if that was goodbye for the year.

Sarah Marsalis never phoned but I knew she was coming up.

I reached into my shirt pocket and pulled out the tired piece of paper I'd been carrying around all day, unfolded it, and read it again.

The hand written note had been faxed to the Café. Minnie had given it to me this morning when I paid for my breakfast.

To C.E. Brody: Your Kitzenjammer Valve arrives tomorrow on the two o'clock bus.

Lust, love and like. Any one will do, two is better, but all three? You might as well sign over the deed to the ranch.

I wondered which ones were us, then realized there was something irrational going on, at least for me.

Yeah she was gorgeous, yeah she was fun, yeah she liked my dogs. But she was also a cop. And a recovering alcoholic. And our lives were miles apart. And she'd kicked me in the shins and pinned me to a floor and threatened to break my arm—and even shoot me. The woman certainly had a temper.

But there was just something about her.

She lit up my life and I couldn't wait to see her again.

Damn woman.

I scattered the coals in the fire, gazed up at the mountains, shook my head, then headed for my cabin with my dogs at my side.

Life is full of mysteries.

From the Author

No one accomplishes anything all by themselves and I am indebted to the following people who each played a part in creating this novel.

I extend my thanks…

To my father, ninety-six years young, whose guidance and encouragement has always been there.

To my sister Esther, whose enthusiasm and support for anything will make it happen.

To Lela Gahwiler, Joey Baird, and Charlotte Henning, who graciously took the time to read my early manuscripts, and politely pointed out all my typos and errors (and there were plenty).

To Mark Perry, whose surreal and stunning photograph, 'A Bad Day For Flying', was used for the image on the cover.

To Mark Smith at Chrismar Mapping Services, who created yet another first rate map.

To Glendon Haddix and staff at Streetlight Graphics, who took all the bits and pieces and magically assembled them into a book.

To Dave Sharp at Tintina Air in Whitehorse, who gave me all the time in the world to talk about flying a Beaver, and his wife Megan, for the best complimentary coffee mug in aviation.

To Janet Sanders at Alpine Aviation in Whitehorse, who ordered up a beautiful sunny day at Schwatka Lake, and pilot Andrew Swenson, who took me flying in the company Beaver, serial number 66.

And finally, thanks to the colorful five percent, those larger than life Yukon characters I knew and worked with during my twenty years in the north. In case you were wondering, one of them actually did tow his clothes around the lake to do his laundry.

May the spirit of the Yukon live on.

About the Author

Ken Baird operated a Yukon gold mine for ten years. A former receiver-manager and private pilot, he now lives in Florida.

Yukon Revenge is his second novel. His first novel, Yukon Audit, won the 2016 Indie Book Award for Best Thriller.

CPSIA information can be obtained
at www.ICGtesting.com
Printed in the USA
BVHW070734080121
597261BV00001B/15